The Last Cruise

ALSO BY KATE CHRISTENSEN

THE
LAST CRUISE

~~~~~ *a novel*

Kate Christensen

DOUBLEDAY *New York London Toronto Sydney Auckland*

Book design by Maria Carella
Jacket design by Jaya Miceli
Jacket photograph by Loïc Venance/AFP/Getty Images

Library of Congress Cataloging-in-Publication Data
Names: Christensen, Kate, 1962– author.
Title: The last cruise : a novel / by Kate Christensen.
Description: First edition. | New York : Doubleday, [2018]
Identifiers: LCCN 2017030311 | ISBN 9780385536288 (hardcover) |
    ISBN 9780385536295 (ebook)
Classification: LCC PS3553.H716 L37 2018 | DDC 813/.54—dc23
LC record available at https://lccn.loc.gov/2017030311

MANUFACTURED IN THE UNITED STATES OF AMERICA

10 9 8 7 6 5 4 3 2 1

First Edition

For Brendan

The Last Cruise

~~~~~ *part one*

THE THEATER
OF NOSTALGIA

chapter one

As Christine walked out of the air-conditioned terminal into the balmy, sweet air of Southern California, she inhaled sharply and started to laugh. She might as well have traveled to another planet. It was summer here. The air vibrated with sunlight. Bits of mica glinted in the pavement, making it sparkle. She walked through clumps of people with deep tans wearing shorts and sandals. When she looked down to steer her luggage cart over the curb, she caught a glimpse of the winter pallor of her own skin, dead white.

The cabbie helped her stow her luggage in his trunk. "You brought everything, I guess."

"I'm going on a cruise," she told him, trying to temper her giddy elation with apology. In the cab on the way to the hotel, she leaned her head against the back of the seat and watched the palm trees roll by. She wanted to drift on the fumes of the wine she'd drunk on the plane, lose herself in thought, but the cabbie was energetically chatty, with a musical but guttural accent she couldn't place. He had shining black hair and chalky skin, and he was skeletally skinny. She decided he was a vampire, which added a dreamlike, sinister undertone to his chattiness.

He was also, apparently, a self-appointed ambassador to Long Beach. "We are the seventh-largest city in California," he was saying. "We are the second-busiest seaport in the United States, as well as the Aquatic Capital of America. There are many boats to charter for excellent dolphin and whale watching. And the beaches. Five and a half miles. You have heard of Misty May-Treanor?"

Christine shook herself awake, trying to focus.

"Olympic gold-medalist beach volleyball star?" He peered at her in the rearview.

"Right," she said. She added, as if to justify her ignorance of this local celebrity, "I'm only here till tomorrow afternoon."

"Go to the Aquarium of the Pacific," he said, undaunted. "It is the second-most popular family destination in Los Angeles after Disneyland. And go aboard the *Queen Mary*."

"I'm about to be on the *Queen Isabella* for two weeks."

He was silent, possibly offended at her equating the two ships. She asked, "How long have you lived here?"

"Eight years," he said.

"Where are you from?"

"I moved here from Wisconsin."

"I mean originally?" She peered at his medallion, but his name was obscured by the large plush whale affixed to his dashboard.

He went quiet again, as if she had made another faux pas, this one even worse. Christine had never met a cabdriver in her life who was offended by this question, but of course there was always a first time.

In front of the hotel, under the porte cochere, the driver reached back and took the money she handed him, and when she waved away the change, he nodded with aggrieved gratitude, not meeting her eye.

"I apologize," she said, her door open, one leg out of the cab, her bag slung across her shoulder. "I shouldn't have asked where you're from. That's none of my business."

He finally looked directly at her with a small, tight smile. "I am from Wisconsin," he told her. "Have a nice stay in Long Beach, ma'am."

Christine had just turned thirty-six; she couldn't help taking that "ma'am" as a small slap in the face. She glared at the oblivious driver, regretting the guilt-induced generosity of her tip, while a valet transferred her bags from the trunk of the cab to a wheeled cart.

The dim, high-ceilinged lobby looked like the interior of a

modern bank, with a polished stone floor and a wall-long desk with several perky young corporate-looking people standing in a row behind it.

"Christine Thorne," she told the desk clerk, a plump blonde with a smoothly tanned, button-nosed face. "I have a reservation for one night. Under 'Valerie Chapin.'"

"Two queen beds?" said the woman, whose name was Rhonda, according to her nametag.

"That's right. My friend's arriving late tonight."

"No problem. I'll just need a credit card and ID, please."

Christine fished out her card and driver's license and handed them over.

"Wow," Rhonda said. "You've come a long way. Must be cold back there in New Hampshire."

"I actually live in Maine. Well, right on the border. For some reason, my mail comes through the New Hampshire post office, so that's officially where I'm a resident. But I'm really from Maine."

"Is there that much of a difference? Winters are shorter in Maine, or what?"

Christine gave her a look of gentle admonishment, the same look the cabbie had given her, she realized. Maybe all Americans were touchy about their provenance. "They're just different, I guess," Christine said. "But I'm definitely a Mainer. Six generations on my father's side."

Rhonda was looking at her with a vacant expression of bright interest that suggested another guest was standing behind her, waiting. She handed Christine a key card. "Will you be needing assistance with your bags?"

"Yes please," Christine replied, looking back at the valet with mild embarrassment. She wasn't used to people carrying things for her, but those bags were heavy. For a moment, she feared she didn't have enough cash after the cab fare to tip him. Then she remembered the five she always kept stashed in a side pocket of her shoulder bag; she'd put it there years ago, back when she still lived in New York. She'd never had to use it before.

"So what's the weather like back east right now?" said the valet as they stood side by side in the elevator. He had the gravelly voice of a heavy smoker, which struck her as odd, since she didn't think people smoked in Southern California.

"It's cold and wet," she said. "We call it mud season."

"Here, it's summer year-round," he said. "I get sick of it, to be honest. Well, only a little."

In room 712, he set her bags down professionally, one on the luggage rack, the other aligned with the closet door.

"Many thanks," she said, handing him her emergency fiver.

"Thank *you*," he said.

She kicked off her sturdy walking shoes (brand-new Merrells, free of mud) and padded in bare feet to the window to slide open the stiff drapes. Across from her was a painted mural of a pod of whales or dolphins swimming on the side of an enormous building; maybe that was the famous aquarium. She'd ask about it tomorrow. She owed the cabbie that much, she supposed. Even though he'd called her "ma'am."

Standing in front of the full-length mirror, she appraised herself honestly. Maybe she did look middle-aged, or at least unfashionable, here in this place of eternal youth and glamour. The cream-colored pedal pushers and long-sleeved black T-shirt that looked spiffy at the Portland Jetport had felt rural and frumpy the instant she'd stepped off the plane in L.A.; almost all the women in the airport wore yoga pants, stretchy low-cut tops, and wedge sandals. And her body, which was serviceably strong, youngish, and healthy, all she needed in Maine, had likewise begun to feel bulky and sexless next to all these super-slender Cali babes with their turbocharged boobs and butts like clenched fists of muscle.

Her cell phone buzzed.

"Hey," she said, picking it up and flopping onto the bed. "How's Sukey?"

"On the mend," came Ed's voice. "She ate her dinner without a fuss and took a good crap outside just now, no diarrhea. How was the flight?"

"Long. I treated myself to some wine. They make you pay for everything now. I had a salad, too. Kale." They both laughed. They grew mountains of the stuff every year.

"It's so quiet here," he said. "When are you coming home, again?"

Home, Christine thought with a funny, fond internal quailing.

Ed Thorne was ten years older than Christine, slight and handsome, with a square jaw and a small nose and bright blue eyes in a long face. In the early days, when they'd first fallen in love, he'd been so passionate, he had surprised her with his lustiness, his excitement, his desires and sexual openness. But they had quickly become a pair of oxen, yoked together, a farmer and his wife. This past year, she'd been distracting herself from Ed's yearning for kids with impossible fantasies about one of their apprentices, a local boy who slouched around the farm bare-chested in falling-down jeans that showed the waistband of his boxer shorts. He drove Ed nuts with his inefficiency while he drove Christine nuts in a wholly different way, with his pouty bee-stung lips and sculpted biceps.

"I'll be back before you even notice I'm gone," she said.

"Sure," Ed said. "How's the weather?"

"Weirdly warm. It feels wrong. But I love it."

"How's Valerie?"

"I haven't seen her yet. She's on a late flight from New York. Won't be here until midnight or something. I'll probably be sound asleep by then."

She yawned and heard him yawning on the other end of the line. It was three hours later there, dark already, and he'd been awake since before dawn, as had Christine. She pictured him alone with the dogs, looking absently at his solitary reflection in the big window by the woodstove, the house creaking in the cold, settling in for the night.

After they rang off, she lay on the bed for a while, holding the warm phone in her hand. She stretched out luxuriantly. She wasn't used to having a whole bed to herself. Ed flailed and twitched and rolled over in the night, waking her up, and then it always took a while to fall back asleep because she was nervous that he would jostle her again. She closed her eyes, sighing with tiredness. The mattress was nice and firm, and the pillowcases were starchy and fresh-smelling. Valerie wouldn't be here for hours.

She was just falling asleep when her stomach growled loudly and woke her up. That airplane-issue kale salad had been hours ago. Suddenly hungry, she got up and slid back into her shoes and put her key card into her bag. Down in the lobby again, she found the bar, a scattering of mostly empty tables tucked into a corner on the other side of the escalators that went down to the restaurant. She chose a corner table on a soft banquette, lit by the evening sun. Her body told her it should be dark by now, and that she shouldn't be hungry. She felt a pleasant jet-lagged sense of unreality.

The man sitting alone at the next table gave Christine a quick once-over; she could feel his stare although she wasn't looking at him. To her relief, he looked away again, having evidently deemed her not worthy of interest. So she glanced back at him. She had the brief impression of a chesty, muscular body, a pugnacious nose, dark short hair. He looked like a stevedore, like he no more belonged in this fancy hotel than she did. No doubt he had reached the same conclusion about her.

She ordered a margarita, no salt, and fish tacos.

"Good choice!" said the waitress, who was so pretty and well built that Christine had to take her in in sections: sleek muscular upper arm, aquiline nose, silky highlighted long hair, starfish eyelashes.

"Great," said Christine, smiling up at her.

The air felt liquid with permanent warmth. The people seemed liquid too. The bar felt like an aquarium. Inland Maine was all granite and hemlocks and interesting weather; its people were rugged workers, private, without artifice. Here, languid bodies displayed themselves openly. People spoke and laughed as if cameras were following them.

Her next-table neighbor was looking at the waitress too, but more pointedly, in a way that suggested intention.

"Are you going on that cruise?" the waitress asked Christine. "The *Queen Isabella*?"

"How could you tell?" Christine asked with a laugh.

"Lucky guess," said the waitress.

"I'm going on that cruise," the man next to Christine said. He had an accent similar to her cabdriver's, Eastern European undergirding fluent English. "I was just called in at the last minute."

Christine turned to look at him, frankly this time, since he'd spoken: a knuckle of a nose, dark eyes, strong jaw, and a hungry expression.

But he wasn't speaking to Christine. He was looking up at the waitress.

"Well lucky you too, then," she said.

"May I have another beer, please?" he asked.

"Sure. Where are you from? Your accent."

Wisconsin, Christine almost said.

But the man said, "Budapest. I'm Mick."

"Laura," the waitress told him.

Christine opened her book so she wouldn't appear to be eavesdropping. It was some long, engrossing thriller she'd found in the used-book bin in her local supermarket, along with a few other mildly interesting-looking castoffs she'd stockpiled and managed to fit into her bursting luggage.

"So are you excited for the cruise?" Laura was saying to Mick.

"No. I'm a cook, so I spend the whole time down in the galley, I hardly get any air, and I don't get to talk to people much. It's basically a long lonely time at sea for the workers on board."

"That sounds hard," Laura said. "Wow. I hope they pay you well."

Christine heard genuine warmth in her voice and wanted to warn her: *Don't tempt a starving man with raw meat.*

Sure enough, Mick succumbed. "Maybe you'd like to have a drink with me later, that would be great."

"Oh," Laura said. "Thanks, but I can't."

She took his empty glass and began to move off.

"Also, I'd like a hamburger," he said.

"And how would you like that?"

"Very rare, please." He held her there by the force of his eye contact. Christine could feel it without even looking at them. "I just arrived from another cruise," he said. "I thought I was going on vacation. Then the office calls and says, 'Hey Mick, the other guy can't do it, you gotta help us out, it's a special, a one-off, we need our best chef.'"

His American accent was spot-on. It made Christine wonder whether the Hungarian thing was fake, to impress Laura.

"Well, that sucks," said Laura. "I hate it when I have to cover for someone and I've made plans already. But you know, it's the job, right?"

"You know exactly what I'm talking about," said Mick. "You really can't have a drink later? Just a quick one. I have to be at the docks at four."

"I have plans already," said Laura, the warmth drained from her voice, shading into formality. "But thank you."

"Yeah," said Mick, "I should have figured."

"Well, I'll be right back with your beer and burger. And your margarita!" she said to Christine as she walked off.

"Thanks," said Christine, glancing up and looking quickly back down at her book. Mick sat very still, staring after Laura. She could feel how fixed his mind was. Maybe he was drunk. Of course he was drunk. She hoped Laura would be careful when she got off work.

After a while, a different waitress, this one dark and small and tough-looking, brought an enormous round white plastic tray and lowered it onto the table in front of her: the tacos. The steam rising from the hot fish made Christine ravenous.

"There you go," said the waitress as she put Christine's margarita down.

"I'll be right back with your order, sir," she said in Mick's direction, walking off.

Christine could feel Mick watching her as she took a bite of her tacos. They were delicious, the grilled fish fresh and tender, the lime slices ripe and juicy, corn tortillas warm and soft. She gobbled it all down, taking periodic sips of her sweet, tangy drink, which she happily noticed was heavy on the tequila, and let her attention wander around the room, carefully not looking at Mick. At the bar, a girl who looked fifteen or so stood talking to a man on a barstool, leaning in close to him. She wore a leather jacket, and below that, apparently nothing. Her small, globelike butt cheeks glowed. When she bent slightly at the waist, Christine saw her bikini bottoms flash, but then the girl straightened and was once again half naked. The man she was talking to put an arm around her and pulled her into a half hug. He must be her father, Christine told herself, knowing she was wrong. More likely her roommate's father.

She finished the tacos and downed the last gulp of sweet-tart melted ice in her drink, and sat back, panting gently. She was a bit tipsy, she realized, but whether this helped or worsened her sense of displaced alienation wasn't clear. It was amazing that you could get on an airplane in Portland, Maine, before one o'clock in the afternoon, change planes in Chicago, and get off in California at just after five o'clock in the evening. She felt as if most of her psyche was still hanging somewhere over the Midwest.

When the short, dark waitress finally brought Mick's burger and beer, Christine signaled for the check and absentmindedly ruffled the pages of her paperback while she waited.

Mick turned abruptly to her. Startled, she met his gaze. His dark eyes, unexpectedly sharp and intelligent, studied her, and for an instant she imagined she could see straight into his brute, embittered soul, and he could see back into hers, whatever it looked like. Probably bland and unremarkable to him, she thought, and she looked away, embarrassed, as the check came and she signed it to her room, and left the bar.

When she stepped outside, it was almost dark. She braced herself for the familiar bone-deep chill, tensing her arms close to her body and hunching her shoulders, but the air was still bathwater temperature, much warmer than the air-conditioned hotel had been, and her nose filled with the green, sweet smell of vegetation, a pleasurable shock after the sterile winter. She could feel her whole body relax into the unexpected relief of it. Strolling along the harbor path, she passed a few dawdling people, probably hotel guests like her, maybe fellow cruise-goers. She stopped to stare at the lights on the water. The harbor was a giant crescent around a calm and gleaming bay. Pelicans perched on the docks near moored sightseeing ships. Farther along, a ska band played an old Bob Marley song at a slightly slower-than-normal tempo, *"Lively up yourself, and don't be no drag."* The singer's accent was Latino. Christine stopped to listen, found herself sitting in the cool grass watching a small group of toddlers spinning around to the music, jigging up and down, calling to their parents to watch them.

The sight of these small, exuberant people made her anxious. She and Ed had been married for seven years. He wanted children. She didn't. There was no rational explanation for why she didn't want them. It was just a feeling. But she knew it was hard for Ed to understand. She wished she could tell him exactly how she felt on those bleak winter days, when the world was muffled with frigid snow, and she would look around their small rough farmhouse, and out at the white-shrouded woods and rocky meadows, the frozen lake, the middle of nowhere. She pictured herself as a nineteenth-century farm wife, bearing children in pain and danger, nursing and tending and rocking and nurturing them one by one as they arrived, along with all the other daily and seasonal chores. That had been her great-grandmother's life, even her grandmother's. The silence and isolation. The endless hard work: cleaning, washing, chopping wood, canning. It was the same work Christine did now, but in those days she would have done it all by hand, without a vacuum cleaner or a chainsaw, heating water on a woodstove, without any regular contact with the outside world: no telephone, e-mail, Internet. The reality of marriage back then, the rock-bottom duty of it all, always made her shudder—half pleasantly, because it wasn't actually her life. But it was close enough.

She resurfaced from her thoughts to discover that she was striding along the harbor path again. At some point she'd left the band behind, the dancing children, and now she was headed toward a grassy knoll, on top of which was a lighthouse. It could have been on the Maine coast.

Christine took off her shoes and sat, resting her chin on her bent knees, pressing her bare soles against the coarse sweet-smelling grass of the short hill, feeling a shivery pleasure in her solitude, a sense of possibility opening up before her as she gazed at the rosy water in the lowering light. Far out on what looked like islands was a gaggle of tall, spindly, insect-like oil rigs, gently bobbing as they pumped. Nearer in, the lights of the harbor glowed brighter as the sky got dark. Pelicans plummeted with open beaks toward the water. Even though they were rapacious predators, they looked appealingly clumsy and top-heavy. In the harbor, a freighter lay low in the water, stacked high with shipping containers, waiting to be unloaded by the cranes on the dock. She wondered what they were full of: maybe sneakers and cheap clothes from China or India, made by children in airless shacks. Or stuff made in shabby Third World factories, electronics or plastic toys or flimsy designer knockoffs of watches, bags, sunglasses. So much junk in the world, she thought: so much useless trash. Off to her right, in the next harbor over, hulked the grand, black-hulled *Queen Mary,* with her trio of raked funnels and black-on-red livery. Maybe the *Queen Isabella* was behind her, already in berth.

It struck Christine as completely absurd that she had just flown across the entire country and was about to get on a boat and sail to Hawaii. Back home, people went on cruises that left from Portland or Boston and sailed down the Atlantic coast to the Caribbean, or up to Nova Scotia and Prince Edward Island. Not that she'd ever been on a cruise before. She hated cruise ships. If Valerie hadn't invited her and insisted through Christine's repeated demurrals, Christine would never have agreed to do it.

But now that she was here, sitting in this seductive warmth, she was glad that she had. She felt the farm and Ed recede in her mind on a wave of tequila, along with her dog's illness, the long and harsh winter she'd just endured, the spring planting cycle starting up anew, training the summer's two apprentices. She knew all the hard work that waited for her as soon as she got home. She had been born into that work. She'd tried to escape it, had gone to journalism school, moved to New York and succeeded there, but Maine had called her back, in the end, as it did so many of its natives. *Come back now, take care of me,* it had called querulously, the opposite of a siren song, and she'd gone back, to marry a farmer, as Barnes women did.

Her phone buzzed. She took it out and looked at the screen. It was a text from Valerie. "Flight canceled. Taking the 6AM tomorrow. I'll meet you at the ship, I guess? Hope you're having fun!"

She wrote back, typing slowly with one thumb tip because she'd never learned to use two: "How horrible, so sorry. It's great here. Call me when you land tomorrow."

Feeling lighthearted at the prospect of a night alone in her own bed in her own room, Christine got up, slid her feet back into her shoes, and headed back along the path, toward the music, the dancing babies, the lights.

chapter two

The nonstop El Al flight from Tel Aviv to Los Angeles took fifteen hours and landed on the same day it left. During that entire day, as the plane followed its imaginary dotted line across the globe to crackling, tinny music (Miriam still thought in old newsreel images even though the last one she'd seen in a theater had been sometime in the 1950s), she worried about her violin, which was securely tucked overhead in its Bobelock crescent case with its strings properly loosened.

Miriam worried about her violin actively, as she would worry about a dog or a small child that might start whining or need its diaper changed. She tried to sleep for a few hours with her head smooshed on a little pillow against the window, but her body could never get comfortable on a plane. She found that if she didn't keep things moving, it all tightened up and ached.

Also, Isaac, her ex-husband, sitting next to her in the middle seat, was snoring. They had both grown up in the United States and emigrated to Israel in the mid-1960s. There, they had met as soldiers during the Six-Day War, in 1967, and had been married from 1971 until the late 1990s; it was hard for her to pinpoint when or why, exactly, the marriage had ended. They had finally gotten around to finalizing their divorce sometime later; again, the exact date eluded her, maybe because it didn't matter, in the end, since neither of them had ever remarried. Their passports proved that she and Isaac still shared a last name, his family's: Koslow. It was so close to Miriam's family name, Kosner, she hadn't seen the point in changing it back.

They even lived in the same Tel Aviv high-rise building, which wasn't exactly an old-age home, or even assisted living, but it was chock-full of old people, and there were nurses and doctors on staff and a dining room on the mezzanine that served kosher food soft enough for the toothless and bland enough for the dyspeptic. Isaac's larger apartment had a view of the Mediterranean, while Miriam, who lived on a lower floor, had a view of an unremarkable section of downtown Tel Aviv. Isaac was richer than Miriam because of a family inheritance, and she hadn't taken any of it in the divorce. All she had was what she made, performing with the Sabra String Quartet, which she and Isaac had formed in 1975 with Sasha Spektor and Jakov Strauss, and giving violin lessons. She couldn't afford to retire; not yet, anyway. Sometimes she thought about just moving in with Isaac and selling her place, not that he had offered that as a solution, but she was fairly certain she could bully him into it. So far, she had been able to keep going without resorting to that, but it was her backup plan in case her savings weren't enough when she got too decrepit to play music anymore. The Sabra Quartet had been performing together for more than forty years and was starting to fray around the edges: they were all getting old. They were in their last years together. They all knew it.

And yet here they were again, on yet another long plane ride, flying halfway around the world to play for their billionaire friends and benefactors, Larry and Rivka Weiss, on their two-week cruise to Hawaii. Miriam couldn't wait until the whole thing was over and she could be home again.

The stewardess, who had been working her way down the aisle with the drinks cart, had almost reached her row. "Stewardess" was the wrong word now. Flight attendants, you were meant to call them. Language was always changing, both English and Hebrew, and it was sometimes impossible to keep up. Everything was so politically correct now. Everyone was so sensitive. And being bilingual made it more complicated. Miriam didn't mean to screw up, she just couldn't help it. She had to tell herself not to say *"schwartze"* and *"faygala"* anymore, but sometimes she forgot.

The stewardess was smiling at Miriam, her head cocked with inquisitive politeness, as if she'd just shouted a question at a daft person, which she probably had. She was a gorgeous young thing, an olive-skinned, sloe-eyed Sabra with raven hair and lush lips. They were a dime a dozen in Israel, but it didn't make them any less appealing. Miriam thought they were the most beautiful women in the world.

"Tomato juice, please," said Miriam in Hebrew. "With some vodka on the side. I'd like Smirnoff if you have it."

"Bloody Mary mix?" the girl asked. "It's kosher."

"No!" Miriam said, in English now. "I hate that stuff, ecch, celery salt. Straight tomato juice. Kosher, I don't care about. Do you have any plain potato chips?"

"The snacks cart is right behind me," said the girl.

Isaac was awake and awaiting his turn to order. The sound of him drawing in his breath with a slight wet catch in his throat caused Miriam to clench her jaw and dig a fingernail into her palm. She had known this man almost her entire life and she had wanted to strangle or eviscerate him so many times, she no longer even noticed the urge when it came upon her.

Of course he was going to ask for a seltzer.

"Seltzer, please," he said in English. Isaac had never quite gotten the hang of Hebrew, even after all these decades, although he spoke it well enough when he had to. Miriam knew how proud he was; it made him insecure not to speak a language other than his native one, even though all the newly arrived Israelis of their generation had learned it together from scratch in the ulpanim. "Can I have the whole can?"

As the jet thrummed through the thin, high altitudes above the earth, they drank their beverages side by side, Isaac taking little sips of his, Miriam slugs of hers. The carbonation made his nose twitch. The vodka entered her bloodstream and made her feel fiery and young again. She crunched her potato chips. He sniffed, nibbled at his chocolate chip cookie. She closed her eyes and hummed, very lightly, her second-violin part to one of Schubert's slow movements, she couldn't remember which one right now. She could feel Isaac there next to her like a part of herself. Divorced or not, she knew that he was envious of her cocktail. He was allergic to liquor. It inflamed his cheeks and made him nauseated. One sip was enough. He'd been a great pothead in his day, but his lungs were too old now to tolerate it, so he ate it baked into sweets, which he loved.

On the plane, in the row behind them, sat the quartet's other half with Jakov's cello in the middle seat between them. Sasha, the first violinist, was drinking black coffee. Jakov was drinking red wine. They were an interesting pair: Sasha looked like a swarthy hawk with his strong tall body and sharp short hawk's beak of a nose and Russian black eyes and black-and-white wavy hair that hadn't thinned with age. Jakov the Lion's former wild mane of ginger curls had faded to a fluffy white-gold, but his face was still cherubic and catlike with pouting lips and slanted gold-green eyes. Miriam still thought both men were nice to look at, and for a while, way back when, she'd yearned to schtup them both. Not at the same time, necessarily; or maybe at the same time, sure, why not, since it was all purely hypothetical and always would be.

Really, Sasha was the one she'd always had a crush on, for as long as she'd known him. Once, fifteen years ago, during the slow movement of Schubert's *Rosamunde* Quartet, she and Sasha, side by side on their violins, had shared an interval of soulful communion with the music and each other. She was stirred for days afterward, all fluttery around him. He was the same around her, too, but they hadn't dared act on any of these feelings. Never mind that he was married. This was separate from that. This was music, this was work, this was their shared livelihood. And Isaac. They couldn't do that to Isaac. It would destroy the quartet. Besides, playing music together was sexy enough, most of the time. Except of course when there was squabbling or discord, which happened frequently, as it did in any family. The quartet was like a four-way marriage, she sometimes thought. But all this time, secretly, Sasha had been the one she wanted to be married to, for real. And she'd always suspected he felt the same about her.

Miriam hadn't had a romantic relationship with anyone since her divorce from Isaac. Maybe because of her ongoing yearning for Sasha, combined with their travel schedule and performing lives, she'd hardly had any sex at all, just a toss or two a decade or so ago with her sweet, helpful neighbor, Moshe Gross, and a brief affair with, of all people, her daughter-in-law's uncle, Ira Goldstein, whom she'd met and flirted with at her first grandson's bris. He was a cultured, intelligent man, courtly and generous and lusty. Their affair might have lasted, but he lived in Berlin, and neither felt like relocating, and Miriam traveled so much already, they couldn't figure out how to meet often enough to sustain their feelings for each other. So that was that, it all fizzled out, *pffft*. They'd lost touch long ago.

It was nice, daydreaming over her glass of tomato juice and vodka about her past sex life. It allowed her to forget that she was worried about this upcoming cruise for a number of reasons, Isaac's recent intonation issues and her own arthritis among them, Jakov's backstage tantrums over tempi, about which he and Sasha had never agreed, and Sasha's emotional fragility since his wife had died abruptly last spring of an aneurysm, which had caused him to miss the occasional entrance, something he had never once done in all these years. But the main thing she was worried about was playing the *Six-Day War* Quartet, a long and difficult piece that Rivka Weiss herself had written, on commission, for the Sabra Quartet last year. They hadn't had a chance to perform it yet; this would be their first time. Rivka of course was going to be on the cruise, with her billionaire husband, Larry, who was one of the owners of the ship. And Rivka had made it known to them that she was excited to hear her quartet performed. The problem was that they had hardly had any time to rehearse it yet, and worse, "The Weiss," as they called it, ominously, was spiky, dissonant, and contained a full fifteen seconds of silence during the Andante. Miriam's second-violin part was full of tricky double-stops that were nearly impossible to play in tune, as well as scampering, atonal arpeggios that demanded intense concentration.

Miriam was sure her part had been written with a certain punishing vindictiveness. Rivka had never liked her, for some reason that Miriam couldn't understand. But the Weisses had funneled a generous amount of money in the Sabra's direction over the years. The quartet depended exclusively on Larry's goodwill for their most lucrative yearly gig, the summer concert series at the Jewish Folk Art Museum. Their fees from that series alone paid Miriam's apartment dues and expenses for the entire year. And Larry was on the *Queen Isabella,* the very ship they were sailing on. So they had to play the Weiss on this cruise, and they had to play it well, despite the piece's extreme difficulty. And they probably had to play it more than once, because after the first performance, Rivka would have notes for them, no doubt. She always had critiques, elaborate, poetic, demanding, and impossible to obey: *"The opening fifteen bars of the scherzo have to be drawn out, slowly, slowly, slowly, like pulled taffy, like a sigh, like the slow fall of water into a bowl from a great height."* That had been written on the actual score. It reminded Miriam of the vague, pretentious notes Debussy used to add to his music, smacking of insecurity and control issues. "Which one is it like?" she had snorted to Isaac. "The taffy or the water? Or the sigh?"

Miriam finished her drink and put her head back on her pillow and shut her eyes.

"Three more hours," said Isaac in the direction of Miriam's ear. He hadn't spoken in a very long time. He coughed to clear his throat. The sounds of his rattling phlegm caused her to snap her eyes open and make an annoyed clucking sound, which made Isaac huff. "I'm choking," he said.

"Choke quietly," she said. "I'm trying to sleep."

As Isaac continued gently snorting with the remnants of his choking fit, Miriam gave up on sleep and turned around to look through the crack in the seats at Sasha, directly behind her. He was awake and staring straight ahead, his face blank, sagging, his eyes dull. Such a handsome face, it made her so sad to see him like that, collapsed in grief. She wished she could cheer him up.

"It's almost over," she said. "We land in less than three hours."

He didn't respond. Was he going deaf? That would be a catastrophe.

She turned around again and opened her book, fretting.

*

The plane landed with a heavy jolt. Isaac clenched his fists on his thighs. Miriam reached over and took his hand. "We made it," she said. He squeezed her hand, and like that they were friends again.

After clearing customs, the four of them walked a little stiffly out into the early evening sunshine, wheeling all their instruments and bags in various carts. While they waited on the curb for a cab big enough to fit them all, Miriam inhaled through her nose. The smell of this place was so familiar, so anciently known. She had been born and raised in Los Angeles, then schooled in New York City at Barnard and Juilliard, before she'd left Greenwich Village in the early '60s as a young Zionist, all fired up with newfound political Jewish fervor, to make aliyah and live on a kibbutz. She'd lived in Israel ever since. Sometimes, though, she wished she could go back to Los Angeles, the city of her birth. But inertia, money, and the quartet had kept her in Tel Aviv. It was so easy to live there, with its beautiful climate and geriatric-Jew-friendly benefits. It was almost like living in Southern California, but better, because their water problem was figured out with desalination and recycling of gray water. And in Tel Aviv, she didn't have to worry about earthquakes, landslides, fires, or tsunamis. The only thing she feared was the people, all the chauvinistic zealots and rioting hotheads. And given the choice, she preferred to live with the dangers she knew best, the ones she understood.

Still, her earliest memories were here. And it felt good to be back, smelling the smells of her childhood. She wished she could stay a few days instead of driving straight to Long Beach and getting on a boat tomorrow.

When they had stowed all their gear in the back of a mini-van, with Jakov's cello taking up half the back row of seats, they strapped in and the young Hispanic driver inched out into the thick LAX traffic.

L.A.'s freeways were not so familiar to Miriam; she hadn't had a driver's license when she'd lived in Los Angeles, or even in New York. That had come later, in the 1960s, in her early twenties, when she'd learned to drive in a jeep in the Sinai Desert. But she remembered driving all over the city as a little girl in her parents' Chevrolet, stuck in the bench backseat between her two older brothers, cigarette smoke blowing on the hot breeze from the front seat. Her parents were always chain-smoking. She remembered her father's bald head gleaming with sweat where his yarmulke didn't cover, her mother's brassy, stiff wig curls staying in place no matter how windy it got. Her father had been a high school math teacher. Her mother had been a pianist, and a very good one, who'd given up any chance of a career for the usual reasons Orthodox women gave up the idea of a career in those days. But she'd taught piano lessons in their Boyle Heights apartment.

All at once, Miriam was there again, in the old neighborhood. It came back in one whoosh of memory: their cool, sprawling second-story apartment in the Wyvernwood; dust motes swirling in the light near the projection booth when the movie started in the Brooklyn Theater; the Breed Street shul with its carved benches and painted murals and stained-glass windows; the B-line streetcar that rattled and jolted through the traffic and was so much fun to ride. She remembered hearing the Kol Nidre sung during the High Holy Days in her grandparents' Wilshire Boulevard Synagogue with its beautiful domed, gold beehive ceiling, her stomach rumbling with hunger along with everyone else's. She could hardly remember her bat mitzvah. She'd been so nervous. Daniel Fischel! He was there, and as she'd sung her haftorah portion, she'd looked up and met his eyes and almost forgotten her place.

Her first kiss had been with Daniel at the Brooklyn Theater. They were both fourteen, so it had been 1956 . . . What was the movie . . . ? Something very dramatic, with what's-her-name, that's right, it was *Giant.* Miriam could remember the taste of the butter from the popcorn on Daniel's mouth. His hot hands on her waist. Her first love. That romance had ended when her family moved to the San Fernando Valley in the late 1950s, when the freeways were built through the old neighborhood and the Jewish population became increasingly leftist and radicalized. Miriam's last two years of high school in the Valley had been dull, no boyfriend, a lot of schoolwork and practicing her violin and hardly any fun, because she was so focused on straight A's and escaping to New York to start her real life. She had left at seventeen on a full scholarship to Barnard. So that was all, that was Los Angeles, it was all Boyle Heights for her.

And it was gone, all of it. Her parents and brothers were all dead. She had no family here anymore. When she'd gone back five years ago to visit her old neighborhood, she had found it so changed she didn't recognize it. The Boyle Street shul had been abandoned and wrecked, graffitied, with pigeon feathers on the floor. The Brooklyn Theater, which had closed decades ago and been turned into retail stores, was razed, and now there was an empty lot there, unless they'd already built something else on top of it. And there were no more streetcars, not since the early '60s.

The minivan had been crawling along the 405, but the traffic cleared as if by magic and they picked up speed and whipped along. Isaac, Jakov, and Sasha all looked completely *farmutschet,* three old men who'd just flown around the world. Miriam imagined she looked as tired as they did. The Kol Nidre was going around in her head now, that most sacred of prayers. She was imagining the version recorded by Itzhak Perlman and Cantor Yitzchak Meir Helfgot in 2012, so soulful, so moving for her to listen to, truly the embodiment of sacredness in music. Miriam thought Itzy and Yitzy (as she called them to herself) probably liked each other a lot, listening to the recording. You could always hear in the music how the musicians felt about one another. She knew that was true of the four of them.

"Los Angeles is so dirty," said Isaac. He was sitting in the front, next to the driver. Miriam and Sasha sat in the forward passenger seats, and Jakov was in the back with his cello. "Such a dirty town. The air is brown, there's trash everywhere."

"That's not true," said Miriam. "The air's been cleaned up a lot. Where do you see trash? Show me."

"It's not that I see it right now," said Isaac, turning back to look at her. "I didn't say I saw it right now. I'm making a general statement."

"The water's not so good either," said Sasha. "What's left of it . . ."

"Who cares?" said Jakov from the back seat. "We're here for one night. Then it's all ocean breezes and purified drinking water for two weeks. I read that cruise ships have the cleanest drinking water."

"Cruise ships," said Isaac. "All you hear about cruises lately is people getting sick because of other people not washing their hands after they go to the bathroom. I'd rather stay on dry land any day. I'd rather perform in a department store."

"I like a cruise," said Jakov. "The food is always good, and the audiences are usually too drunk to notice when you flub a note."

"I never flub a note," said Isaac. He coughed with agitation.

Sasha still wore the blank, sepulchral expression Miriam had noticed on the plane.

"Sasha," she said now, "what's wrong with you?"

"I'm dreading the Weiss," he said.

"Oh, I was dreading it the entire plane ride."

"I don't think I can play it anymore."

"*You* can't? I'm the one with the impossible part! Your part is all gliss and legato."

"Is that what you think my part is? Have you ever played it?"

"The whole Weiss is unplayable," said Jakov. "And unlistenable."

"I like it," said Isaac. "It's exciting."

"The Weiss is not exciting," said Miriam. "It's horrible."

"So what should we do?" said Sasha. "Are we really going to play this thing on the ship?"

"If we don't," said Miriam, "Rivka will hate us, and Larry will never hire us again. But I'm okay with that if you are."

"Of course we're playing it," said Isaac. "And we'll play it well. Stop being such babies. We'll rehearse it for the first few days and then we'll play it one night in the middle of the cruise sometime."

A dread-filled, resigned silence hung over the van. The cab came off the freeway and slid through the streets of Long Beach down toward the harbor. When they pulled up at their hotel, Miriam paid the driver with their business credit card and tipped him, squinting through her reading glasses at the damned machine. The display was hard to read when she was this tired. Yawning, holding their aching backs, they climbed from the minivan and stood blinking under the hotel's porte cochere with their instruments and luggage. Swiftly, bellhops swooped in and collected everything, ushering them all into the lobby, toward the front desk.

Their four rooms were on four different floors. It was one of the stipulations they made when they traveled, along with airplane seats in different rows. Their booking agent had screwed up this time with the plane seats, but at least he'd gotten the hotel right. Up in her stark, drab room on the ninth floor, Miriam ran a bath and undressed. Just as she was about to sink into the warm water, her room phone rang, that ugly electronic bleating all the phones had now. The little screen on the bathroom phone identified the caller as room 1216. She picked up the handset, looking at her naked reflection in the mirror in the bright lights. Never had she looked older or uglier in her entire life. And she prided herself on keeping her looks into old age, and her figure, too. She was slender and her face was still pretty firm, but her reflection looked a hundred years old, wizened. What did they make these hotel lights and mirrors out of? It made her want to jump out the window. No wonder hotel windows didn't open.

"Mimi," said Isaac when she picked up, "can you come quick?" His voice was urgent, high. He spoke English.

"Where?"

"To my room. I need you to look at something."

"I'm about to get in the bath. I'm falling down with exhaustion. Can this wait until tomorrow? Or can you get Jakov to come look at it?"

"I have something on my . . . my scrotum," he said. "Jakov can't look at it."

"For God's sake. You men are so delicate. He has one too, you know. It's no mystery to him. What's on your scrotum that you need me to come and look at it right this minute?"

"It looks like a cancer."

"Go to sleep, Isaac. It won't kill you before morning." She hung up the phone and stared at it. Then she called the front desk. "Please hold all my calls," she told the person who answered. "Especially from room 1216."

She climbed into her bath and scrubbed herself well, ignoring all possible signs of skin cancer, although there were two or three suspicious-looking moles and an unhealed sore on her shoulder that she'd been a little worried about. She refused to be a hypochondriac like Isaac. She'd die of skin cancer first.

chapter three

Mick stood on the dock watching as forklifts unloaded pallets into the *Queen Isabella*'s delivery bay, to be picked up by other forklifts and cube-waltzed into her belly before being conveyed to the storage rooms below. He was still a little drunk, but he was an expert at working under the influence, any influence, for any length of time. He could work for thirty hours straight and put himself into a waking trance, drunk, stoned, or high, and never drop anything or miss a detail. His hands and his brain had struck an agreement: his brain did what it wanted, and his hands ran the show. That was how he survived this job.

He shoved his hand into a box of asparagus on a waiting pallet. The stalks were damp. Any wetter and he'd have to reject them. He nodded at the forklift driver. It was almost five o'clock in the morning. The sky over the harbor was the color of eggplant. Inland, the horizon showed streaks of eggshell and cream. Everything looked like food to Mick; not edible, but in need of attention, quality control, prep. The air smelled like diesel exhaust. He felt as if he'd never be allowed to lie down and sleep again. His eyelids crackled with dry sand. His mouth was so parched he sucked his own tongue. *Az Isten verje meg* . . . he was thinking in Hungarian, he was so tired. He allowed himself to slump, standing with his eyes closed for five long, ticking seconds, a micro-nap, as his brain rebooted itself. Then he straightened up and got back to work.

A pallet of broccoli came by. He thrust a hand into a random box and felt the springy green firmness of a flower. In four days, it would be limp and browning. But for now, it was perfect. Thank God. He hated sending broccoli back; he always needed every stalk. Broccoli was the cornerstone of the plating garnishes, a staple of the salad bar, a key player in the vegetable-of-the-day medleys. He had a good idea of the *Isabella*'s menu, but didn't know yet precisely what it entailed. He'd find out soon enough. He had a meeting with the executive chef at 0730.

Normally, the job of overseeing the deliveries was done by the storekeeper, but this cruise was small and just a one-off, so they hadn't hired one. Mick was one of three executive sous-chefs, working directly under the executive chef in either the one main restaurant galley or the buffet galley, he didn't know yet which. He was usually a station chef, a line cook; this was a promotion. He suspected it was only temporary, since he was filling in for someone else, but if he did a good job, it wouldn't go unnoticed. Nothing ever did on a cruise ship. Anyway, it was nice to be outside, on land. He'd spend enough time in the belly of this ship in the next two weeks. He might as well get all the fresh air he could in the meantime. Not that this air was particularly fresh.

He rummaged around and pulled an oyster out of a box marked WASHINGTON STATE. He fished a shucking knife out of his jacket and opened it, slurped the sweet-briny nugget from its bed. He scowled at the forklift driver as if it were possibly bad and shucked another one, making the guy wait. The second was as energizing as the first. He nodded at the driver and the pallet moved on.

That waitress last night, what had gotten into him? The look in her eye. She had run away and sent the other one over, the short dark one, and had stayed on the other side of the room. He was a drunk creep now. Fuck it. It had been too long since he'd touched a woman. He never got involved with anyone on a ship, not out of faithfulness to Suzanne, who had never been faithful to him, but because he didn't have time or energy. Women on cruise-ship crews were young and luscious and decadent, for the most part. They drank and got stoned and slept around and had as much fun as they could, even though they were working the same long hard hours everyone else worked. He needed to fuck one of them soon. He needed Suzanne.

His hand snaked into a box on the next pallet and encountered a neatly packed row of rotund things with rough prickly skin and hard spiky tops. They felt like tiny magueys grafted onto the tops of miniature barrel cacti. They were fresh, firm and full of turgor. He thought of aloe, with its thin green slime, good for kitchen burns. But this wasn't a succulent. Then all at once his mouth was filled with the memory of a fruit: juicy, tart, sweet, fibrous. He felt a powerful craving for grilled chunks, with pork, soy sauce, something spicy. Pineapples. The cruise was going to Hawaii: of course. He waved the pallet on.

The *Isabella* rose sleekly from the water, much smaller than the last ship he'd worked on. That had been a five-month stint on a vast white behemoth that accommodated four thousand passengers, most of them Americans who had opted for the package that included unlimited sodas from dispensers that read a chip in their ship-issued plastic cups. The ship itself mirrored the people on it, oversized, out of proportion, expelling ground-up food waste and treated sewage into the ocean, spewing colossal clouds of exhaust into the sea air, a giant pissing, shitting, farting beast. While the kitchens in its massive belly disgorged ton after ton of French fries, pizza, and grilled slabs of steak upward to be chewed and swallowed and deposited into smaller, individual massive bellies, belowdecks the foreign-born, mostly Third World crew worked long, hard days, slept little, ate little, gave themselves over to keeping this untenable system, the dream vacation, going.

But this ship was a different animal entirely. He had learned from the brochure the office manager had handed him that the *Queen Isabella* had originated in a more elegant, scaled-down era, before cruise ships got put on steroids and turned into so-called "floating cities." She'd been built in France in the early 1950s, renovated and refurbished in the 1970s, sold to Cabaret Cruises, an American company, and re-renovated and re-outfitted in 2002. She had just two raked funnels and only five decks from the waterline up, and carried a fraction of the thousands of passengers they crammed aboard those supersized monsters. Her lifeboats hung from davits, low down. Her curved stern swooped high over the water. Her bow rose at a sharp angle.

Mick had been told very little about this cruise, but he knew that it was the *Isabella*'s last before she was retired: a two-week cross-Pacific jaunt that would take them to three ports of call in the Hawaiian Islands followed by a reverse trip back. The tone was meant to echo and imitate her first cruise in 1957: retro menu, classic cocktails, cabaret singers, jazz bands, string quartets, old movies, blackjack and baccarat in the casino. Everyone would be expected to dress for dinner. There was no Internet service, and no one under sixteen was permitted on board.

All of this Mick approved of, not because he hated contemporary music, or kids, or the Internet, or informal clothes, but because he loved cooking the classic old dishes from vintage menus: oysters Rockefeller, lobster Newburg, clams casino, steak Diane. He liked aspic. He liked Hollandaise sauce and champagne sherbet and avocado halves stuffed with shrimp salad; he liked real cocktails, martinis and highballs. He romanticized that time of honestly fancy food and drink, back before farm-to-table became an elitist idea claimed by the rich instead of what the peasants ate, before the magic tricks of molecular gastronomy with its emulsions and foams, before "craft cocktails" in Mason jars made with infusions and smoke and fey garnishes. Growing up in Budapest at the end of the twentieth century had been something like having a 1950s American youth. It felt familiar to him, cozy and civilized.

So he didn't dread this cruise as much as he'd dreaded the last one. Two weeks of making food he knew, and then he'd finally get to see where things stood with Suzanne.

His hand was shoved deep inside of a box of onions, looking for the dry-papery rasp that meant they were fresh. He sniffed his fingers. There was a trace of mold. That was bad, but the onions felt okay. He'd get someone to sort them and use up the moldering ones fast. Another wave of exhaustion penetrated to his bones. He waited for it to recede. It didn't. He stumbled and caught the edge of a pallet to keep from falling. Automatically, his hand found the inside of a box. Wet, slimy, and jagged. He pulled his hand back: broken egg. There was never just one. He was too tired to care, and it smelled fresh enough on his hand. He waved it through. The albumen tightened around his fingers as it dried. He fished a sanitary wipe from a pocket and wiped his hand clean, then fished out and put on the latex gloves he should have been wearing all along. Another pallet: iceberg lettuce. Images of wedge salads with bacon and Roquefort dressing rose in his mind, antic, dancing, plates tilted and spinning. He squeezed a few heads. They had crunchy heft and enough watery give. Okay then, on they went. Then his hand was inspecting a T-bone steak, prodding, massaging, pinching gently. He sniffed his latex-covered fingers, inhaling the mineral tang of flesh and blood. The water shimmered with fresh, early sunlight. A pelican was strutting along the dock. Everything kept closing in on his eyes, zooming dark then expanding again. *Sleep,* his brain commanded. He needed a catnap before his meeting with the executive chef, whose name he hadn't been told yet. Otherwise he'd be incoherent and crazed-looking on his first day of work.

After the last pallet went into the hold, he staggered behind it into the *Queen Isabella* and went along the wide central passageway. His quarters, he was sure, weren't ready for him yet, so for now he'd have to improvise. Various crewmembers in uniform rushed by him, not registering his presence. He didn't know the precise layout of this particular ship, but he could figure it out.

He climbed through the stairwell, up and up, then saw sunlight under the door marked EXIT, pushed it open, and found himself on an empty deck, of all the lucky breaks. It was lined with deck chairs. With any luck he could lapse into a restorative coma for fifteen minutes or so before anyone saw him. He walked swiftly to the end of the deck, ducked under a railing, and climbed into a private nook. He stretched out on a flat, cushioned deck chair, put one arm over his face to shield his eyes from the sun, and was almost instantly in a deep, animal sleep.

His dream was vivid and felt real. He was swimming under-water with a school of large fish who bumped up against him and blew bubbles in his direction but otherwise left him alone, as he did them. The water was bathtub warm. The sun shone high overhead, glinting on the surface above him, and he didn't seem to need to breathe. That was it, the whole dream. It went on and on until a loud noise woke him up, a hollow metallic clang nearby.

His arm flew off his face and he sat up, wide awake, aware of where he was and why, being in the long-practiced habit of tran-siting from sleep to wakefulness in a split second. He replayed the noise in his mind as he scanned the deck: whatever it had been, the deck was still empty. He had slept a fairly long time, according to the position of the sun, which had thrown his balcony into shade as it rose. Maybe half an hour. Too long.

He leapt up off the deck chair and headed back to the door to the stairwell, hoping it hadn't locked behind him. He'd been too tired to remember to prop it open. He checked his phone: 7:27. He was going to be a few minutes late to the first staff meeting, a seri-ous offense. If the door was locked, he was fucked.

The door was unlocked: his second piece of luck of the day. He flung himself down the stairwell. His mouth was still dry, and his eyes burned. He wondered how his breath smelled and decided it was better not to think about it. His armpits, same thing. He burst through the lower door into what he hoped was the right corridor, and walked fast in the direction he hoped would take him to the meeting room. He ran his fingers through his hair and brushed his hands over his jacket to make sure it wasn't askew. Equally crazed people rushed all around him. It was now 7:30 on the nose. He followed another guy in a chef's jacket around a corner, up another flight of stairs, and down another corridor. The other guy pushed open some swinging doors and there they were, the galley crew, sitting in what looked like the breakfast buffet room around the longest table. Without the guy ahead of him, Mick never would have found this room. Now he was plausibly on time. He glanced at his savior's face: very black, young, clean-shaven, with a close buzz cut. He'd thank him later. Maybe he'd find an ally. The guy wore a yellow neckerchief: chef de partie.

His neckerchief! The office manager had issued it to him just hours before, along with his checked pants and jacket and toque. Mick pulled it from his pocket and looked at it: it was black and silver, signifying his elevated status. He tied it around his neck as he slid into an empty chair between two kids in green neckerchiefs: low on the totem pole, one male, one female. They both gave him sidelong looks, ascertained his rank, and sat up straighter. For the first time, Mick fully grasped the fact that he was one of three sous-chefs who shared the second-in-command position here.

"Hello, everyone," said the man who had to be the executive chef, because he was the only person in the room who didn't have to wear a neckerchief. He didn't look like much: slight and pale with a long, toothy face, freckled, bespectacled. "Welcome to the *Queen Isabella*." His accent might have been South African, maybe New Zealand, Mick couldn't tell. "I will assume we're all here. Because you don't want to be late, ever, for anything, or I will cut off your head."

No one laughed. No one was expected to.

Some poor straggler came in then. No one but Mick dared to turn and look. It was a girl in an orange neckerchief, he saw: poor sacrificial lamb. The rest of the staff stared at their leader, who pinned the latecomer with a laser stare.

"Well! And you are late because . . . ?"

"I couldn't find the room, Chef," she said. "I got lost. I apologize and I promise I will never get lost again as long as I live." She was cheeky, defiant, under a veneer of caution. Her accent was Spanish maybe, or Mexican or South American.

All the melodrama, the theater, the interpersonal power displays of the professional kitchen, Mick couldn't stand any of it. He already hated this guy. She was one minute late, and this room had been hard to find. Why not let her come in and sit down quietly and get on with the fucking meeting?

"I will hold you to that promise," said the executive chef. He stared at her for a couple of beats while she found a chair and sat down. "As I was saying. Hello, everyone. I'm Laurens van Buyten, as most of you know."

Mick stared at him. *That* guy. Why hadn't he realized? Why had no one mentioned it to him, the guy in the main office, the woman who'd given him his uniform and marching orders, anyone? Van Buyten was the most famous chef in the business. If cruise-ship chefdom had a movie star, this was the guy. He was Belgian, a hotshot, and he was young, Mick's age. He'd come up through European fine-dining hotel kitchens and New York restaurants. Now he judged cooking shows and was rumored to be opening his own restaurant in Amsterdam. And he was maybe thirty-four.

Somehow Mick had managed never to land in Van Buyten's kitchen before. He'd only heard about him from other chefs who'd suffered under him and lived to talk about it. He was one of those guys who watched you quietly while you dug yourself deeper into the weeds, just stood there seeming to grow bigger and bigger, swelling with power and swaying slightly like a king cobra, his tongue flicking in and out, while you burned yourself on a handle and fucked up the timing of a filet of expensive fish and dropped the ladle of sauce on your foot, then he struck like lightning and stopped your breathing with toxic venom and your eyes bugged out and you died. Or so the rumors went.

Of course now would be the first time Mick had to work directly under this sadist, these particular two weeks when he was wrung out and his brain was fried and he wasn't even supposed to be on this ship. Of course.

Mick watched his new, temporary boss, trying to identify his tell or weakness—because everyone had one—in order to use it to keep him off-balance, to keep him from wielding too much power over him, since he already recognized him as someone who would do so any chance he got. Chef Laurens sat at the head of the table, leaning back in his chair with his left arm dangling behind him, holding a pencil in his right hand whose eraser he was using to trace circles on the tabletop in front of him while he looked waywardly through smeared glasses up at the ceiling, at the door, along the table, down at his hand holding the pencil, never directly at anyone. He spoke with a clipped, rushed cadence, as if he were carefully controlling a tumult in his head, parceling out a whole welter of stuff in pips and nuggets to keep the deluge dammed, controlled. So he was shy and emotionally chaotic. What chef wasn't? Mick was too.

As he made eraser donuts on the tabletop, Laurens described in his flat voice the adventure they were about to embark upon together, re-creating the menus of a once-grand ship for its last cruise. This was clearly his attempt to inspire slavishness in the breasts of his peons for the duration of the voyage. He wanted to win them over before he scared the shit out of them, classic cult recruitment love-bombing. Looking around at the faces of the troops, Mick had to admit he was doing a pretty good job. These multiethnic kids, most of whom had likely never heard of half these dishes, actually looked eager to cook Welsh rarebit and con-sommé madrilène under the direction of this pale despot.

Laurens reached into a satchel by his feet and pulled out a fat, worn book. He held it up so everyone could see it.

"*Mastering the Art of French Cooking.* You all know it?"

The room erupted with nods.

"This is your bible," he said. "Everything is in here. As you know, Julia Child was a stickler and her recipes are formidably labor-intensive. But this is our book for the next two weeks. Every staff dinner, we will say a prayer to the late great Julia. Now for the buffet."

He consulted a paper at his right elbow.

"Miklos Szabo," he said, pronouncing it perfectly. "Why don't you tell us what you've got planned."

Mick raised his hand. So he was on buffet. Good to know. Laurens fixed him in his sights as Mick cleared his throat. Every face in the room turned toward him, every set of eyes fixed on him.

"Call me Mick," he said, unsmiling, playing the gruff but fun-damentally good-hearted Eastern European bloke whose good side you wanted to be on because you didn't want to see his bad side. He knew the theatrical power tropes of the professional kitchen as well as anyone. "Hello, Chef, everyone."

He spotted a couple of kids who'd worked under him before, good kids who caused no trouble. He looked at everyone's face for signs of incipient flaws, potential for insurrection. He saw only shiny eyes, neatly groomed heads, spotless uniforms, perky neckerchiefs, like a scout group, a fresh-faced crew for the old *Isabella*'s swan song.

"Chef Laurens has laid out the main dining room menu," he went on. "So let's talk about the buffet." He lifted one side of his mouth in a half smile to stall for the second or two it took him to shake a plan loose from his gummed-up brain. For a bad split second, his mind went blank. Then he opened his mouth, and words came out. "Tonight we're going to bring together two fun food trends from the era of this ship's first cruise: Hawaiian and barbecue. Since this is a Hawaiian cruise, right?"

He took a breath, trying to decide how much of a lecture he should give them.

"When soldiers came home from the South Pacific," he said, "postwar Americans discovered canned pineapple, their fencepost drug to Hawaiian cuisine."

"Gateway," muttered the girl who'd come in late.

He ignored her and went on, trying to sound knowledgeable, like a leader. "And barbecue had become very popular as well in the suburbs, not the slow-smoked kind, but Dad grilling meat over coals on the patio while Mom made cold salads like macaroni, Jell-O, and potato. This postwar America was a very nice place. We want our passengers to experience that. Now, times feel less safe, much less secure."

He sensed a bit of restlessness.

"Tonight," he said, and they snapped to attention again, "for our welcome buffet, we're offering a suburban version of a Hawaiian cookout, like a luau, but with suckling pigs on spits instead of the whole pig cooked in a pit on a beach. Pineapple spareribs, fried rice, we'll do shrimp kebabs and grilled mahi-mahi with a fruit slaw, fruit everywhere, in salads and centerpieces, flowers. And we'll have ukulele music and tiki torches and dancers in grass skirts. Someone needs to coordinate with the entertainment director."

While he talked, Mick felt himself returning from his exhausted walkabout in the nether regions of his psyche. His dream of swimming underwater with all those large fish had been about his job. It had been about fourteen- or sixteen-hour days belowdecks in the steamy kitchen bumping up against other cooks, not needing to surface or even breathe, not needing to leave his medium for any reason, because, he remembered now, this was where he felt most at home, his natural habitat. He was ready for this.

The meeting swept on. When it was over, and everyone had dispersed to work in the galleys, to find their quarters, to hammer out unfinished contractual business in the main office, Chef Laurens looked at Mick and summoned him over with a tip of his head.

"The person who was late," he said. "Please deal with her appropriately. Make sure she knows that is unacceptable on my ship."

"Yes, Chef," said Mick.

"I don't know you. You're with Cabaret?"

"For the past eight years," said Mick. "I just came off five months in the Caribbean and the Bahamas on the *Illusion*."

"Ah," said Laurens. "That explains it. Well, this should be a cakewalk. Four hundred passengers and no tricks." He sniffed. His freckled pale nose twitched slightly, but he didn't sneeze. He pushed his glasses up on his nose. He was a gangly, weedy schoolboy, by all appearances. It worked to his advantage, so that when he struck, it would be as terrifying as a meek rabbit attacking viciously out of nowhere with a snake's fangs.

There was nothing further. Mick was apparently dismissed. Okay, then.

He walked to the window of the buffet room, taking out his phone. There was a signal here. He dialed: it was early afternoon in Paris.

"Meek," Suzanne said in a breathy exhalation. *"Allô, chéri."* She was in bed with someone. The guy was right there, maybe even fucking her while she held the phone to her ear. And meanwhile, her caller ID had told her it was Mick, and she'd picked up the phone. "Just a second. Hang on." He waited. What was she doing? he wondered. Getting out of bed, leaving the guy there to wait for her to come back when she finished with her call. Throwing her robe on over her naked body, tossing her hair back, lighting a cigarette, opening the casement windows and stepping with the phone onto her little balcony, out into the skin-tingling chill of a spring day in Paris.

He should have been there; he should have been the one fucking her. This call was costing him a lot of money, and for what? It was torture.

Her voice came back to his ear then. *"Allô?"*

"I'm calling to say goodbye," he said.

"So you are going. For how long?"

"Two weeks. I could be in Paris by May fifth."

"May fifth," she repeated. She hesitated.

It wasn't enough. He loved her. He couldn't take it anymore.

"Or maybe I won't come," he said. "I don't know. I should go to Budapest and see my father."

"No," she said. "Come, we'll figure it out."

They always spoke English, although Mick's French was passable. He was used to it; English was the lingua franca on the cruise ships too. He only ever spoke his native language with fellow Hungarian crew, when there were any, which was almost never.

Suzanne was a philosophy professor at the Sorbonne, of all the unlikely things. She was ten years older than Mick, quintessentially French, cerebral and unsentimental, highly sexual but not especially sensual. She loved to fuck, that was all. Mick looked tough and solidly practical, a hardworking Magyar, but he was a secret cornball romantic who swooned at beautiful music. He was smart enough, he'd read books, but he was no university professor. They were unsuited to each other in every way that he could see, and yet he adored her, heart and soul, and he thought she loved him back, in her way. They'd met in Bali five years before, and since then, he visited her every chance he got. Meanwhile, she slept with whomever she pleased and assured him it didn't matter. He slept with no one and assured her it did. The thought of her with another man made him implode with jealousy, but there was nothing he could say: he lived at sea. She owed him nothing. They'd exchanged no assurances of fidelity, ever, and he told himself with stalwart, difficult fairness that he had no right to ask that of her.

Now he had to be away from her for two more weeks. That wasn't so long, in the scheme of things. But as he pocketed his phone, he had a sad feeling that this was it, it was over, it had to be. He couldn't subject himself to this constant heartache anymore. It wasn't worth it, no matter how much he loved Suzanne.

It was getting late. He had just enough time to locate his quarters. Down in his assigned windowless closet-sized cabin belowdecks, his roommate's bags were on the floor by the bunks, and the top bunk had been claimed by a toiletry bag and a jacket, but the guy wasn't there, to Mick's relief. In solitude, he stowed his things, took a quick shower, shaved his stubbled face, and then it was time to get to work.

The buffet galley was already going full tilt when he came in: kids were breaking down ingredients, prepping vegetables, roasting bones for stock, assembling the components of that night's featured buffet entrées. One kid was stacking oysters in ice at a stainless steel worktable; the guy next to him pulled meat from steaming-hot lobsters. The galley already smelled like a flesh carnival, a stink of sweat and brine and steam and meat. Mick inhaled the familiar smell: he loved it.

He looked around for the girl with the orange neckerchief, the one who'd been late to the meeting. She was peeling mushrooms at her station.

"Your name?" he said as he approached her.

"Consuelo," she answered. "Yes, I was late, Chef."

Their eyes met, locked, and for an instant there was a flash of something in her eyes, an insolent familiarity, as if she thought she knew him and therefore didn't fear him. Her orange neckerchief meant that she was only one rung below him. She had evidently read him closely while he'd spoken in the meeting, the way he'd been reading Laurens. He hadn't forgotten her correction of "fencepost drug." He wished he'd said that on purpose to find out whether anyone would be cheeky enough to speak up. Well, he had *her* number too: she was an arrogant little shit.

He kept his face still. "Once more and you're gone," he said.

"Yes, Chef," she said. She was not at all apologetic, as if she were angry at the circumstances that had made her late instead of being sorry for being late or taking responsibility for her fuckup. Granted, it had only been a minute, and he'd been on her side, but this attitude was a bad sign. He waited, silent. "It won't happen again," she said.

chapter four

The Aquarium of the Pacific was exemplary: bright, modern, well organized. Christine paid the hefty entrance fee and wandered into the lobby, clutching a brochure, bedazzled by the soaring wall of fish swimming through plants and sunlight in the great hall. It was still early, and the place had just opened, but it was already overrun with screaming children in school groups or attached to parents.

Most of the exhibits were small, individually curated aquariums filled with bright patterned fish darting through lavishly weird neon coral, undulating jellyfish, and otherworldly plants. Next to each tank was a placard describing each species' level of endangerment, its fragile ecosystem, the degree to which its particular habitat and population were currently being damaged by the greed and carelessness of humanity. It was like walking through a museum of ancient jewelry in bright boxes, Christine thought, everything there to be looked at and admired, but never to be worn again. From a distance, it looked as if the tanks were filled with glittery confetti, blown sideways with undulating streamers of algae in the gusts of current from the filters. But up close, the fish were bright scraps of pure life, lurid nuggets of color with faces whose expressions were as idiosyncratic and quizzical as Christine's own.

She stood staring at one large, calm yellow-and-brown fish, its big eyes looking back at her. She wondered what the fish thought of its life imprisoned in a glass box, whether it longed for the open ocean, whether it had ever known the wilderness. She decided it had probably been born in the aquarium. Maybe it had no idea what it was missing, or, conversely, how lucky it was to be safe in here instead of exposed to predators and the elements out there.

Dodging two hip-high, screaming human boys who went barreling by her, Christine headed to the window of a large sunlit tank where seals and sea lions swam around and around, either in a catatonic state of bored desperation or a blissed-out transcendent trance, it was hard to tell. The boys had already pressed their faces against the glass as their father took shots of the seals swimming by, eyes closed, stomachs up, long and sleek. Their bewhiskered faces were beatifically cynical, like Renaissance paintings of saints' heads. They appeared to be entirely unaware of the people on the other side of the glass, but Christine caught one peeking back at a little boy, who squealed with excitement.

"He winked at me," he yelled to his mother, who was two feet away from him. "He *winked* at me! Mom!"

"That is so *cool!*" his mother shouted back at him, looking around as if to make sure everyone in the hall was hearing this conversation.

"He didn't wink at *me*," his brother shrieked at them both.

Christine walked down a dark corridor and out into the sunshine of the aquarium's big courtyard, where there were more exhibits, colorful little tropical birds called lorikeets bustling around an enormous cage full of bamboo and trees, many kinds of sharks crammed together into a big shallow lagoon, and other, smaller tiled pools full of rays, like a sort of aquatic petting zoo. Children reached their hands in and tapped and rubbed the rays, who didn't seem to mind.

She bought two small cups of sugar water at a little stand and went through the escape-proof doors into the lorikeet "forest," a big, netted aviary with dozens of little birds, each colored in sections like a flower or ornamental jewel, bright blue, red-orange, and green, with red-orange eyes and a curved beak. Three lorikeets at once flew aggressively at her. One flapped into her hair and clawed at her head for purchase, another landed with a thud on her shoulder, and two more perched on her arm and wrist. They were heavier than they looked and felt like thrumming balls of energy and kinetic life. She had to hold her arms out like a crucifix as more came at her, diving into the little paper cups and jostling with their beaks to gulp down the precious sugar water. As soon as the cups were empty, the pretty, voracious, powerful little lorikeets flew away as quickly as they had come, leaving scratch marks and droppings behind on her shoulders and arms.

Little fuckers, she thought, half laughing, half relieved to slip through the escape-proof doors at other end of the cage. As she washed her hands at the sink outside, she thought that these birds were like human kids: shitting, hyperactive, sugar-addicted monsters. She wandered over to the pool filled with circling, listless sharks, and made her way up a concrete ramp to a penguin habitat. She had always loved penguins, those most improbable of creatures, dignified, mournful, physically compelling, the Buster Keatons of the animal kingdom. Some of them were falling off the ledge into the water and arcing through the depths; others seemed to be involved in a formally intricate spring mating dance on the ledge. They looked happy enough in their artificial cage, with no predators, no stress, all the food they wanted. But as with all the other aquatic animals, the wall next to their exhibit held a placard about endangerment and extinction and global climate change, and how, in the wild, their species was threatened and struggling to survive.

Depressed, Christine left the penguins and walked on an upward, curving ramp past a shorebird sanctuary filled with egrets, ducks, and plover. Back inside the building, she found herself in a long dim hallway studded intermittently with more bright, glass-fronted boxes filled with doomed sea life receding into the darkness. It was the sea-floor section of the aquarium. It looked almost like a haunted house, or a house of mirrors, with a dark, magical, unreal gloom, a relief after the starkly sunlit reminder of the planet's impending doom.

She stopped to look at a replica of a tropical coral reef. The coral lagoon was filled with fish, wildly colored and patterned, with aptly cartoonish names like Clown Triggerfish and One Spot Rabbitfish and Humbug. They floated around the coral, wriggled through waving plants, looking peaceful and contented despite the fact that the coral was, on close inspection, fake. Christine remembered a scene from a nature show she'd seen on TV a few years before, a shark raid on a coral reef at night. Sharks zoomed out of the black depths like gangsters and attacked the sleeping fish, wrecking the coral and eating everything in sight, then swam away, leaving it all devastated. Yes, this coral was artificial, but at least these fish didn't have to worry about being attacked. Things could be worse, she supposed.

Farther down the hallway, she caught sight of a placard that said GIANT OCTOPUS next to a tall, narrow tank. There didn't seem to be anything in there but a couple of lobsters and some plants. She bent down and studied every crevice between the rocks and in the fake coral, but there was no sign of the octopus. Where was it? Had it escaped? Had it died? She went over to a young woman in a brown AQUARIUM OF THE PACIFIC T-shirt who stood behind a group of children thronging the petting tank full of creatures.

"I can't find the octopus," Christine said to her, startled to hear a note of actual panic in her own voice.

The young woman, whose nametag said LIZA, looked thoughtful in the professional, practiced way of someone who spent her paid days catering to people's questions and befuddlement. "Oh, he's in there all right," she said. "He's probably just hiding."

"He's not," said Christine. "I looked everywhere for him. I think he got out."

Liza left the children to do whatever they wanted and followed Christine back to the octopus tank.

"Octopuses are amazing at getting out of their tanks," Liza said as they stood looking in together. "Another aquarium just lost one of theirs. It squeezed through a hole the size of a nickel and went through pipes connecting three different tanks and back into the ocean. They really travel, they're very curious and smart. But so far, ours has stayed put."

"It doesn't look like a big enough tank for a giant octopus," said Christine.

"Oh, he's fine in there. Don't worry! We all love him."

"What is there for him to do in that tiny tank, all alone?" Christine felt a tightness in her chest. She couldn't seem to draw a breath.

Liza gave her a sidelong look. "He probably crawled behind a rock. He'll come out again, I'm sure! He always does, eventually."

She went back to her post behind the petting zoo. Christine stayed in front of the tank, breathing shallowly, her pulse fluttering. She hadn't had an actual panic attack in years, since her twenties in New York. But she couldn't stop picturing the intelligent, solitary octopus searching its tank obsessively for a nickel-sized hole to slither through, yearning to compress its body and slide along a narrow pipe to freedom in the open ocean.

Christine forced herself to move away. With her head down, she walked quickly past the remaining exhibits, through the lobby, and straight out the door.

Back out in the warm, bright air, she sat on the nearest bench on the marina, with her eyes closed, taking deep breaths until she'd finally calmed down enough to walk back to her hotel. She looked forward to seeing Valerie, having a drink on board the ship. She couldn't wait to sail away.

*

"How's your cancer this afternoon, Isaac?" Miriam asked her ex-husband. They sat in a couple of armchairs, waiting for Sasha and Jakov to join them in the lobby so they could all take a taxi to the ship together. "Do you still want me to look?"

"In the light of morning I think I may have overreacted to a negligible discoloration," he said. "I was exhausted from the flight and wasn't being rational."

She laughed. "That's not like you at all."

"It is exactly like me."

Miriam caught sight of Rivka and Larry Weiss coming from the elevators, making their slow way through a crowd of people wearing nametags thronging the area by the check-in desk, a convention of some kind. She was surprised to see them; she had expected them to stay somewhere far fancier, more elite and sumptuous. For that matter, she also would have expected them to cruise on a private luxury boat rather than an aging, crowded commercial cruise ship; no doubt they owned at least one yacht. But she knew the Weisses prided themselves on living as normal a life as possible. They made a point of mentioning this whenever they could. And this cruise was a sentimental journey for them, commemorating the anniversary of their first meeting on board the *Queen Isabella* thirty-five years before.

"If it isn't my favorite musicians," came Larry Weiss's penetrating voice.

"Hello," said Rivka in her husky growl as Miriam and Isaac stood up to greet their benefactors. "Are you ready for the cruise?"

"We're very excited," said Isaac.

Miriam exchanged air kisses with Rivka and let Larry plant a smooch on her cheek. "Absolutely," she said, looking with stiff politeness at them, feeling as if her face had been rubbed with ice. She was never sure how she felt about Larry. He was always breezily friendly in an impersonally general way that held an edge of condescension, but he wasn't overtly horrible like his wife. "We're all very excited."

"You, I believe," Rivka said to Isaac with a thin smile, "but I'm not so sure about your wife." Rivka spoke affectedly, like certain artistes and poetesses Miriam had known, with grandiose dramatic gestures and exaggerated expressions. She also dressed like a poetess, in flowing tunics and tights and ballet slippers. She was bony if you disliked her, gamine if you were generous; the clothes suited her, and her manner could seem elegant and sophisticated if you looked at her in the right light, but Miriam couldn't stand the woman, so she chose to view her solely as pretentious. Well, she was married to a billionaire; she could take it. But then of course she and Larry had met before all of this, back when they were both still struggling to make it, she in the competitive, male-dominated world of classical music, he in the risky, fraught arena of speculative investment. So Rivka hadn't married Larry for his money, and he hadn't married her for her artistic success. They had evidently married for love, and then they'd both worked hard and been incredibly lucky in about equal parts. Even though Miriam couldn't fault Rivka for being a gold digger, she could still hate her in the privacy of her own mind.

But she still had to placate Larry. "We really are," Miriam said with disingenuous brightness. "In fact, we were just discussing today's rehearsal of your quartet. We're going to perform it for you on the cruise."

"And I couldn't be more excited to hear it played by the people for whom it was written." Rivka's slender white-gold bangles tinkled as she lifted both arms and dropped them again. "That in fact is the whole reason I insisted that you come on this cruise."

Miriam knit her eyebrows together, thinking that "the whole reason I insisted that you come on this cruise" sounded like an ominously pointed threat.

Jakov and Sasha came over, followed by a bellhop with their instruments and luggage piled on a rolling cart.

"Hello, dear people!" said Sasha. He looked almost like himself again today, brighter and more alert. Miriam felt a flash of warmth at the sight of him, tinged with relief.

"Come," said Rivka. "We have a minivan waiting outside to take you all to the ship."

"Let's go, you nudniks!" Miriam flapped her hands impatiently at her distinguished colleagues. She couldn't help it, she was agitated and eager to escape.

Somehow, over the course of the next few minutes, she managed to disengage from the Weisses and hustle the three old men into the van and oversee the stowing of all their instruments and luggage and tip the two valets. She buckled herself in with a long, relieved sigh. One hurdle leapt over: getting out of the hotel. There were many more, of course: getting everyone aboard, then settled, then calm and focused enough to run through Rivka's quartet at least once before tonight. They'd have to find a practice room. Life was nothing but a series of hurdles.

The driver turned onto a bridge that crossed to the other side of the harbor, and immediately they were stuck in traffic, a glum morass of windshields and bumpers inching along toward the docks. Miriam's mind drifted to tonight's performance, during cocktail hour in the main dining room, as the ship steamed out to sea. They'd agreed on their lightest, most shamelessly crowd-pleasing program: Vivaldi's *Four Seasons* followed by Mozart's *Eine Kleine Nachtmusik.* Miriam planned to wear her sleeveless purple sheath dress. It always made her feel glamorous. Playing those warhorses, she'd need to keep her morale up however she could. Maybe a vodka and tomato juice beforehand. But even this pleasant thought did little to blunt her dread of the cramped quarters, the crowds and claustrophobia, all the inconveniences of shipboard life. And the Weiss quartet: she couldn't forget that for one minute.

*

Down in the galley, Mick inspected fifteen suckling pigs. They were coming along nicely; this was good, because they had to be carved and served at the sail-away party in three hours. They'd had to flash-brine them; normally they steeped overnight, but there hadn't been time for that. They lay nestled like nursery-rhyme characters, tucked in their baking pans, bedecked with pineapple rings and shiny with glaze made of sea salt, Coca-Cola, pineapple juice, and liquid smoke to goose the flavors along. Looking at the innocent little bodies, their baby-piggy faces so trustingly soft, eyes closed as if they were only sleeping, he was reminded out of nowhere of a cannibalistic recipe he'd once read about, some tribe's ritualistic slaughter of young female virgins who were then marinated in wild herbs and spring water for a few days, tenderized with pineapple and wrapped in banana leaves, and buried in fire pits to slow roast.

He'd always thought that sounded delicious. If he had to eat human flesh, a juvenile female would be his first choice.

Western culture's proscription against human flesh had always amused him. A culture that considered edible such stuff as brains, snails, fungi, frogs, fermented vegetable matter, eyes, and intestines seemed mildly hypocritical when they eschewed their own apparently tasty and undeniably plentiful kind. No doubt the primary reason the taboo against cannibalism existed was that human meat was so delicious. Otherwise, there would be no need for it. The Vietnamese loved duck embryos cooked in their own eggshells, which they downed with beer. In Sardinia, they ate sheep's cheese in which flies had laid eggs and maggots had helped the innards of the cheese to rot. Cambodian fried tarantulas were a delicacy; Mick had never eaten them but imagined he would not like them very much. He had also never eaten Norwegian cheese made with a whole sheep's head, an actual fermented, reeking head on a plate, presumably served with a knife and a loaf of bread; he had no desire to, either. He wasn't a super-macho food sensationalist, he wasn't addicted to that adrenaline high of showoff gross-out consumption for its own sake like a lot of the food guys on TV, but as a matter of course, out of curiosity, he'd eaten ants and grasshoppers in Mexico, worms in California, cockroach-like beetles somewhere else, he couldn't remember, and blood sausage everywhere. Why were these considered edible and human flesh not? Meat was meat.

"Behind you, Chef," said Consuelo, squeezing around him with a tray of something hot. She was in charge of running the buffet-galley meat station. These were her roasting piglets, in other words, and Mick was standing right in her way with his ruminations and woolgathering.

He moved away from the oven and back to the task at hand. At the moment, while keeping an eye on the so-far highly efficient progress of tonight's ersatz luau, he was conducting an in-depth, largely mental inventory of his stores and their levels of freshness and perishability. The guy who was supposed to be here, a non-verbal Serbian meathead named Anto who was nonetheless one of the best executive preps in the business, liked to work off the cuff, improvising like a blind musician with whatever he had on hand. Normally on cruises, the stores were all arranged and earmarked and synced according to location, date, and so forth, programmed into computers and marched out with clockwork precision to fulfill the predetermined menu's promises, but Anto was famous for his wild hairs of inspiration and flights of fancy involving many ingredients and a sudden attack of genius. The higher-ups tolerated this because he always, according to cruise-industry legend, pulled it off with panache. Passengers often requested repeats of dishes he'd thrown together. Some of them became menu staples.

But Anto had slipped and fallen hard on his ass a few days before, apparently (so Mick had been able to gather from one of the chefs who'd been working with him) while rushing somewhere with a heavy tray of an hors d'oeuvre he'd been in the process of inventing, involving chestnuts, bacon, habanero peppers, port wine, and goat cheese. He'd slipped a disc and that was that. He was out of commission for a long time, poor guy. Management had tapped Mick to take his place, largely, as far as Mick could tell, because he was available, his primary qualification. His first time in this higher-ranking job, as it happened, was going to be a two-week ordeal of seat-of-the-pants navigation without a chart or flight plan, with the likes of Consuelo as his first line of defense. He'd just have to pretend he was Anto and get the job done.

"Excuse me, Chef," said Consuelo at his elbow. He found himself staring into a walk-in filled with seafood. He had been handling cool, firm mackerels one by one, as if he were still inspecting deliveries on the wharf before dawn. "I want to consult about the piggies."

"Go ahead."

"How can we get more flavor into them? I'm worried about the flash-brining."

"The liquid smoke should do it."

She handed him a skewer to taste. "Ham kebab," she said.

He wrapped his molars around the back piece and slid the whole thing at once into his mouth. Fresh pineapple chunks interspersed with chunks of ham and drizzled with honey, then grilled. Salty, fruity, sweet, meaty—simple, but classic.

"Good," he said. "Needs a splash of soy. Not too much, the meat is already salty."

"Yes, Chef," she said. "My team is working on pork belly sliders."

"Something spicy on the sliders. What kind of bread?"

"No buns," she said. "We're breading and frying squares of pork belly, with pineapple and bacon in the middle, spicy mayo, toothpicks."

"Okay," he said.

She waited for an instant, as if she was expecting more of a reaction from him. Determined to bring her into line, he inclined his head to dismiss her. Immediately, she went back to her station.

The entertainment and cruise director, a tiny blond American with a silly name he instantly forgot, had been thrilled about the Hawaiian-themed launch-night buffet party. She'd passed Mick on to one of her staff, a young Korean American man named Park. "I *love* it," he'd cried. "I will round up the tiki lamps!" Mick liked working with gay American entertainment staff, possibly because they liked working with him. He also, incidentally, liked being touched by American men, gay or straight. His job was lonely and hard and he didn't have much physical contact with anyone, aside from bumping into people on the line accidentally. Entertainment people were demonstrative, theatrical, handsy. Mick knew that American men weren't socially permitted to touch one another the way men in other cultures could as a matter of course. Straight American men were terrified of being perceived as gay. Gay American men were often careful to hide it on the job. But entertainment staff seemed looser, less worried about all that, though it was still an issue, Mick knew. So when they touched Mick, it felt extra tender, always slightly sexual with a whiff of nervousness, no matter what the toucher's sexual orientation was. And the entertainment staff were separate from the hierarchy of the kitchen staff, although the two teams worked closely together, so Mick could relax around that crew without worrying about breaking protocol.

Park had a big, sweet face and a cuddly, bouncy personality. He was interchangeable with all the other American entertainment staff, male or female, that Mick had known through the years. They seemed to breed them in the Midwest in particular. Park was from Illinois.

"Joliet," he'd said with unforced cheer. "Forty miles in distance but really a million miles in all other ways from Chicago. A prison town, used-to-be steel town, and I'm *very* glad to be out of there."

He'd asked Mick about growing up in Budapest, and then Mick had mentioned Suzanne, the fact that he should have been with her in Paris right now. Something in his tone must have given away how lovelorn he felt, because Park had stroked his arm and assured him that true love was never smooth, and he himself was heartbroken right now over a crewmember who'd just broken up with him, and he was *here,* on the *Isabella,* so Park would have to avoid him for the next two weeks.

This meeting cheered Mick up quite a bit.

He picked up another mackerel and looked it in the eye. He envisioned a whole school of them, grilled, arranged in scalloped stacks on a platter of seaweed salad, garnished with pickled lemon rind and charred caper berries, drizzled with spicy aioli. So he wasn't in Paris with Suzanne, so what? He was going to let himself have some fun on this cruise.

chapter five

You're really here," said Valerie as she and Christine hugged by the ramp leading up to the boarding deck of the *Queen Isabella.* "I can't believe I got you to leave the farm and fly all the way across the country."

"Are you kidding?" said Christine. "I need a vacation like you would not believe."

"Should we get on this thing?" Valerie asked, squinting up at the towering ship. People jostled around them to board.

"I can't wait," said Christine.

Valerie laughed. "You have to have fun the entire time, in fact I command you to. Seriously. This is a work trip for me. I need you to be my proxy."

As they joined the slow line of passengers spilling up the gangway onto the ship, Christine stole a gander at Valerie's impeccably urbane outfit. She wore a gray shirtdress with a white collar and black wedge espadrilles. In her bony cleavage nestled a pendant, a brass owl with glowing red garnet eyes. She wore stylish black glasses. Her short dark auburn hair curled against her neck. She was severely thin, even more so than usual. Christine felt like a bumpkin next to her.

"It's so intense," Valerie was saying as she checked her phone for messages, updates, texts. Her voice was staccato, clipped. Christine had forgotten what New Yorkers could be like, coming at you like hungry highly-strung wild animals, scanning for prey, chattering away. "The pressure I'm under, it's crazy. And then the whole fuckup with my flight, I barely slept, and the guy next to me farted these toxic methane clouds the whole fucking flight. Oh my God, I can't wait to unpack and take my shoes off. Oh look, a text from Julian. Like I care. And another one from, oh shit, I forgot that whole thing, okay, it's okay." She mashed at her phone with her thumbs.

Christine had met Valerie twelve years before when they'd started together, freshly arrived in New York, as assistants at *Babe,* a hip women's magazine with a young, feminist slant. The magazine had folded after three years, but their friendship had endured. Christine was always the stable, responsible Maine girl who supported Valerie, perennially lovelorn, through multiple emotional crises. She invited Val to sleep over when she was heartbroken, and gave her advice and generally acted as her big sister, or even mother, or even, she'd often thought without resentment, stand-in boyfriend. Christine generally had boyfriends, but she always included Valerie, who had become her roommate, in movie nights and takeout meals. And Valerie had always given Christine a lot in return. She was dashing and fearless and intrepid. She forced Christine to try new things, be more ambitious, and push harder for what she wanted. In the past seven years, ever since Christine had moved back to Maine and married Ed, Valerie had remained Christine's connection to her old life in New York, kept her in touch with the world of journalism, given her all the latest gossip. She'd allowed Christine to feel that she hadn't completely dropped off the map. And in return, Christine had remained Val's sounding board and solid shoulder—from a distance, but still and always there.

"How is Julian?" Christine asked. She felt oddly shy with her old friend as they unpacked in their tiny cabin, cramming their dresses onto hangers in the doll-sized closet, stowing toiletries on the little shelves in the minuscule bathroom. She hadn't seen Valerie since last June. She'd forgotten how focused she was, how ferociously professional. Christine felt a mild queasiness at the thought of spending two intimate, close-quartered weeks together. There was hardly room to walk around their luggage, which they'd piled on the floor. The two beds were separated only by a little night-stand. The decor was '70s-sitcom drab: beige and powder-blue patterned bedspreads, a small round table by the window with one chair, a long low laminated bureau below a painting of the ocean at sunset in lurid neon oil. Christine would have felt cramped alone in this room. Sharing it with Valerie, she suspected it would be possible only to sleep and shower here. Even that would be tricky.

Valerie gave a hard snort of a laugh. "That is so over."

"Why?" Christine asked, although she was secretly unsurprised. "I thought you liked him."

"Do you want the short version or the long one?"

"Long, please," said Christine. She was still feeling shaky from her weird experience at the aquarium, and Valerie's serial tales of romantic failure were generally entertaining, if increasingly worrisome, since she seemed to be getting simultaneously lonelier and less practical in her choices of men, as far as Christine could tell from her e-mails. In truth, it pained Christine that Valerie's dim view of men was so reliably and regularly confirmed by the accused themselves, as if she had an unerring instinct for finding the ones who conformed to her low expectations.

"Actually, it's short no matter how I tell it," said Valerie. She didn't look at Christine. She was concentrating on arranging a dress on a hanger, and her voice was clipped, so Christine couldn't gauge her feelings. "It was a disaster. The end. I need to conserve my energies. I'm not good at anything except work. And masturbation. No more men, Christine, I mean it."

Valerie was right: she was very good at her work. At thirty-two, in addition to running her own successful news and culture website, called PaperCuts.com, she had recently published a *New York Times Magazine* cover story exposing "the shadowy world of hidden workers in the new global economy," as the tagline summarized it. She'd been approached by a handful of interested editors in the weeks after it ran. She was in the process of signing a six-figure deal to expand her piece into a book.

"Your life couldn't be going any better, it seems to me," said Christine.

"On paper it couldn't," Valerie said. She closed the closet door, nudging it with her hip to make it stay shut. "Okay. You go up to the sail-away party and I'll stay here and type my notes."

"Notes?" said Christine. "What notes?"

"I talked to a crewmember while I waited for you on the dock. He told me about the system they have for sorting the luggage and delivering it to each cabin and suite." While she talked, Valerie pulled out her laptop and set it up on the little desk by the balcony door.

"You already conducted an interview?"

Valerie's tone softened. "With Orpheus. What a name. He's Jamaican. He has a dreamy accent, they all do. No one on the crew is American, he also told me. They're all foreign-born. And the ship itself is registered in Panama for tax purposes even though it's American-owned."

There was a knock on the door. Christine was closest, so she opened it. A young black man in a uniform stood in the doorway with a wheeled cart, which held a champagne bottle in a silver ice bucket, a small shiny gold box, and a cream-colored envelope. "For Miss Valerie Chapin," he said, pronouncing her name with a lilting accent.

He wheeled the cart in and wedged it between the two beds.

"What the hell," said Valerie, flinging herself across Christine's bed and plucking up the card. "It's from my new editor. 'Dear Valerie, bon voyage, work well, best, Lisa.' God, how thoughtful, I like her already. Although 'best' is not my favorite sign-off. So corporate. But whatever."

The steward hovered. He was small and slender and very pretty, there was no other word for him. His short black hair was neatly parted on the side, but one tiny cheeky spit curl was pasted against his temple, and a diamond chip glittered in one nostril.

"My name is Trevor," he said, addressing Valerie. "I'll be your room steward for the voyage. Please inform me of all your needs and requirements, and I will do my utmost to fulfill them."

Christine had been fumbling desperately in her pockets for a bill of some kind to tip him, knowing she had nothing.

"Trevor," Valerie said, putting out a hand to stop Christine. "You get your tip at the end, right? That's how it works?"

He gave one brief flutter of his long lashes, a butterfly's flick of surprise. "Correct, ma'am," he said.

"If you call me 'ma'am' one more time, you're not getting a dime," said Valerie. While she talked, she opened the small gold box on the cart and plucked out a truffle and handed it to Christine. "It's 'mademoiselle' from now on. I love your accent. Where are you from?"

"Haiti, mam'selle," said Trevor.

Christine caught a glint in Valerie's eyes, the rapacious intentional charm of a wolf espying a lone Bambi in the woods. "Do you have a minute, Trevor? Can I ask you a few quick questions about your job for a book I'm writing? Sit here, it'll only take two minutes, and then you get to be in a book."

"Okay, mam'selle," said Trevor, perching with dainty obedience in the armchair.

Christine left Valerie with her subject and went out into the stuffy narrow hallway, which was as ugly as their cabin: blue-and-gold patterned carpet; embossed, swirled gold wallpaper; fan-shaped sconces with bright bulbs blazing in them. She skirted passengers going in and out of their staterooms, dodged stewards with carts, climbed some stairs, and finally burst out of the stairwell and inhaled the fresh air. As she climbed an outdoor flight of metal stairs, the ship's horn let out a blast. The engines rumbled underfoot. The ship gave a lurch, and just like that, the *Queen Isabella* set off.

Christine joined a crowd of people standing at the railing. She watched as the Port of Long Beach fell back into a blue haze, saying an unsentimental but ritualistic-feeling goodbye to the pelicans, the oil rigs, the shipping-container cranes, the harbor, the aquarium, and the grand old *Queen Mary,* soaring so much higher than the *Isabella;* her black-capped funnels were among the last sights Christine saw before they were truly at sea.

On a small stage by the swimming pool, a jazz trio struck up a snappy rendition of "Take Five." Uniformed waiters appeared with trays of retro snacks. As they went by, Christine scored a Ritz cracker spread with pimiento cream cheese, then a pig in a blanket, and then an oyster broiled in its shell, smothered in green sauce and breadcrumbs. Soon she'd make her way to the bar and order a very dry and icy martini with three fat olives on a toothpick, and later she'd meet Valerie at the restaurant for a fancy dinner, and she wouldn't have to cook it herself or pay for it, and she could wear one of the dresses she'd brought, and high heels, and she'd put her hair up. She could indulge and not feel guilty. Ed wasn't here to look askance at the wastefulness of it all, to wonder aloud what the point was. There was no point, really. And that was enough for Christine at the moment. As she looked around for the next tasty morsel, she remembered that eating was supposed to be the entire point of a cruise; the whole commercial venture was predicated on the simple equation of appetites and their satisfactions. Unable to muster any argument with this, she gave herself over to it, letting her perceptions and appetites coexist happily.

As the blue forms of land receded farther and farther into the distance, Christine wandered around the deck, picking more snacks off trays, until she found a small semiprivate nook on a balcony. She eased onto a wooden deck chair, leaned back, and gazed out at the open ocean, feeling like a character in an old movie. The Pacific was totally foreign to her. She was used to the Gulf of Maine's heavy rocking chill, the steady winds constantly ruffling its blue-gray surface, water that never warmed up fully even on the hottest summer days, so when you plunged in, your skin burning from sunbathing, the shock of icy brine made you hold your breath and your skin tingle as if it had been mildly burned. This was a different ocean altogether, misty and amiable, a placid, pale green, gently rocking bath splashed by frank sunlight. Even the air smelled warm, with whiffs of blooming underwater algae that thrived in body-temperature shallows. She pictured the weather turning rough, hard winds sending high white-foamed waves cascading against the upper decks, the ship juddering and pitching, and shivered with happy imagined horror. The forecast for the next two weeks held nothing but sunshine and calm seas.

She picked up one of the cruise brochures lying on the side table next to an ashtray. The *Isabella*'s shape on the cover was reduced to a few lines: her bow was slender and high, pointed and aerodynamic, her stern curved like an Art Deco bar, half a flying saucer, out over the water. The ship had three cross-shaped masts interspersed with two funnels that slanted back like the much-larger *Queen Mary*'s. Her foredeck was clear, so her unencumbered nose cut through the water. The highest decks rose steeply from her middle, planted there like a building.

On the first page was a map of the ship. "C" and "B" decks were at the bottom, where most of the crew and staff worked and lived and where the stores and engine room were. Then came "A" deck with the restaurant, buffet, and galleys, and above that the main deck, then the sun, promenade, bridge, and pool decks above. The pool deck had a raised solarium at the stern, more suites and cabins in the middle with a catwalk on either side, and up front, a bar by the swimming pool. Christine resolved to spend the bulk of her waking hours there, drinking and reading and swimming and soaking up the sunlight. It was the least she could do, since Valerie had to work the entire time. She stretched and yawned.

On the next page she found a bullet-point list of facts about the *Queen Isabella*. The ship's body was 674 feet long and 86 feet wide and 28,600 gross tons. Her record speed was 26 knots, and her cruising radius was 20,000 miles, whatever that meant. She had a passenger capacity of 976, although on this, her final voyage, the brochure said, the guest list had been cut down to 400 so that everyone could stay in upper-deck staterooms and suites, and to make "the cruising experience feel more intimate and exclusive." Christine wondered uncharitably if this was because the lower passenger cabins were unfit for habitation, maybe beginning to mold and decay. Or else they just hadn't been able to fill the ship with passengers.

She looked up from the brochure at the mild carpet of rippling water under the sky, two parallel planes through visible space of pure vanishing blue that appeared to meet at the soft gray horizon line that kept receding as the ship plowed on. Voices were amplified by the warm spray in the air, increasing in volume then fading out and replaced by others as people moved about the deck. To her relief, she heard no children's shrieks or squeals or whines. The cut-off age, she had been told, was sixteen, but even teenagers seemed in short supply. There was one sullen-looking, slightly overweight college-aged girl in a blue sweatshirt sitting in a chair reading the same brochure, seemingly as engrossed as Christine in the *Isabella*'s facts and background. She looked up and met Christine's eye and immediately looked away. She struck Christine as the kind of girl who would keep to herself for the duration of the voyage, watching the drunken, carefree adults around her with satirical sharpness, recording her observations in a journal. Christine had been the same way at that age.

The third and fourth pages of the brochure were taken up by a history of the *Queen Isabella*, written by Tye and James Blevins, whoever they were. Christine braced herself for the usual groan-worthy cheeseball prose of restaurant menus or cheap museum placards, but she was pleasantly surprised and even amused by the cheekily ironic, fairy tale–like tone.

"Once upon a time," the story began, "in 1953, a ship named the *Queen Isabella* was born. This was a heady era, the golden age of capitalism and nuclear energy and a generally held, naively wide-eyed belief in human progress. In those days, it was considered romantic to smoke and glamorous to drink Coca-Cola and patriotic to support the automotive industry by driving cars that looked like bloated fish."

Christine glanced up at the teenage girl. She was absorbed in her own brochure.

"The *Isabella* started out her life as the oldest of identical triplets: the (now-defunct) *Queen Eleanor* and the (oft-renamed, soon-to-be-scrapped) *Queen Melisende*. The three sisters had been commissioned five years earlier, in 1948, by Anne-Marie de Belloc, the reclusive, childless, and (filthy) rich widow of a French industrialist, and were built by Forges et Chantiers de la Gironde at Lormont near Bordeaux on the Gironde estuary. Unfortunately, due to some bad investments and even worse luck, the widow went broke, and by 1953, the year of the *Queen Isabella*'s completion, Mme de Belloc had sold her houses, her considerable stash of jewels, and other holdings to pay her debts. But, by dint of a sleight-of-hand false sale to her maid, she managed to keep her ships. The *Isabella* was put to work immediately, carrying paying passengers and plying the Mediterranean, to support not only Mme. de Belloc, but also her poor half-formed sisters, the *Queens Melisende* and *Eleanor,* stalled in a Marseille shipyard. They languished on the ways for the next two years and, when the former millionaire could no longer afford the rental of their berths, were almost abandoned forever and sold for scrap. Then, at the proverbial eleventh hour, de Belloc, forty-three but still seaworthy herself, managed to wed an elderly Greek shipping magnate, Stavros Chronis, whose fortunes allowed the two sister ships to be completed, outfitted with teak-decked balconies, beveled chrome vitrines, crystal chandeliers, and soaking tubs inlaid with mother-of-pearl."

Christine envisioned Anne-Marie with a blond scalloped bouffant, dove-breasted, hard-faced, but with vulnerable brown eyes. She'd married the rich Greek to save her ships, a marriage that Christine pictured as polite, chilly, and entirely public except when Stavros demanded that his wife fulfill her sexual duties.

"Each ship's accommodations ranged from the two super-luxurious multiroom double-balconied owner's and presidential suites, bulging from the sides with views both fore and aft, all the way down to the inner windowless bunk-bed cells for the crew. During the early 1960s, the Chronis Corporation sailed the now extremely popular sisters under the Greek flag on a leisurely circuit around the Mediterranean: Gibraltar, Valencia, Lisbon, Naples, Cannes, Thessaloníki, Barcelona, Beirut, Athens, and Genoa."

The names evoked in Christine a sunstruck, piney fantasia of olives, retsina, grilled sardines, and hot late nights in seaside cafés.

"Even though the three sisters were virtually identical, equally beautiful and luxurious, the *Isabella* was always the favorite. Maybe because of her status as the first to be launched and sailed, maybe because of the fortuitous historical connotations of her name, Americans in particular (some of whom were at least passingly familiar with Queen Eleanor of Aquitaine but not, generally, with Queen Melisende of Jerusalem) preferred her. The rich and famous of the era booked her suites and dined on filet mignon and oysters Rockefeller at the captain's table, danced the cha-cha and the tango to hot bands in the ballroom, drank martinis and cognac in the Starlight Lounge, smoked cheroots in the casino. Natalie Wood posed for a spread in *Life* magazine aboard the *Isabella*. Buzz Aldrin and his wife enjoyed a luxurious week in one of her first-class suites, as did President Nixon. Joe DiMaggio and Marilyn Monroe were caught necking by paparazzi near the swimming pool. Gene Kelly made a splash in the ballroom for a dazzling night, squiring several starstruck matrons around the teak parquet floor, dipping one so low her diamond brooch fell off, then famously dipping her again at the end of the dance so he could pick it up again and hand it back to her."

Christine laughed aloud: it was all so improbable. And here she was, Christine Thorne from western Maine, spending two weeks on a ship whereon presidents, movie stars, and astronauts had vacationed.

"Just like all great beauties, the *Isabella* grew older and frailer. After her sisters died natural deaths, she was getting ready for her own retirement when Cabaret Cruises swooped in, adding this sentimental favorite to its fleet in 2002 and restoring her, almost completely, to her former glory. For fifteen years, refreshed and fully renovated, she sailed the Pacific Ocean from Long Beach, her adopted home, up to Alaska and down to Mexico and out to the Hawaiian Islands. And now, at last, after a long and fruitful life of dignity, health, and success, the *Queen Isabella* is making her final voyage. Her last cruise will be a celebration of the glorious era of glamour and elegance, a theater of nostalgia."

Christine closed the brochure and leaned back in her chair. She had been aware for a while of a thrumming deep in the bowels of the ship, like a constant presence, a noise she could feel in her bones, the sub-aural hum of the engines. Simultaneously, she noticed the gentle fore-and-aft rocking of the ship as the bow plowed steadily through each rolling impulse of water, muscling through one broad swell after another. She felt safe, unaffected by the scale of the effort, like a flea perched on the back of a smoothly cantering horse. The relationship between ship and water didn't affect her. She was too small, of a whole other scale. Her body reacted only to sun and air while the ship did all the work of moving. It was so relaxing, she found her eyes closing slightly, her muscles giving up their terrestrial battle against gravity. Her mouth went slack, and she felt herself beginning to drool and closed it. No wonder people went on cruises.

"Shut *up*," someone shrieked nearby, a throaty male voice. "No *way*."

"The pool is tiny," came a snotty female voice from the other direction. "I can't believe how small. It smells musty in our room, too."

"We can get off in Honolulu if you hate it."

Sleep, soft and muffling, folded itself around Christine's brain.

*

The Sabra Quartet had spent most of the afternoon before the sail-away party in the ship's chapel down on "A" deck, rehearsing, or rather desecrating, Rivka Weiss's scherzo. This was a dampish, seldom-used closet containing a laminated wood lectern for a pulpit, four heavy wooden pews that could have been repurposed from a defunct Southern Baptist church's fire sale, and a sort of graceless modern stained-glass chandelier, ecumenically incorporating a Star of David, a cross, and a star-and-crescent, dangling from the ceiling on a heavy chain. The room's low-pile mustard-yellow carpet dampened all sound and deadened the air. The walls and ceiling were paneled with dark wood, and the back wall was heavily curtained in gold brocade, further hindering the acoustics. Imprisoned and isolated with their own difficult dissonance, they found themselves looking forward, all four of them, to later, when they'd play the breezy, boringly pretty, decades-memorized *Four Seasons* in the restaurant upstairs amid the genteel scents and sounds of fine dining. Ah, the freedom, such luxury.

For one thing, Sasha couldn't seem to nail his diabolically tricky entrance in the seventeenth measure; but even before that, Miriam's staccato arpeggios, meant to sound like machine-gun fire, bore a closer aural resemblance to chattering teeth. And Jakov's long cello notes, which were intended to be human moans, sounded like kvetching. Only Isaac was able to navigate his part with any conviction, but Rivka had gone comparatively easy on the viola, whose part in the scherzo consisted of a lot of low-pitched blatting interspersed with high glissando screeches. Isaac's part wasn't even that hard to count. Miriam suspected Rivka of favoritism: she had always batted her eyes at Isaac.

The Six-Day War had been written in honor of the Sabra; for one, because they were one of Israel's finest string quartets, but also because they were all veterans of the war. Playing it not only caused Miriam to break out in a psychic rash, it reminded her of being an IDF soldier fifty years before, the sun baking her head through her helmet as she barreled along in a jeep through the sand. Isaac had fought alongside Miriam in the Sinai; that was where they'd met. Sasha had been an Air Force pilot and was responsible for some particularly effective air strikes against Syria. Jakov had worked in Intelligence and had been on the team who'd intercepted the cable from Nasser to the president of Syria, urging him to accept a ceasefire. Why Rivka had thought any of them would be pleased to relive this experience musically was anyone's guess.

"Let's try this again," said Miriam, glancing at Isaac, who looked over his fingerboard at his colleagues, acknowledging their distress with his hoary eyebrows knitted. "Sasha, what if we count you in this time?"

"I'll get it right," said Sasha crossly. "I can count it."

"Hey," came a bright, female American voice in the doorway. "Sorry to interrupt, I had no idea anyone was in here."

A small, dynamic woman burst into the chapel wearing yoga pants and a sports bra with high-heeled tango shoes. She waved at them all, amused by their puzzlement.

"Sorry, I'm Kimmi," she said. "I'm the cruise director as well as the entertainment director, they doubled me up on duties for this cruise because it's so small. You must be the string quartet from Israel. I came in to get a Bible. I'll just grab one and get out of your hair."

She strode to the lectern and looked behind it, into its shelf, talking steadily as she went, trying to minimize any awkwardness she'd caused.

"We're planning a performance for the talent show later in the cruise, a few of us entertainment crewmembers. We wanted something ocean-related, and Park thought of the story of the parting of the Red Sea as maybe a jumping-off point, but none of us really remember the exact text and there's no Internet so we can't Google it." She rummaged around. "Can there really be no Bible? What kind of a chapel *is* this?"

"We might be able to help you," said Jakov. "We're all familiar with the book of Exodus."

"Moses held out his staff," said Isaac, "and the Red Sea was parted by God."

"The Israelites walked on dry land, pursued by the Egyptian army," said Jakov. "Once the Israelites were safely through, the sea closed again, and the Egyptian army drowned."

"That's right," said Isaac. "And there was a pillar of cloud by day and a pillar of fire by night."

Miriam nodded. Here she'd just been playing staccato machine-gun fire that sonically re-created her own army's successful war with the Egyptians, and now they were talking about the Egyptian army drowning while the Jews were saved in the Torah. There were similarities in the two scenarios, but no one had parted the Red Sea in 1967. The Jews had had to fight, with the element of surprise standing in for God's miracle.

"Don't forget the Song of the Sea," she said.

"The Song of the Sea," said Kimmi. "That's what I came to look up! I need the words."

"It's long and I don't know it all, but I can tell you Miriam's Song, which she sings after the Israelites cross to safety," said Miriam. "It's much shorter, and it goes in English, 'Sing to the Lord, for he is highly exalted. Both horse and driver he has hurled into the sea.' Not really talent-show material, though."

"Probably not," said Kimmi doubtfully. "But let me write down the words anyway."

chapter six

Christine came downstairs after her epic nap on the deck chair to find Valerie still sitting at the little table, squinting at her laptop screen through her glasses, typing away. Christine stripped in the tiny bathroom and stood in the weak stream of water in the shower stall, which appeared to have been built for a medium-sized child.

"You have such a nice body," Valerie said as Christine came out of the shower and started dressing. "I'd kill for your boobs."

Valerie's breasts were flat little bumps, but her body was lanky and narrow-hipped, the kind most women envied and yearned for. Anyway, she'd never had any difficulty finding boyfriends; she just had trouble staying interested in them for longer than two months.

"You're sexy and glamorous," she told Valerie. "And I'm ordinary and always have been."

Valerie was still fixated, a frank and frankly sexless appraisal that made Christine feel like a cow at a state fair. "You have amazing arm muscles. Farming kicks the ass of going to the gym."

"Thank you," said Christine with effort.

A few minutes later, wearing her dusky rose shantung sheath, bare-legged and bare-armed, and a short string of seed pearls she'd found in a small Williamsburg thrift shop back in the 1990s, plus the strappy gold stilettos she'd worn at her own wedding, Christine climbed the grand staircase and wandered along the ship's main promenade. Her hair was pinned up with another thrift-store find from her city days, a rhinestone comb sparkling on the back of her head. Her hands, which she'd had manicured in Portland the morning before her flight, looked totally unfamiliar with their well-shaped nails, pinkish gold. Her toenails were a darker shade of the same color, and her feet were weirdly free of calluses.

She checked out her own reflection in a long beveled mirror hanging in the stairwell. She felt confident, not awkward anymore, thanks in part to Valerie's compliments, which felt much less intrusive in retrospect. She felt like a woman. Gone were the mud boots, the dog-hair-bedecked jeans, fleece jacket and knit cap, the drab wool scarf that she joked with Ed had molecularly fused with the skin on her neck. Gone were the sloppy, country-girlish ponytail, the ever-present farmer's smell of sweat, fingernails full of dirt. She had no evening chores, no canvas totes full of wood to bring in from the woodpile, no chickens or ducks or dogs to feed, no dinner to cook, no checklists or orders to look over, no runs next door to Steve and Molly's farm for a quart of sheep's milk and a quick hello. Too bad Ed wasn't here to appreciate this. He loved to tell her in his understated way that she "cleaned up good."

Restless at the memory of the farm, she picked up a glass of sparkling something from a passing tray and took a sip: it was excellent, very dry. The long, burnished wood floor of the promenade glowed as the sconces and lights came softly on, and she stopped by one of the enormous windows to look out at the darkening ocean. Live old-style jazz tootled and honked on the warm breeze from somewhere not too far away; it was the kind of jazz she liked, swinging and danceable. She felt her shoulders moving in time, felt her whole body revved up with the heat of sensuality. The booze warmed her chest. She smelled cigarette smoke from somewhere nearby. Champagne fizzed in her nostrils while she moved loosely to the jazz and let the sea air slip around her skin.

An hour later, Valerie was already waiting for her at the entrance to the fine-dining restaurant. "There you are!" she said. Christine peeked in and saw a long room with a high ceiling, chandeliers, ceiling fans with fat wooden paddles, potted palms, half-moon banquettes. She heard silverware on china, a hum of voices, music from a string quartet across the room, three elderly gentlemen and a lady. "Are you drunk? I hope you're drunk. You're fun when you're drunk."

Once again, the irritation of being both scrutinized and appropriated by her friend returned. Christine tried to slough it off. "They're having a luau in the buffet room, with ukuleles and steel guitar and three girls in leis singing old Hawaiian torch songs. And suckling pigs."

"You want to eat there instead? This place just has a geriatric string quartet and the decor is kind of snoozy. The menu looks great, though. They're serving frigging squab. Pigeon. No joke."

"This place looks great," said Christine as a tall, gray-haired, stiff-backed gentleman in a crisp tuxedo approached to lead them to their table.

"My name is Sidney, and I will be your maître d' for this cruise," he said with a species of British accent. He seated them with thin-lipped formality, pulling their chairs out. "The wine steward will be over immediately." As he unfolded their napkins for them with ceremonious precision, Christine took hers and draped it over her lap, afraid she was doing it wrong, almost expecting him to correct her. "Enjoy your dinner, ladies." He bowed slightly from the waist and glided away. Christine was almost certain that she caught a glimmer of self-mocking amusement in his eye as he turned.

"The staff seem like actors in a play," she said. "Like *Upstairs, Downstairs,* that old BBC show my parents watched. Downstairs is like backstage, where they get to be themselves."

"A play," Valerie repeated. "Christine, this isn't romantic for them."

"I know," said Christine, wondering when Valerie had become so much smarter than she was. They'd been equals once, back when they were younger. Then Christine had gone home to Maine. "I was just babbling. I'm drunk, remember?"

But in fact, Christine wasn't at all drunk, and she had no idea why she'd said that. To keep the peace, maybe. To prevent herself from snapping defensively at the friend who'd invited her on this cruise in the first place, to whom she felt uneasily beholden.

The menus were handwritten in black ink on rectangles of cream-colored stock. In addition to the squab, there were *tartare de boeuf,* Caesar salad, shrimp cocktail, oysters on the half shell with shallot mignonette, a vegetable Napoleon, and a few other classic dishes. It really was like going back in time. She could have been in a fine-dining restaurant decades ago in Boston, rubbing shoulders with bluebloods and Harvard professors. Her parents had taken her and her sister down a few times to expose them to "polite society," as they called it, and Christine had loved it.

The wine steward arrived with an Aussie accent and a thick book full of names of different wines.

"I'll have the house white," said Christine. "As long as it's not Chardonnay."

"House red for me," said Valerie. "As long as it's not Merlot. One glass with dinner every night, two if I'm feeling racy. I seriously do not want to lose my shit on this cruise. You know how I love to lose my shit. It just leads to trouble of the sexual kind, and I have no time for that."

"Wait, no action the entire time?" Christine said, laughing. "Are you not even checking out the men?"

"What men? Everyone's paired up and over sixty. Luckily for us. You're married to a farmer. And I'm married to my book."

When the waiter returned to inquire about the young ladies' desires for dinner, Valerie ordered the steak tartare and the squab, no starch. Christine eyed the menu for a moment, enjoying the choices, then settled on shrimp cocktail and steak Diane. "I'll take her starch, too," she added.

Valerie snorted. "Farmer," she said.

Christine settled back in her cushioned chair, feeling lucky and glamorous. "So what did you learn today at school?"

Valerie pushed her glasses up her nose and fiddled with her bangs.

"I'm trying to figure out the hierarchy," she said. "It's going to be hard to penetrate the crew and staff. They're so separate from us when they're not working, and passengers are definitely not welcome in their world. And while they *are* working, they never seem to have time to talk. Also, Cabaret is a really powerful corporation, so they don't want to say anything that might jeopardize their jobs. I don't know. I think what I have to do is find out where they hang out on their time off, when we get to Hawaii, and get drunk with them, or pretend to get drunk. That's the only way I'm ever going to learn anything real. But I have to stay sober. Seriously."

A few hours later, Christine found herself on the dance floor in the Starlight Lounge, chaperoning a brazenly tipsy Valerie. While Christine had been drinking steadily and enthusiastically all day, she had eaten well and paced herself and so had managed to keep her wits about her. Valerie, on the other hand, was drunk in the manner of someone who had been determined not to drink and then caved and gave herself over to it with precipitous abandon.

"You're too gainfully employed for me," Christine overheard Valerie saying to the man she was fake-ballroom-dancing with. He was a news photographer by day and video artist by night named Jake who, it turned out, lived three blocks away from Valerie in Brooklyn. He worked for a celebrity news-and-gossip website called PopRocks.com that Christine had never heard of.

"Hey," Valerie said into Christine's ear as she and Jake went waltzing by, "should I go make out with Jake in a lifeboat?"

Christine was entrapped in the determined arms of Jake's colleague, Theodore, a serious, slightly pudgy journalist who was "actually a poet." Christine was only dancing with him because Valerie had accepted for both of them. But Theodore was mistakenly flattered and intrigued, and Christine kept having to maneuver his eager body a safe distance from her own while he crooned along with "Blueberry Hill" into her ear in a not-bad baritone.

"I don't care," said Christine, laughing, but they'd already danced out of earshot.

"How about you?" Theodore asked. "Do you want to make out?"

Her wedding ring was apparently invisible to him. "I'm married," she said.

"So am I," said Theodore, pressing himself against her.

"Oh please," said Christine, strong-arming him away from her. "Stop it, seriously."

When the song ended, Christine went over to Valerie and tapped her on the shoulder. "I'm cutting in," she told Jake, linking her arm in Valerie's. "We have to go."

Valerie let herself be pulled without protest out of the Starlight Lounge and up to the pool bar at the top of the ship. "Oh my God, Chris," she said in Christine's ear. "Thank you."

Behind the bar stood a tiny, pale, dark-haired woman. "I am Natalya," she told them in a flat bored voice, placing napkins in front of them as they seated themselves on two stools in the center of the bar. "I am happy to serve you. What's your pleasure tonight?"

"I'm already drunk," said Valerie. "So I think I'd better take it easy."

"Really?" said Christine.

"Fuck no," said Valerie. "I'll have a martini, very dry, stirred, straight up, olives. Let's do this."

Christine laughed. "Make that two."

A moment later, with casual flips of her wrists, Natalya set two brimming martini glasses on the napkins in front of them. "Enjoy," she said in her dead voice.

"Cheers," Valerie said, knocking her glass against Christine's, and licking the booze off her wrist. Christine chewed a big, hard, gin-soaked green olive and looked around at the hanging strings of light, the rustling palm fronds, the surface of the pool, shimmering and rocking. She felt the ship underneath her, light but solid, felt its buoyant forward momentum from the powerful engines firing many stories below. Because of Valerie, she had been thinking all night about the workers who kept the ship running for all the vacationers whose pleasure came at their expense. But she was unable to feel terribly guilty about it at the moment. The olive left a rich, oily, salty film on her tongue that made her instantly crave another one. She took a gulp of the icy martini. It went down her gullet as smooth and hard as liquid glass.

"Natalya," said Valerie, a little too loudly.

"Yes," said the bartender from the shadows. "Another round?"

"Not yet," said Valerie. "I'm wondering if you have time to talk to me about your job. I'm a journalist. I'm writing a book about workers. I'm on this cruise to collect stories from the people who work on this ship. I'm not here for fun."

"You look like you are here for fun," said Natalya. Her tone was insolent. "I am sorry but I have no time for talking." She had been standing idly, gazing out at nothing, but now she picked up a rag and began to swab the bar top.

"See?" Valerie murmured to Christine. "They don't want to talk to me. Oh well. Who can blame them? I wouldn't want to talk to me either."

Christine gave her a little nudge of pretend agreement. They both laughed.

*

Mick was almost done shaping the sausage patties. Next to him in the cold room, Consuelo was slicing strips of bacon with a long, sharp knife and layering them in a shallow stainless steel pan. Their breath steamed in the air. They had been discussing the night's weak spots, strengths.

"Nice job on the sliders," he said now. "They couldn't get enough of them."

"Thanks, Chef." He felt her swell with pride. Its warmth filled the space between them. Good. He had systematically beaten her down through the night. Now he had her; she was on board.

Mick was dying for a cigarette. He only smoked after his shift these days. Consuelo stacked the last neat, thick bacon slice and sealed the pan with plastic and slapped a strip of tape on it and took a Sharpie from her apron pocket and marked it with "Bacon," her initials, and the date. She stripped off her latex gloves and trashed them while Mick finished the last little meat patty, sealed and marked the pan. His gloves came off; he flexed his fingers, ready to get out of the kitchen and head for the crew lounge to throw himself into a chair, light up, and crack a beer. His crew would work for a few more hours, and the night service crew was just arriving for their shift, but his work was done until 0600 tomorrow morning. He thought ahead, mentally making Hollandaise. He hated fucking brunch. The worst meal ever invented. Including fucking high tea. Forget it. It was a good idea not to think one second beyond that first long, slow, cold, bubbly gulp of beer prickling in his nose, that first inhalation of smoke piquing his lungs.

Consuelo followed him out of the cold room, expertly dodging the other cooks rushing around, the old kitchen dance. On his way out Mick said his good nights, checked everything again, but there was nothing else for him to say or do tonight; they'd had their post-closing meeting already, the ones who were done, and Paolo was in charge of the night crew, thank God. Mick knew him from other cruises; he was Argentinean, a fruit bat, a prima donna, but a hard worker and solid under his theatrics and tantrums.

In the locker room, he and Consuelo stripped casually, without looking at each other. Aprons and jackets went into the laundry bin, checked pants followed, clogs and neckerchiefs went into their lockers; then, standing back to back, they silently dressed in jeans and black T-shirts. He slipped on the leather jacket Suzanne had given him and turned around to see Consuelo, identically dressed, in the mirror.

"Nice outfit," he said, laughing.

Consuelo flicked a quick grin at him, already moving on to wherever she was going—a date, judging by the look on her face, shining and expectant, wide awake. She was in her mid-twenties, twenty-seven at the oldest. Mick remembered being that young, only seven or so years ago, but it felt like decades. The endless supply of energy, the boundless anticipation.

"*Buenas,* Chef," she said, and was out.

In the staff lounge, he went to the bar and ordered a bottle of ice-cold Belgian beer and closed his eyes and shivered as the first chug went down his parched gullet. He was badly dehydrated from his hangover earlier, the stress of this new setup, forgetting to drink water through his shift. He drank again. The beer was almost gone already.

He knew that smoking was allowed on the *Isabella* as part of this cruise's late-'50s retro theme, but Mick wasn't sure that extended to the crew. He didn't care at the moment. He fished his pack of cigarettes out of his jacket pocket, tipped one out, stuck it in his mouth, and flicked his lighter.

There were three distinct groups of people in here, the various mafias converging at the end of their work shifts, none of them Hungarian, as usual. He heard Jamaican-accented English from the crowd nearest the door, Spanish against the wall, and Russian in the corner. He looked around for an empty chair, flopped into the one nearest him, leaned back, and closed his eyes.

"Hey."

It was Consuelo, giving his shoulder a light tap as she moved past. He caught a whiff of her perfume, some spicy combination that smelled like cloves, musk, and a flowery depth, but not sweet, a deeply carnal smell.

"Hey," he said back, squinting up at her.

She kept moving past him, lithe and focused as a fillet knife. He watched as she went over to the Spanish-speaking contingent and thrust herself into their midst, then he reminded himself that she worked on his station, and he was her boss, and he shut his eyes again.

The staff lounge was traditionally the place on any ship where the crew came to unwind, if they were lucky enough to have one. Crew lounges often got crowded and wild, with half-naked dancing, drugs, fights, heavy-duty make-out sessions. In the lounge, you could do what you wanted, because management usually stayed away. Apart from the crew mess where they ate their meals, drinking here and working out in the crew gym were the only two social release valves the workers had during their time at sea, when there was no shore leave. This bare-bones room with its makeshift bar and motley assortment of chairs and tables, mismatched castoffs and discarded leftovers, was the only place on the entire ship where they were allowed to drink besides their quarters, which were too small for more than a few people to fit into. But at least the lounge had plenty of alcohol. The dank, dark, cramped little gym next door with its two treadmills, one elliptical machine, two weight benches, and a smattering of suspiciously moist yoga mats was much less appealing.

But it was strangely quiet in here, Mick thought. First nights were generally loud, wild, and late, the new crew getting acquainted or greeting friends they hadn't worked with in a while. Maybe most people hadn't come off their shifts yet; he didn't know the schedules of the waiters and housekeeping staffs.

Just then, one of the Russians said something loudly and their entire table ignited in laughter. The guy tending bar, a voluntary position paid only in tips and social prestige, was evidently a Russian too: he yelled something across the lounge and threw a bottle of vodka over to the table. The guy who'd shouted caught it and opened it and drank from it, then wiped off the top and poured straight vodka into everyone's glass with a flip of the wrist and a flourish.

The mood at the Jamaican table was dreamy and contemplative; maybe they'd found a place to enjoy a post-work spliff. Mellow, heavy-lidded, they peeled the labels off bottles of beer and bobbed their heads to the music on the sound system, some kind of synth-heavy pop with a female singer. Mick had no idea who she was. Her voice was husky, twitchy with alley-cat yowls. It was the aural equivalent of Consuelo's perfume.

But the stoned, spaced-out Jamaicans were raucous compared to Consuelo's table. Talking in low voices with their heads close together was not Mick's usual notion of a group of Spanish speakers. In his experience, Hispanics and Latinos loved to mix it up when they drank, interrupting each other, flaring into opinionated rants and half-flirtatious arguments and hot riffs of arguing banter and hard laughter. These people were talking one by one, quietly, and everyone seemed to be listening instead of jumping in. Mick's Spanish was passable, just good enough to make out the gist of a conversation. He listened hard, but their voices were too quiet, impossible to eavesdrop on.

Consuelo, who was facing Mick, caught his eye and kept her face impassive as she held his gaze. He had no idea what she was trying to telegraph to him. She thought he was hot and desired him passionately? He should mind his own business? He should fuck off? Probably the latter two.

He shut his eyes again and let the music and beer fill his head.

He felt another quick tap on his shoulder a while later with another whiff of her perfume. He opened his eyes as Consuelo slid into the chair next to him and sat facing the same direction he was facing, toward the bar, where the Russian bartender was smoking and leaning on the bar top and yelling over at his increasingly drunk compatriots. He had a grim face, colorless hair, and a huge nose. He saw Mick looking at him and held up a beer bottle. Mick nodded and caught the bottle as it flew toward him, twisted off the top, drank.

"Hey," said Consuelo. "You looked like you were having a nice nap."

"Thanks for waking me up," he said. "Looks like a serious discussion over there. Are you talking about economics or science or something?"

"We're plotting to take over the world," she said.

She looked serious, but Mick was learning her sense of humor, he thought. He laughed; she didn't. "Where are you all from, anyway?"

"Most of us are from Mexico, a couple from Guatemala. We know each other from past cruises. You know Rodrigo, right? He's on our station. And Yvete is a croupier in the casino. A couple of others are room stewards. A couple of waiters."

"They're your friends?"

Her face went still as she looked over at the table. "In a way. Friends, yeah, sure."

"What were you really talking about?"

"How pissed off we are about the layoffs. You know they're canceling all our contracts after this cruise?"

Mick stared at her. "No," he said. "I haven't heard anything about it. Are they really?"

"I guess you're in the clear, man. Also, do you know who's on the boat? One of the owners of Cabaret. Larry Weiss. Should we poison his steak?"

"You think it would solve anything?"

"It would make me feel better."

Mick nodded at her empty glass. "You want another glass of wine?"

She shook her head. "I'm going to sleep. My new boss is a bastard. I have to stay on my toes."

She winked at him and got up, banging her knuckles softly against Mick's.

chapter seven

Miriam unpacked her toiletries carefully, trying to keep them from getting mixed up with Isaac's. Of course Rivka, in her willful ignorance of their divorced state, had put them into a room together, with a double bed no less, when she'd made the arrangements for them. As soon as she realized this, Miriam had marched straight up to a crewmember and demanded a room of her own. The ship was less than half full; surely they could accommodate her. But the boy had disappeared and Miriam hadn't seen him since. She had had to rush to get to their rehearsal in the chapel, so nothing had been done, and here it was after dinner, and she was exhausted. She'd slept with Isaac endless times before, she supposed she could do it one more night, but tomorrow she was going to raise hell and get herself her own damned private cabin. She didn't care if they docked her pay, she wasn't spending two weeks lying awake next to this snoring old man, checking his damned scrotum for him every time he decided he might have cancer.

Isaac was still up in the casino with Larry and Rivka, watching Larry shoot craps and flirting with Rivka, on whom, Miriam suspected, he had a crush. She hoped he'd stay up there all night. But she knew he wouldn't, and she also knew that she wouldn't be able to sleep until he came back. She would lie awake, expecting him to come along any minute and rattle the key in the lock and turn the light on and make a racket getting himself into his pajamas and heaving himself down next to her, jostling her and disarranging the covers. Why bother falling asleep if she'd just have to do it all over again?

She climbed into the bed on the side farther from the bathroom, since Isaac had to get up in the night because of prostate issues, and God forbid he should have to go all the way around the bed. She plumped up her pillows, settled herself against them, opened her boring Norwegian crime novel, and began to read. Ten minutes later she was sound asleep with the book open in her lap, the lamp on, and her reading glasses still on her nose.

She awoke with a small gasp and floundered up from the depths of a deep, untroubled sleep to find Isaac, lying on his back next to her, staring up at the ceiling. He looked over at her.

"Good morning," she said. "You were so quiet, I hardly knew you were there."

"I lay here awake all night, not moving."

"You didn't."

"Of course I didn't."

She sat up slowly, rubbing her eyes with the heel of one hand, bracing her back with the other. Sunlight streamed through the porthole. She got out of bed and stretched her arms skyward, as she did every morning, then bent over and tried to touch her toes. She repeated this ten times, grunting. Isaac heaved himself up out of bed and looked out the porthole. His white hair stood up around his head, sunlit, like a nimbus. He looked to Miriam like a saintly Einstein in pale blue-and-white-striped pajama bottoms and a white undershirt. It was not at all awkward to be sharing a bed with him again. It felt familial, like sleeping with an aunt or a cousin.

"I didn't hear you come to bed," she said.

"I tiptoed into the room like a mouse, so terrified was I from years of sleeping with you. You always flew into a rage if I woke you up. And I knew I'd lie there all night, too afraid I'd snore. I'd never sleep in a million years."

"But you slept."

"I slept very well," he said. "Did I snore?"

"If you did, I didn't hear it."

"So maybe you're going deaf."

"Eccch," said Miriam. She went into the tiny bathroom and turned on the shower.

*

In the buffet breakfast room, Christine collected a cup of black coffee and a bowl of yogurt with a scoop of fruit salad on top. Armed with her morning's requirements, she headed up to yesterday's nook and lounge chair, which she now thought of as her exclusive spot. Valerie was still asleep; Christine expected her to be out cold until early afternoon.

She arranged her breakfast on the table next to the chair and took from her bag the copy of Evelyn Waugh's *A Handful of Dust* that she'd filched yesterday from the ship's library, a windowless inner room on the sun deck with wingback armchairs and mahogany shelves and tasseled standing lamps. It was well stocked with books, including leather-bound editions of novels by Wodehouse and Cather and Wharton, much better than the schlocky charity-box crap she'd brought from the supermarket in Maine.

Instead of reading, she looked out at the view as she drank her coffee. The water swelled, rising and falling in heavy rhythm. The ocean looked like a miniature mountain range in constant liquid motion, dark fluid granite peaks veined with white, shifting, collapsing, forming new peaks. The dome of air from sea surface to sky-top was shot with bits of quick gold, charged with ions, dancing with refracted sunlight.

Nearby on the deck, there seemed to be a kerfuffle going on between a tall, indignant old man and a baffled crewmember, who looked hapless and very young.

"Oh, for God's sake," said someone behind her. "Good luck, Sasha."

Christine turned and beheld an elderly woman a few lounge chairs over, staring down the deck in consternation. She was small and slender, and she looked simultaneously elegant and fierce in her gray long-sleeved T-shirt and peg-legged white trousers, her chestnut hair pinned up with a sparkling clip. Her small face was swathed in oversized sunglasses.

The woman noticed Christine and politely took off her sunglasses to look her directly in the eyes. "He's up in arms because they're making us share rooms. The ship isn't even half full, but they won't change it. I have to sleep with my ex-husband, can you imagine?"

The tall man walked off down the deck as the crewmember began straightening deck chairs, looking hangdog.

"Is that him?" Christine pointed to the tall old man's very straight retreating back.

"No, that's our first violinist. My ex-husband plays the viola. The cellist is around here somewhere. We're a string quartet."

"Oh," Christine said, recognizing her. "I heard you playing during dinner last night. You were wonderful."

"Thank you," said the woman. "We've played together for a very long time. I'm Miriam, by the way."

"Christine," said Christine.

"Do you mind if I join you?"

"Not at all," said Christine, hoping her face didn't betray her hesitation. She had never been particularly fond of talking to strangers first thing in the morning.

Miriam brought her coffee over to the empty deck chair next to hers. "Are you from Los Angeles?"

"Oh no, not at all," said Christine. "I'm from Maine. I've never been on a cruise before."

"Lucky you. I've been on far too many. Well, it's my job. And it pays well. We usually get our own rooms, though."

"I'm sharing a room with my friend," said Christine. "She invited me, so I can't complain, but I didn't realize how small they were going to be."

"They're usually bigger. But this is an old ship. And at least you don't have to sleep with your ex-husband."

Christine laughed. "I'm still on my first, and he's at home."

"Good for you. Kids?"

"No. Not yet. Do you have any?"

"I have two," said Miriam. "A boy and a girl, the lights of my life. Rachel and Avner, their names are. I have grandchildren, too."

Christine felt an unaccustomed urge to pry, or maybe it was just curiosity. She found herself liking this woman. "Did you always know you were going to be a mother? Or did you decide at some point?"

"It wasn't a choice," said Miriam. She seemed to welcome Christine's interest. "It was an important thing for us all to have children. Our population was decimated, Israel needed people, to work and learn and carry on our traditions, we needed soldiers in the army, we needed the next generation of Jews."

"That makes sense," said Christine. "For me it's completely different. I think all the time about overpopulation and extinction and climate change."

Miriam put a hand on Christine's arm. It felt surprisingly heavy and strong, like those little birds at the aquarium. "Two more won't make a difference to the world. But they will make all the difference to you."

"Maybe," said Christine.

Miriam peered closely at her. "How old are you?"

"Thirty-six," said Christine. "I know, I'm getting old."

"Oh, you're so young. Just don't stay stuck. That's the real mistake. Whatever you decide." Miriam suddenly looked ancient and wise to Christine, all her elegance revealed to lie lightly on her, like a shimmer of fairy dust. But her eyes blazed as brightly as a girl's. "Don't be afraid of change."

Christine felt a rush of relief, hearing this, although she wasn't sure why. "Thank you," she said. "That's a good way to look at it."

"I've never been afraid of change," said Miriam. "That way, you don't have to regret the things you didn't do."

"What's it like, having your ex-husband in the quartet with you?"

Miriam laughed. "It's a little like being married still, only without the headaches, because I don't have to live with him. We live in the same building and we work together, but I have my own apartment, I can do as I please."

Christine tried to imagine herself and Ed divorced, still working the farm together, but living apart, with their own individual lives outside of farmwork. She found the idea very attractive and didn't quite know why.

"That sounds great," she told Miriam.

"He still drives me crazy, so it's half great," said Miriam, waving a hand as if to send the other half of Isaac packing. "Neither of us remarried and we're together all the time, so it's like we never really split fully."

"I work with my husband," said Christine. "We're together all the time, we work hard on our own land, and it's a good life." She hesitated. Sitting here in the hazy sea air, so far from land, gave her a feeling of safety, as if whatever she said would stay here in the ocean. "But sometimes I feel invisible," she added slowly. "Like I'm disappearing." She felt instantly sheepish for confessing something so fanciful.

But Miriam, to her credit, didn't laugh. She didn't say anything. She just went on watching Christine with her keen warm gaze.

*

Mick was supposed to meet Chef van Buyten at 1100 hours in the small office off the main galley. When he arrived at 1058, the two other executive sous-chefs were there already. They'd been introduced in the meeting the day before, but he'd forgotten their names. One of them was French, that much he remembered. The other was Asian, Japanese maybe. They were the same rank as Mick, but technically slightly above him in station, since they worked in the main galley, and Mick was running the buffet.

The Frenchman, small but wiry with muscle, sat backward in the chair by the inner wall, his shaved bullethead covered with a pugilistic stubble of black hair. He wore thick, black-rimmed glasses made even thicker and blacker by the echo of his thick, black eyebrows. He was also heavily tattooed, at least on his fore-arms and neck; the rest of him was hidden in his whites. Instinctively, Mick had no interest in provoking him. He knew the type. Quick-tempered for no good reason, prickly and unpleasant, and not as good as he thought he was, which Mick suspected was the real source of his bad temper.

The other sous-chef glanced up briefly as Mick came in. His black hair was neatly clipped. He was soft-bodied and round like a baby, and had a huge head with a sweet round face, but his eyes looked weary and old.

"Mick," Mick reminded them both. He sat in the empty chair farthest from the desk.

"Kenji," said the Japanese dude. He had a seemingly natural puckish expression he managed to parlay into a glower.

The Frenchman's thick lips twisted. "Jean-Luc," he said with apparent bitter condescension.

Mick almost laughed, but checked himself.

"Chef," the three of them said in ragged unison as Laurens came in and sat abruptly in the chair they'd left him, the one behind the desk. His pale, freckled face held no expression. He bared his teeth at them all, but it wasn't a smile, and his eyes flickered from one face to another. "First, I'd like to hear from each of you how you think it went last night. Kenji, you first. Talk to me about the fish."

"*Oui,* Chef," said Kenji. "I think most thing come out good. I think we have good rhythm, my team perform well. When we get hit with a lot of order for two hour, we stay cool, don't lose our shit. Rodrigo did good, cooked perfectly. Stefan had some trouble with his timing a couple time at the beginning. All in all we did okay, very good. I was proud of them."

"What could you have done better?" Laurens fired back. "What did you fuck up? What went wrong?"

Mick waited for Kenji to get defensive, bluster, try to cover his ass. Instead he said, "Nothing wrong, Chef. Stefan had trouble with tricky timing of fillet of sole at first but he learn quick. We did very well. No send-backs. Everyone happy, Chef."

Laurens kept his gaze on Kenji for a moment. Kenji looked back, unperturbed. His eyes even ticked closed a millimeter. Mick was impressed: this guy had sangfroid. Either he wasn't afraid of Laurens or he was an excellent actor.

"Mick," said Laurens.

Mick snapped to. "*Oui,* Chef."

"Did you talk to the insubordinate girl who was late?"

"Consuelo. I did, Chef. I stayed on her ass all night. She's in line now. No more trouble from her or I will answer for it."

"I heard good reports from Sidney about the buffet. Passengers were pleased with your pig roast and the entertainment. All around, a success."

Mick had been aware of Sidney all night last night and had worked hard, unobtrusively, to make sure his initial impression was good. The maître d' and head of the waitstaff was an elegant, punctilious, demanding Welshman, and everyone who knew him and had worked with him before apparently deeply respected him. No one seemed to know anything about him, apart from the fact that he was something of a legend among Cabaret kitchen crews. He was like the Godfather. He could make you, he could break you, and no one ever questioned him. And he was effortlessly proper; he brought civilization with him like his own personal corrective. He was therefore superbly effective. And a positive assessment from Sidney, coming from Chef himself, was worth a gold brick or two in galley currency. Mick tried not to beam. He felt Jean-Luc sending him a sidelong death ray.

"I put Consuelo in charge of developing and executing the hors d'oeuvres," Mick said. It always looked good to deflect praise onto your staff whenever possible, and Consuelo deserved this, especially after she had gotten herself in Laurens's bad graces right off the bat. "She came up with the sliders and the kebabs. People seemed to love them. Sidney is correct."

"Ah," said Laurens. "Was there anything you could do better as we go on?"

"Tonight, the theme is elegant and fancy. Gourmet in 1950s

style. Canapés to start. Caviar and blini. A beautiful spread of classic food using lighter, more contemporary recipes and techniques."

"Ah," said Laurens again, noncommittal, blank. "Thank you. Okay. Jean-Luc," he added as if it were an afterthought.

"*Oui,* Chef."

"Your assessment of last night. Your station had some serious trouble."

"The squab," said Jean-Luc. "Didier, he know now what he did wrong."

"Didier," said Laurens, "was not in charge of cooking perfect squab. You were. What happened?"

"Squab," said Jean-Luc with hatred. "Didier overcook it. *C'est simple.* Now he know not to do that."

"Anything else?"

"I would like to do the flambé of the steak Diane on the floor individually. It is impressive and also, the steak is better."

"Talk to the waitstaff, see what they think."

Jean-Luc opened his mouth to launch into something about tableside pyrotechnics, Mick was certain, and he also knew that the waitstaff would comply with whatever the chefs wanted them to do, they always did.

"Lobster thermidor," said Laurens.

Jean-Luc shut his mouth. Blinked. "Excuse me, Chef?"

"How do you make it? All three of you. I want to hear your preferred method and recipe."

"Lobster thermidor," said Kenji. "Yes, I know it. It was invented in France in a theater restaurant. Lobster steamed, de-shelled, packed into the clean shells and covered in a cream sauce with sherry and mustard, then grated Gruyère on top, then broiled."

"Nothing else?" said Laurens.

"That is how I would make it, but I have not ever had to."

"You never made it out of curiosity? It's a classic."

"No, Chef," said Kenji coolly. "I would welcome the opportunity."

"Beh," said Jean-Luc, "it's too much work for what you get, it's too rich, and very expensive. In Paris we did a version much easier, much faster. We make the sauce ahead of time, no shells, plated the lobster meat, *et fini,* but it's not a good return. You cannot taste the lobster under all the sauce. It's a waste of money and ingredients and time, Chef."

Laurens held Jean-Luc's gaze for a couple of beats, during which Mick gathered himself, thinking.

"Mick, anything to add?"

"I made *homard thermidor* in Budapest at the restaurant where I learned to cook. It was a three-step process for the sauce, and it was excellent, delicious, and worth the trouble." He paused and added pointedly, without looking at Jean-Luc, "Expensive, yes, but not more than filet mignon. We made the custard separately in a bain-marie, then folded it into the sauce, tempering it, very slowly. For the sauce we did not use cream; we made a roux as for a béchamel and then added to it a glaze of lobster stock, wine, and sherry with a sprig of tarragon, a pinch of nutmeg. Then you slowly temper together the béchamel and glaze with the cream custard, adding a little dry mustard, until it is very glossy, thick, then pour just the right amount, not too much, over the tender lobster meat. And broil with a little grated Gruyère to finish, then a hit of paprika, and finally, we served it over buttered egg noodles with a small pitcher of the sauce on the side."

"I'm hungry," said Laurens with a half-smile so faint, Mick was sure he'd imagined it. "Can you make me one for lunch?"

"*Oui,* Chef," said Mick.

"Also," said Laurens. "One more thing. Mick, you'll replace Jean-Luc on the meat station for this cruise. Jean-Luc, you're running the buffet galley now. I think that is a better use of our resources."

"*Oui,* Chef," Mick said. "I'd like to bring Consuelo over too."

Laurens flashed a look at him. Mick knew he'd stuck his neck out too far now with Chef, but he held his eye contact without wavering; he had just learned from Kenji's example that holding Laurens van Buyten's gaze was the way to impress and disarm him. Of course: he was a bully, and like all bullies, he could be disarmed only with fearless strength. Any emotion on the part of his prey, any sign of weakness, and he smelled blood.

"She's tough," Mick added after a beat or two went by without a firm no. He guessed that this was one of the highest compliments in Laurens's lexicon. "Her sense of timing is good, she knows the recipes of this era."

"Well then," said Laurens. "Consuelo can switch with Didier. Okay?"

"*Oui,* Chef," said Mick calmly. His second promotion in three days, and he'd secured a place for his underling.

"Is this clear, Jean-Luc?"

"*Oui.*" Jean-Luc swallowed a toad in his throat. "Chef."

chapter eight

The main galley roared and clanked, the air vibrated with heat. In the midst of the controlled chaos, Mick wrestled a gigantic tray of briskets into an oven and turned to a forty-quart pot of simmering beef stock. Nearby, Consuelo braised duck legs. She looked neat and calm, swathed in an apron, her dark hair tucked under a scarf, focused on her work. After last night, Mick was now very aware of her. He found himself watching her, studying her. She was slender and strong and had a flat, moonlike face with full lips and almond-shaped eyes and a high, pale forehead. Her face wasn't beautiful, but she had a macho samurai-like implacability alongside a Hispanic formality and, he thought, an underground sensuality. He imagined that softening her would be a challenge, but once you had her, she would surrender all at once. He thought of the way a mushroom resisted, sliding drily in the hot pan in clenched refusal until all at once it ran with juices and went limp and rich and fragrant.

Mick recalled his promise to himself that he would make it a point to get laid on this cruise. Of course he could not have anything to do with Consuelo—never someone who worked with him, especially an underling in such close proximity all day—but the fact that he was allowing himself to think about her in this way only proved how much he needed it. He imagined himself in that parallel, luckier life he would have been leading right now if things had gone as planned: in Paris, in Suzanne's bed drinking red wine, naked, smoking, talking about where to go for dinner, or should they stay in . . . and then he stopped thinking about Suzanne altogether.

There were no windows in the galley. Giant vents sucked up the smoke and circulated the air, but they couldn't do much when the kitchen was in full swing. Around him, the huge stainless steel room was all monochromatic hard polished surfaces, some fogged with steam, some bright with reflected light from the red-hot electric burners, some gleaming. The air was so thick and wet, Mick felt as if he were breathing hot seawater. He remembered his dream of swimming below the ocean with big friendly fish; had that been only two days ago? That was what he felt like now, shoulder to shoulder with his fellow cooks, no one saying much, everyone fierce and intent, staying out of one another's way with practiced expertise and finesse. He knew this work, he knew exactly how to take charge of a meat station, although he had never run one before. He had been in Consuelo's place for years. He had observed. And he'd been very keen to get a chance to prove himself. And the fact that Laurens van Buyten of all people had put him here . . . He could not fuck up, could not distract himself by imagining himself eating coq au vin with Suzanne at a table outside somewhere, licking the meat juice off her fingers, gathering his forces to fuck her again when they got back to her small aerie in the Marigny on a quiet, twisting lane, with its billowing curtains and high ceilings and the tiny kitchen he loved to fill with provisions he didn't have to cook and could heap on a board after sex to eat picnic-style on her enormous platform bed, peaches and tomatoes, *boules* and cheeses, charcuterie with cornichons and grainy mustard, chocolate and pastries, and wine, always wine . . .

"Right behind you, Chef," said Consuelo, passing by him fast, so closely he felt the air whoosh against his back, but she didn't touch or even graze him.

He snapped out of the impossible reverie and went to the walk-in and brought out a crate of quail. One by one, he began spatch-cocking them, pressing them into the cutting board and snipping out the backbones with shears to flatten them. He loved working with quail. They were a simple thing, little bodies that looked vulnerable, froglike, in the roasting pan; their bones were tiny, delicate, and their meat was tender, mild, responsive to whatever flavors it was bathed in. Tonight it would be paprika, fines herbes, and sea salt, cooked fast in butter in a hot pan, served on a bed of roasted potatoes with a side of julienned vegetables, so simple, yet so easy to get wrong: quail had to leave the pan still faintly pink at its core or else it dried out. But if you did that, you were rewarded with a delicacy beyond chicken, or pheasant, or duck, a tiny rich morsel of meat racked with wee bones that demanded slowness in its consumption, a conscious suspension of gluttony, a Zen focus in which dismantling this perfectly made small creature took your entire attention.

He was aware, in the back of his brain, that Laurens was sitting in his office right now, eating the lobster thermidor that Mick had made. This time, he had used Julia Child's recipe as per Laurens's implicit directive at the first staff meeting, which called for mushrooms and cognac and cream, and required him to cook the lobsters in a quick vegetable-infused broth. It was intensely fun to make and completely different from the method he'd been taught by Chef Viktor at the Eszterházy Restaurant. He'd grinned to himself the entire time he'd been cooking it, glancing happily between the book and the stove. It had been a while since he'd taken such a childlike pleasure in cooking. He'd made two: one for Chef, the other for Consuelo and himself to share. Of course Chef had recognized its author when he'd brought it in to him.

"Julia Child's recipe," he'd said, inhaling the steam that rose from the sauce.

Mick and Consuelo had devoured theirs, standing side by side at their station, grinning at each other. Then they'd thrown the plates and forks in a dish tub and seamlessly resumed whatever they'd been doing.

"Hello?" came a female American voice through the swinging doors. Mick ignored whoever it was. Let the prep cooks handle her, whatever she needed. "Excuse me?"

He went on spatchcocking quail. Press, snip, snip, stack.

A woman appeared at the end of the station, her head cocked

playfully sideways to show that she knew she was intruding and was half apologetic about it, but she needed to talk to them so here she was. She was youngish, tall and skeletally thin, with curly, short reddish hair and glasses, a long, pale face, her upper lip curved and long and almost prehensile.

"I'm Valerie Chapin," she said. "A freelance writer, I'm working on a book, and I wondered if I could take up a few minutes of your time. Not now, of course, but sometime during the cruise?"

Consuelo had watched her sidelong as she talked and then, without a word, vanished into the cold storage room.

Mick kept one hand on the quail he'd just finished, the other on his knife, and stilled his hands. "Maybe," he said as curtly as he could. "You have to go through Chef van Buytens."

"I'm so sorry," she said, giving him a keen look, half flirtatious, with a predatory edge. "What is your name? Maybe we could meet later tonight or tomorrow, whenever you like, I'll be available."

Mick gave her a quick glare and resumed working.

She waited there, standing and watching him work, longer than he would have imagined was possible, even for someone as rude and arrogant as this woman clearly was, but finally she gave up and left the galley.

Consuelo returned. "Who the fuck was that?"

"She said she's a writer," said Mick.

"What does she want with us?"

"I told her to fuck off."

"She's a guest."

"I was polite."

"You were polite," repeated Consuelo, infusing the words with all the amused skepticism they could contain. Mick realized he was being teased. She was subtle. On hearing of her promotion to the meat station thanks to Mick's recommendation, she had nodded at him briefly, a typically economical gesture Mick had interpreted as her version of clicking her heels together with joy.

"I want to talk to her," said Consuelo. "On my break."

Mick squinted at her. Consuelo's face held a blank expression that revealed nothing. Mick went back to his quail. He felt a twinge of unease, but there was no reason for it, at least nothing he could pinpoint, so he let it go.

*

After another decadent dinner in the fine-dining restaurant, Christine and Valerie went back up to the crescent-shaped teak pool bar. They perched on high stools amid a talking, laughing, drinking crowd. People swam in the pool and floated on rafts. The same jazz band from the night before had set up on the other side of the pool. Valerie, who seemed to have thrown her determination to stay sober overboard, was halfway into her second martini. "Meanwhile, this hot Eastern European chef was a total dick," she said. She had been telling Christine about her slow progress so far with conducting interviews. "He ignored me, anyway."

"He was probably working," said Christine. She flashed on the drunk, tough-looking Hungarian guy who'd sat next to her at the hotel bar in Long Beach, the one who'd hit on the waitress and made her run for cover. "I wouldn't mess with professional chefs. They're all supposedly ex-cons and thugs."

"Just my type, right?" Valerie took a cigarette out of a chrome-plated cigarette box she'd pulled from her pocket and lit it with a sleek lighter. Christine hadn't known she was in possession of all this equipment. Valerie had quit and started again through the years so many times Christine had lost track. Valerie loved renouncing vices, but she equally loved taking them up again, as if this cycle of abstinent virtue and decadent self-destructiveness were a private, seasonal rhythm that anchored her in some way. Christine, who always felt ploddingly steady and sensible, adored this about her friend.

"Who do these chefs think they *are* in their stupid white aprons and *Crocs*?" Valerie said, exhaling a stream of smoke as she talked. "I mean, seriously. Why does cooking bring out the douchebag in men? Actually, writing does too. Actually, everything does."

"Farming doesn't," said Christine. "At least, not as obviously."

"I'm gonna stalk that fucker and make him talk to me," said Valerie. "He's too high up the food chain for my purposes, but now it's a point of pride."

"In other words, he's hot," said Christine.

"A hot douchebag," said Valerie. "Just my type."

"So let me ask you something. Why didn't you try to get a job on a cruise ship if you wanted the real story? Like Barbara Ehrenreich. Instead of interviewing workers, work alongside them."

"I'm doing the Studs Terkel thing instead," said Valerie. "Like an update of *Working.* The socioeconomic landscape he was writing about has totally changed. I want to give contemporary workers that kind of voice. I see my cruise-ship chapter as an answer to David Foster Wallace's snarky essay, which frankly hasn't aged well."

Christine laughed; this was so like Valerie, to appropriate the work of writers she admired while bragging that she would write something better. "It is? How?"

"Wallace just went on a cruise by himself as a skeptical dude with an attitude. Don't get me wrong, it's a brilliant and funny essay, but that all seems too obvious now. We get it. The world is so much bigger now, so much more complicated. And I want to go deeper. I want to uncover the real story. There's a class structure on this ship, there's an economy, there's a system that mirrors the global one. There are thirty different nationalities in the working staff, the waiters and bartenders and cooks and room stewards and engineers and dishwashers. No Americans. All the Americans are above decks, in entertainment and on the bridge and among the guests. But below, it's all foreigners, most from Third World countries. All cruise ships are the same."

"That's really interesting," said Christine. "Seriously."

"Hey, can I play you an interview I just did?" Valerie took out her iPhone. "I managed to get one of the cooks to talk to me, she works under the guy who snubbed me. I want to know what you think. Here." She thrust her phone at Christine.

"Now?" said Christine, looking down at Valerie's phone. After only one day without using one, it was jarring to look at the small lit-up screen.

"It's short," said Valerie. She clicked on an icon marked ISABELLA INTERVIEWS and handed Christine a pair of earbuds, which Christine obediently put on.

Valerie hit play, and a woman's accented voice spoke into Christine's ear. She sounded Spanish and tense. *"I can give you a couple minutes but then I have to be back at my station."*

"What is your name and nationality?" Valerie's voice said.

"Consuelo Fonseca. I'm Mexican. From Acapulco."

"How long have you worked for Cabaret?"

"Six years."

"Can you tell me a bit about your job?"

Christine heard an angry, scornful sound, a snort. *"Sure. I'll tell you a couple of things. We work sixteen-hour days for pathetic wages. Most of us, our contracts are being canceled at the end of this cruise."*

"They're firing you?" came Valerie.

"Yeah. And you know why? So they can hire refugees to do the work we do, but for less money and longer hours. I'm talking desperate people, from Syria, Sudan. The owners of this company are shit. One of them is on board. I read an interview with him online where he said that the reason Third World workers like us are good at our jobs it that we're culturally suited to them." Her voice deepened as she imitated him. *" 'The Filipinos always smile at the customers even when they're tired from working so hard because they're so happy and it's such an honor to work for Cabaret. Workers from India are great like that too, always smiling, happy to work aboard these ships. Mexicans are the same. Always cheerful.' "* She snorted again. *"Look at me, so fucking cheerful. It's bullshit."*

"So why did you stay with Cabaret all these years if the conditions are so bad?"

"Because there's nothing for me in Mexico, no jobs, the economy is shit, and I'm sending money home and spending nothing. I don't have time to spend money. I'm young and I can take it. My parents are depending on me. I need this stupid job. Like everyone else on board this ship. We all need these jobs."

"*But you don't think they should hire these other workers? They need the jobs more than you do, even.*"

"No. *I don't think that.*" Consuelo's voice was acid. "*What I think is that they should stop treating us like slaves and not get rid of us to hire cheaper labor.*"

"I get it," said Valerie.

"*So they're dumping us and hiring desperate people, even more desperate than we are. Syrians running away from hell. Africans who will do anything to have a safe place to sleep, a tiny bit of money for their families. They'll be treated like labor animals. It's completely fucking wrong.*"

"*Wow.*" Christine heard real surprise in Valerie's voice. "*I didn't know that.*"

"*Okay,*" said Consuelo. "*I have to go now.*"

There was a click. Christine took off the earbuds.

"That's horrifying."

"I know, right?" said Valerie. She finished her martini. "Want to go in the pool and lie on one of those big rafts?"

"In our clothes?"

"Why not? I'll leave my phone here. No one will steal it."

They arranged themselves head-to-toe on an empty raft, cradling their drinks. Christine kicked gently against the pool's edge and sent the raft bobbing and floating into the middle. The surface of the water rocked and shimmered. Light from tiki lamps shot upward and dissipated in the still air. There were a few other people, dog-paddling with foam noodles, lounging on fat inner tubes, but no one paid attention to them. It was as if they were in a self-contained little bubble, a sanctuary of sorts. Christine looked down at her bare feet glowing like pale flat fish above the blue water, bobbing around with the bright neon purple and pink floating things. It reminded her of the aquarium, which gave her a fresh jolt of that same panicky, desolate feeling she'd had looking in at all those creatures in their tanks, reading all the plaques about the dying oceans. But there was something else too, something more immediate and personal. She felt a resurgence of the long-quashed yearning that had been awakened by her conversation with Miriam that morning.

She lifted her head. Being around Valerie's fast-talking nervous energy made Christine aware of how slow and stolid she had become. She could feel Valerie's brain working now, even when she was silent, the energy of her thoughts running ceaselessly. Christine remembered being that way, back in her old life. Now, there were whole swaths of time when her thoughts seemed to stop, when action took over completely and she became a functioning machine, carrying out her tasks. She thought with an odd, unaccustomed longing of her old walk-up apartment in New York, on Orchard Street, the sour, fecund smell of the old tenement stairwell; she remembered climbing up the four flights to her apartment's battered front door in stylish leather boots, heavy plastic bags of groceries wrapped around both wrists. It was odd how real it felt to her, more real than the farm, as if her entire life since going back to Maine had been some sort of hallucination, as if she'd never left that life of late nights in bars and reading books on long subway rides and jostling through crowds of varied, interesting people.

She hadn't been looking to escape from that life, not consciously. But one fall weekend, she had gone up to Maine to visit her parents in Standish, and incidentally to interview a farmer friend of theirs named Ed Thorne for a piece she was thinking of writing on the rising popularity of small organic farms in New England. She had driven her mother's old Subaru over to Fryeburg on a clear, crisp day to find Ed heaping a pile of pumpkins into the back of his truck to take to the farmers market the next morning. As Ed liked to put it, it was love at first question; she sat on his porch all afternoon with him, drinking mead he'd made with honey from his own bees, and then sat all evening at his table, eating the dinner he cooked, food he'd raised and grown himself, and then she spent the night with him, and the next night, too. It was a relief to admit it to herself: she was tired of being broke, in debt, stressed-out about money and bills, the hustle of freelancing. Six months later, she left New York and moved back up to Maine to live with Ed. The piece never got written. That had been almost eight years ago.

"Val," she said now, "I have to make a decision. Ed wants kids, and I don't."

Valerie sat up, rocking the raft, splashing them both. "You never told me that. What do you mean, you don't want them?"

"I'm not sure."

"But don't you need them to collect eggs and harvest stuff and put wood on the fire?" Valerie laughed. "All I know is *Little House on the Prairie.*"

"I don't want to turn into a mother," said Christine. "My mother."

"Listen, I get it, I don't want kids either," said Valerie. "At all. But if I were married and lived on a farm, I'd totally have them."

"Sometimes I miss my old life."

"You never loved New York, and you didn't love journalism either. You were good at it, but you always said you hated the bias and slant and trashiness of it all."

"Maybe so," Christine said. She went silent, let the whole subject go, feeling disappointed and slightly depressed. She had expected Valerie to say something different; had wanted her to, even.

Someone jumped into the pool near them. Water sloshed into Christine's ear and gin went up her nose. She coughed. The raft bobbed on the wake. Overhead, the Milky Way sprawled across the length of the sky, a violently lavish expanse of light, exactly as it did on clear nights in the sky above the farm, but it looked more dazzling and savage here. Christine felt a burst of wild, open excitement. Here she was, drunk on a raft in a pool on a ship on a dark ocean, thousands of miles from home. Anything was possible.

~~~~~ *part two*

THE FLOATING
WORLD

Something had been happening to Miriam on this cruise. Maybe the Pacific Ocean had something magical in its ions, maybe its wind strummed her cells, Aeolian harp–like, and produced harmonies and frequencies she could feel but not hear. But she had been feeling a little giddy since the ship had left port.

It was Sasha.

While they performed the *Rosamunde* Quartet on their second night at sea, she had felt a leaping of their souls toward each other in midair, wafted by the music.

It was crazy to articulate it thus to herself. It was insane. She was the most sensible of musicians, the most determined to attribute the sweet power of a tremolo, the foreboding of a shift to a darker key, a melody's progression from blitheness to awe, to the mathematical relationships between notes and the fact that the human ear and psyche were attuned viscerally to these things the way a dog's ears picked up high-pitched noises and caused a tumult of barking. These music-fed emotions weren't real, they were no more than notes, bowings, changes; sure, they conjured real feelings. But they didn't themselves *cause* them.

Still, she could not account for the exalted joy she felt from the opening notes of the first movement. She felt as if the music itself were lifting her soul from her rib cage and transporting it somewhere overhead, where it met Sasha's soul in a dance. That was the part she couldn't explain; she didn't believe in souls, let alone that they could just fly, willy-nilly, from the breasts of elderly violinists, and encounter each other somewhere above their heads.

And yet, it had happened. It felt as real to her as her feet felt on the floor. She turned to her right as she played and looked at Sasha, and he turned to his left and looked over his fingerboard at her, and they both raised their eyebrows at the same time as if to say, *Yes! This is an odd thing that our souls are dancing together overhead! But they are!*

So she wasn't imagining it.

They had played this quartet more times than she could remember. It was one of Schubert's greatest quartets, the full expression of his genius; it was imbued with the composer's humane and profoundly emotional melodic voice. The conversation between the four instruments was a lamentation and a rejoicing at the same time, sorrowful but light. *"Schöne Welt, wo bist du?"* the first movement asked. "Beautiful world, where are you?" Her second-violin part moved restlessly around the median, as if questioning, and Isaac's viola and Jakov's cello undergirded her. Sasha's melodic first-violin part was sure and true, as if he were leading them all together into a leap of faith that if they played this piece through to the end, they would find it, the beautiful world. He soared up toward it.

Miriam soared with him, left her body and herself behind and willfully went with him somewhere, where the two of them were conjoined in a twisting dance . . . Honestly, nothing like this had ever happened with any other piece of music. It was too much. Maybe it was the setting, the light, the romance of the ship. They were playing in the open air, up on the top deck, near the blue-green lit-up swimming pool, under a starlit sky, in candlelight, with torches lit, potted palm fronds rustling and the ocean wind scouring the ship's surfaces with its salt-rasping tongue. In the dim light, Miriam saw her old friends as if they were young again. All their faces looked awake, sharpened, excited. She knew hers did too.

And there it was again, Sasha's gaze, seeking out and meeting hers as he played unerringly. They both knew these parts by heart. His eyes were reassuring and playful and full of love, and she felt her own eyes answer him. It was that night again, the one so many decades ago, the night she'd felt herself falling in love with him the first time they'd played the *Rosamunde.* The feeling hadn't gone away since then; it had just been in abeyance, held in reserve somewhere, invisible.

Long into the early morning hours after that performance, Miriam lay in bed, too thrilled to sleep, listening to her ex-husband's gentle snoring, not bothered by it at all. She was happy to be awake, happy to be a violinist, happy to be on the Pacific Ocean again, her natal sea, the ocean that felt most like home to her. But she wasn't thinking about the ocean. She could only think of Sasha, how kind he was, how graceful and determined, how handsome his face had looked tonight in the starlight and candlelight. He had been so unhappy since his wife died. He'd been a shadow of himself. Tonight, he had come back to her, the Sasha she'd always loved.

She loved him, and she always had.

The thoughts she was having! Like a silly young girl. She'd never had these thoughts about Isaac, and he was her life's mate, the father of her beloved children. Sure, she had loved him when they were younger, even though he hadn't made her heart do flips. They'd always been friends and partners, making a life side by side, until they'd eventually started fighting all the time and gotten sick of each other and ended the whole thing. He'd never made her swoon, never given her these crazy, ridiculous thoughts of souls and dances and exaltation. She'd never felt this way about anyone, ever. Except, of course, for Sasha.

Well, here they were on a ship together, maybe for the last time in their lives, or one of the last times, since the quartet would not be able to perform for much longer; their minds and bodies were all failing in various ways. That night may have been the last time they would ever play the *Rosamunde,* their final performance.

Miriam had to get up out of bed and breathe the fresh air and stand outside and look out at the ocean; her whole skin was tingling, her mind was encased in a bubble that wanted to float out of her skull. The music had ended, but the feeling remained. After being a professional musician for more than half a century, the idea that music might cause something real to happen, might inspire feelings that were true and actual, was a revelation to her. She had heard it could happen, but she'd never believed it, no more than she'd believed in religious visions or near-death tunnels of light or astrological predestination. She was rigorously pragmatic. She was empirical, grounded, and above all else, skeptical.

Schubert had undone her. Of course it would be Schubert. No other composer could slide his melodies straight into the heart so you wept without knowing why you were weeping. His music had the effect of the greatest poetry, of the most humane and beautiful and heartfelt words, but wordless, far more direct, elemental almost.

She got out of bed and silently put on her bathrobe. Pocketing her room key, she eased the door shut behind her and went along the corridor to the door that led out onto the walkway. Outside, she leaned against the railing and looked down at the dark ocean, watching small curlicues of whitecaps glowing in the still-dark early morning air.

The door opened. Someone came out onto the walkway and moved with purpose toward her. For a moment she feared it was Isaac, come to tell her to go back to bed, dammit, was she nuts, did she know what time it was, it was three o'clock!

But no, it was Sasha. She'd known he'd come out, she realized. He was wearing his bathrobe too. She looked at him, and he looked at her, and both their faces were alight, open, and smiling.

"Since Sonia died," he said to her in a quiet voice once he was at the railing standing next to her, "I've begun to feel this way again."

"This way again," she repeated, as if she were asking, but she was really assuring him that she knew exactly what he meant. He had invited her into that strange, ardent, mysterious dance, and she had responded, had let her own playing answer him. But tonight wasn't the first time he had sought her out in the *Rosamunde.*

All of a sudden, it all made sense to her, clearly, and even though it was nuts, illogical and absurd, she believed it.

*

The breeze was alternately brisk and balmy, cool with pockets of warmth, like a mountain lake. The hazy air looked as liquid as the salt water, and the ocean held as much light as the sky. To Christine, standing at the railing looking out to sea, the entire world was a blue-gold fantasia punctuated with spray, shaded with pastel colors and shadows. She hugged her bare arms, her hair blown by the mild salt wind, her eyes bedazzled by the sunlight on the diamond-bright sea surface that shimmered in glinting, changing points of color all the way to the horizon. The waves were a cohesive, unbroken sheet of heaving water, turned by the sun into pure light and reflection, gone shapeless with brilliance.

While Valerie worked, Christine drifted around the ship, doing as she pleased. She felt a distance between herself and everyone else on board, crew and passengers alike, almost as if she were invisible. She listened in on other people's conversations. No one seemed to mind or notice. She felt encased in a shield that conferred absolute social solitude. It made her relaxed and jumpy at the same time, comfortably anonymous but uneasy at this enforced idleness, no one needing her, nothing to do but observe and think and indulge herself. In the open-air breakfast bar on the patio by the pool, she got a cup of coffee and a freshly baked pastry. She read her book in the shade of an umbrella to the sounds of splashing and laughter and conversations around her. She had finished *A Handful of Dust* and had exchanged it for *A Passage to India*. It was sheer luxury to reread literary classics. After a few hours, when she got hungry again, she ate lunch down in the buffet, a sandwich, a salad, a glass of wine. After lunch, she went up to the solarium at the very top of the ship and fell asleep in a deck chair. Her nap was wine-drugged, comatose, filled with exciting dreams. She awoke as the slanting afternoon sun sent a shadow creeping over her skin, sat up and slid her feet into her sandals and made her way down the stairs to the pool bar.

"Christine," said the bartender, her new friend Alexei, reaching for the shaker, "how has your afternoon been?"

"Another perfect day," she said, yawning, and they both laughed. "How are you?"

"Things could be worse," he answered. He was elfin and pale, with a pouf of yellow hair. She worried about him, and what would befall him when this cruise was over. The recording of Valerie's interview with that chef, Consuelo, now permeated every interaction she had with the ship's workers.

"Do you like your job, Alexei?" she asked as he poured her martini into a glass.

"Making a drink for a beautiful woman on a beautiful ship at sea. Who would complain?"

"I hear they're canceling all your contracts," she said before she could stop herself.

He put her martini in front of her. "Yes," he said. He didn't ask how she knew. "But there are ten other cruise lines, maybe twenty. I'll take a vacation and then I will get another job."

She stared at Alexei's face for any sign of panic or outrage, but his expression remained blankly benign. She took a gulp of booze and watched a group of adults in the pool playing water polo, splashing and dunking one another with vicious fun. She turned to face the ocean and watched the light on the sea surface, tracking the occasional cloud mass that sailed over the horizon to engulf the lowering sun before sailing on again.

She made her way along the deck and down the external staircase, two flights. The promenade was a wide, glassed-in, teak-floored hall that ran most of the starboard-side length of the ship, with double doors all along its inner wall that led to equally grand public rooms, the Starlight Lounge, the casino, the smoking room. The windows were multi-paned, gigantic, providing a glass barrier against the sea spray but no impediment to the view of the open ocean.

Now, the sun was dipping below the horizon through a misty curtain of faraway rain, staining the sky a lurid combination of intense cantaloupe pink and mango yellow that had just begun to fade. People strolled along in twos and threes, enjoying the sunset, doing laps. The light in the promenade was tinged with gauzy gold; it felt as if it came from the past, and Christine was sure she saw a ghost out of the corner of her eye, far down the promenade, and then another one, human-sized impressions of electricity in the air, kinetic disturbances of the light. Superstitiously, she felt that these imprinted echoes of long-gone people were good luck, and their eeriness somehow magically broke the slight unease she'd been feeling on this much-vaunted last cruise, with all its freighted symbolism and sentimental melodrama.

She turned back to the seemingly infinite parallel surfaces of the sky and water and let her eyes blur into a daydream. Soon it would be time to dress for dinner.

*

Scorching heat and sweat on his forehead and fiery steam and the fleshy demands of meat were a special kind of hellish earth-air-fire-water combo Mick dealt with every day and loved perversely, even the burns on his wrists and hands, the tiny abrasions and cuts and splashes of hot fat. He welcomed it all. It quieted his brain, this stainless steel inferno of raw and charred meat and the quick flash of knives.

For the first two days of the cruise he'd thrown himself into impressing Chef, keeping his hard-won respect, showing him he'd made the right decision. Laurens had confirmed the rumor Mick had heard: that he was leaving the industry after this cruise and opening his own restaurant in Amsterdam, of all the beautiful, fun, cool fucking cities.

"I'll be hiring chefs to come and work for me very soon," Laurens said. He was sitting behind his desk with his fingers steepled. His tone was noncommittal, cool. Mick, hovering in the doorway with that night's menu for his approval, couldn't tell whether Laurens meant he might be interested in hiring Mick himself, or whether he was speaking hypothetically about his plans.

"You're currently looking for chefs, then?"

"I'm always looking for talented people who aren't afraid to contribute to my vision," said Laurens. "I want to be impressed. I want to feel inspired and excited. I want people I can trust to execute my ideas. It's a rare quality I'm looking for."

And he fixed Mick with a direct, challenging gaze. Mick was sure now that he wasn't imagining it: Laurens was considering him as a potential hire for his new restaurant.

Until he'd proved himself and given Laurens something to be impressed by, Mick resisted articulating it consciously in the privacy of his own skull; but maybe, his subconscious hummed with percolating urgency, maybe, if Laurens liked Mick's work, he might have a place there for him. The prospect of working on land, in a restaurant, with a regular schedule, living in an apartment, was so tantalizing that at the moment he felt that, if he had to do so in order to leave the cruise industry and work for Laurens van Buyten and live in Amsterdam, he would slice off his left nut, stick it on a skewer along with his left pinkie finger and his right ear, roast it all to dripping perfection, and feed this kebab to a starving dog in a cage. Luckily, Mick had skills and experience, and generally, that was all getting a new job required. But he had to shine. He had to dominate. He could not fuck up.

This was his first chance to distinguish himself after the initial success of the lobster thermidor. Chef hadn't said a word to Mick about it until the following day, when he'd taken him aside and informed him that this dish would be one of three entrées on the menu for the second of the five captain's table dinners for the cruise.

"Make it exactly as you made it for me. Do not alter one molecule. It was perfection. We're also offering filet mignon with a red wine reduction, and for the vegetarians, a truffle risotto. It's a beautiful, classic menu and the lobster is the pièce de résistance. It's also the only entrée we won't be offering on our general menu. It will be exclusive to this dinner."

"*Oui,* Chef." Mick, jubilant, watched him walk away, then turned back to the duck à l'orange he was working on for tomorrow's Home

Cooking Night in the restaurant, to be offered along with boeuf bourguignon and paella, a dish Mick loathed both to eat and to cook because it was complicated and labor-intensive and in the end a waste of good seafood, because the rice just took over, but luckily the guys on the fish station were in charge of it.

"What the fuck did he want?" Consuelo asked when Chef was out of earshot. The question was rhetorical: she had heard every word.

"More lobster thermidor," said Mick. "Get ready to outdo the last one."

"We're meat, not seafood," she said, tipping a tray of roasted bones into a hotel pan in a hollow clattering rush.

"Not for the captain's table dinner. He also wants filet mignon with red wine reduction."

She grunted. "Easiest thing in the world."

"Then it's yours," he said.

She cocked her hip against the counter edge and folded her arms and fixed Mick with a sideways, hooded glare.

"So you're his butt boy," she muttered.

"What?" said Mick.

"Nothing," she said. "Congratulations."

"No," he said, advancing toward her, making her back up to get away from him. He stopped when they hit the end of the station. His face was right in hers. "You do not talk to me like that on my station."

He held his face close to hers, so close their breath commingled in the short air between them. His eyes pinned hers. She stared back at him. Her irises were the color of cinnamon, reddish brown, flecked with the pale gold of ginger. He could smell that scent she wore, very slightly, rising in fumes from her warm neck, emanating from the thrum of her elevated pulse. It had no effect on him here. He felt clear, unconflicted. He was management. So be it. That was how you moved up in the world, you took opportunities when they came, and you acted with authority when you had to.

"Do you understand me?" he said, his voice even. "I want an answer."

"Yes, I understand you," she said clearly. "Chef."

He stayed there for a few beats to make sure she got his point.

They moved apart, got back to work. Rodrigo arrived, took his place on the line, the meat station swung into high gear, and the night went on, like any other night.

chapter ten

Christine opened her stateroom door to find Valerie at the small table by the window, in her bra and underwear, painting her nails.

"It's almost time," Valerie said. "We have to go up in ten minutes."

Somehow, by befriending the Brazilian lounge singer who was the girlfriend or mistress of one of the senior officers, Valerie had finagled invitations for herself and Christine to the captain's table dinner. It was black tie, and apparently the two or three celebrities on board would be there, as well as the captain and senior officers and ship's owner. All day, Christine had been half dreading the stuffy formalities and enforced small talk, but Valerie had insisted that she come along.

Well, at least she had the right clothes for it. Before the cruise, Christine had bought a strapless emerald-green gown with a low bodice and a tight mermaid skirt in a vintage thrift store in Portland, a vaulted former bank where the rouged-and-mascaraed old woman behind the counter always made everyone check their bags because "hoboes" liked to come in, she said, and "steal my wares." Trying on the dress, looking in the store's warped mirror, Christine had felt a rare shock of pure pleasure. It had been so long since she'd dressed up. Along with a gauzy gold shawl and a rhinestone necklace to go with it, her haul had cost almost four hundred dollars. She had charged it to the farm credit card, and she hadn't told Ed.

Now she imagined his face when he got the bill. Well, it was her money too.

After a quick shower, self-conscious as always under Valerie's frank gaze, but now more accustomed or at least inured to it, she slid on the satiny, well-cut gown, zipped up the short side zipper, and bent forward to nestle her heavy breasts into the bodice. She brushed her hair and put it up in a loose knot with a hairpin.

"No makeup?" Valerie asked.

"I look like a cheap whore in makeup."

Valerie studied her. Their eyes met in the mirror. "Put on some lipstick, that outfit is begging for it."

"It'll just smear all over my tooth and come off on the rim of my glass."

Valerie shook her head. "Put on some lipstick."

To appease her, Christine uncapped a tube of dark red lipstick and ran it over her mouth. She grinned at Valerie. "See? Cheap whore."

"You look perfect," said Valerie with a sigh.

The captain's dining room was off by itself down a short private hallway from the fine-dining restaurant. There was a small crowd already in the teak-paneled lounge, which had a hand-painted mural of a jungle scene above an inlaid mother-of-pearl mahogany bar. Behind the bar stood Alexei, the bartender who made Christine's martini every afternoon. The captain held court in the center of the room in his whites and insignia and brass epaulets and buttons, clustered with three similarly attired senior officers, an intimidating scrum of nautical authority. Christine recognized a young female Disney star standing by the bar holding a champagne flute, talking with theatrical self-awareness to another young woman Christine also recognized, a hip-hop singer named Tameesha. So these were the cruise's celebrities.

Valerie strode up to a gorgeous woman who could have been a foreign movie star.

"Beatriz," said Valerie, "hi!"

"Valerie!" Beatriz hugged Valerie, then looked her up and down. "You look *stunning.*" She pronounced it "stoning" in a husky voice and an alarmingly sexy accent. Her skin was flawless; she exuded a heady warm scent so potent, Christine found herself leaning closer to breathe her in.

Valerie preened at the compliment. She was wearing a shapeless but wildly stylish charcoal-gray dress made of a dull, sturdy material with a square neckline, short sleeves, a simple Empire bodice, and a long flared skirt. It had been designed by a Williamsburg wunderkind, and had cost so much money that Valerie wouldn't tell Christine the amount, even after Christine told her how much her own dress had cost.

"Thanks so much for getting us invited," said Valerie. "This is my friend Christine."

"Nice to meet you. And now, we need a drink," said Beatriz as she led them over to the bar.

"I'll have a cosmo," said Valerie to Alexei. Although she was aggressively au courant about almost everything else, she was endearingly un-snobbish about food and drink; Christine had always loved this about her.

"I'll take a glass of white wine, please," said Christine.

Alexei winked at her as if they were old friends. "I have a beautiful, very cold white Burgundy. You will not be disappointed."

Beatriz and Valerie talked in low, fast voices, their heads together, while Christine sipped the chilled, dry, spectacularly good wine and eavesdropped. Nearby, the Disney star was saying something earnestly to the hip-hop singer. Christine remembered her name: Cynthia Perez. In real life, up close, she looked exactly the way she did in photographs, with an enormous round head like a doll's and small, pretty features. "So I was like, 'If you have to discuss this right this freaking minute, let's go somewhere quiet so she doesn't hear you.'"

"She was listening, right?" said Tameesha, who was tall and willowy and big-eyed, a humanoid grasshopper.

Before Christine could figure out what this conversation was about, she was flanked by two elegant black men. They were, she guessed, about her own age, in their mid-thirties. One of them wore a plum-colored velvet jacket and black checked trousers; the other was in a tuxedo. Their faces were lean and sly. They appeared to be identical twins.

"Hello," she said to the starboard brother.

"I'm Tye Blevins," he said. "And this is my brother James."

Christine appreciated their courtliness, which matched their outfits. "Are you having fun on the cruise?"

"Oh, we love the mid-century era," said James. "We're cultural historians. Tye is a history professor at Yale. I write historical mystery thrillers. We thought it would be a lark; there's an old word you don't hear anymore. Our last chance to sail on the *Queen Isabella.* For us, it's all about how convincing the period details are."

"So," said Christine. "Are you convinced by the period details?"

"We were the historical consultants for this cruise," said James. "So we'd better be convinced. Otherwise we're all in trouble."

"Are *you* convinced, that's a better question," said Tye.

"I've been drifting around for days, feeling like I'm in a time warp," said Christine. Her chest was warm from the wine. "Wait. You guys wrote that thing in the brochure, about the history of the ship, right?"

"Guilty as charged," said James.

"I thought it was really interesting," said Christine, snatching a small dark snack from a passing tray that turned out to be caviar and crème fraîche on cocktail rye. She put it into her mouth to free her hand and quickly took another one before the waiter moved away.

Valerie, hoisting her cosmo aloft, tipped her head at Christine. She was standing with the captain of the *Isabella,* a tall, bald, cinematically handsome white man with salt-and-pepper sideburns and broad shoulders. He looked the part so completely, white teeth and twinkling eyes and all, that Christine almost laughed aloud.

"Excuse me," Christine said to the Blevins brothers. "My date beckons."

"Captain Jack Carpenter," Beatriz was saying, "this is my new friend Valerie Chapin."

"Pleasure," said the captain, turning to look at Christine while he shook Valerie's hand. "Hello there."

"This is my friend Christine Thorne," said Valerie.

He looked Christine up and down with blatant appraisal. "Where did you come from?" His accent was midwestern.

"Maine," said Christine. "A farm, actually."

"Oh. What kind of farm?"

"Vegetables and chickens. It's small. My husband and I own about twelve acres."

"I grew up on a huge farm in Wisconsin," he said. "We grew corn. Nothing but. It's nice to have a little variety, don't you think?"

Christine glanced at Valerie, who narrowed her eyes in a smirk.

"This is such a beautiful old ship," said Valerie.

"Yes?" he said, turning away from Christine with a hint of reluctance.

"You must love being in charge of it."

"She's a great relic, for sure," said the captain, smoothly refocusing his attention as if he'd hit a button on the control panel in his forehead and his internal rudders had swiveled, far below. "I hope you're enjoying the cruise."

Just then, a young woman in a Cabaret crew uniform approached the captain and began to speak rapidly into his ear.

"It's a bit of a working vacation," said Valerie to the air where the captain had been standing a second ago. She shot a grin at Christine, pretending to confess to her imaginary listener. "I'm talking to a lot of interesting people for a book I'm writing."

"You're a writer?" asked Tye Blevins, who had been talking until now with seeming total absorption to Cynthia Perez, but apparently with one ear cocked at their conversation. "I'm a writer too. Dry academic stuff. What are you working on?"

"It's still early days," said Valerie, her face instantly alight with the pleasure of discussing her work with anyone who took an interest in it. "I'm going for a portrait of workers at the lowest levels of various industries, the people on the ground who keep things running. Who are they, what are their experiences."

Tye's eyes were lasers. "You're interviewing the staff on board?"

"Oh God no," said Valerie, waving the question away with breezy firmness. "I'm on vacation."

"Right," said Tye. "I get it."

"Hello, everyone," called Kimmi, the cruise director. She raised a glass of champagne to the room at large. "Welcome. We have a special group tonight, and it's good to see you all getting to know one another."

"Hear, hear," said the captain, who had freed himself from his underling and now stood next to Kimmi, holding his own glass up. "Welcome, everyone. Cheers."

Two of the waiters flung open the tall double doors at the end of the lounge, and Christine walked with everyone else into the small dining room. She gazed around. The arched ceiling was painted sky blue with a few fluffy clouds, its rim edged in gold leaf. The walls were paneled in bamboo. Amber-colored teardrop sconces protruded at intervals. The long table down the middle of the room was draped in white linen and set with china, silver, and crystal, tall white tapers burning in candelabras. Next to each plate, Christine saw a hand-lettered place card and an individual glass bud vase containing a single white peony in full bloom. Open French doors led out to a balcony beyond the sideboard and small bar. Warm air blew in and made the flames flicker.

"Dude, we've been slumming it till now," said Valerie, lifting a bud to her nose. "Finally, the VIP treatment."

The Sabra Quartet played in an alcove. Miriam gave her violin a little dip in greeting when Christine caught her eye.

*

The quartet had agreed on the sweetly gorgeous, deceptively simple Borodin for tonight's program, followed by Rochberg's modern offbeat variations on Pachelbel's overplayed Canon, and then the Tchaikovsky as a digestif, because it was exciting and sparkling and energetic and would send everyone away in a good mood. These three quartets were easygoing staples of the Sabra's repertoire, not too taxing for any of them, which was all to the good, because both Isaac and Jakov claimed they'd come down with mild stomach bugs. Miriam suspected it was just a touch of seasickness, pure and simple, but they both adamantly denied it, as they always did, on every cruise.

During the Borodin's first movement, the dinner guests drifted into the dining room with the captain and senior officers. As Christine walked in, Miriam ogled her admiringly, noting how well she carried herself. The green dress suited her figure, and she had the height and the curves to carry it off and the broad shoulders to offset the strapless bodice. And the girl next to her, the friend who had brought her on the cruise, what was her name? Nicole? Melanie? Valerie. She looked exactly the way Miriam had expected her to look, based on Christine's brief description of her: slinky, audacious, twitching with self-regard. Miriam watched her position herself vis-à-vis Christine and flick a glance at her friend, a quick naked dart of some pure emotion that was almost certainly envy.

Miriam could empathize. She herself had been sexy as a young woman, a "dish" as they called it back then, but she'd never been a beauty; she'd always known it and had focused on cultivating both style and moxie, and not worrying too much about her looks themselves. And as she got old, she accepted the double-edged necessity and luxury of fading away into the background to observe invisibly, as she was doing now. Had she been beautiful, she would have mourned the loss. Instead, she had achieved over her lifetime a cheerful, confident ease in herself that felt, in old age, like female triumph.

As the first movement ended, Miriam watched Larry Weiss come into the dining room, tall and imposing in a tuxedo, with Rivka tottering on his arm in very high heels and a fitted cream-colored sparkly dress, the usual gauzy scarf fluttering over her bony shoulders. The Weisses as a matter of course glanced over at the quartet with impersonal, proprietary affection, but did not, apparently, notice Miriam watching them. Larry went over to the bar while Rivka and Valerie introduced themselves and stood chatting. To Miriam, watching from afar, they seemed to be two of a kind: ambitious, shrewd, stylish women. Rivka, like Valerie, had a dramatic, near-skeletal chicness that offset her own odd looks. But unlike Miriam, she had refused to accept invisibility in her old age, and she was rich enough to have the luxury of any and every mitigating means available. Her armor included plastic surgery, a subtly youthful coif, flowing scarves, eye-catching jewelry. Like Valerie, she was all tautness and attitude. Both of them caught and held attention like bare fishhooks hung with glittering lures.

Sasha lifted his violin and glanced to his left. As she had done for fifty years, Miriam turned to the right and caught his eye, the signal. As the corner of his mouth lifted slightly, she almost melted with love, but, always professional, she only nodded back at him slightly, as did Jakov and Isaac to her left. Instantly, the quartet was a unit, coalesced. Sasha brought his violin down to bring them all in, and the scherzo began.

*

Christine found herself seated between Tye the Yale historian and a dashing chief officer named Tom. The captain sat at the head of the table flanked by Rivka Weiss and Cynthia Perez, with Kimmi at the foot between Larry Weiss and Philip the hotel director, a slender man who had a voice so deep it sounded like a foghorn. Christine had been sure at first that he was just putting it on to be funny, but he'd kept it up all night.

All four of the ship's top-ranking officers were American, white, male, ostensibly Christian, and ostensibly straight, although of course you never knew. And all of tonight's guests were a mixture of black, Hispanic, female, Jewish, and possibly gay. Christine noticed this with the same half-conscious bemusement with which she speculated about the waiters. Were they Filipino, Mexican, Malaysian, or

Dominican? They were all dark-haired and -skinned, but according to Valerie, Cabaret hiring practice dictated that there couldn't be too many people from the same country, or who spoke the same language, to prevent them from organizing against their working conditions. So Christine deduced that Cabaret deliberately hired a variety of similar-looking waiters who spoke different languages, which she found disturbing on several levels.

The waiters, wherever they were from, moved efficiently around the table with hand-lettered menus, pouring wine. "Oh, lobster thermidor," said Tye Blevins on Christine's right. "They served it once in New Haven. An even blacker black tie event. It's cool. It comes right in the lobster shell."

The muted, entangled, melodic sounds from the stringed instruments, the wafting heat from the candles, and all the wine made Christine feel overheated. She slipped off her shawl, intending to drape it over the back of her chair, but a waiter was there at her elbow to take it. "Let me know when you'd like to have it again, miss," he said very quietly.

As the salads were served, iceberg wedge with Roquefort dressing, Christine glanced at the head of the table and met the captain's eyes. She realized with a flattered rush that his gaze felt frankly lustful. She leaned forward with feigned innocent absorption in what James was saying across the table from her, to show off her cleavage. Inwardly, she was laughing at herself for being so blatant, but she was totally unable to resist this temptation. The captain's blue eyes looked hot and glinting when she darted a glance back to him to see whether he was still watching. All through the dinner, as she ate the luscious lobster dish and drank her wine and made conversation with everyone around her, there was a thin, buzzing wire stretched tightly between her and Captain Jack, so tightly that if one of them leaned back, the other felt the pull. Christine allowed herself to enjoy this even as her wedding ring shone on her left hand. She was far from her husband, in the middle of the ocean, and this was harmless, for God's sake.

At the foot of the table, Larry Weiss had assumed control of the conversation. His voice was penetrating, sharp as a radio. Christine had never met a billionaire before. She wondered if they all, like Larry, existed in this weird ultra-concentrated, individually wrapped atmosphere. It was nothing he said or did. He was understated and subtle. But his abstract, intangible assets somehow magnetized him, transferred themselves to his body itself, so he was able to be rich and powerful without doing anything. He seemed preternaturally relaxed. He laughed, a full, genuine laugh, ringing and merry and warm, and for some reason, against Christine's own will, she laughed along with him although she hadn't heard the joke. It was impossible not to.

Between the entrées and dessert, Kimmi stood and dinged her wineglass. The table went quiet. "Ladies and gentlemen, allow me to present to you the chef whose cuisine you've been enjoying on this cruise—coming to us from Brussels, Belgium, Chef Laurens van Buyten!"

A pale, slight, bespectacled man swathed in white materialized behind her from out of the candlelight.

"Thank you," said the chef, formally, in a clipped, accented voice. "It is nice to see you all. I am very honored and delighted to be the executive chef on the famous *Queen Isabella* for her last voyage." He paused with professional calm for the patter of applause, then went on. "I have brought Chef Miklos Szabo to talk a little bit about one of the dishes we've made for you tonight."

And there was that guy Christine had seen in Long Beach, in the hotel bar. He was swathed in white like his boss, but he was as different-looking from him as one European white man could be from another of roughly the same age. Laurens looked like someone who'd been bullied and teased in school and was touchy and sensitive because of it. Mick, by contrast, was broad-chested and pugnacious-looking. He looked like he could have been doing the bullying.

"Lobster thermidor," Mick began without any pleasantries or preamble, and with an accent so slight he could almost have been American, "was invented in 1894 in a restaurant called Marie's in the theater district of Paris. Tonight, I used the recipe by the late Julia Child from her book *Mastering the Art of French Cooking,* in honor of the era when the *Queen Isabella* was built."

"Thank you very much, Chef Mick," said Laurens van Buyten during the ensuing applause.

"I'd like to add," said Chef Mick, who appeared to Christine to be trying to impress his boss, "a small story of when I was a young student, in Budapest."

Laurens's face remained impassive, but Christine thought she detected a very slight but clearly displeased flare of one nostril.

"To pay for my university, I learned to cook from the chef at the Eszterházy Restaurant, which was part of the Hungarian Folkloric Theater. Chef Viktor taught me to serve lobster thermidor over buttered egg noodles, a Hungarian touch. Tonight, I have done the same in his honor. I hope you have all enjoyed it."

Laurens clapped Mick on the shoulder with one hand. "Thank you, Chef," he said. "Please save your private memoirs for old age."

Mick grimaced at the low murmur of laughter from the table and made a hasty, apologetic gesture that Laurens ignored. Then he was gone, banished to the galley, Christine surmised, in disgrace for stealing his boss's show and overstepping.

"And for dessert," Laurens said, "we have a classic that was a great hit in the 1950s, back when the *Isabella* was first built . . . Baked Alaska, or *la surprise du Vésuve* à la Julia Child."

The lights were dimmed. To even more applause, the battery of waiters streamed in, each one carrying a tray on which a meringue had been set aflame. The scent of burning rum filled the air.

By the time the diners had looked up from their plates with nearuniversal expressions of childish happiness, the chef had gone.

"And finally," said Kimmi, "I would like to present Tameesha, who hails from our very own home port of Los Angeles, California."

Tameesha stood with her hands by her sides, her head thrown slightly back and her eyes closed.

Even Christine was familiar with her two or three enormous hits; they were as impossible to forget as advertising jingles, repetitive tuneless ditties, half spoken, half intoned with Auto-Tune through electronic effects. She had always assumed that Tameesha couldn't sing, was just all attitude and provocation.

But instead she started crooning "You Send Me," by Sam Cooke, in a tender, full-throated, easygoing voice, as familiarly as if she'd been singing it for years. Her face was filled with a kind of pleasure Christine had been missing for a long time in her own life: the joy of allowing her full self to come out, not holding anything back.

When she had finished, bowing at the vigorous applause, the captain handed around a box of cigars. Christine took one, and then, when several of the men wandered out to the balcony to smoke, she and Valerie got up and joined them. The night air was soft and clean and salty. The moonlight made a gleaming path on the dark waves that ran far below with a low calm murmur. Christine and Captain Jack glanced at each other again, but it was friendly now; the flirtation had run its course. It couldn't go anywhere but to ground. Oh well, she thought, feeling half disappointed, half relieved.

"It's nice to meet you, sir," said Valerie, walking straight up to Larry Weiss. "This is a great ship."

"Thank you," said Larry as he turned to face Valerie, leaning against the railing, rolling his lit cigar in his long fingers. "Yes, my wife has a bit of a sentimental attachment to it. This is our anniversary cruise. We own a perfectly nice private yacht, but I think she prefers the *Isabella*."

"It's definitely peaceful," said Valerie. "It's amazing how far away from everything we are, out here."

"It's an escape," Larry agreed. "No cell phone service, for one thing. I'm usually on three of them at once, all day every day. I feel helpless without my earpiece. But I could get used to it."

"There's always the return trip," Valerie said.

Larry sucked on his cigar. The end sparked, ashes blew off in the breeze. "Oh, we're just going one way. Getting off in Hawaii. Got to get back to work."

Smiling, nodding, Valerie leaned into the warmth of his easy, mellow charm. "What kind of business are you in, if you don't mind my asking? I apologize for not knowing."

Christine listened with frank admiration. Valerie had always been so good at flattering powerful people, getting them to talk without knowing they were revealing anything. As a journalist, Christine had always been leery of intruding, thanks to the ingrained New England etiquette of minding your own business. And her native blunt honesty had likewise made it hard for her not to blurt out her real purpose in questioning them.

As Larry answered in broad and general terms, and Valerie asked another seemingly innocent question, Christine stared down at the water. She was drunk, she realized. Below the ship, the ocean looked like a rolling sheet of thick black oil. Electric light fell in choppy bands on its surface. She felt a cold, gripping sadness in the pit of her chest. It had come seemingly out of nowhere, like her reaction to the octopus in the aquarium. She hoped she could stave off these crises of hollow, trapped dread until she was back in Maine, planting seedlings, hatching chicks, again caught up in the cycle of renewed life.

chapter eleven

Mick hadn't meant to go on and on about his fucking youth in fucking Budapest in front of Laurens and the captain and senior officers and all those passengers. Walking out of the room in disgrace, he wanted to stab himself in the head. He had always prided himself on being adept at reading the people he worked for. He'd honed the skill growing up with his father, who was low-key and affable until he exploded in violence toward whoever or whatever was closest at hand. As a small boy, Mick had learned to identify unerringly the almost imperceptible signs of an impending tantrum. A twitch in his father's lip presaged a punch in the head; if he asked a question, unthinking, and his father hesitated before answering and then spat a terse, monosyllabic answer, Mick knew to get out of his way until the next day, or he'd find himself shaken upside down a little later on. He was lucky, he figured; the hardest lessons, he got early, when he was young enough to absorb and use them as an adult. It had stood him in good stead in the world of professional kitchens, where chefs were as often as not broken in some way, damaged, or abused, or neglected, or bullied, or wrecked by drugs or alcohol, or hardened by being in gangs or prison, or all of the above. The abused became the perpetrator of violence; the bullied went on to crush the weak; the hardened went on to beat others down. It was the way of the species.

Mick was proud of his own self-control in kitchens. He didn't throw tantrums. He didn't hit people or tongue-lash them. He wasn't a bully or a tyrant. But tonight, he'd lost his self-control.

And, as always in his life whenever he got too cocky, too desirous of attention, too hell-bent on proving something, someone slapped him down. He thought of that someone collectively as "the gods," but it always had a human face. When he was little, it was his father. Later it was chefs he worked for, women he wanted to impress. Most recently, it was Suzanne. And tonight it had been Laurens, the person whose respect he most wanted at the moment.

He fled from the room, his head hot and seething with shame. Finished with his work for the night, he went straight down to the crew lounge, still in his whites, since he'd put on spanking clean ones for the presentation upstairs.

The lounge was crowded. He stormed to the bar and ordered a shot of whiskey and a beer.

"Looks like someone had a bad night," the bartender said. His name was Trevor; he was a Haitian room steward, slight and very young, with hooded eyes and skin so dark it glistened. Sometimes he sang along with the music on the PA in a trembling falsetto.

Mick downed the shot, took a long slug of the beer. "A little better now," he said. "I'll take another shot."

He sat alone in the lounge watching the mafias converge, consult, conspire. Tonight it was primarily the Jamaicans, the Greeks, and the South Africans, with two Indian guys over in one corner, keeping to themselves and talking in low voices in what was probably Hindi. The groups had no apparent common currency; they sat apart, in discrete cliques as delineated as schools of fish, eight or so in each group, men and women, mostly young, healthy, good-looking. Normally, in and between these ethnic and nationalistic huddles, there was flirting, there was drunken but mostly good-humored posturing, there was loud talking, blowing off steam. Tonight was weird, like the first night had been. The conversations felt private, without theater, and the atmosphere in the room was tense, thick, loaded.

"What's up tonight?" he asked Trevor. "There's something going on, I can feel it."

"Oh yeah," said Trevor. "I can't keep the drinks going fast enough."

Mick caught the flicker of Trevor's eyes toward the South African group. "So what's going on?"

Trevor gave Mick a measured look, assessing him, reading his loyalties. Trevor knew exactly what was up, Mick thought, but he wasn't telling. Maybe because Mick was senior kitchen staff, so he was high enough up in the chain of command to be considered an outsider, or worse, management.

"Bad day all around, I guess," Trevor said, pouring. He set the squat brimming glass in front of Mick. The amber surface trembled slightly with the vibrations of the ship. He stepped back with his palms flat on the bar top. While Mick downed the new shot, Trevor sang in his high, trembling voice, *"You go to my head, and you linger like a haunting refrain."* His lips made a soft purse on each "you" with a tilt of his head, as if he were blowing kisses at Mick.

"Nice voice," said Mick. "You should sing in the talent show tomorrow."

"It's for passengers," said Trevor. "Let all the old ladies do their thing."

"Crew can perform."

"What are you performing?" Trevor asked. "A striptease?"

It was flattering to be flirted with like this. If only Trevor were a girl, Mick thought.

"I don't want to scare anyone," he said. "I'll wait until the Halloween show for that."

"There's no Halloween show for us," said Trevor quietly, his voice cutting under the hubbub. "You know Cabaret is canceling our contracts, right?"

"I heard. That's terrible."

"They didn't cancel yours?"

"Not that I know of."

"The rest of us, after this cruise, we're done. Fired. Out of a job."

"I'm sure the other cruise lines will take you on," said Mick. "Experienced workers? Isn't everyone always expanding?"

"Easy enough for you to say," said Trevor, not flirting anymore.

"I'm sorry," said Mick.

"Also easy for you to say."

"Listen," Mick said. "I'm only a boss on this cruise. I got bumped up because they were short a man. Normally I'm with all of you, working under the same conditions, same hours, same pay scale. Don't treat me like one of them. I'm not one of them."

Mick felt turbulence at his right elbow as someone jostled him, sliding onto the barstool next to his. He smelled that spicy scent she wore.

"Hey," he said to Consuelo.

"Hey," she said back.

Trevor's fluid expression immediately went jovial again. "What's your poison?" he said like a noir-movie bartender, with a pretty good New York accent.

"Give her whatever she wants," said Mick. "She works with me, she works her ass off. I owe her."

"Yes you do," said Consuelo. Mick could feel heat, perhaps from a recent hot shower, coming off her skin; her face looked scrubbed. Her hair was slicked back, and she'd rolled up her sleeves to reveal, or maybe show off, the tattoos on her sinewy, slender forearms: on one, a small blue Earth with the words EN PELIGRO DE EXTINCIÓN arched over it in Gothic script; on the other, CHINGA TU TIO SAM across a miniature of the old American army-recruitment-poster figure in his top hat; and above it, a simple cartoon Popeye-style ship's anchor with a tiny, intricate monarch butterfly perched on it, whatever that meant. Beata, Mick's little sister, had sported similar symbolic protestations. Seeing these tattoos on Consuelo made him miss her.

Consuelo looked past him at the Greeks over in the corner and then flickered to the South Africans. "Trevor, what's the word?"

"Sad," said Trevor. "Mick refuses to do a striptease for the talent show."

"I would pay him not to do one," she said. She tapped a finger on the bar top while she thought. "Wine, please. Anything red, whatever." She turned to Mick. "How'd it go upstairs? Did they like the food?"

"I fucked up," he said. "Chef was pissed."

She took a gulp of wine like a hungry animal at its trough. "What did you do?"

"Talked too much."

"Chef is a fucker." She drank greedily again.

"He's all right. It was my fault."

"No," said Consuelo, "he's a tyrant."

"He has to be. It's part of his job."

"No, he's worse than most. Control-freak asshole."

"Are you drunk already? You can't say that to me. I'm your boss, technically."

"Fuck that," she said. "Outside of the kitchen, no one is my boss. And after this cruise, I have no job."

She was still sparking with heat, but now it struck him that the source was internal. It was anger. Not at Mick, but at something connected to him, associated with him, his temporary executive power. Flames crackled in her skull and shot their light out through her eyes. And it wasn't only Consuelo he was feeling it from. Even Trevor's flirting with him held a flash of insubordinate aggression under the fawning sweetness.

Mick reached along the bar and picked up someone's abandoned cigarette pack. Trevor raised an eyebrow, but went on washing glasses without a word, so Mick took one of the cigarettes and lit up.

There was a dark thing growing here in the crew lounge, like smoke from a damp, slow-burning dirty fire, expanding into a choking fog. Mick didn't like it. And he didn't share it. The *Isabella* was, so far, a pretty good ship to work on, with an American captain and officers and a small passenger list and good conditions, except for the crew's quarters, which were damp and moldy, but how much time did anyone actually spend in their tiny dark room except to sleep? So they were being let go, so what? They'd find jobs on other ships. Cabaret wasn't the only company, not by a long shot. This entire crew could apply to Disney, Royal Caribbean, Holland, Princess, Carnival, Norwegian, any of the other fleets, and they might even find better pay and conditions.

But of course it was tough to have to find a new job. Mick hoped he still had a job with Cabaret after this cruise. His dream life in Amsterdam with Laurens was probably out of the question now. But even if his contract was terminated along with the others', he would roll with it, start planning for what to do next; he would waste no time being angry, fomenting resentment. He would go out with his head up, professionally. That was how he functioned. As long as he had a job, he did his work as well as he could and banked his paychecks. But of course he was lucky, compared to his coworkers. Many of their countries had been through revolution, coup, oppression, dictatorship, poverty, war, upheaval. Mick had been born during the end of Goulash Communism, Hungary's mild version of Soviet rule. Budapest had been dubbed "the happiest barrack." By the time he was old enough to notice his surroundings and form memories, the ravages of the war had largely been repaired, and Hungary had made a calm and seamless transition to democratic voting. As a teenager, Mick had hung out with his friends at the Moscow Square subway station in his Tisza shoes, feeling hip and retro, all of them freely mocking the uncoolness of the Soviet era while fetishizing its remnants and relics as newly chic. School trips took children to Memento Park to see "Stalin's Boots" while teachers tried to educate them about the former communist regime that had already given way to a free market economy. They'd been lucky. They all knew it. It was good to be Hungarian, to live in their beautiful peaceful city while just to the south, armies fought bitter inter-ethnic wars and everything collapsed and splintered. Now, of course, Hungary's government was sliding into autocracy, but Mick wasn't there to experience it. His homeland was a faraway place, existing only in memory.

"So where are you going to go after the cruise ends?" he asked Consuelo. Trevor had gone off to pour vodka for a knot of dour, pale Russians. "What's your plan? I assume you've got a plan."

"Of course I have a plan."

"Another cruise line?"

She looked sidelong at him and spoke carefully. "I'm done with cruises."

"Are you going back to Mexico?"

"I'm going to get famous."

"Right," he laughed. "That's an excellent plan."

"That's my plan," she said, unsmiling, forceful.

"How are you going to get famous?"

"You'll see me on TV."

Mick stared at her. Then he grinned, not taking the bait. Right, of course, this was how she joked. He stood up, yawning. "My curfew is now. Good night."

"*Noches,*" said Consuelo. "*Hasta mañana,* boss."

"Don't go," Trevor called along the bar. "I almost had you."

Down in his quarters, Mick undressed and took a shower, then fell into his lower bunk, naked except for a pair of clean underwear. The room was cramped, like all crew quarters: two bunks, small bathroom, old carpet, sallow fluorescent lighting, no window. His roommate was a chef on the all-night galley crew, room service and breakfast prep. As management, Mick should have had his own, larger room, but no matter; he and his roommate almost never saw each other. There was nowhere to store anything, so they pulled clean clothes out of their duffel bags, which were crammed against the wall, and shoved dirty laundry into the corner. This was how Mick had lived for years. He was used to it. By the time he got into his hard narrow bed, he was tired enough to sleep standing up in a cold rainstorm. This low down in the ship, below the waterline, there was little movement, but the hum and vibrations of the engine were ever-present. For Mick, it was like a white noise machine, a sleep aid that masked late, drunken, loud voices in the hallway, the throb of music from the room next door, every sound but the ones in his own private dreams. Over the years, he had grown to like sleeping underwater, the wild ocean just a hull's width away, just an inch or two, from his dreaming head.

*

Late that night, after the captain's table dinner, Miriam and Sasha stood outside by the railing, feverishly kissing. He was so tall, her neck bent backward. It made her even dizzier. His bristly cheek chafed her smooth one. His teeth knocked against hers. His body felt young and urgent. Her hands went under his shirt, and she pressed her hot palms on his flanks while his hand snaked into her dress to cup her breast. She swooned. They hadn't had sex yet, but they were like a couple of teenagers all of a sudden. Miriam felt that if she couldn't lie naked in a bed next to Sasha soon, she might explode. She was fifteen again, a young girl in an old woman's body.

They badly wanted to tell the others, because they very badly wanted to switch bedrooms. Miriam was hoping Isaac would agree to move over and bunk with Jakov in the stateroom with two single beds so she and Sasha could share the stateroom with the big bed. But that meant Isaac would have to leave his place by his ex-wife's side so she could sleep with his colleague and friend instead. They were, technically, divorced. But somehow that didn't matter. Miriam didn't know how to tell Isaac. Sasha didn't know how to tell Jakov, who had nursed a long crush on Miriam himself, in spite of the continued existence of his own very devoted wife, Devorah. Miriam couldn't believe Isaac didn't see the sparks shooting off her skin, didn't notice the lusty fire in her eyes, didn't feel the new passion raging in her.

Miriam had known Sasha for her entire adult life, but now she realized she'd hardly known him at all. He seemed deeply mysterious to her, this man she'd worked and traveled with for more than forty years. She knew he was handsome, he was kind, he could be bossy, he was a brilliant violinist, he was occasionally overcome with emotion, especially when he played Schubert, and he had loved his wife and still loved their three children. She knew he'd grown up in Brooklyn in an Orthodox household. She knew he'd rebelled against his father after graduating from the Mannes conservatory and had become a lefty political activist for a while before emigrating to Israel, and shortly afterward had met Sonia, who became his wife. Miriam had always liked her, but she was a tough bitch, with good reason. Her parents and older brothers had all been killed in the Holocaust. She had been hidden as a child by a generous, heroic family in France until the war was over. Then she'd been sent to her Polish aunt, who'd miraculously survived Auschwitz, and who had brought her to Israel as a young girl.

Sasha had always been devoted to this force of a woman, but something had always pulled him to Miriam, she knew, just as she had always been pulled to him. Their spouses were so different from them. And they were the same kind of person, both of them practical and responsible on the outside, but inside they were frustrated romantics.

They whispered all these things, and so many more, into each other's ears and necks and mouths, embracing on the deck for hours. As they ran their hands over each other's bodies, Miriam felt how much strength was still there, how much juice and vigor. They laughed with giddy joy. And then they wept with how much time had been wasted, and was gone forever.

"Finally," said Sasha.

"At last," Miriam echoed him.

"I've loved you all along."

"I've loved you, too."

Oh, they were glorious, those headlong passionate hours.

But how would they tell Isaac? And Jakov, too. If Jakov had been the one whose wife had died, he would have charged right at Miriam like a lusty bull. But his wife was still alive, that lively, opinionated woman who cooked like a dream, hence Jakov's girth. So Jakov couldn't blame Sasha or begrudge him or Miriam their happiness, but he wasn't going to be thrilled to hear the news of their love affair.

And Isaac—he'd never had to share Miriam with another man. The two short-lived affairs she'd had, he'd never known about because she'd protected him from knowing. She'd been discreet for his sake, and also for their children's, although when she'd recently confided in her daughter, Rachel had applauded. Rachie had always gravitated to Sasha, even as a squinty-eyed, impatient, precocious little girl. Sasha had always known how to talk to Rachel. He'd never condescended to her. He'd treated her as if she were his equal, his contemporary. Miriam realized with a whole new rush of happiness that her daughter would be over the moon about her and Sasha, her skeptical sour-patch of a daughter who was never over the moon about anything.

"Let's tell them in the morning," said Sasha. "It's time."

"At rehearsal," said Miriam. "I can't wait another minute."

"Neither can I."

"I'll say it," said Miriam. "I'm the one who has to. You leave it to me."

After they parted in the hallway in front of her door with one last lingering kiss, Miriam got into bed and lay awake the rest of the night while Isaac snored beside her. At dawn, to avoid facing him, she got up and fetched some coffee and paced along the promenade until it was time for their rehearsal.

When she arrived at the chapel, Sasha was alone practicing his part for Rivka's piece. Without the rest of the instruments to give it a context, it sounded even weirder, even uglier, as if he were a teenager screwing around with atonal dissonances, trying to annoy his mother.

"My darling," he said.

Her chest felt like a giant slow bubble was rising in it, just because of the sound of his voice and the sight of his familiar but suddenly thrilling face.

He put his violin down and stood up and embraced her. The feel of his hands firm on her waist, his warm breath against her temple, made her press her face to his.

"You look as beautiful still as you ever have," he said with amazement as they pulled apart, smiling at each other.

"So do you," she said. "As handsome."

They kissed slowly, with their mouths open, breathing hard.

"We'd better stop," she said, chuckling. "They'll be here any minute. They shouldn't walk in on us before we tell them."

Sasha sat in his chair again, picked up his violin, and noodled around while Miriam got hers out and tightened and rosined the bow, tuned the strings, put on her reading glasses.

Isaac arrived first, and then Jakov. Miriam felt her hands shaking slightly at the sight of them. Her heart thudded as she put her violin down and looked at Sasha. He looked steadily back at her, willing her to be the one to say it. It had to be her.

She and Sasha had been speaking in English. But now she said in Hebrew, "Jakov and Isaac. I have to tell you something. Sasha and I have fallen in love."

"What was that?" said Isaac with a confused expression. He'd been staring into his viola case, lost in thought, as he often was in the mornings.

Jakov had heard Miriam just fine. He stared at her, and then at Sasha, and then at Isaac. Then he looked back at Miriam with a fierce expression. "Say it again," he said. "Go on."

"Sasha and I have fallen in love," she repeated. It was much easier the second time. She was so relieved, she felt like laughing, but she restrained herself. It would be so impolite to Isaac, whose befuddled vague expression was shifting, sharpening, comprehending, and then in an instant, trying to compose itself into dignity, acceptance, pride.

"Mazel tov," he said to Sasha, and then in English, "She's nothing but a headache."

All three of them burst into laughter, but Jakov was scowling. "This is unprofessional," he said. "This isn't good. You're acting like a couple of idiots. Please stop it. You're old and you're losing your minds."

Isaac cradled his viola against his stomach and caressed its curves with his thumb. "Jakov," he said, "surely this is my battle to fight, not yours."

Jakov twanged the C-string of his cello. It gave a deep burp.

"Sure," he said. "Fight away. Only you're not fighting. You're divorced, or so you say. Well then, why can't I say something? This quartet, it's my entire livelihood. You think it's funny? Be my guest, laugh."

"Why is this bad for the quartet?" Sasha asked mildly. "What Miriam and I choose to do in our personal lives is our business. We're telling you as a courtesy."

"Actually," said Miriam, "we're telling you because we want to switch staterooms. To be honest." God, it felt good to just say it, after tiptoeing around in secrecy for two days. She went on boldly, "In fact, Sasha wants to switch with Isaac. We want to share a room."

There was a silence. The room's walls seemed to vibrate a little from the shock waves emanating from Isaac and Jakov.

"Sleep together," said Isaac, pale, his laughter gone. He clutched his viola in both hands against his belly and stroked it as if it were an upset, high-strung cat.

"That's right," said Sasha, as if he'd just realized that he had a part in this little drama too. "It's true. Do you mind changing rooms with me, Isaac? We can do it this afternoon."

"Do I mind," said Isaac in a daze, "do I mind."

"Of course he minds," said Jakov, "and I do too. I don't want to bunk with you, Isaac. You snore."

"He does snore," said Miriam. "But Jakov, I'm sure you do too. And anyway, why should I have to put up with it? I put up with it for years already."

"I can't hear myself," said Jakov. "But him, I'll hear."

"Stop it," said Isaac. "This isn't funny. What do you mean, sleep together? You two? In the same bed? Sasha. Tell me. Is that what you're saying?"

"Yes," said Sasha, "and what are you, her father? Am I some boy come courting her? I'm asking you to switch rooms with me, that's all. You don't need to know anything else. It doesn't concern you."

Miriam looked around the airless, ugly room with its mustard-yellow rug and hideous paneling and ridiculous little pulpit. As a place of worship, it was sadly lacking. As a place of high interpersonal drama, it was comic. Isaac's thin hair floated in wisps above his scalp and caught the light. Jakov's shirt had some egg yolk on it from breakfast, and his face was crumpled from his pillow. Even Sasha looked old and funny in this room, and Miriam was certain that she did too. A giggle rose in her throat. She couldn't hold it down.

Isaac began to weep. He looked down at his viola, careful not to let tears splash onto the glossy wood. His thin chest heaved. His soft stomach convulsed. "Miriam," he said. His voice was plaintive and stricken. "You would do this to me now?"

Miriam crossed the room and put her hand on his back and rubbed gently between his shoulder blades as she'd done for their children when they were sick or upset. "Shhhh," she said as he leaned into her. "This doesn't mean I don't still love you, *neshama*. You're my children's father. You're my life's mate. Don't cry. I deserve to be happy. I deserve to be loved by a man. You and I, that part of us is over, remember? But you're family to me still, and you always will be."

Isaac took a breath and shook his head. "I know that, Miriam. I know. I just needed a minute. Now we should rehearse and no more talk about this." He wiped his eyes with the back of one hand. "And yes, Sasha, I will exchange rooms with you, and Jakov, we will snore together in beautiful harmony."

Miriam felt she had never loved Isaac as much as she loved him right then. His back had been quivering. She could feel what a blow this was to him and how much it cost him to summon his generosity. But he had done it. This was a demonstration of love he had never shown her when they were married.

Miriam looked over at Jakov. He was gazing at her with tender, stricken sorrow. But he had no say in the matter, and everyone knew it, Jakov most of all.

They all sat in their seats and ran through the *Six-Day War* Quartet, and for the first time, they played it without a single mistake.

*

Valerie was sitting up in bed, staring into her laptop screen, tapping away with one earbud in her ear. A pot of coffee sat on a tray on the nightstand.

"Did you read the history of the ship in the brochure?" Christine asked as she brushed her hair.

"No, why?"

"It's an interesting story," said Christine. "You might want to talk about it in your story about the cruise."

"This ship is only interesting because it's old."

"She's beautiful, too. And a lot of famous people have sailed on her."

"You're such an elitist," said Valerie breezily, still typing.

"Why is that so bad?" said Christine. "So I like some things more than others because they're better, so what?"

Valerie didn't answer, so Christine went into the bathroom and closed the door. She looked into the mirror as she brushed her teeth and made a snarling face. Her mouth was misshapen by the brush, rabid-looking with the foaming toothpaste. She had been reveling in dressing for dinner every night in beautiful clothes, and drinking martinis and dancing and being flirted with by Brooklyn hipster dudes and cruise-ship captains. It had all reminded her that she was still youngish and even attractive. But this morning she had woken up with a sense of caution, hearing her mother's voice telling her to know her place, not stick her neck out, act right so people wouldn't talk. She vowed to reclaim her low-profile New England humility. She was much more comfortable that way.

"Maybe you should include a chapter about farmers in Maine," she said to Valerie as she took her bathing suit off the balcony railing where it had been drying and stuffed it into her bag. "We're struggling low-level workers, by any standards. It's hard to raise crops and livestock in rocky, thin, acidic soil and Zone Four winters and short growing seasons. It's kind of insane that we do it at all, much less succeed at it."

Valerie went on typing as if Christine hadn't spoken. Her

silence wasn't hostile, Christine thought, but more like the oblivious absorption of a professional to whom a layperson was speaking words that had nothing to do with her, and were therefore outside of the realm of her attention.

"And speaking of struggling," Christine went on, opening the door, "it's time for my busy day by the pool. You coming?"

"I'll meet you up there in a bit," Valerie said without looking up. "I just have to finish this. God, I wish there were fucking Internet in this fucking ocean. I'm kind of dying without it. Or cell service at least. I can't even text anyone."

"Who would you text if there was?"

"No one," Valerie said. "You."

They both laughed as Christine headed out the door.

chapter twelve

Mick arrived eighteen minutes early for his shift. Laurens hadn't shown up yet, but that was normal. Still, Mick's mouth was dry and his heart was beating too quickly. He wanted to dive into work immediately, immerse and submerge himself in physical labor, the harder, the better. It was the best way, really the only way, to block out mental stress. And he was nervous and on edge. It wasn't just Laurens's curt dismissal of him after his fuckup, dashing his hopes for a job in Amsterdam, nor was it whatever he'd been sensing in the crew lounge last night, the anger and tension of the layoffs. Mick was angry at himself. What the hell was he doing on this cruise, anyway? Why had he agreed like a lapdog to forgo his vacation, bribed by a promotion that meant nothing in the end? And no extra pay. And no Suzanne, no Paris.

Consuelo was already on the line, prepping braised pork chops. She flicked a look over at Mick, but didn't say anything. The rest of the crew was there too, hard at work. No one seemed startled to see Mick arrive early. They were all involved with their various meat projects, searing and breaking down and braising. A glance at the meat station was like a snapshot of controlled carnage: flesh, bone, blood, gristle, skin. It was like a surgery room, all gleaming stainless steel and sharp, specialized instruments, and the chefs were swathed in white like doctors, working silently as if they were saving and healing live bodies rather than cutting up dead ones.

Mick hauled many pounds of thawed vacuum-sealed racks of lamb out of the cold storage room. At his station, he slid the first untrimmed rack from its plastic package. With his butcher's knife, he removed the shoulder blade by paring it away. He made an incision at the rib-tip end where the shoulder blade had been removed, then peeled away the fat, slicing with the knife to free it gradually while using his other hand to pull it off in an unbroken swath. He set the pure white fat aside for sausages. Then he fine-trimmed the remaining fat and trimmed the tendon, scored the membrane down the center of each bone, and pulled fat away to expose the bones so they stuck out all in a row, naked and elegant. His attention had to be unbroken, his hand precise; if he slipped even a little, he could cut himself or wreck the expensive meat. This was New Zealand lamb, leaner and smaller than American and full of grassy, gamy flavor. His knife was freshly sharpened, its blade so keen it melted through the fat. He found himself humming under his breath.

He flipped the rack over and, with his boning knife, trimmed the flap of fat and membrane from the exposed two inches of bone. He used the butt-end of his knife to get the bones perfectly clean, as clean as ivory. He stacked the first beautifully frenched rib rack in a hotel pan and moved to the next and did the same thing all over again, and then again. Time melted by like the fat under his knife. Then he was aware of Consuelo at his side, restless. He glanced over at her.

"Hey," he said. "Good morning."

"Chef," she said. "Can I talk to you a minute?"

"Let me finish these up."

"You're finished, it looks like."

It was true; he was cleaning the bones of the last rack.

He set his knife down, going over the marinade recipe in his mind. "Go ahead."

"This is a general question," she said. She looked as bleary as Mick felt. Her face was puffy, and her eyes were bloodshot. "Why did you sign on with Cabaret?"

"Why not?" said Mick. "I wanted to get out of Budapest. I was going nowhere."

"Okay. And where do you see yourself going after this? You

asked me that last night. Now I'm asking you. Are you staying with Cabaret? They didn't cancel your contract, right?"

"I don't know," he said slowly, squinting. "Maybe, maybe not." He peeled off the gore-smeared latex gloves. "Now I'm ready to get back onto land again. Chef Laurens is opening a place in Amsterdam. But that's out now, right. So I don't know. No idea."

Consuelo's face was hard, blank, and her eyes stared into Mick's. He couldn't tell what she thought of this plan, or why it was so important for her to grill him about his future. And he didn't have time to ask, because Laurens was there, silent and small and pale, inspecting everything and taking in the morning's progress without seeming to look directly at anyone, but not missing a single detail. Mick was sure he'd notice if anyone had missed a spot shaving or was hung over, and would draw his own conclusions and keep his own counsel about them until it was appropriate for his own purposes to air them.

"What's going in your marinade for the rack of lamb?" he asked Mick, standing at his elbow, checking the frenched racks. His tone was bland and everyday. He broadcast no punitive static. The air between them was clean.

Mick's knees softened very slightly with relief. "Mustard, garlic, soy sauce, rosemary, olive oil," he said.

"Good," said Laurens.

Mick inhaled a full lungful of air for the first time, he felt, since the captain's table dinner. His future was not wrecked. He'd overreacted: his ancient lizard brain had sent him into a fight-or-flight response to grave danger when there was, in reality, none. This was the downside of growing up with his father. Mick could pick up signals, but he couldn't always interpret them correctly, since his internal decoder had been calibrated for his father alone. And he no longer existed for Mick, except in the past.

Consuelo had slipped back to her station. Laurens moved over to watch her stirring bacon, carrots, and onions in butter. Without looking over directly, Mick could sense her bristle at Laurens's approach and then relax again as he moved on to Miguel. Between

Mick and Consuelo, the air roughened slightly with turbulence caused by Laurens's presence, then all at once it calmed down and everything was okay. Mick had no idea why. He went on putting together his marinade, but now he felt like himself again.

*

Miriam awoke from the deepest sleep she'd had in what felt like years to find herself in her and Isaac's bed. It was late afternoon already. In the first instant of full consciousness, she discovered that she was naked. Worse, she seemed to be entwined around Isaac, her body curled around him, her front pressed to his back and her legs snaked around his, and he, horror upon horrors, was also naked. Then she awoke fully and nuzzled her face into the back of Sasha's neck.

After their rehearsal in the chapel, Isaac had moved all his things across the hall and down four doors, and Sasha had done the reverse. The two old men were as gracious about it as possible. They tried very hard to banish awkwardness with as many jokes as they could tell, Isaac expanding on the theme he'd struck earlier about how miserable Sasha would be with Miriam and how glad he, Isaac, was to finally see her handed off to another man, and Sasha riffing with mild self-deprecation on his own lack of worthiness to take on such a formidable woman. Miriam laughed inwardly to overhear these two men discuss her, for the sake of their ancient friendship and Isaac's pride, as if she were a valuable prize (Sasha), a cross to bear (Isaac), and a force to be reckoned with (both). Jakov had absented himself, wisely, and was sitting with Larry and Rivka in the buffet. The lunch special was beef Wellington, and Jakov had professed great excitement about this.

"Brioche crust, it said on the menu!" he said as he headed off to the dining room.

As for Miriam, she and Sasha fell into bed together as soon as the move was made. It was exciting, but also a bit anticlimactic. They did not have sex; they were both too overwhelmed with emotions and the strangeness of this and the newness of each other's bodies and the beauty of falling in love so late with someone so well and deeply known, yet also unknown. It was an afternoon of sighs and gazes, caresses and embraces, many words, many silences, and a few brief spells of guilt over Sonia and Isaac. But those didn't last long. For God's sake, who had time to bemoan former spouses?

"*Boker tov, yalda yafa,*" Sasha muttered now.

"It's the middle of the afternoon, and it's Miriam," she whispered. "Not your wife."

He chuckled. "Did you think I was Isaac, just now?"

"For one terrible instant. So I didn't want to give you that same shock, although for you, I know it wouldn't have been terrible."

She could feel his penis. His "cock"? It was hard, anyway, and she was glad of that. Starting tonight, they'd get to sleep together for the rest of the cruise, maybe the rest of their lives. When they got back to Tel Aviv, who knew what would happen. She had her place in the high-rise with Isaac several floors above her, and Sasha had his and Sonia's house in Jaffa, but it would make more sense financially, as the quartet retired, for them to join forces. Also, she wanted to live with Sasha. Miriam had never been averse to getting ahead of herself, especially in financial and practical matters.

"Did you fall back to sleep?" Sasha asked. "Wake up, I miss you."

She laughed. She loved him so much. "Where do you want to live after the cruise, when we get back home?"

He didn't hesitate. "With you. Can you come to my place? We can't live near Isaac. We should get married, anything you like."

Her chest warm with joy, she said, "As a proposal, it's maybe a little casual. But as a proposition, I accept."

A little while later, they got out of bed and dressed without showering, looking at each other's bodies with childlike curiosity and unabashed love.

"I remember in the 1970s, at the Dead Sea," said Sasha. "Remember? You wore that black bathing suit. So sexy! Like Sophia Loren. For Sonia's sake I had to look away. You look exactly the same to me now. I can't believe I finally get to see you like this. I finally get to sleep with you."

She waved away the compliment, laughing.

"Tonight," he said seriously. "Tonight, I promise to make love to you. Don't worry, I still can. With you, I can do anything."

Dressed, their hair combed, but without any other attention to their appearance, they ventured into the hallway hand in hand. They didn't say so, but they both hoped they could spare Isaac the sight of them together, so soon.

Isaac was nowhere to be seen. But there was Rivka Weiss, of all people, coming toward them along the hallway, wearing a tailored white silk pantsuit, her hair impeccably mussed under a broad white hat.

Miriam saw her first, then Sasha. Then Rivka saw the two of them, coming out of the same stateroom hand in hand, looking rumpled in the manner of people who have been naked together carnally and recently. People who, in Rivka's eyes, had absolutely no business doing so.

"Oh!" she cried, her sculpted eyebrows raised as high into her taut forehead as her recent Botox treatments would allow, which wasn't very. "Where is Isaac? I was—I was just looking for him. To see if he wanted to take a walk along the promenade before the talent show."

"Good evening, Rivka," said Miriam calmly. "I have no idea where Isaac is, I'm sorry."

"All right," said Rivka, still looking askance at Miriam.

"By the way, we got divorced more than twenty years ago," Miriam added in her own defense, but Rivka didn't hear her. She had dashed off on her spidery legs, teetering on her wedge sandals, fleeing from the sight of these wicked adulterers, from such insurrection on the part of her very own musicians.

*

When Christine and Valerie arrived just after dinner, the air-conditioned Starlight Lounge was already half full of mostly gray heads and hands fanning programs, chattering voices rising from the small tables and semicircular booths. The lounge was a large interior room with no windows; it was on the promenade deck, but it felt underground, louche. The small raised stage had a sparkly linoleum floor that resembled ersatz starlight, its blue faux-velvet curtains parted, footlights beaming upward. Waiters circulated with trays held high, serving fancy, colorful cocktails in giant glasses garnished with tiny paper parasols and wedges of exotic fruit. Paddle fans turned overhead.

The talent show wouldn't start for a while, but there were plenty of people to watch in the meantime. The other passengers had proved to be an odd and entertaining group, Christine thought: mostly older American couples, the usual suspects on any cruise, but there was a wide variety even in this normally homogeneous assemblage: a gaggle of California hippies; several well-preserved glamour babes and their younger male companions; a few dignified black couples who looked out of place only because they were so well dressed and conservatively elegant compared to everyone else; and quite a number of gay pairs, both male and female. There were also, of course, a number of fat, pinkish human adults in mass-produced clothing, but fewer of these than Christine had expected, because she had expected an entire boatful.

"This should be fun," said Valerie. "I predict five drunk strip-teases, four lip-synching drag queens, three bad comedians, two okay musicians, and a semiprofessional emcee."

"Are these seats taken?" said a voice.

Christine looked up. "Miriam! Have a seat."

She hadn't seen Miriam since the captain's table dinner, and hadn't been able to speak to her. But she seemed like a different person now. An unmistakable glowing aura radiated from her.

"This is Sasha," Miriam said, gesturing at the handsome gentleman at her side. He had black eyes and a well-shaped nose, broad shoulders and a full head of salt-and-pepper hair. He wore a cotton button-down shirt and blue jeans. He was sexy, no matter how old he was. "Sasha, this is my new friend, Christine."

"I'm happy to meet you," said Sasha as they seated themselves in the two other chairs at the table.

Christine widened her eyes at Miriam, and Miriam twinkled her eyes back at her. "And you must be the friend Christine has told me so much about," she said, turning to Valerie. "Forgive me, I've forgotten your name."

"Valerie," said Valerie, who couldn't hide the fact that she had no idea who these old people were and didn't care.

"And what are you young ladies doing on this boat full of old people?" asked Sasha. He had a low, gravelly voice tinged with an accent.

"Oh, I'm trying to get a little work done," said Valerie. "I'm a writer."

"I'm on vacation," said Christine.

"What do you do?" Sasha asked.

"I'm a farmer," said Christine. She was getting a little tired of saying this every time she met someone. She wished she had something more interesting to offer about herself.

"Great combination," said Sasha. "A writer and a farmer."

"Oh. We're not together," said Valerie. "Though if I had to marry a girl, it would totally be Christine."

"I used to be a writer," Christine said, feeling defensive. "In New York."

"So how long have *you* two been married?" Valerie asked in a skeptical voice. Miriam and Sasha exchanged an amused look.

"I was married for forty-three years, and my wife passed away last January," said Sasha. "Miriam and I have just fallen in love after more than half a century of friendship and working together."

"Oh," said Valerie. She looked consternated by this for some reason.

"That's amazing," said Christine. "I'm so happy for you, Miriam. Both of you."

Their drinks arrived, tropical and festooned, tart with just the right amount of sweet. Kimmi flew onto the stage out of the velvety darkness and grabbed a microphone. "Thanks for coming, everybody! So I'd like to introduce tonight's first act, a singer from Brazil. Give it up for Beatriz Oliveira! Accompanied by our very own house band, the Kool-Tones!"

The jazz quintet off to the side raised gleaming horns in a salute, the drummer simmered his sticks on the floor tom, and Valerie's friend Beatriz took the stage in a skintight fuchsia dress.

"*I'm feeling mighty lonesome,*" she sang in a smoky whisper. "*Haven't slept a wink . . .*" Her interpretation of "Black Coffee" began with all the appropriate pathos, but as it went along, she sounded increasingly defiant, like a woman who was not resigned yet to her fate. Her face opened like a flower in water, blooming, her eyes alight with a glinting, self-possessed sexual straightforwardness that belonged to the present-day era, her own time. "*My nerves have gone to pieces, my hair is turning gray . . .*" As she sang, Christine watched Miriam and Sasha out of the corner of her eye. They were holding hands on top of the table, leaning into each other with abstracted yet fully awake expressions. He drew her in close, Miriam looked giddy with joy, and Christine felt a pang of vicarious envy. She missed being in love. Marriage wasn't about heady, swooning romance and it never had been, she knew that full well and accepted it, but the small whiffs of vicarious helium she was breathing in were enough to set up a powerful and irrational yearning for it, just once more, in some small way, the way a reformed alcoholic seated next to a happy drunk at a dinner party might crave some booze.

"They're so lucky," Christine whispered to Valerie, nodding toward Miriam and Sasha.

"I bet you miss Ed right now," Valerie shot back.

"No," Christine said bluntly. "Not at all."

Valerie leaned against her, and they both laughed in the old way, with a shared sense of generalized scorn for men, glad to be unencumbered, independent, free.

chapter thirteen

Laurens was on Consuelo all night. He abruptly left the pass, where he'd been overseeing plating and garnishes, to stand directly behind her, as close as he could get without touching her; so close, Mick knew, that she could feel his exhalations from his nose on the back of her neck. Every now and then he'd correct her flatly, jabbing his finger to point at the offending action. "You waited too long to turn that," he said. "Three seconds too much and a chop is ruined." A minute later: "Don't heat the fucking sauce till it boils, you break it that way." Mick could feel Consuelo tightening, bracing herself, maintaining control and calm through strict, years-long internal discipline. Laurens was cool and icy; she was cooler, icier. Mick would have reacted exactly the same way. She was a pro, and he was proud of her. There was no reason for Laurens's treatment of her tonight except that Laurens probably sensed that she wasn't subordinate enough. She took too much pride in her work and invested too much ego in it for his liking, for the good of the kitchen's overall morale, and so she required further taking down. He was doing his job, and she was doing hers.

"Yes, Chef," she said for the tenth time, stepping aside so Laurens could show her the way he wanted the meat plated. Almost nine minutes had gone by since he'd stepped back to correct her, and she hadn't cracked, not even a little. Her eyes were on her work, not flickering, not slitting. Her hands were steady. Laurens was testing her, poking at her, determining her weaknesses, and she was rising to it. But Mick kept close tabs on her anyway. He'd vouched for her and brought her with him to the main galley. So if she exploded at Laurens, or flashed any temper, Mick would be called upon to step in somehow and smooth things over. All his antennae were tuned in, his muscles tensed for intervention.

Laurens lifted the sauté pan of sweetbreads Consuelo was cooking in butter and held it under his nose, breathing in their steam, then shook it gently, assessing their turgor. "Did you blanch these?"

"Yes, Chef," said Consuelo.

"When you sauté sweetbreads, blanching robs them of flavor."

"Yes, Chef," she said.

Mick felt a surge of pride in her. She was tough. Laurens was right, also. She shouldn't have blanched them.

"It makes them easier to slice but it's lazy. They're better unblanched." Laurens put the pan back down.

"Yes, Chef," said Consuelo. Her voice sounded steady and earnest.

Just as Mick relaxed his grip and started to submerge himself in his own rhythm of work, Consuelo turned to Laurens, casually, as if she were about to add something to her submissive agreement.

"I have a question, Chef," she said. Her voice was low and calm. "What if I told you that you were wrong and the sweetbreads are better this way? What would you do to me? Would you send me to my room?"

Laurens stared at her as if she'd lost her mind. He didn't move. He had no expression at all.

Mick inhaled sharply and choked on some spit and began coughing hard. He bent over, low down, so he didn't spray the food.

"I disagree with you, Chef," said Consuelo. "The way I make them, they come out both tender and delicious-tasting. Look. Try some."

While she spoke, she sliced off a piece of sweetbread with her eight-inch chef's knife's razor-sharp blade, impaled it on the tip of the knife, and dipped it into the sauce waiting to coat each serving, a rich-looking tomato sauce. She held it out to Laurens, stuck on the point of the knife, right in front of his face. It dripped red.

He looked at her. His face was white, and his voice held no emotion at all. "We will discuss this when dinner service is over," he said. "Now, back to work, everyone."

Consuelo winked at Mick and carefully ate the bite off the tip of her knife. "It's fucking perfect," she told him with a cold smile.

"Back to work, you heard him," said Mick, not smiling back. No point in saying anything. The damage was done.

His ears thudded with his heartbeat. In the back of his throat, he felt the itch of another cough, but he suppressed it.

It had all happened in one minute, at the most, but he felt as if the waves of energy that powered the kitchen had been profoundly disturbed. For the rest of his shift, the rhythms were off. Laurens was tightly wound, and the tension in the room caused everyone's movements to slow, bodies to fight for balance. All the other chefs seemed to be trying to stay on top of things and be perfect to make up for Consuelo's unthinkable, terrible insurrection.

The rest of the dinner shift was as weirdly tense a night as Mick could remember in all his years working in a kitchen. People looked at one another furtively, grimly. No one looked at Consuelo. Mistakes turned into minor catastrophes and were surfed over, corrected, dealt with. Mick and Kenji, on opposite sides of the galley, exchanged quick eye contact a couple of times, telegraphing irritated bewilderment to each other with a flick of their eyes. Kenji's fish station hit the weeds several times. A tray of charred cod had to be thrown out when black smoke churned from the salamander. A pot of béarnaise sauce was scalded beyond repair. On the meat station, Mick had to micromanage Rodrigo and Tony in addition to keeping his own stuff going. Consuelo was the only one in the kitchen who had been letter-perfect all night. Her sweetbreads, the waiters reported, were generating raves.

"Compliments to whoever made these," one of the waiters had said, loudly, so that everyone could hear. "From the old lady who doesn't like anything. The one who sent back her filet mignon the other night."

Consuelo didn't respond. She barely acknowledged the compliment or looked at the waiter. And she didn't look at Mick once all night. Of course she knew he was baffled and upset with her, that he was watching every move she made. Her insolence surrounded her; he could feel it bubbling, hot, rash, triumphant. The piece of sweetbread dripping with sauce at the end of her sharp knife, extended toward Laurens's face, was seared on his memory.

Goddamn her, he thought, even though what she'd done wasn't so bad in itself. She'd disagreed with Laurens's assessment of her technique and offered him a sample of her work as proof that it was up to snuff. But in reality it was far worse: she had challenged and even threatened the executive chef in front of the whole galley. They had all seen it, and they all knew what it meant. And Laurens knew it too. That was the unforgivable thing. Not the letter of the act, but the spirit. In the old maritime days, on an eighteenth-century ship, the captain might very well have had her thrown overboard. Instead, Laurens would put her off the ship as soon as they came into port in Honolulu.

As well he should, Mick thought. Although Mick wouldn't necessarily have run a kitchen the way Laurens did, he preferred working under a control freak like Laurens to a chef who was more lax and volatile. He liked rules, liked knowing where he stood. The harder and more exacting the work he was required to do, the more comfortable he felt. This only doubled his anger at Consuelo: Laurens wasn't even that bad! And yet, in spite of himself, Mick couldn't help worrying about what would happen to her now. And this combination of protectiveness and anger reminded him of the way he'd worried about his younger sister, Beata, with her buzz-cut hair and tattoos and blackout drinking and stash of drugs and all-night raves in the ruin bars, stupid girl, coming home totally fucked up, defying their father to hit her the way Consuelo had defied Laurens to fire her. Authority, male: not their favorite thing.

Mick had simply wanted their father to run a more orderly and efficient household, to be an effective head. Beata had been emotional, egotistical, whereas Mick was always pragmatic, interested primarily in survival. Beata had died in a motorcycle accident at nineteen. She had been sparky and charismatic, just like Consuelo; they also shared outsized pride and temper and a cavalier refusal to play the game, a self-defeating stance that only ever bit them in the ass. And it made Mick sad. He liked Consuelo. He wanted her to do well. She was a talented chef, bright, skilled.

But then he remembered that she'd fucked things up for him, too. Whatever ground he'd regained with Laurens after his faux pas at the captain's table dinner was lost. He had failed to keep Consuelo in check. It wasn't his fucking fault, but he couldn't tell Laurens that when he and Laurens inevitably discussed the incident later. Instead, Mick would have to take responsibility for her, apologize, act contrite. It made him seethe with frustration. It was one thing to watch someone torpedo her own job, another thing entirely to be implicated in her behavior and held responsible for it.

He managed to get through the shift by going from one thing to the next, trying to focus on what was at hand, immediate. And when it was finally over, the last meal served, the last tray of leftovers stored, the equipment clean and wiped down, the floors swabbed, they all straggled over to the pass and gathered around in their usual raggedy ranks for the end-of-night meeting. Most nights had gone extremely well, which meant that this gathering was usually short, sweet, punchy, and even festive, with bottles of beer handed around, maybe a pan of leftovers passed with a fork, everyone exhausted, sweaty, relieved. But tonight the galley was silent. The tension from earlier had deepened to a blanket of smog. Kenji raised an eyebrow at Mick, who answered with a shrug so small his shoulders barely moved.

Laurens had been in his office for the last few hours, between service and the closing staff meeting. It was a power move, like everything he did. He never fraternized with the other chefs or staff. He wasn't given to lingering. As always, his arrival in the galley caused the room to go quickly silent. Everyone stood still. Consuelo waited next to Mick, holding her knife case, though she breathed evenly, her arms loose by her sides. Mick was impressed in spite of himself at her cool. His own hands were clenched.

"Hello, everyone," said Laurens. He looked very pale. His eyes were rimmed red. He held one arm across his stomach as if he were protecting it. He stopped at the head of the pass and looked around at their faces, stopping on Consuelo's while he spoke, looking directly at her. His voice sounded a little weak, but he didn't hesitate. "We had a situation tonight. It could not be handled during service without disrupting the passengers' dinner. I am going to deal with it now. Consuelo, from the beginning you have been a problem in this kitchen, and what happened tonight was inexcusable. You will be put off the ship in Hawaii. Please leave my kitchen now and do not come back."

Consuelo hefted her knife case lightly from hand to hand. "Yes, Chef," she said in a clear voice. Mick imagined for an instant that she was about to take her fish knife from the case and stab Laurens through the heart. But instead she walked out of the galley, her back very straight, her gait unhurried. The door swung behind her.

"And everyone else," Laurens began, but he stopped as one by one, without a word, the crew turned and followed Consuelo out.

"Hey, what are you doing?" Laurens said to their departing backs. "I didn't dismiss you."

No one answered him. Mick watched in astonishment as the most obedient and lowliest of his staff, every ranking color of neckerchief from dishwashers to line chefs, filed out the door. He tried to catch someone's eye, anyone's, but no one would look at him. The displaced air of their bodies blew against his cheeks along with an animal smell of sour sweat.

Laurens turned to Mick and Kenji. They were the only two left in the galley. "What the hell is going on here?"

Kenji looked at Mick with the same baffled expression. "I don't know," he said.

"Me neither," said Mick. "I've never seen this happen before."

The three of them stood and stared at each other for a moment in silence. Mick heard his own heartbeat loud in his ears. "I think it's a protest," he said, remembering the atmosphere in the crew lounge these past nights. He could hardly believe he was saying this, but it was the only thing that made sense.

Laurens coughed. "You're fucking joking, right?" He leaned against the counter, one hand clutching his stomach. The skin of his face was stretched so tight the knobs of his cheekbones gleamed in the overhead glare. "Where's the night crew?"

"I don't know," said Kenji. "They should be here."

"Chef," Mick said. "Are you all right?"

"Yes," said Laurens. Something rippled across his face, a spasm of some kind. "Please go and inform the night crew that they have duties to perform. I want them here now. Go and find Paolo. I'll be in my office." He turned and made his way slowly toward the far end of the galley. But before he'd even reached the door to the first storeroom, he collapsed to the freshly mopped floor. At first Mick thought he had skidded and tripped, since the floor was gleaming wet, but instead he lay propped on his elbows, vomiting.

Kenji grabbed a clean torchon off the counter and helped him up. Mick wet another torchon at the prep sink, wrung it out, and handed it to Laurens.

"This is bad," said Laurens, gasping, clutching his stomach as he mopped his face. He leaned over and vomited again and kept heaving.

"Let me take you to the infirmary, Chef," said Kenji. "You need a doctor."

Mick took it as a clear sign of how sick Laurens was that he didn't try to argue. "Find Paolo," Laurens called to Mick as Kenji helped him out of the galley. "We need the night crew in here."

*

Miriam couldn't help smiling at Kimmi's unflagging energy and enthusiasm as she introduced and applauded one act after another, a jazz guitarist, a retired opera singer, an amateur stand-up comedian.

Kimmi was nominally the Sabra Quartet's boss on the cruise, and as such, she was easygoing and not unduly concerned with protocol; not a stickler, but not lax, either. She was professional and fun, but there was more to her than that. Every time Miriam saw her, she was making an extra effort to be humane and responsible, talking confidingly to an elderly man as she helped him up the stairs by making it look as if she'd just taken his arm, joining a solitary diner whose spouse was under the weather, rousing torpid midafternoon sunbathers by the pool to get up and swivel their hips to a Frank Sinatra song, which they did with laughing good cheer. She was doing double duty on this cruise. As the entertainment director she was responsible for fun, and as the cruise director she was responsible for morale, and she took both seriously.

During a sweet rendition by two old men of an Everly Brothers song, Miriam's attention was caught by one of the waiters. He walked quickly, head unobtrusively down, toward the Weisses' table, which was near the front of the stage. Miriam watched as the waiter leaned down and whispered something in Larry's ear. Larry put a hand on Rivka's shoulder, whispered in turn into her ear. Rivka stared up at him as Larry stood and followed the waiter to the back of the lounge, threading the thronged tables, and out the door.

"Where's he going?" Sasha said into Miriam's ear. So he had noticed too.

"I don't know," she said. "Maybe we hit an iceberg."

"Through the years our love will grow," the crooners sang in close harmony. *"Like a river, it will flow."* Rivka was nervously glancing over her shoulder at the door. Miriam considered going down to her table and asking her straight-out what the waiter had said, but of course Rivka wasn't likely to confide in Miriam; she'd probably snub her, make her feel like an idiot for sticking her nose in.

"Our next act is a young and talented piano player," Kimmi announced when the two old men had finished. "She's a sophomore at U.C. Berkeley, majoring in chemistry, but if that doesn't work out, I think music might be a good plan B for her. See what you think. Everyone, Allison Goodwin! Come on out, Allison!"

A spotlight followed young Allison as she walked quickly and shyly onstage in a boxy navy-blue dress. Miriam recognized the slightly plump, socially awkward girl; she had sat at a table near the quartet at dinner the night before, listening avidly to the music and ignoring her parents, her mother's loose laughter and copious consumption of white wine, her father's ham-fisted flirtation with the two women at the next table.

Overhead the stage lights blazed. The baby grand had been pushed to the front of the stage, its lid lifted. Votive candles flickered on the tables. Cigarette smoke curled in the candlelight and dissipated in the air blowing strongly from the vents overhead. Allison sat very straight, lifted her right hand slightly, and then brought it down on the opening run of Rachmaninoff's Piano Sonata no. 2, the cascading notes tumbling effortlessly from her fingers in jagged rocks and fluid gullets of water and tree trunks rushing downstream: colliding, almost violent, powerfully beautiful.

She was a prodigy, this girl, thought Miriam. It was a rare treat to hear another classical musician, a real one, perform on a cruise. But the former soldier in Miriam had split off from the music; she couldn't help glancing over at Rivka again. As an Israeli, Miriam was prone to jumpiness in crowded public places. Her caution had shaded into paranoia as the years went on. She made hasty exits when she went alone to matinees in the afternoon and someone came in who didn't look right. She left buses before her stop when a fellow passenger prayed to himself too conspicuously. She fled from pedestrian malls, leaving her tea undrunk on a café table, at the sight of a Palestinian with a backpack and no clear reason to be loitering across the walkway. Every time, she wanted to shout as she left to warn everyone else, but she knew this would be crazy, and she could be arrested for disturbing the peace, for causing panic at a false alarm. So she had to content herself with private reconnoitering, retreating from apparent peril that always, every time, turned out to be nothing. Still, she would rather be on the lookout, sharp, overreacting, than to be caught asleep and dull-witted. When the bomb came to rip her apart, she would at least see it coming. She wanted to die on her toes if she had to die at all.

She stood up and touched Sasha on his shoulder. Without looking up at her, he put his hand over hers and held it against his warm neck. She leaned down and murmured in his ear, "Come with me, let's get some air."

When she got to the back of the lounge, he was right behind her. He whispered, "Should we go back to our room?"

"I would love that," she whispered back. "But I've been wondering about Larry."

"Wondering what?"

"Why he left," she said.

He didn't miss a beat. "What are you worried about?"

Three cheers for the Israeli army, she thought; even half a century later, the training was ingrained.

"Rivka seems very worried about something," said Miriam. "I'm sure it's nothing. A business call. But you know how I overreact. It's a terrible habit."

Sasha cupped her cheek with his hand and gazed at her. She waited for him to laugh at her, her mouth twitching, ready to laugh at herself with him. "I think," he said, "we should go and find Larry, and you can ask him yourself."

They opened the door to the lounge and walked hand in hand along the promenade deck, softly lamp-lit, breezy, empty of people. The burnished wooden floor gleamed. The enormous windows held reflections, barely glimpsed through the corners of Miriam's eyes. Through the closed doors, she heard faint voices in the casino as they passed it, laughter and shouts and the clack of the roulette wheel.

"Do you smell smoke?" said Sasha, stopping. He tilted his head toward the opened doors at the aft end of the promenade to inhale deeply through his nose.

"Cigarettes?" said Miriam, doing the same. Then she caught it: an acrid burning smell, just a whiff. "Yes," she said. "I smell smoke."

"A fire."

Miriam stared at him, inhaling through her nose. Yes, it smelled like there might be a fire somewhere. Of course she didn't want anything actually to be wrong, the thought terrified her in fact, but even so, she was gratified that Sasha had believed her. And that, for once in her life, she might actually be right.

chapter fourteen

Mick entered the crew lounge and spotted Consuelo right away. She was at the bar, surrounded by a crowd, including several members of the galley crew. Trevor stood behind the bar. Everyone was focused on her. She was holding court like some sort of heroine in a movie.

She caught sight of Mick, and her face blazed. "Hey, boss," she called with half-affectionate insolence.

Crewmembers moved out of his way to let Mick through, then closed around him again, quiet. He could feel clearly that he was now an outsider in this room. He looked at her and around at the silent, wide-awake faces. "Does anyone want to tell me what's going on here?"

Consuelo took a deliberate sip of her wine, watching his face over the rim of her glass. "Walkout. We quit."

"All of you?"

"Yes. They're firing us anyway. No severance. Nothing. Let them make their own fucking food, clean their own fucking rooms. We've got over half the crew with us."

"This is crazy," said Mick, looking around at them all. "You'll be screwed if you do this. No cruise line will hire you. They'll blackball you. All of you."

"So what?" said Consuelo. "They treat us like shit."

"I didn't treat you like shit," Mick said. "Laurens didn't either. He's a fair boss. He's tough, but he's not mean or crazy. Think about this. It's not too late to stop it."

"Sorry, *Chef.* This is a done thing."

Mick looked at her for a moment. Then he looked around at the others, their expressions all set, determined. He had no idea what to say, how to respond. All he knew was that he no longer had any authority over Consuelo, or any of them, for that matter.

"Okay," he said wearily. "It's your ass, not mine. Has anyone seen Paolo? Laurens wants the night crew in the galley for their shift."

"He's with us," said Consuelo.

"But he's management," said Mick, genuinely shocked. "Why would Paolo walk out?"

"Solidarity," said Consuelo. "You can join us too, if you want. It's not too late." She grinned cheekily at him.

"And it's not too late to drop this whole thing and go back to work," said Mick. "What are you trying to get out of this?"

"What do you mean? The action speaks for itself. We'll get huge publicity, too. TV news, the Internet, it will be everywhere."

So that was what she'd meant the other day about getting famous.

"I mean," said Mick, "are you trying to bargain with the owners? 'Cause they won't bargain. They never do. They don't have to."

"Yes, they will," said Natalya, the Russian bartender. "Otherwise, good luck to them, finding replacements on short notice in Hawaii for the rest of the cruise. We'll have leverage."

"You won't," said Mick. "This is really stupid. You're screwing everybody. Yourselves, and the rest of the crew, and the passengers most of all."

"Cabaret went too far this time," said a guy Mick didn't recognize. "We are reacting the only way we can. It's their own fault."

"You won't get anywhere with Cabaret," said Mick. "And the rest of us will have to pick up your slack for the rest of the cruise, and no one else will hire you. It's not like you have a union to fight for you."

"We do now," said Consuelo. "This is our union."

"Oh man," said Mick, shaking his head. He could feel how useless it was to try to reason with these people. They were excited to do this, even if it was just to screw Cabaret. Walking out was their main objective; vindictive payback. How was he supposed to argue with a room full of defiant, righteous, angry workers who had nothing left to lose? And besides, they weren't wrong.

Without saying another word, he turned and walked out of the crew lounge, stood for a moment in the hallway, trying to decide what to do. He badly wanted a beer, but the crew lounge would probably enforce a "no management" service policy now. He vaguely contemplated going to the restaurant to get a beer from the bar refrigerator. Or he could go to the small break room where upper management theoretically congregated. Mick had never been in there, and despite everything going on, he still didn't consider himself management. The crew lounge was where he felt at home, and now that the lines had been drawn, he had nowhere else to go.

He became aware of a chemical, noxious smell. It was coming from one of the vents. He inhaled hard through his nose a few times: smoke. It was unmistakable. Then all at once, the fans stopped, the lights went out, and the hallway was black and silent.

*

"Where is our waiter?" Valerie said, craning her neck to look around. She got up and went to the bar, leaving Christine alone at the table. Miriam and Sasha had gone off somewhere, probably to neck on the promenade. Christine barely noticed. From the first notes of the piano piece, she had been caught up in its drama, swept away by restless torrents, made dreamy by peaceful interludes. And the girl who was playing was young but masterful. With a start of surprise, Christine recognized the teenager she'd espied just before they'd sailed away from Long Beach, the sullen, gimlet-eyed girl who'd been reading her brochure in a nearby deck chair while Christine had been reading hers.

And here she was again, pouring her soul into the piano. Just as she was pounding out the dizzying final passages of the piece, the stage lights went out. The air-conditioning died, and the lounge became instantly hot, dark, and stuffy. The music stopped. A murmur filled the silence. Christine looked around at confused faces, shrouded in the half light. The votive candles on the tables flickered, jewelry glinted, tips of cigarettes winked throughout the room. Kimmi, confused, tapped the dead mike on the darkened stage.

"Okay, everyone!" she called. Her voice sounded small and weak without the mike. "Everyone, as you can see, the power just went out. I'm not sure what's going on, but I'll let you know as soon as I know anything."

Valerie slid back into the chair next to Christine and handed her a glass. Her face was sallow in the greenish emergency lighting that had just come on overhead. "The bartenders are gone," she said. "I made it myself. I hope this isn't serious."

Christine took a gulp. It was straight vodka over ice.

The PA system crackled to life, and the captain's voice came through, calm and commanding. *"Hello, folks, this is Captain Jack. You've probably noticed that the power went out. You might have smelled a little smoke, too. There was a small fire, but it's under control, and we're working on getting the power back up and running. It's nothing to worry about, this is temporary, so please try to relax and enjoy your evening and I'll be back soon with an update."*

"Oh my God," said Valerie. "Holy shit."

A few people coughed. Others headed for the exits, propping open the doors to the lounge on their way out.

"Let's get some fresh air," said Christine, picking up her drink. As they left the lounge, Christine realized that the constant vibration of the engines underfoot had stopped, along with everything else.

"What happens now?" she heard a woman's voice ask.

"They'll get the power back on again," said her male companion. "They always do. We just have to wait."

*

Miriam and Sasha stopped on the stairs leading up to the bridge. Loud voices echoed down below.

"The power went out," she said. She heard the astonishment in her own voice. A fine, spitting rain had begun to fall, and the air was dark and heavy, with no wind. In the dim light from the sky, Miriam could make out a thin layer of acrid smoke wrapped around the ship, blanketing it.

"Was it the fire?" she said.

"Probably," Sasha replied. "Let's go to the bridge."

Their feet clanged on the metal staircase as they made their way to the top. They hovered together in the open doorway to the bridge. Under a curved wall of enormous front-facing windows, the long control panel was dark. Dim overhead lights, which must have been battery-powered, illuminated the cavernous room with pale greenish light.

Miriam heard Larry before she saw him.

"This is a bad situation," he said, his loud voice cutting through all the others. "We're dead in the water."

As Miriam's eyes adjusted, she saw him at the back of the room, sitting at a long table next to the captain. They were both speaking at once into handsets. The captain's voice was low and even, so Miriam couldn't make out what he was saying over Larry's sharp projection, but she could hear speakers crackling all over the ship, so she guessed he was making an official announcement. Three young bridge officers had clustered around the conked-out control panel beneath the windows. They were speaking in low voices. Miriam edged in their direction, her ear cocked like an antenna to pick up whatever she could.

"Was it an oil leak, or electrical?"

"I don't know. But the sprinklers didn't even come on. They had to go in and turn them on manually. I heard a couple of the engine room crew passed out from the smoke and had to go to the infirmary."

"I was working on the *Sea Star* three years ago when that engine fire happened. We waited three days for a tow. Three days! And that was in the Gulf of Mexico."

"God. What were they thinking, sending us to Hawaii in this piece of shit?"

Miriam stepped closer to Sasha and took his hand as two more young men in uniform tumbled in through an open door, brandishing flashlights. "What happened?" one of them said. In the greenish light from above, he looked half asleep, shocked out of a stupor. It occurred to Miriam that these kids had probably been sleeping and had come upstairs to begin the night shift.

"Engine fire," said one of the other officers.

"How did it start?"

"We don't know yet."

"Is it out?"

"It's contained, but they're still fighting it."

"Where's the power? What about the backup generator?"

"All we have are basic communications and emergency lights."

"Seriously?"

The other officer jerked his head in the direction of Larry Weiss, who was on his feet now, pacing about the room, shouting into his satellite phone handset.

The officer spotted Sasha and Miriam. "Can I help you with something?"

"We came to find out what was going on," said Sasha.

"The captain just made an announcement that the fire is contained and the ship is safe," said the officer. Miriam opened her mouth to explain that they hadn't heard the captain's announcement because she'd been standing right here while he made it, but the officer gestured to the open doorway to the stairwell. "You'll be safer down with the other passengers."

Larry hung up the phone and turned to the captain. "What a mess. Un-fucking-believable." He turned to the crewmembers nearby. "What? You're just standing there? Why aren't you fixing this shit?" Then he saw Miriam and Sasha and strode over to them and put his hands on their shoulders. "You two," he said. "Get downstairs and follow instructions. And if you see my wife, tell her to go to our suite and stay there."

Miriam felt his hand on her shoulder like a steel clamp as he herded them out of the room.

"What's happening, Larry?" she asked him.

She looked up into his face and met his gaze. He looked startled to recognize her there, surprised to remember who she was, his old friend Miriam.

"It'll be fine," he told her, his tone softening. "Little blaze in the engine room, should be out by now, or soon."

"Will the power come back on?" Sasha asked.

"I'm sure it will," said Larry with his old easygoing confidence. "Don't worry, go back to your cabins and be comfortable. We'll take care of this."

As Miriam and Sasha went down the stairs, she heard his voice again, penetrating, full of punitive anger at the bridge crew, and felt as if, after all the decades she'd known him, she had just seen Larry Weiss clearly for the first time.

*

Mick retraced his steps back to the crew lounge in the glow of the emergency lights. He had already concluded that the power had gone out because of the fire. The next logical conclusion was that the crew who'd walked out had deliberately set the fire to sabotage the ship. It seemed crazy. But then again, he had never in his life witnessed a galley crew walk out on their executive chef. He had no idea what they were capable of doing now, how far they were willing to take this insane protest. Maybe Consuelo had actually poisoned Laurens. She had joked about it the other day. At least, Mick had thought she was joking. Who knew anymore?

When he got to the open door to the darkened crew lounge, he heard shouting, chaos, thumps. A few people were lighting candles.

"What's going on?"

"Why is the power out?"

"Hey," Mick yelled into the crowd. "Did you assholes start a fire?"

Some began to panic at the mention of fire. There were shrieks, curses. Someone standing close to Mick said something in a low, despairing mutter in a language he didn't know.

"A fire," said Mick. "It made the power go out. Does anyone know anything about this?"

"No," came shouts from several people.

"Where is the fire?" said Trevor.

"We should go and help," said Rodrigo.

"No!" He heard Consuelo's voice clearly. She stood with her arm raised theatrically in the manner of a rebel statue, lit by candlelight. Her voice was clear and ringing. "No one leave! It works better for us if we stay together and don't give in!"

"People will be scared," said a young woman Mick recognized from salad prep. "It won't hurt us to see if they need anything."

"We aren't their servants anymore," said Consuelo. "We're equals now. And if we stay here, we have more leverage, if we stay true to what we're doing. It's better for us. No one leave!"

Mick could see how much she loved this role, resistance leader, venting her righteous anger in service of a cause instead of having to keep it suppressed on the line. She was flying high. Not even the news of the fire and the power going out had daunted her.

He pushed his way through the crowd and stuck his face near hers, tapped her on the shoulder.

"Did you poison Laurens? Tell the truth."

"Poison—what?"

"He's throwing up. He went to the infirmary. What did you do?"

She looked shocked, genuinely. "I would never do that," she said.

"Did you people start the fire?"

"No! This is the first we've heard of it. Why the hell would we do that?"

He locked eyes with her for a beat or two. "If there's a fire," she called as he turned into the crowd, "then we're *all* fucked. All we did was walk out."

Exhausted, Mick stepped out of the lounge and stood alone in the dim, smoky hallway. He had no one to confer with. Kenji had taken Laurens up to the infirmary. Jean-Luc was a competitive, pouty meathead and would be of no help to him. Paolo had joined the walkout, and there was apparently no night crew now, either.

He couldn't face going back to the galley alone. He craved a short glass of straight whiskey with a ferocious bloodlust. With no real idea of where he was headed, he found the nearest stairs and climbed upward, out of the smoke. A cigarette, *jaj istenem,* he wanted a cigarette.

*

Christine and Valerie had made their way up to the solarium at the very top of the ship to join a crowd of people. The ship lay on the calm ocean. Smoke from the fire hung over the open decks like drifting clouds of noxious incense. Without the soothing effect of the constant, low-level vibrations of the engines, everyone was full of nervous jitters, as if all the engines had transferred their energy to the passengers themselves, and the sudden lack of propulsion had awakened everyone out of their dreamy languor. Christine heard sharp voices, felt bodies moving around her in restless dislocation and fear.

From the front of the solarium came a bridge crewmember's voice, amplified through a megaphone. She sounded very young, but calm and confident. "Everyone, hello, I have good news! The fire is out, and no one was hurt. And we're working on getting the power back up for you."

There were some wan cheers as flashlights were trained up to illuminate her. Small arrows of rain slanted down through the beams of light.

"Well, folks, we had a small engine-room fire," she said. "Our crew has put the fire completely out with no damage to the ship, and the engineers are working on repairing the generators."

"When will we have power back?"

"As soon as we can."

"Is there a midnight buffet?"

"Not tonight. I'm sorry."

She put the megaphone down for a moment while another bridge crewmember said something into her ear. She listened closely, nodded, lifted the megaphone again, and resumed.

"So we're going to work through the night and do our best to have the power back up by tomorrow morning. Meanwhile, we need you all to stay warm and safe, so the captain is asking that you all go back to your cabins right now. I know it's a bit smoky below, and the air isn't working, so you'll need to open your windows enough to let fresh air in. Keep your doors open if you have inner rooms. There's emergency lighting in the hallways. The crew will be here to assist if you need us. So try to get some sleep, and we hope to have everything back up and running in the morning."

"Oh man, this is fucked up, Christine." Valerie's voice vibrated through their pressed-together skulls as Christine put an arm around her and they leaned into each other. "I'm so sorry I brought you on this disaster cruise."

"It's not your fault," Christine said. "Anyway, aren't you glad I'm here? What if you were alone?"

She could feel Valerie's anxiety subside. She liked having her arm around her friend. It made her feel motherly. It was not a bad feeling at all, this power to soothe and ground someone with your physical presence alone. Valerie's shoulders and ribs felt as insubstantial as wicker.

Christine realized that she was ravenous. It was funny how quickly she had become conditioned to look forward to the midnight buffet. Normally, at home, she and Ed ate dinner at about six-thirty and nothing else till breakfast the next morning. Yet it had taken only a few days of sumptuous late-night spreads to get used to this nightly indulgence.

Laughing inwardly at herself, she realized that she felt irrationally cheerful about this situation, on the whole. This was the way she usually reacted when things went "pear-shaped," as her mother put it. Maybe it was because, when Christine was growing up, any small catastrophe had caused her parents to focus on her and her sister instead of being their usual distracted and worried selves, as if having the barn wall collapse or the tractor break down or the lambing ewe die made them remember that they loved their children.

"Hey," said Valerie. "There's that guy. That chef."

Christine caught sight of him, emerging from the stairwell nearby. Mick, she remembered. That was his name. When he saw Valerie and Christine, his knotted expression eased and he seemed on the verge of greeting them. Then his face went blank and he turned away, as if he'd remembered that he didn't know them, or didn't care if he did, and went off into the darkness.

chapter fifteen

As soon as it was light enough to see, Christine got out of bed and stood in her pajamas by the open window, hugging her arms to her chest to warm herself. The ocean looked pellucid and calm. The cabin felt stiflingly small behind her.

"Oh God," moaned Valerie from beneath her covers. "Did we dream all that?"

Christine turned to address the fetal knot cocooned in its nest of blankets, hair sprouting onto the pillow. "I wish we had."

"What's going on?"

"We're still adrift, I think," said Christine.

Valerie unpeeled the blankets from her head and squinted at Christine. "Well, this is a plot twist I didn't expect. Power outage. My cruise-ship chapter just got a lot more interesting. This could even be a book of its own."

"That might be the one good thing in all this." Christine stretched, hearing her joints crack, feeling her muscles elongate like rubber bands. She yawned so hard her jaws creaked. "I have to get out of here. Want to come?"

"I'm not awake yet," said Valerie, pulling the covers back over her head. "Bring coffee if you can find any," she added, her voice muffled.

In the bathroom, Christine peed and flushed the toilet. Nothing happened. So the plumbing wasn't working: that was bad. Instead of trying to take a shower, which she imagined would be futile now, she pulled on shorts and a T-shirt, brushed her hair. Out in the hallway, it was so quiet she could hear her own footsteps as she padded along on the patterned carpet with its dizzying inter-locking mod diamonds and ovals. No vibrations underfoot meant that the engines were still out. So was the air-conditioning. The door at the end of the hallway was propped open, letting a fresh bright breeze pour through.

It was just past dawn, she guessed, judging by the soft span-gled light on the water. She was alone on the staircase, alone in the hallway. As she approached the open door to the breakfast room, she heard activity and saw two waiters in uniform taking dishes off rolling carts and arranging them on a long table. The room was bleached with light and filled with the sound of the waves, closer down here than on the upper decks, the morning light and salty air contrasting with the kitschy decor, synthetic burnt-orange drapes, sunburst wall-to-wall carpet studded with pink and ocher and magenta, and stackable mass-produced cushioned chairs and institutional tables.

At the other end of the room she recognized Sidney, the maître d', wrestling with a large sliding window on a track. He stopped to rub his shoulder. Then he fished a flask out of his hip pants pocket, unscrewed it, and took a deep drink.

"Can I help you open it?" Christine asked, walking toward him. "It looks like a job for two people."

Sidney shoved his flask back into his pocket. "No no, I can manage. Breakfast isn't ready yet, I'm afraid."

Christine looked around. Besides Sidney and the two other men, there was no one there. Usually the breakfast room was thronged with staff. She watched as Sidney pulled and pushed, straining against the sliding door. It wouldn't budge.

"Here," she said, dragging a chair over to the window. She stood on it, grasped the pane, putting her own hands on it above Sidney's handholds, and tugged with him. The window opened smoothly on its tracks, letting warm sea air billow into the room.

Christine jumped down and returned the chair to its table.

"Thank you," said Sidney. "Couldn't have done it without you."

"Your name is Sidney, right? I know because I've met you every night at dinner."

"And you're Christine Thorne from Fryeburg, Maine."

She couldn't help smiling as she heard her name and that of the little town she called home. "What's happening? Do you know?"

"Well, we're in a bit of a pickle, to tell you the truth," said Sidney. "Nothing you should worry about, though."

"So the power's really out," said Christine. "Can they fix it?"

"Oh, I reckon we'll be all right. That crew knows what they're about down there."

"Is there anything I can do in the meantime? I would love to help out if I can."

"Thank you, but that's not necessary."

He made "necessary" sound like a euphemism for "appropriate." Christine pressed on. "I mean it. Really. I work hard. And I'm good at taking orders."

Sidney hesitated. He was clearly unwilling to say no to a passenger's request, no matter what it was. "Try the galley," he said with dubious reluctance. "They're a bit short-staffed at the moment. Little to-do last night. They might welcome an extra pair of hands."

"Thanks," she said.

He gave a slight bow from the waist and turned away, done with her. Christine hesitated, wondering where the hell the galley was, but she was too intimidated by his demeanor to ask for directions.

*

Mick woke up in blackness, rolled out of his bunk and stood up, opened the door to the hallway to let air and light in, and looked around for his clothes. His roommate was in the top bunk, his face turned to the wall. Mick stared at the back of his head. He couldn't picture his face. What was his name? Silvio? Salvatore? He usually worked the night shift and didn't come in until Mick had left. He should have been in the galley, not sleeping here.

Mick snapped awake remembering the walkout, Laurens, the fire.

He stood still outside his room, listening for the familiar thrum of the engines below him. But there was nothing, only a stifling silence. He headed quickly down the hallway, almost running. The emergency track lights were still on, and the air was dense and smelled of smoke and God knew what chemicals they'd used to put out the fire. He assumed he'd lost most of his staff, and the power was still out. How would he cook with no electric stoves? Frozen and refrigerated food wouldn't last more than a day. They were due to resupply in Hawaii, so there wasn't much food left on the ship. He would have to make a full inventory of their stores, try to make them last until . . .

His thoughts were interrupted by a loud, clear voice behind him. "Hello, good morning, can you tell me where the galley is?"

He stopped and turned. It was that woman from Long Beach, the friend of the journalist. She had an odd expression on her face as she also recognized him. "Oh. Hi." She hesitated, and Mick waited for the other shoe to drop. "You're the chef," she said politely.

"That's right," said Mick. "How can I help you?"

"I want to help *you*, actually," she said. "I just talked to Sidney up in the breakfast room. He said maybe you could use a hand down here. I'm Christine."

He was tempted to tell Christine, brusquely, to go back up to the breakfast buffet and leave all this to the crew, but he wasn't sure there *was* a crew, and she was staring at him with a bug-eyed determination that made him pause.

"All right," he said. "Follow me."

He led her through the restaurant. Everything was still as it had been left the night before: tables set, shelves stocked for service, bar organized and gleaming. Ready for lunch. But with no crew to speak of and no power, lunch would most likely have to be basic, thrown-together sandwiches, which Mick suspected would not go over well with some of the passengers.

He stopped and turned to face her. He might as well tell this one before they all found out. "Here's the thing, Christine. Most of the galley crew quit their jobs last night and walked out. Hard to do on a ship this size, but they've done it."

She didn't look entirely surprised. Maybe she'd already heard. "What happened?"

"They said they won't do their jobs anymore unless management renews their contracts with better terms."

"Wait. Why?" she asked. "Because of the fire?"

"Nothing to do with the fire. This is their last cruise. Their contracts are being canceled, and they're pissed, so they decided to get their revenge."

"How many?" she asked.

"I have no idea. I'm not even sure anyone will show up this morning."

"Okay," she said, clearly startled. "I'm happy to do whatever you need me to do. I'm a farmer, I used to be a waitress. I cook at a soup kitchen every week, anywhere from fifty to a hundred people. I know how to work."

Mick made a frank assessment of her plain shorts and T-shirt, her earnest eagerness to help. Maybe she was okay, not the rich bitch he'd originally pegged her as. At any rate, he didn't have the luxury of turning her down.

"Let's go," he said.

He led her through the doors and into the main galley, which was empty, silent, lit by the emergency track lighting, still smelling faintly of the harsh bleach-based cleanser he had used to mop up Laurens's vomit, swabbing the floor and counters several times to try to wipe out whatever virus or bacteria he was harboring and had left behind. The dead stoves were shadowy through the gloom.

Christine looked around. "I could make coffee."

Mick took a liter beaker from a shelf, filled it with tepid water, and took a long drink. "Can't make coffee," he told her, wiping his mouth on the back of his hand. "No electricity for the burners. Can't boil water, can't cook anything."

"What about cold brew? I could start it now. You let it sit and then just strain it. I could make a huge batch."

"Go for it. Your first assignment."

He went to the locker room, pissed in the little toilet, tried to flush and couldn't, and felt a sudden sense of dread. No plumbing. He put on a clean set of chef's whites. Back in the galley, he tossed another to Christine: she put it on without having to be told. After he'd shown her where the coffee was kept, he went into the first walk-in refrigerator to take stock of the remaining supplies, the perishables that had to be eaten immediately.

A while later, as he emerged with a hotel pan of hard-boiled eggs, he heard voices.

"Morning, Chef," said a young man with an Aussie accent.

Mick didn't recognize the clean-cut blond kid, but he must have been on the morning crew. Or what was left of it. Behind him was a small cluster of people—eight, he counted—all wearing clean white jackets and neckerchiefs, exactly on time for their normal shift. He recognized a few of them from the main galley, one from his own station, a prep cook named Camille, dark and serious, with glasses.

Mick felt himself relax a little. So there was order in the world after all. The remnants of his exhaustion lifted, the scrim of grime around his vision cleared.

"Good morning," he said. "Does anyone know what's going on with the rest of the crew?"

"Most of them are on the main deck," said Camille. "They've taken it over. I think they're planning to stay there until we get to Hawaii."

"Some of them are in the buffet galley," said another young woman. She had an Indian accent, and Mick remembered her, though not her name, from the first day; he had put her in charge of service aesthetics in the buffet galley, because she had seemed to have a good eye. Then he'd come over here to the main galley and hadn't seen her since. "They've taken that over too," she was saying. "They're eating breakfast in there. I'm supposed to be working there, but they said I couldn't stay unless I joined them. But I didn't want to. So they threw me out."

"What about Chef Jean-Luc?" Mick asked. "Isn't he in charge?"

"He's joined the walkouts," said the Aussie.

"Okay," said Mick, trying to hide the shock he felt at this news. "I guess it's just us then. Until others decide to show up. So let's get started."

He looked into their faces: they all looked frankly relieved to have found someone to tell them what to do. He glanced over at Christine, who was stirring coffee into cold water in a soup pot. She looked back at him with the same expectant, trusting expression everyone else had.

"By the way, everybody, this is Christine. She volunteered to help us out. So please treat her as one of the crew. Right now she's cold-brewing some coffee, which is the only way we're going to get it since the power's still out, so you should be extra nice to her." A couple of weak smiles. Good. "We'll put out breakfast for the passengers first. Simple stuff like cereal, milk, fruit, hard-cooked eggs, anything immediately perishable. You two," he said, pointing at Camille and the Aussie, "go up to the breakfast room and see what they've got, what they need. The rest of us are going to make a quick inventory of our stores, starting with the perishables: meats, dairy, fish, vegetables." He could feel himself slipping into autopilot, running through the service as he had done a thousand times for executive chefs, trying to impress them. The pitch was the same, but now that there was no one to impress, he heard himself delivering it in a warmer tone, with less of an edge. "We'll have to use as much of that as we can today. Lunch will be simple: cheese sandwiches, fruit salad, bags of chips, that sort of thing. As you all know, we can't use the stoves. The desalination pumps are down, so we'll have to ration whatever we have in the tank. Service will be paper and plastic from now on. For dinner tonight, we're going to make a shitload of ceviche to use up as much of the seafood as we can. And salad, mostly lettuce, also cucumber and anything else that might spoil. We're going to use the outdoor grills to cook meat, since we have plenty of charcoal left. But the main thing now is to figure out what goes bad first, and that's what we'll serve. Okay?"

There were nods all around, a chorus of "Yes, Chef."

"Good," he said, and found himself clapping his hands together and rubbing them, the way Laurens did at the end of staff meetings. "Let's get to work."

*

It had been her first night alone with Sasha in their shared cabin, and Miriam had spent most of it worrying about Isaac, down the hall in the cabin with Jakov. She missed him. She always knew how to comfort him, and he her. They would have kvetched and moaned together. Instead she had tried to match Sasha's quiet forbearance all night. He had settled himself in their double bed and lain awake for hours, brooding in silence. He was always stoic and self-contained, philosophical about discomfort. When she tried to talk to him, to caress him, he responded at first but lapsed back into worried fulmination, so she left him alone. Maybe he had been thinking of his own wife. At some point it had hit her with sheepish sadness that she was being foolish; maybe she was too old to start over, too old to have a swooning new love affair.

Dawn came as a relief to both of them, it seemed to Miriam. As soon as it was light enough to see, they dressed wordlessly and left their cabin. The hallway, lit by windows at either end, looked like a lunatic asylum that had run out of medication: old people staggered around, some still in pajamas, others in misbuttoned shirts and rumpled shorts.

"Finally it's morning," a woman said, clutching Miriam's arm. Her eyes were ringed with pigmented circles. Her lips were cracked and pale. "I was sick all night. I have nothing left inside to throw up."

"Me too," said someone nearby. "What was in our dinner last night?"

"The toilets aren't flushing!"

"Mine's all stopped-up!"

A bridge officer appeared in the hallway. "Good morning."

"Can we get some breakfast, do you think?" said someone.

"Breakfast is being served in the buffet."

"What about the plumbing? It's broken."

"We're working on that," said the officer. He looked painfully young to Miriam, mid-twenties at the most.

"Thank you," she said to him as she walked by. "You're doing a good job."

"We're trying," he said. "I am so sorry about this, it's awful for you all."

Isaac and Jakov's room was the last door before the stairs. Miriam put her hand on Sasha's arm for him to wait, and knocked. Jakov opened it. He wore pajamas and held a washcloth over his eye. "I knocked against something in the night," he explained, disappearing into the small bathroom. Miriam stuck her head into the room. Isaac was sitting up in his own bed, his legs still under the blankets. "I'm glad to see you got through the night all right," she said.

"This is not what I would call 'all right,'" said Isaac.

"I know," she said, feeling a rush of tenderness toward him. "Do you want to come with us now? We're going to the breakfast buffet to see if there's anything to eat."

Isaac waved her off with a mournful expression. "Go, go," he said. "I'll see you later."

She nodded at him and went, shutting the door behind her. She joined Sasha and the rest of the herd as they went hobbling to the stairs, along a hallway, and into the breakfast buffet room. It was heartening to see the sunlight streaming in with fresh air through open windows, two staff members in uniform behind the long tables, breakfast arranged: small boxes of cereal, fruit, bread and butter and jam, cheese, napkins. Even the garish patterned carpet cheered her up a little. The storage refrigerator had been opened, and its drawers were filled with small, single-portion containers of milk and juice and yogurt. Most of the service tables, draped in white linen tablecloths and holding empty electric chafing dishes, had been pushed over by the open sliding doors to the balcony, through which fresh air blew steadily off the ocean.

"What, they can't cook anything?" came a plaintive voice that belonged to an skinny elderly redhead in a flowered muumuu who could have been one of Miriam's cousins.

"The stoves don't work," said Sasha. "They're electric. We need the generators for them." He turned to Miriam. "I'm going to go see if I can help fix them. I used to be a good mechanic, when I was young."

"Yes," Miriam said. "You should, of course you should."

He gazed at her tenderly. "Will you be all right, my beloved? Can you eat something?"

Just like that, Miriam melted with love for him, all over again. "I'm perfectly all right," she said.

He embraced her, and she clung to him for a moment, feeling all her fears and worries from the night before turning into fear for his safety. There might be another fire down there, some sort of catastrophe.

"Be careful," she said, anxiously.

When he'd gone, she joined the crowd clustered by the food and collected a container of yogurt from the open refrigerator, a banana from the mound of fruit on the serving table, and a plastic spoon, and looked around for somewhere to sit. The cavernous table-filled space made her feel as if she were in school again, casing the cafeteria for allies. Then she spotted Rivka Weiss slumped all alone at a table by the window, her small head wrapped in a lime-green turban. Her face was averted, looking toward the ocean.

What was *she* doing here, Miriam wondered. Rivka never came to the breakfast buffet room. She and Larry had the palatial owner's suite near the top of the ship, where she probably had her breakfast brought to her on a private balcony off her bedroom. Why had she come slumming it down here?

"Rivka," said Miriam, walking up to her. "Good morning, how are you? Can I sit with you?"

Rivka looked up with a snap of her head. "I don't mind," she said automatically, before she'd even registered who it was. "Oh, Miriam," she said, and turned back to look out at the bright water and hot sky.

Miriam was startled by her ravaged face, tormented and creased, probably by a pillowcase, without its usual artful makeup. Her arched, plucked eyebrows and downturned pale mouth, the turban swathing her coconut of a skull, made her look like an invalid in the immediate aftermath of major surgery.

"I'm so sorry about this mess," said Miriam as she settled herself in the chair opposite her. "Have you heard anything more about what's happening?"

"Larry is leaving the ship." Rivka glanced at her again, her mouth working, saliva gathering at the corners, her eyes wide with pinpoint pupils. She had taken something, a sedative maybe. "He's trying to get a military helicopter to come and get him. They only have enough fuel to take two or at the most three people at this range. I'm not going with him. I'm staying here. I can't believe he would do this."

"You should go," said Miriam, feeling perversely charitable. "We'd all do the same if we were you, and no one will judge you."

"He says it's because he has an extremely important meeting with some Chinese investors," Rivka said. "But that's a big fat lie. He could reschedule it. He just wants to get out of here, that's all. There's no way the engines can be fixed. They'll announce it soon."

"Oh. I hope that's not true," said Miriam.

Rivka didn't seem to hear her. "They came to get him last night to tell him the ship was on fire. And the first thing he did was to call for a *helicopter.*" She stabbed a bony finger at the table. "This is *his ship*! He's responsible for it! For all of you!"

"But what can he do for us, really?"

"Stay here and suffer with the rest of us!"

Miriam was tempted to put her hand on Rivka's to soothe her, but she was starting to feel angry at Larry herself.

"There's a meeting with the captain and officers later this morning," Rivka said. "Would you do me a favor, Miriam? Would you come with me? If I have to face Larry alone right now, I might kill him. Apparently the meeting is in a place called the 'war room,' which strikes me as appropriate."

"I'd be happy to go with you," said Miriam.

She couldn't imagine what had changed overnight, why Rivka

was treating her all of a sudden as a necessary ally, a confidante, even. For the first time ever, she almost liked Rivka for her staunch horror at her husband's entitled defection from his own crippled ship. She remembered with disgust how Larry had herded her and Sasha out of the bridge last night, his hand like a sharp claw on her shoulder, the way he'd yelled at the bridge crew when it clearly wasn't their fault. It made her sad, more than anything else, to see him behave that way, a man she'd liked and trusted for so many years. And it also made her feel queasy, that this was the person who had sustained the Sabra Quartet, provided the bulk of their livelihood and supported their performance career. She hated having to be beholden to such a jerk, having her outrage tempered by ancient loyalty and gratitude. Larry probably saw the Sabra as a tax deduction, a worthy cause to offset all the terrible things he did to have all that money. Well, the quartet was getting too old to play anymore. After their retirement, they could have nothing to do with Larry Weiss, ever again. Small comfort, but she'd take it.

chapter sixteen

The galley air was thick and sour, even though all of the ship's doors and windows had been opened to let air circulate through the lower decks. Christine could feel occasional hot burps from outside permeate the inner crevices of the ship. It was no hotter today than yesterday or the day before. It was the lack of air-conditioning that felt strange, one more dubious luxury she had acclimated to in a few short days. In Maine, almost no one had it or needed it. Now, she felt its absence acutely as she stood at the prep counter, making cheese sandwiches. The cheese was sweating in the heat, half melted. The tomatoes and cucumbers were limp. It was a big comedown from the usual midday feast.

Working alongside her was a young married couple, Camille and Lester, who'd grown up together in a small village in the Philippines. Over the course of slapping hundreds of slices of cheese between hundreds of slices of bread, Christine learned that this was their first cruise working together in all their years with Cabaret, four for her, five for him. "So at least we're together," said Camille. She was a short, dark, skinny girl with a round face, glasses, and heavy straight black bangs. She looked like a teenager to Christine, but she must have been at least in her mid-twenties.

Lester had small, darting eyes, a thick scar running down one cheek, and an angular, anvil-shaped head. His piratical looks were, Christine had realized within two minutes of talking to him, completely at odds with his personality.

"It would be terrible to be separated right now," he was saying in a gentle, thoughtful voice. He was almost in tears, imagining this hypothetical separation from his wife. "Especially if she was the one stuck here."

Camille put a latex-gloved hand on his shoulder. Lester covered her hand with his own latex-gloved one.

Christine looked up as Mick appeared by her side, handing out drinks. "You have to keep drinking," he said, passing her a bottle of iced tea, still somewhat cold. "It's hot down here, especially if you're not used to it."

"Thank you," she said, blowing a lock of hair out of her face with a sideways grimace.

All morning, she had been trying to square this competent, thoughtful, caring man with the drunk meathead who'd hit on the waitress in the hotel bar, the showoff at the captain's table dinner. He didn't seem like the same guy at all. He had brought her into the galley crew effortlessly, without making her feel awkward or intimating to everyone that she was some sort of princess, slumming it.

When the sandwiches were done and stacked on a tray to be brought upstairs, Christine took off her latex gloves, scooped out a cupful of coffee from the pot she'd left to steep, and headed out of the galley to her cabin.

"This might be the weirdest coffee you'll ever drink," she announced, opening the door.

There was no answer. The lump in Valerie's bed was, Christine assumed, Valerie herself, still sleeping, so she set the cup on their shared nightstand. Valerie groaned and sat up. "What time is it? What's happening? Did they get the power back on yet? It's so hot in here."

"No power yet," said Christine. "But coffee."

"Thank you." Valerie picked up the cup, took a sip. "Is everyone freaking out? Are we getting rescued?"

"I don't know. Half the crew walked out last night just before the engine fire. They didn't set it, I don't think, but they've taken over the buffet galley and set up camp on the main deck."

"Holy fuck," said Valerie, coming instantly awake. "You're kidding, right?"

"No. It's true. They're on strike. They're trying to negotiate with the owner to get their jobs back, but on better terms. The rich guy we met the other night at the captain's table dinner, remember?"

"Okay," said Valerie. "I need to go and talk to them right now." She downed the rest of her coffee and leapt from her bed, went into the bathroom and closed the door.

"Don't use the toilet," Christine called. "We can't flush it."

The door opened. "Wait, what?"

From her pocket, Christine took a wad of small yellow plastic sacks with biohazard markings on them and gave them to Valerie. "Bio-bags," she said. "Crewmembers were handing them out earlier. We're supposed to leave the full ones in our bathroom, and they'll collect them."

"This sucks," Valerie muttered as she closed the door again.

"Also," said Christine when Valerie emerged looking grim, "no showers."

"No showers." Valerie stared at Christine. "When are they going to fix it?"

"I don't know," said Christine.

Valerie slid a cotton dress over her head, stuck her feet into sandals, and picked up her notebook on her way out the door. "I hope I can remember how to take notes by hand."

*

The ship felt as if it were set into a block of concrete, no motion anywhere, nothing but flat sea and hard sky. Miriam was sweating from every pore. The back of her neck felt swaddled in an electric blanket. Rivka clutched her arm as they went along the catwalk toward the bridge.

"Good," Rivka said into her ear as they stepped into a small room off the bridge, "Larry's not here yet."

The so-called war room was empty except for Captain Jack and two senior officers, who stood poring over a vast oceanic map on the table. Two younger men in lower-ranking uniforms stood uneasily behind them. It was a small room, just a teak-lined cubbyhole really. Behind the men, on a long countertop, was an array of blank computer screens and instrument panels, now defunct.

The officers didn't notice the two old women, which was just as well. Miriam could read music and words and land maps, but not ocean maps. She stared at the unfurled paper with its longitudinal and latitudinal lines, the huge expanse of blue covered with numbers and dots, thinking wistfully about her daughter, her son, her grandchildren. She wondered how Isaac was doing. She'd left him in the shade on the pool deck with Jakov, who was feeling queasy and bilious in the heat. Sasha was still down in the engine room, but what he was doing down there was a mystery, since the engines were, as far as anyone knew, completely kaput.

Larry Weiss entered, flanked by two more senior officers. He stood by the window with his arms crossed high on his chest, his legs apart, ignoring his wife, who ignored him back. Miriam could feel them both bristling. The brightly sunlit little room seemed as crowded and full of faces as a rush-hour subway car.

"Hello, everyone," said the captain. He looked unruffled, almost relaxed, unlike the rest of them. His gaze slid past Miriam. "First things first: Jim, how's it going down there?"

"No luck with the engines," said a strapping young man with a crew cut. "But my guys are on it. They'll keep working till we get back to port."

"What's the backup generator situation?"

"We've got bridge communication, the PA system, and sat phones, plus the shipwide network of emergency lighting, but that's about it." Jim had a hangdog expression, as if this were his own personal fault. "That means no AC, no vacuum pumps for the plumbing, and no refrigeration or propulsion."

"So we have basic communication capabilities and limited light-ing, but nothing else," said the captain.

"That's correct, sir," said Jim.

No one looked at Larry Weiss.

"Tom," said the captain, turning to another young man on whose uniform the clusters of insignia and brass appeared to be second only to the captain's, "when can we expect to be hauled out of here?"

"Cabaret is sending tugboats, but they're still days away. HQ is looking into sending additional supplies and water if we need them."

"An airdrop," said the captain. "Okay. No power, no tugs yet, lim-ited food and water. Elhadji, what's the weather look like out here?"

"Clear skies all week," said one of the lower-ranking men behind the captain. "Fingers crossed."

"Crossed fingers won't save us in a storm," said the captain. "Chen, are we set with the lifeboats? Manual winches good to go?"

"Yes, Captain," said a younger officer. "And we'll organize another muster drill this afternoon."

Although Miriam always wanted to know the worst, the men-tion of lifeboats was frightening. Rivka's fingers had been squeezing her upper arm so hard it almost hurt.

"Good," said the captain. "Phil, what's the report on the gal-leys? How's morale?"

"Chef Laurens is very sick," said a deep-voiced officer. "But Chefs Mick and Kenji have taken over in the main galley. Tonight they're planning to do a cookout on the pool deck. We'll have drinks and music, if possible. We want to keep people happy."

"Lots of booze," said the captain. "Keep it flowing. But not too much. We don't want any man-overboard situations." It was evi-dently meant as a dark joke, but no one laughed. "And also, keep those bio-bags in circulation, make sure they use 'em, otherwise this boat's going to stink like a barnyard."

"Aye-aye, sir," said Phil. "My team is on it."

"Now," said the captain, straightening up and crossing his arms. Miriam didn't know a thing about the formalities of nautical command, but the captain's dramatic show of authority seemed intended to impress Larry Weiss. "We have another situation to add to the engine and generator failures. Eric, why don't you brief us on the latest with this illness we've been seeing? Chef Laurens isn't the only one, is he?"

"The medic says it's norovirus," said a bald senior officer with a mournful face. "About eighteen, twenty people are pretty damned sick already. It's fairly common, as we all know, especially on cruise ships. And there's no real way to treat it, you just quarantine the patients and let it run its course. But it's gonna be hard to keep things sterilized with no plumbing and limited water. This bug tends to spread pretty fast in the best of conditions."

Everyone in the room looked unhappy, including Larry. Clearly this was news to most of them.

"We've established a clinic on the promenade deck," Eric was saying. "It's the best we can do for now. And we're going to need all the hands we can get." He said this to the captain, not challenging him, but implying a question.

"Well, about that," said the captain. He hesitated, not with uncertainty, Miriam thought, but for effect. He looked directly at Larry. "As most of you know, right before the fire, we had a situation in which about half of the crew walked out."

"Yes, Captain," said Larry with a hint of annoyance. "I'm well aware of the situation."

"Then you know they've set up camp on the main deck. And they seem to have taken over the buffet galley as well, at least until Cabaret agrees to reinstate their contracts, in which case they would be willing to resume their duties."

"Bullshit," said Larry. "It's a publicity stunt. I'm not reinstating any contracts. I don't even have the authority to do that without approval from the CEO of the company and the board of directors. Honestly, this is outrageous. Criminal, in fact."

"Mr. Weiss," said the captain with elaborate courtesy. "Perhaps if you just agreed to have a conversation with the leaders of this protest."

"No way," said Larry. "Absolutely not. First of all, I don't negotiate with terrorists. And second of all, how do we know they didn't set the fire themselves? Do we know that?"

Captain Jack seemed frustrated, Miriam thought, which made sense, since he clearly couldn't dictate the workers' terms, couldn't do anything but defer to Larry. "Well, it's critical to the well-being of this ship that we get them back to their stations, in uniform, as soon as possible. Otherwise our situation could disintegrate further."

"Sorry," said Larry Weiss without looking at all sorry. "You can let them rot or throw them overboard. I don't give a fuck what happens to them."

Miriam almost gasped aloud. Rivka's grip was cutting off the circulation in her arm.

"Anyway," said Larry, "what I want to know is, why the hell don't we have power? Where is the backup engine?"

"With all due respect, sir," said the captain with cautious geniality. "The company decided to use the space for extra cabins instead. Better for revenue, that was the rationale."

"Well," said Larry, "that should never have happened." He looked around the room for someone to blame. But since there clearly wasn't anyone, he changed tack. "Well, luckily I've arranged for a military helicopter to come this evening. It can only make one trip, and it can only take limited weight. I'm airlifting the executive chef out, he's dangerously sick and he needs a hospital."

"My hero," muttered Rivka.

"My wife and I will be leaving the ship as well," he was saying. "So you all will just have to sit tight and wait for the tugboats to arrive."

"I'm not going," Rivka said. "I'm staying here with the people whose lives are *your* responsibility."

"No," said Larry. "You're coming with me."

"No, I am not," said Rivka. "I'm staying right here, and you should too. This is *your* fault. *You* canceled their contracts. *You* wouldn't pay for backup engines. And now you're ditching the ship?"

Everyone in the room, including Miriam, stared at her.

"Okay," said the captain. "Meeting dismissed. Except Elhadji and Chen, I need you two for further instructions."

Rivka marched out and along the catwalk. Miriam hurried after her.

"I want the whole quartet to move up to my quarters," Rivka said as she hustled along. "All four of you, as soon as Larry's off the boat. I've got room, no sense wasting it."

"Thank you," said Miriam, matching her stride.

"No," said Rivka. "It's for me. I want company. You're doing this as a favor to me."

"Is a helicopter really coming to get him?"

"If Larry wants a helicopter, he'll get one." They started down the stairs. "And a new wife. Goddamn it, I'm thirsty."

*

The sun hit their faces with a hot blast as Christine and Valerie emerged from the stairwell and out onto the expansive main deck. It was the lowest and largest outdoor deck on the ship, and from it, the higher decks rose in a terraced block. At some point during the night or early morning, the aft section of the main deck had been converted into a makeshift camp. Corners of bedsheets had been tied to high railings and awnings in taut rectangles to make ceilings for shade. Bunk mattresses were lined up underneath, each made with sheets tucked in just so, pillows plumped, cotton blankets folded at the foot, everything crisp, orderly. So this was what happened when a bunch of room stewards went on strike and set up a tent village, Christine thought. It was all so impeccable. The crisp military neatness was at odds with the mood among the crowd on deck, young workers out of uniform, wearing their own clothes, lounging on deck chairs, at ease for once. They were quiet, seemingly relaxed. At first glance, they could have been a group of young passengers, enjoying a sunny morning on a cruise. But a pall hung over them like the smoke from last night's fire, and on closer look, the casualness of their postures seemed forced, provisional. Their faces were tense and alert. Their voices carried to Christine as she hesitated by the stairwell doorway. She heard several foreign languages at once, for the first time since she'd come on board, of which she recognized only Spanish.

Valerie left Christine's side and inserted herself among them, claiming an empty deck chair in a circle of young women. Perched on the edge of the chair, she eased her notebook from her bag and opened it discreetly, scratching with her pen on a blank page to make sure it worked as she asked a question, listened to the answer. Christine watched from the doorway as Valerie began writing quickly, her usual chaotic discontent concentrated into one hard knot of purpose. The women seemed eager to have someone to talk to, someone who appeared to be on their side.

Christine thought of Lester and Camille below in the galley, how purposeful and sure they'd seemed to her. In contrast, these kids—as Christine thought of them, since most of them seemed well under thirty—looked defiant on the surface and nervous and scared underneath, unsure of everything. This was clearly not an ideological movement, politicized and telegraphed to a larger world. They seemed more like a provisional, loosely knit faction of strangers, bound by desperation and need. Christine felt uneasy, standing there where she didn't belong, watching, with nothing to offer them but silent compassion.

The young woman Valerie had been talking to stood up and led Valerie over to another group, offering her a seat with them. One member of the group seemed already to know her: a wiry, striking, Hispanic-looking young woman Christine didn't recognize. She started talking rapidly to Valerie, watching her intensely as Valerie wrote everything down, almost reading over her shoulder. Christine guessed this might be the same angry young female chef with the masculine-sounding name Valerie had interviewed a few days earlier. Christine was too far away to hear what they were saying, but she saw from the woman's body language and the way the others seemed to coalesce around her, paying her close and respectful attention, that she was one of the leaders of the group.

Valerie buzzed back over to Christine. "They're not giving in," she said with quiet excitement. "Not until Larry Weiss agrees to negotiate with them. He's refusing to even talk to them, so they're at an impasse. I'm going to find this rich asshole and try to get a statement from him, anything I can use."

"You're getting involved?" Christine wanted to caution Valerie to leave this alone, but she knew it was useless. This was her job.

"Are you kidding?" said Valerie. "I have a frontline scoop on the first-ever official walkout on a cruise ship. Of course I'm getting involved! Want to come with me?"

"No thanks," said Christine, feeling her old discomfort with the more predatory, brazen aspects of journalism. She left Valerie to her interviews and headed back to the galley, back into the flow of work again, back where she belonged.

*

When the emergency blasts sounded, one short followed by one long, Miriam was sitting in Isaac and Jakov's cabin with Jakov, who wasn't feeling well. Miriam suspected that he was suffering from heart trouble. He had been diagnosed with a bad heart several years before, and he'd been eating nothing but meat and cheese and buttery pastries for days.

"Do I have to go too?" he said as the instructions to go to their muster stations came over the PA system. "I don't think I can stand up."

"You stay here. I'll say you're sick and you went to the last one. Remember your muster station number?"

"Eight!"

The quartet had attended so many muster drills on so many cruise ships over the years, they could all put on life jackets automatically by now. Strapping hers on, Miriam made her way down to the assembly deck. Days ago, when they were still docked in Long Beach, the first muster drill had been festive, full of laughter and cheering. This time the mood was more grim. Miriam found Sasha and Isaac already wearing their life jackets, standing by the railing as their station leader took roll call and marked each name and cabin number off a list on a clipboard. The forty or so people assigned to Miriam's lifeboat stood in a ragged, sticky mass. No one laughed or cheered. Several people tugged at their life jacket straps as if they suspected they were defective. Others peered with fretful skepticism over the railing at their lifeboat as if assessing its seaworthiness as well as the likelihood that they'd actually have to get in it.

When Jakov's name was called, Miriam said, "He's sick. He couldn't make it."

The young deck officer, an Asian boy in an orange safety vest, scowled at her as if Jakov's absence were somehow her fault. "Everyone has to attend muster drills, ma'am," he said with frosty admonishment.

"He can hardly stand up," said Miriam. She heard an edge in her own voice. "He knows where to go and how to put on a vest."

The officer ignored this and went on calling names.

"What a putz," muttered Isaac in Miriam's ear.

She was too stricken to laugh.

After lunch service was over, Mick left the galley and went down to his tiny cabin. He stripped off his clothes and wet himself thoroughly in a forbidden trickle in the shower, then turned off the water and lathered his hair and soaped and scrubbed his entire body. He rinsed off quickly, dried himself with a rough towel, put on a clean T-shirt and pair of checked pants, then his chef's whites from the morning, and headed back to work. In the crew lounge, the ragtag members of his small galley crew had put together a hearty but sensibly expedient staff meal of whatever odds and ends were most likely to go bad first: day-old loaves of bread and a few ripe soft cheeses, kiwifruit and raspberries on the edge of spoiling, flats of smoked trout and salmon that had been opened already. The crewmembers were spread around the tables, popping open cans of cola and bottles of tea, eating and drinking ravenously and quickly, since they weren't sure when their next meal would be.

Mick had never been in the crew lounge during the daytime. Sunlight filtered in through small high windows to reveal a shabby little foxhole, institutional-looking, with scuffed linoleum floors dusted with cigarette ash, greasy particleboard bar, smeared laminated tabletops. At night, in the glow of electric candles, it had felt almost romantic in here, certainly cozy, sitting elbow to elbow with his crewmates, getting drunk to loud music. Now it reminded Mick of a social room in a low-security prison. He felt a burst of anger, but at whom, he wasn't sure. The cruise line? Consuelo? Bad luck? It felt older, deeper somehow. Maybe it was Suzanne, or his father. Maybe it was himself.

Mick sat alone and ate in silence, listening to the others talking amongst themselves. They were speculating about the crew who'd walked out, most of them with scorn that was nonetheless, Mick sensed, tinged with reluctant envy. We have to keep it together, he thought, glancing around. Over the years, he had heard stories from other crewmembers of minor disasters on cruise ships, engine fires, shipwide viruses, people falling overboard, ships stranded and floating without power for four or five days, food and water shortages. But the passengers were what worried him the most. Invariably, whenever things went bad, they turned into a bunch of angry, abusive, hysterical toddlers en masse, demanding immediate solutions from the overworked crew, making their lives a living hell. What was going to happen with half the crew already refusing to work? This was going to be a nightmare.

He glanced over at Christine. She was sitting with three young crewmembers, eating as fast as the rest of his crew, swilling iced tea and looking very American and out of place. She could have stayed upstairs, where she would have been taken care of, but instead she was down here in the hot galley with a motley bunch of cooks. And she looked unperturbed about it, relieved even. He felt a half-reluctant sense of kinship. This was exactly what he would have done in her place.

When they finished lunch and went back to the galley, Kenji was waiting for them. "Chef Laurens is very sick," he told Mick with his usual sangfroid. "He's in the infirmary. I just came from seeing him. He's going to leave the ship soon, a helicopter is coming, he needs a hospital."

Mick stared at Kenji for a few seconds. Laurens was gone. No more shot at a job in Amsterdam. It was done, finished. Consuelo had scuttled his chances, and the engine fire had sunk them along with whatever stomach virus Laurens had caught. Oh well.

"So it's just you and me then," he said to Kenji.

"I guess so," Kenji said. He quirked an eyebrow. "Your girl last night. She took a lot of people with her. They're not working anymore. And Chef Jean-Luc told me to go fuck myself, he's not working either."

"Fuck Jean-Luc back," said Mick. He had never liked that snooty asshole anyway. "And Consuelo's not 'my girl.'"

Kenji flashed him a sympathetic look and rested a fist on his shoulder. For him, Mick thought, this might have been the equivalent of a bear hug. "What are we doing for dinner, Chef?"

"Ceviche, grilled meat. We'll use the braziers, cook on deck. We need to eat this stuff now before it goes bad."

"Sounds good."

While Kenji went off to direct the kids on the meat crew, Mick worked alone, salvaging the fish that was still edible, mixing it with citrus juice, minced red onion, and cilantro. He splashed lime juice a little too liberally in the bowl and looked up, half expecting Laurens to be hovering with an attitude of faint but chilly disapproval, questioning his decisions, frowning. But there was no one there.

He set the ceviche to steep in the still-cool walk-in. When he came out again, Jean-Luc and Paolo were standing by his station, arms folded. They weren't wearing their whites. He hadn't seen either of them since the previous night.

"Hey," said Jean-Luc, chin set. "Mick."

"What do you guys want?" Mick said.

Paolo gave a small bow; he was harmless, a diva. "Some meat," he said. "And one of the braziers. We're cooking on the main deck."

"Why not on the pool deck with the rest of us?" Mick was aware of Kenji and the rest of his crew around him, watching this scene as they went on working. "It would be a lot easier that way."

Jean-Luc made a clucking sound, shook his head. "I thought you had some balls, man. I thought you sympathized with us even if you didn't join us. But I was wrong. You are Laurens's puppy dog, just like Kenji."

Paolo sniggered. Mick could feel the back of his neck getting hot. He didn't look at Kenji, but he could feel his neutral, interested gaze from across the galley. Down the counter, Mick was aware of Christine listening too.

"Take what you need and get out of my kitchen," he said.

"Thank you, Chef," Paolo sang out. He turned to grab a platter of meat, but Jean-Luc held him back.

"One minute," said Jean-Luc. "Hey, Mick. What do you think is going to happen to us when we get to land? Have you thought about what Cabaret will do to us, to make all this go away? I'll tell you what. They are going to blame us for the fire, the sickness of Laurens, everything. They are going to prosecute us for sabotage, make us pay for the damages out of our own pockets. For something we didn't do! They are even talking about throwing us in jail."

"Bullshit," said Mick. The suspicion he'd had the night before bloomed again anew. "How do I know you didn't start the fire, anyway? Poison Laurens?"

"Of course we didn't do that," said Jean-Luc. "And you are being naive. The owner of the company is on board, you know. Everything I said? It comes straight from him, we heard this a little while ago. Cabaret will crush us. That's what he said. And who do you think is going to be stuck with the bill, eh? That's how it works. When there is trouble, when there is a disaster, *we* are the ones who pay."

Mick looked around the galley. Kenji caught his eye and moved one shoulder, barely, as if to say, *I'm not getting involved in this.*

"So I want to ask you, all of you," Jean-Luc was saying. "What are you going to do about it? Are you going to stand there and say nothing while your fellow workers are locked up like criminals? Do you really think they will let you keep your jobs for not standing with us? Of course not. You will all be fired, just like the rest of us. Heads will roll, man. This whole fucking ship. And if we don't fight back now, those heads will be ours. All of ours."

Mick could feel the anger coming off Jean-Luc in waves along with the rank smell of his sweat. The room was quiet and tense.

Christine's voice broke the silence, clear and firm. "We have a boat full of people here waiting to get rescued. How is everyone going to eat if you all walk out? I'm on your side, I'm sure we all are, but that doesn't mean we're going to let people go hungry."

"Who is this?" Jean-Luc said to Mick. "She's not one of us."

"I'm a passenger," said Christine before Mick could answer. "And look, I know you guys are scared, but I think you're over-reacting. Even if what you say is true, even if Cabaret is going to come after you when you get back, there are journalists on board, like my friend Valerie, who I'm sure you've talked with, who can help you get the truth out. You obviously didn't do anything. This is Cabaret's fault for mistreating its workers and not having proper safety measures in place in case of an emergency. But honestly, all that is going to be much harder to sell if you start acting hostilely toward the passengers. That just makes it look like you have something to hide. It makes you look guilty as well as malicious."

"She's right," Mick said, silently thanking her. "The passengers haven't done anything to you, right? So if we want to keep working, that's our fucking choice. And we all need to stick together now. We're all in trouble."

Jean-Luc's neck puffed slightly. Then he shrugged. "Whatever. *Allons-y,* Paolo. Let's get out of here."

They ducked out of the galley, each carrying a platter stacked high with raw meat, Mick heard Jean-Luc mutter, *"Poutain de merde."*

He looked around at his crew. "Everybody good?" They nodded. "Good," he said. "All right. We need to start firing steaks in an hour. A couple of people can go up to get those grills going with Chef Kenji. The rest of you, let's finish the meat prep."

There was a reassuring chorus of "Yes, Chef" as they all resumed their tasks. After Kenji had gone off with his grill crew, Mick moved down the counter and stood next to Christine, who was scooping ground meat out of a large bowl and forming patties with it. "Thanks for saying that, earlier," he said. "If you keep helping me out like that, I might have to promote you."

"That would be great," said Christine. "I want a raise, too. How do these burgers look?"

"A little big," said Mick, reaching into the bowl. "About this size is better."

They worked side by side forming burgers, trimming chops, making a dry rub for the ribs. Mick felt a strange sense of ease working with her, almost as if this were all natural, as if they were getting ready for a Sunday barbecue in the backyard instead of throwing together a meal of the most perishable stores for a few hundred scared people on a dead ship in the middle of the ocean.

At one point, more passengers trickled into the galley to volunteer for kitchen duty: Dora and John, an elderly black couple in matching baggy white T-shirts and tracksuit pants; and Freddie, a middle-aged white woman with a frizzy fuchsia-and-silver mane and a creased, bronzed face. "I cooked in my kids' cafeteria," she announced in a husky smoker's voice. Dora was slightly stooped from the weight of her shelf-like chest, and big glasses hid almost half of her face. John looked even older than his wife; his grizzled face shone with sweat. But they all three seemed game and willing, despite the heat, so Mick gave them clean whites and put them to work.

When everything was ready for service, he sent a few of his crew ahead with tongs and grill tools to coordinate with Sidney and whatever was left of his service team, sent others to run trays of hamburger buns and condiments, ceviche and salads to the pool deck upstairs, and then climbed up with Christine, Kenji, Lester, and Camille, each of them carrying a platter.

The sun had set and the ship rested on a flat field of water whose edges disappeared into the darkening horizon all around it, just turning violet, pure, without a hint of a sunset. The pool shimmered in the light from the tiki torches, its surface still and undisturbed. A crowd of younger passengers had gathered by the bar, their faces glowing in the light from the tiki flames, looking weirdly carefree in their summer camp outfits and tousled hair and tans. They looked as if they were at an actual party. Mick recognized Trevor behind the bar, kittenish as always, but instead of a Cabaret uniform he wore a tight black short-sleeved shirt unbuttoned to his clavicle, and a white pukka necklace to show off his brown chest. His hair was gelled into little ringlets. He could have been on his way to a Caribbean beach nightclub. Standing with him behind the bar was that friend of Christine's, the writer who'd interviewed Consuelo. She was splashing various liquors into plastic cups, stirring mixers into them, garnishing them haphazardly, and handing them out to one and all, taking slugs of her own drink all the while.

Mick and Christine set the meat down next to one of the smoking braziers while Lester and Camille and Kenji took the other. The third grill was missing; Jean-Luc and Paolo must have moved it down to the main deck for the walkouts to use.

"Your friend," said Mick to Christine as they slapped their steaks onto the smoking grill, "seems to be our new bartender."

"Tell Valerie to make me a nice strong vodka," said Christine. She looked good with her sleeves rolled up, her hair pinned back, a pair of tongs in her hand. Too bad she was married, and a passenger, thought Mick. Really too bad.

"What are you drinking?" he called over to Lester and Camille, who were pouring more charcoal briquettes from bags into the other grill.

"Maybe a beer?" said Lester.

"Two beers, please," said Camille. "Thank you, Chef."

"Beer," Kenji said as he passed by with a hotel pan full of marinating chicken parts.

Mick moved through the crowd. At the bar, he waited for Christine's friend Valerie to finish serving a guy in shorts and a T-shirt, smoking a cigarette. Mick envied him. His own pack was still in his jacket in his galley locker. He considered bumming one, but despite everything, he was still on duty.

He caught Trevor's eye as he spun a martini shaker. "Hey. Why aren't you down with the rest of your friends?"

"Tips," Trevor said with a smirk.

"Me too," said Valerie, joining in.

"Did Alexei and Natalya quit?" Mick asked.

"They *started* the whole thing," said Valerie. Her eyes were bright behind her glasses. "They were the leaders. Along with Consuelo and two other Mexicans. You're Mick, right? Didn't she used to work for you?"

"Wait. So half the crew quit?" asked the guy in the shorts with the cigarette before Mick could answer. "Right at the same time as the fire started?"

"They told me they didn't start the fire," said Valerie. "If that's what you're thinking."

"They told me that too," said Mick skeptically.

"Where are they all now?" asked the shorts-wearing guy.

"Down on the main deck, having their own party," said Trevor. "Getting some fresh air."

"How many people are down there?"

"Fifty maybe," said Trevor, looking directly at Mick. "Sixty, seventy, something like that. More joined today."

"I'm calling it Occupy Main Deck. Like Occupy Wall Street," said Valerie. "Did you have any Occupy stuff where you're from?"

"We have TV news. America is very entertaining."

"I talked to them earlier. Then I tried to get the rich-guy owner of Cabaret who's on board to negotiate with them, but he totally shut me. He threatened to have them all arrested for sabotage. He's a prick." She turned to Mick. "What are you drinking?"

"Two vodkas, three beers. One vodka is for your friend Christine."

"Where is she?" Valerie asked.

"At the grill over there."

"Excellent," she said. She handed him the drinks one by one, her eyes locked on his. Out of nowhere, an electric-eel jolt zinged his groin and shocked him. He remembered his vow to himself to get laid on this cruise. God, that had been a million years ago, on the docks at Long Beach. "I'll trade you all this booze for a rare steak. I like it bloody."

"Sure," he said, turning around quickly.

Holding the drinks to his chest, he squirmed his way through the crowd. People thronged the grills, drawn to the smoke and the smell of meat. The band near the pool was playing a rollicking gypsy tune Mick recognized from childhood. Hearing an accordion among the horns, he looked over and saw Kimmi, of all people, squeezing the bellows and working the keys like an old beer-hall pro.

After he distributed the beers, he handed Christine her vodka. She knocked her plastic cup against his in a sideways toast and took a slug. "Thanks," she said. "I needed this."

"Why aren't you over there? If I were a passenger, I'd be getting drunk with that crowd."

"I'm not good at being a passenger. Doing nothing."

"I thought that was the point of cruises. Doing nothing."

"That's not so good for me," she said. "If I don't stay busy, I think too much, and if I think too much . . ."

She fell silent. They worked side by side without speaking for a while, flipping hot steaks onto a platter, slapping fresh raw ones with a sizzle onto the hot grill.

"This way, I can drink while I work and have the best of both worlds," said Christine. She had evidently been following her own train of thought.

"I know what you mean," said Mick, going along with it. "Cheers to that."

She laughed, a rich chuckle. He grinned at her and felt a spark ignite in the air between them. She clenched her jaw and looked down at the steaks, and he remembered again, with even more regret this time, that she was married. Maybe she had felt that spark just now too. And maybe he was flattering himself.

A crackling squawk came from above. Everyone looked up to see a young deck officer in a white uniform and cap standing on the catwalk, shouting through a megaphone. "Everybody, a helicopter is approaching. For your safety, we need you to please clear the aft deck. That's the back. Please move to the front of the ship, everyone."

Mick heard the chopper before he saw it, ratcheting its way over the ocean, coming low out of the twilit sky. Bridge officers appeared on the pool deck and began herding everyone forward. The crowd streamed toward the railing, chattering, with their drinks and plates of food, as the chopper made a downward arc with a stuttering roar and came to a stop, hovering with a slight wobble thirty feet above the decking outside the solarium. The gigantic, whirring blades washed the top decks of the ship with gusts of downdraft. Mick closed the hood of the brazier to keep ashes from flying everywhere while his crew scurried around, securing paper plates and cups and napkins.

Slowly, a large cage-like basket descended toward the decking, and Mick watched as two officers helped Laurens van Buyten into it. He was holding his stomach, looking weak and unstable. The basket was winched skyward. From the open door to the body of the helicopter, a pair of arms reached out and helped Laurens into the cabin, and he disappeared. The basket descended again, and when it hit the deck, a tall man Mick didn't recognize climbed into it and shook the hand of the captain. The basket was winched aloft a second time as the captain stepped back and gave a brief upward wave that was almost a salute. The second man vanished the same way Laurens had, through the door into the cabin, without even a glance down at all the people watching him go.

"Who is that?" Mick shouted to Christine over the roar.

"That's the owner!" Her upturned face glowed in the lights. Tendrils of hair flew around her head.

"The owner of the ship?"

"The owner of the ship! How do you not know that?"

"*Mi a fasz!*"

The Hungarian epithet sounded funny even to Mick's ears. They grinned at each other in the wind.

"Who was the first guy?" Christine shouted.

"My fucking boss!" Mick shouted back.

The helicopter rose slowly, pivoted to put its head down in a wide banking turn, and buzzed away like a giant dragonfly, back the way it had come. In its wake, there was a vast silence, a collective feeling of depressed letdown. As the winking lights receded toward the horizon and the sound of the engine faded, people trailed back to the pool, the buffet table, the tables and chairs. The band's instruments lay abandoned on lounge chairs. A group started to gather around the bar as before, but now the conversations were muted, the festivity dampened. Mick's crew drifted away, probably down to the main deck to join the walkout crew's party. Mick stayed with Christine at the grill. They worked side by side in silence, handing burgers and steaks to the few people who came up asking for them. No one seemed very hungry anymore.

Sparks from the brazier floated upward and twisted high into the darkening air with the smell of charred flesh. It was like a burnt offering to one of the ancient gods, thought Mick with a tipsy half-superstition, wishing those gods still existed. The atmosphere around the ship had been churned and disturbed by the helicopter, as if its coming and going over the horizon had made an invisible rip in the fabric of the sky that had sealed shut again behind it.

Looking out at the ocean's vast and wild void, Mick felt a deep sense of dread. They were completely alone out here.

part three

THE SONG
OF THE SEA

When Miriam stepped out onto the balcony to do her morning stretches, she was assaulted by the sunlight, even though it was still early. It was their fourth morning adrift without power or propulsion. There was no breeze. The air hung like a gauze curtain, trapping the heat against the water. She tried to take a deep breath as she touched her toes, but her lungs felt compressed by the heavy air. How was this the middle of the Pacific? It felt more like the inside of a coat closet. Behind her, in their bed, Sasha was still asleep, lying on his back naked, one arm flung upward on the pillows above his head, the other hugging his stomach. She envied him, being so deeply asleep. She felt wide awake and restless. Her entire body itched from prickly heat and lack of a shower.

The day of their expected arrival in Hawaii had come and gone, and since then everything, it seemed, had worsened. News had filtered from the bridge through the ship that one of the tugboats had had to turn back because of engine trouble, and another one had been sent out to join the first one, so the pair wouldn't arrive to tow the *Isabella* to land for at least two more days. The slower return journey would take five days, at least, which meant another week on board before they reached the Port of Long Beach again. Some cruise, thought Miriam.

On the plus side, Cabaret had promised an airdrop of supplies that afternoon. It was about time, because food and water were running low. The crew had rationed bottled water, two liters per person per day, but people helped themselves freely to alcohol, and no one tried to stop them. If they wanted to dehydrate themselves and stay blotto, that was apparently their business.

Meanwhile, the lower decks were fetid with the stench of overflowing toilets steeping in the heat, uncollected garbage, and rotting food, while the upper decks looked like a crowded tropical refugee camp. Almost fifty people were sick with norovirus, with more succumbing every day. The makeshift clinic on the promenade deck was crowded with stricken crew, passengers, and officers alike, all of them vomiting and feverish, racked with intestinal pain. Miriam felt terrible for them, being so miserably sick on top of everything else. Though the crew had managed to rig two of the toilets in the clinic with hoses and swimming-pool water for the sick people, everyone else was using the now-obligatory bio-bags. Miriam hated pooping into a plastic bag so much, she'd become severely constipated for the past three days in order to avoid it, and she knew she wasn't the only one.

The crewmembers who'd walked out on their jobs, those who weren't sick, were still camped out on the main deck. They stayed there day and night with nowhere else to go and, now that Larry had left the ship, no one to bargain with. They spent their unproductive futile protest in cruise-like activities: drinking, card games, sunbathing, playing guitars. Miriam felt a half-resentful pity for them, all those poor kids with no future and no chance of winning their jobs back. They were stuck here, just like everyone else, mired in frustration, anxiety, and helpless inaction. What good was any of it?

As for the crewmembers who'd stayed on the job, still wearing their now-rumpled and stained uniforms, they had no water or power to do laundry, wash dishes, mop, vacuum, or cook, but they tried stoically to keep things clean and orderly, serve three meals a day, presenting at least the appearance of dedication to their jobs. Since the tiny windowless crew cabins belowdecks were too airless and hot and reeking for habitation, most of them slept outside on the main deck in lounge chairs or on mattresses, side by side with the crew who had quit, and the passengers they were supposed to be serving. These various factions seemed to coexist peacefully, for now. That was the one advantage of the heat: it tamped down tempers, the tantrums and fights that never felt far from erupting, if only because it was just too hot to yell or throw things or punch anyone in the head. Also, everyone seemed united by one common purpose: to get the hell off the ship and back to land.

At least, Miriam thought with half-guilty relief, her own living conditions had improved. At Rivka's insistence, the whole quartet had moved into the owner's suite after Larry had left in the helicopter. Compared to their cabins far below, Rivka's suite was a palace. It sat in the middle of the bridge deck, spanning the width of the ship so there were windows and balconies on both sides, which created a cross-breeze whenever any air moved. The rooms were decorated in striped beige-and-cream wallpaper and fluffy white rugs over cool white-plank flooring. It was all very luxurious and bright, and Miriam felt grateful to be able to stay there, never mind that it was Rivka's fault that the Sabra was on the ship in the first place.

Jakov and Isaac had daybeds tucked into separate alcoves in the living room, and Sasha and Miriam got the smaller, unused second bedroom, with a balcony of its own and a queen-sized bed. Rivka had offered the room to Miriam and Isaac first, which required a lengthy explanation from Miriam that she and *Sasha* were a couple now, and forced Rivka to acknowledge, at long last, and with much disingenuous blinking and stated confusion on her part, that Isaac and Miriam had been divorced for at least twenty years. In the end, Rivka had acquiesced with a bemused skepticism that made Miriam want to slap her, but there it was.

As she crept quietly through the spacious living room out to the catwalk, Miriam heard Jakov groaning in his sleep on his daybed. He had a fever, pains in his chest, and a dry cough. It wasn't the norovirus; he'd had worsening heart trouble for years, which wasn't contagious, so he'd been spared the infirmary quarantine. But Miriam was worried about him. He seemed to be getting worse, like everything else around here.

She made her way down the stairs to the breakfast room, passing a few people sitting in the stairwell of the upper deck. More stood at railings, looking out at the morning sun on the ocean, while others lay sleeping in deck chairs under motionless white bedsheet ceilings. Unlike the military precision of the crew's camp, the passengers' cobbled-together tent city looked scruffy and ragtag, all sagging sheets and rumpled blankets. The passengers themselves looked little better, on the whole, their general mood seeming to hover between anxious waiting, festering outrage, and a collective paralysis of will, gone slack in the heat. People sprawled in underwear and T-shirts on mattresses, publicly asleep and half naked, vulnerable as homeless bums in doorways. Others wandered around aimlessly, looking wild-eyed, dazed, hair sticking up, Band-Aids stuck on various places, chests peeling, noses red from sunburn. Miriam's heart went out to them, so far from home, normally dignified and settled people with houses, grandchildren, histories, longtime careers and jobs they'd retired from or still had.

From the breakfast buffet room, she fetched a plastic cup of the food the kitchen crew had provided: raw oats and cut-up, overripe fruit, soaked overnight in water to make a half-fermented, pasty gruel, and ladled out of a large soup pot. They were calling it "muesli" in a feeble attempt to make it more appetizing, but it looked revolting.

Ascending to Rivka's suite out of the grimy chaos of the rest of the ship, Miriam felt the usual twinge of guilt that she got to live in luxury when so many others, some no younger than she was, had to sleep on deck chairs in the open air. What was worse, most of them had *paid* for this cruise. She had to remind herself again of all the lawsuits that would be filed when they got back to land, the millions of dollars in payouts Cabaret would have to make to these people for their many days of discomfort. From that perspective, it almost seemed worth it, but of course not entirely.

"Don't bother with that, I can't eat it," Jakov said, waving away the food as she held it out to him. He lay flat on his back on his couch in boxer shorts and undershirt.

"You need to eat something, Jakov," she said, lowering herself into the chair by his bed. He hadn't eaten anything in two days. "Even if it's just a couple of bites. You need strength to recover."

"What are you, my mother? I have no appetite! This might be a good thing." He patted his belly.

"Oh Jakov," she said. She wished there were enough water to give him a cool bath, ice to offer him to suck on; things she'd done for her children when they were feverish. But she didn't want to eat that stuff either, to be honest. He closed his eyes again, and she got up and carried the cup of food to the balcony off Rivka's bedroom. The door was open, and Isaac and Rivka sat looking out at the ocean. Miriam sat down beside them in an empty chair.

"How is Jakov?" Isaac asked, rousing himself.

"Not too well," said Miriam. "He won't eat. Does anyone want some breakfast?"

Rivka ignored her. Isaac took one look at the cup and looked away again without a word. Just to spite them both, Miriam forced herself to take a bite of the sweet, sticky gruel. It wasn't so bad once she got started. She was hungry.

"Where is Sasha?" Isaac asked, managing to infuse the question with pathos, jealousy, accusation, and genuine interest, all at once.

"Still asleep," said Miriam. "He lies awake all night. He wishes he could do something to help. But those engines down there aren't anything like the ones he learned how to fix in the war."

"The big hero," said Isaac.

"Well, he *is* a hero," said Miriam, possibly a little too defensively. "He wishes he could help save us."

"While we sit here like pashas," said Isaac.

She laughed. Isaac looked pleased, as if he had won something. He had always been able to make her laugh, even when they were fighting.

"And Larry, sitting in a hotel room in Honolulu," Rivka burst out. "Speaking of big heroes. I hope he chokes on a fishbone." She stared belligerently at Miriam and Isaac. "Do you know how much money he has? And Cabaret, do you know how much their yearly profits are? They could double everyone's salary, all the workers in the whole company—triple, quadruple, even—and not feel a thing. Do you know, just the other day, I heard Larry talking about how it isn't good for workers to be paid too much or be treated too well, because it makes them soft and lazy. He said that! Larry! My husband!"

"That's horrible," said Miriam, uneasily. Rivka's rage helped nothing, as far as Miriam could see. It just made everything worse, in fact. What was the point of dwelling on all this?

"He never used to be like this," she said. "He used to be the nicest guy I knew. Kind, generous, with a strong work ethic, and every other kind of ethic. How did he turn so corrupt? I don't think I realized what a terrible person he'd turned into until I saw him get into that helicopter. I'm finished with him now. That was it."

"He's been very generous to us, the Sabra Quartet," said Miriam with feeble and half-hearted loyalty. "For many years."

Rivka turned to look at Miriam. Her eyes glittered. "Do you want to know something else? This ship is a rusted piece of junk. They painted over the rust. You can see it! Just painted right over it. They cut so many corners it's a wonder this thing even floats."

Miriam felt Rivka wanting her to share in the outrage, to echo it back to her and draw it out of her even more so they could sit there in a hot, sticky web of it all day. She got up, too agitated to sit still any longer.

"I have to go," Miriam said, tossing her empty cup and spoon in a wastebasket for the crew to pick up when they came through. For all she knew, they were throwing it all into the ocean at this point. And who could blame them?

"Where to?" Isaac asked accusingly.

"I can't sit still," Miriam told him. "I think I'll wander around and see if I can help somehow."

"Write if you get work," said Isaac.

*

Christine was awake and lying in bed, looking out through the open balcony door at the dawn, when Valerie came in. Her eyes looked red-rimmed.

"Hey," said Christine. "Where were you all night?"

"On the main deck," said Valerie. She stood over Christine, panting gently, as if she'd just been sprinting. "I've been listening to the crew's stories, taking notes as fast as I can write. God, I hope I can do this justice. It feels so much bigger than one chapter of a book. The story of this cruise could be a whole book in itself." She paced around, restless, clicking her ballpoint pen, riffling the pages of her notebook. "The whole industry is so corrupt, it's almost hard to believe some of these things. Murders and rapes on ships, covered up. People disappearing, and falling overboard. The workers are basically owned by the company. They even tell them when they can go to the bathroom! These people have absolutely zero rights. No wonder they're striking. They have nothing left to lose."

Christine got out of bed and pulled on yesterday's grubby shorts, put her hair up in a ponytail, and rubbed some lotion on her face. "I'm off to work," she said. "You're on the night shift, I'm on the day shift."

Valerie laughed. "I hope your boss lets you take breaks. I hope he feeds you. The food that most cruise workers get is horrible. It's crap. While the passengers eat like lords and ladies."

"Well, now we're all eating crap together," said Christine. "I just hope there's enough to go around."

"I can't remember when I last ate anything." Valerie sat on her bed, opened her notebook, and began scribbling notes.

"You need to eat," said Christine.

"Yeah," said Valerie absently.

"Can I bring you some food?"

Valerie didn't answer. She didn't even look up as Christine walked out.

When she got to the galley, Mick was already there, his cheeks stubbled, dark hair standing up in tufts. No one else was around yet. He looked bleak and tired, but seemed to brighten as soon as she came in. He handed her a warm can of Coke. She popped it open and took a swig as they stood shoulder to shoulder, aiming their flashlights into the pathetically empty storeroom. For the first few nights, they had grilled whatever they could on the braziers. All the fragile perishables had been used up, along with the sturdier fresh food, the potatoes and onions, eggs, apples and carrots. Now, the oats and nuts were gone. They had plenty of rice and pasta and polenta, but no way to cook them. Yesterday, they had run out of bread after using up all the stacked cases of thawed frozen loaves.

"These cruise ships don't give you much extra," said Christine. "It's lucky there's an airdrop coming."

"How about raw cornmeal mush with sugar? There's maybe enough for two days. And after that, wheat flour mush with sugar."

"Well, there's plenty of sugar." They stared at the two enormous bags, unopened. "And oil," she added, looking at the three ten-gallon drums. "We can mix oil with sugar, I guess."

"With maraschino cherries," said Mick. "Two cases. I don't know why. We also have capers."

"Hey. There must be some rats on board, right? Don't all ships have them?"

"Rat tartare with capers," he said without missing a beat.

They had been flirting in the past couple of days, enjoying the easy attraction that fizzed between them as if it were their mutual reward for working so hard.

"The trick is to catch them," said Mick.

"I'm pretty sure I can think like a rat. I know I could eat one. I've eaten squirrel stew before, and it was actually pretty tasty. If it comes down to starving or eating a rat, it's not even a choice."

Mick's laughing eyes caught hers in the sharp light of the electric torches.

Their gaze held a moment too long, on purpose, before they went off to see about lunch.

An hour or so later, as they were putting together a sorry meal of scraps, Christine heard Valerie's voice coming from the gloom near the swinging doors.

"Christine. Where are you?"

"I'm over here," Christine called out.

She turned to see Valerie standing at the end of the prep station. "Come upstairs with me," she said. "There's a party going on, some people hanging out."

"Oh. I'm okay here," said Christine.

"Come on, you need some fresh air. Hey, Chef, can she take the day off?"

"She can do whatever she wants," said Mick, who was going through a box of spices at the end of the counter.

"Want to come with us, Chef? You look like you could use a drink."

"I have to make lunch," Mick said.

"What's on the menu today?"

"Irish tea crackers and peanut butter," he said.

"Mmm," she said, smacking her lips, flirting with him. "Sounds delicious."

Christine felt churlishly glad when Mick turned away from Valerie and moved down the counter.

chapter nineteen

Passing the open entryway to the bridge, Miriam caught sight of Kimmi sitting behind the steering console. She was swiveling her chair back and forth with one foot on the ground, the other tucked up underneath her hip, staring straight ahead through the windows, although there was nothing but the static shock of brightness outside. Two young crewmen in rumpled white uniforms stood on either side of the room, flanking her, looking out at the horizon.

"Nothing," Kimmi said, without turning her head as Miriam went in to stand next to her. "Not even a seagull. Gosh, it's empty out here."

"Where's the captain?" said Miriam.

"Sick," said one of the crewmen. "He's in the infirmary. Along with most of the bridge crew."

"It's norovirus," said the other crewman. "This thing is bad."

Miriam shook her head. "We're cursed," she said. "The fire, then this norovirus. And half the crew quit."

"Trouble comes in threes," said Kimmi somberly.

"I hope that means there won't be any more of it," said Miriam.

One of the young officers bestirred himself, looked across the bridge at the other one. "As long as there's no storm," he said. "As long as they get here in time."

Miriam felt a cold grip of dread in her chest. A storm would be very, very dangerous without propulsion or navigation. The *Isabella* would be helpless.

"So they're letting me hang out in this chair," said Kimmi.

"I'm keeping watch for any sign of life out there. That's my job right now."

When Kimmi turned, Miriam was shocked: her eye sockets were hollow, her heart-shaped face a puzzle of hard planes. Her lips looked painfully chapped, dusted with dried salt from the air.

"Have you seen anything?"

"Not one thing," said Kimmi. "No plane, no ship, nothing but floating garbage."

Miriam looked out with her. Far below, on every side, the ocean ran ceaselessly on, a vast, slow system with its own pulses and energy and no land to interrupt it for a thousand miles or more.

"At least the garbage gives us something to look at besides water," said Miriam.

Kimmi gave a small, dry laugh. "I'm glad you came in. Eduardo and Ivan and I have run out of things to say to each other. Right, guys?"

Miriam looked at the two young officers. The port one was short and dark and moonfaced, the starboard one tall and blond and long-faced. She recognized them, but only vaguely. "I'm Miriam, by the way," she told them. "I'm a violinist with the string quartet."

"Eduardo," said the tall fair one. "Safety officer."

"Ivan," said the short swarthy one. "Deck cadet."

"Last men standing," said Kimmi. "The senior officers are all sick, so these boys have the bridge, what's left of it."

"Maybe you should give yourselves promotions," said Miriam.

"Oh no," said Eduardo earnestly. "We can't do that."

"This is only my first year," said Ivan.

"They can't even joke about it, God bless 'em," said Kimmi. "It's no fun at all. They're fine with me sitting in the captain's chair and pretending I'm in charge, but they won't let me call them my staff captain and first officer. The guys on night watch are just as bad. Sticklers for protocol. Cabaret trains them to be as loyal as soldiers."

"Why are no other Cabaret ships coming to help us?" Miriam asked. "Or anyone?"

"There's no one else out here," said Ivan. "This California-to-

Hawaii route isn't well traveled, not by cruise ships or container ships or tankers, not even airplanes. Cabaret doesn't do this route very often. This cruise was special."

Miriam cleared her throat to steady her voice. "So why doesn't the U.S. Navy send a carrier ship to pick us all up? Why doesn't another Cabaret ship come and get us?"

Ivan and Eduardo exchanged a look, as if they were trying to gauge how much to reveal.

"I want the truth," said Miriam. "Please. I can take it."

"There's an old saying," said Eduardo. " 'The safest ship is the one you're already on.' "

" 'The safest ship is the one you're already on,' " Miriam repeated. "You mean it's dangerous to move people from one ship to another?"

"Very dangerous," said Ivan. "Hundreds of people, in the open ocean?"

"Not to mention expensive," said Eduardo. "That's the main thing, I'm sorry to say. In emergencies, they charge you ten times as much because they can get away with it. And the lawsuits if there were any accidents . . . which is highly possible, in fact it would be unusual if there weren't some accidents, given how many people we are and how perilous the maneuver would be. It's a different matter if there are only ten or twenty trained crew on a stranded ship and another one nearby, that's worth the odds. But Cabaret can't risk it for us, for all these reasons. We're much better off floating here until the tugs can come get us and tow us home."

"But what if a storm comes?" Miriam said. "What if we capsize?"

Ivan and Eduardo exchanged another look.

"That's why we have lifeboats," Kimmi said with bright assuredness. "But don't worry, we won't need them. The tugboats will come soon. For sure."

Miriam looked back at Eduardo. "When are they supposed to get here?"

"A day or more," said Eduardo.

"How long will it take them to tow us into port once they finally get here?"

"A while," said Eduardo. "Maybe five, six days."

"There is an airdrop of supplies coming today," said Kimmi. "On the plus side. Food and water and maybe engine parts, I don't know for sure."

"That is good news," Miriam said, hoping, for Sasha's sake, that the parts would come. "Is there anything I can do to help?"

"We're okay here," said Kimmi. "But you could try the infirmary."

"I will," said Miriam.

She left the three of them on the bridge, staring out together at the barren wasteland of water, and made her way down to the promenade deck. In the infirmary, she found the ship's medic, Mike Pruitt, whose brushy light-brown hair and wire-rimmed glasses made him look more like a pastor or a tax accountant than a doctor.

"How are things down here?" she asked him.

"Pretty bad," he said. His glasses were slightly fogged. He looked harried and out of his depth and apologetic. "And with norovirus, there's not much you can do for it, medically. Time, hydration, rest. Keep it contained. But on this scale, it's pretty intense. It's a bad one."

Miriam looked at all the dozens of deck chairs lined up against the inner wall of the promenade deck, a long row of field cots filled with people who were clearly suffering, some in stoic silence, some vocally. She heard sighs and groans of pain and muttered laments. Several people, pale and agitated, waited by the doors to the two bathrooms with working toilets, the only two on board. She felt nervous, being here, and frankly terrified of catching this awful thing herself.

"Can I do anything to help?" she asked.

"Try Flaminia," he said. "She might be able to think of something."

A couple of days ago, when the norovirus epidemic became serious, a retired nurse named Flaminia had come out of the crowd of passengers to offer her services. She was a glamorous seventyish Italian woman who seemed far more confident than Mike Pruitt.

She collected asthma inhalers, unused pain medications, antibiotics, and anti-diarrhetics from the crew and passengers, and was now rationing them to the patients who needed them the most.

Miriam found her in the little room off the grand hallway that had been turned into the makeshift dispensary.

"Antibiotics," said Flaminia, holding up a bottle as Miriam entered. "Look, here, how much is left in this bottle. They took half the course and then they stopped taking them. Very bad practice. Not that these are any use against this virus."

"I came to see if I could help you. I'm Miriam. I'm with the string quartet."

Flaminia gazed at her for a moment as if skeptically assessing her potential usefulness. "The restaurant crew brings water, the stewards help with cleaning," she said. "But maybe . . ."

"I have no nursing training, but I did raise two children," Miriam added.

"There is really very little we can do for them," said Flaminia. She added in a half whisper, "Three people already have died."

Miriam stared at her, horrorstruck. "People died?"

"Shhh," said Flaminia, putting a finger to her lips, glancing at the open door. "The crew doesn't want us to know. They're afraid of panic. They even tried to hide it from me, but how could they. I saw them, removing the bodies, very early this morning. This is a terrible epidemic. More will die tonight. Nothing we can do about it."

"Where did they put the bodies?" said Miriam, aghast.

Flaminia gave an expressive, pragmatic Italian shrug. "Maybe overboard, who knows?"

"Oh, how awful." Miriam braced herself with a hand on the table. "I won't tell anyone, I promise. But what can I do? What do you need?"

"Play something, maybe. Music. For the patients." Flaminia ticked her tongue against her front teeth and nodded. "Yes. Some music might be very nice for them. Make them forget they're sick."

"I'll go and get my violin," said Miriam. "I'll be right back."

She hurried out and climbed the stairs back up to the owner's suite. There she found Isaac and Rivka exactly where she'd left them earlier, sitting side by side on the main balcony, staring in silence at the horizon.

"Isaac," she said. "Come. I need you. Get your viola. We're going down to play for the sick people, the nurse asked me."

He made a face like a fussy baby confronted for the first time with a new food. "Right now, you want to do this?"

"What, you're too busy? Yes, right now!"

"The two of us? Play what?"

"Anything. One of the five thousand pieces we know. These people are dying, Isaac!" He eyed her, hesitating. "Forget it," she said.

She turned back into the suite, fetched her violin out of the closet, and went out along the catwalk. When she got to the top of the stairway, she stopped and turned back to see Isaac, lumbering toward her, shading his face with his hand to block the sunlight, carrying his bulky viola case. In that moment she felt that in all the years they'd been together she had never been happier to see him.

*

As soon as Christine left the galley with her friend, Mick's mood dropped. He felt sluggish, depressed, on the verge of unleashing his pent-up anger. They should have been in Honolulu days ago. He'd been eligible for shore leave on this cruise. But instead he was stuck in this dark, airless, infernally hot kitchen while food supplies steadily dwindled. He didn't know where else to go.

Kenji had been hit by the norovirus two days before, and had joined all the other quarantine sick people writhing in deck beds on the promenade. So Mick was in charge. But there was so little left for anyone to do that the crew had started spending most of their time up on the main deck with the walkouts, doing nothing, waiting. Christine was the only one who came down to the galley regularly. And now that she was gone . . .

The dark galley air felt thick with a residual static-electric energy, reverberated with all the furious work that had gone on down here before the engines died. So many people, so much heat. It made him weirdly nostalgic. He almost wanted to crawl into a supply closet and hide there, like a little kid, hoping that if he squeezed his eyes shut and counted to three, it would all be the same again when he came out, the galley full of people, food, action, with bright lights gleaming on stainless steel, the air roaring with the vents and air-conditioning, the stoves flaming with heat.

He remembered the captain's table dinner, when he had given that impromptu speech about Chef Viktor, how Laurens had reacted, the withering scorn. *Save your private memoirs for old age.*

Was his story really so boring? So inappropriate? All Mick had done was to put the dish into a personal context. It had taken less than a minute to tell. For the first time, instead of shame, he felt a hot tongue of rage. He hadn't deserved that rebuke. He should have walked out proudly, unfazed, happy with the success of his dish. Instead, he'd felt crushed. And why? Because some Belgian prick's ego couldn't handle someone else stealing his spotlight for one measly second? What did it really matter?

He poked his flashlight into the dry-goods storage room to see what else he could salvage from the old cases of canned fruit cocktail, Spam, deviled ham, and Campbell's cream soups, asparagus and mushroom and celery. Mick had no idea why most of this stuff was on board. Laurens had insisted that everything be made fresh, from scratch. Maybe the stores were meant to feed the crew, or to fulfill special requests from homesick American passengers who needed a room-service fix of the supermarket foods they were used to. Whatever the reason, Mick was glad to have it, even though much of it probably dated back to the Cold War. He hoped it wouldn't give everyone botulism, because they would need all of it, starting now. Subtracting the norovirus victims, and counting the entire crew, including the walkouts, there were almost five hundred people on board to feed. Even the canned food wouldn't hold out for long.

"Right in here," he heard a familiar voice saying behind him. It was Consuelo. "I think there's at least three cases."

"Let's take two of them," came the French-accented voice of Jean-Luc. "It's ours as much as theirs."

"Hey," Mick said, turning to flash his light on them. "What are you doing?"

Consuelo jumped a little. Her hair was loose, hanging in wild dark strings around her face, which was dark from the sun. Her arms looked sinewy and tensed for trouble. She wore a sweat-stained T-shirt and a pair of grubby trousers. "We're running low on food," she said. "We're hungry. We need supplies."

"And you were planning to just come in here and steal mine?"

"It belongs to everyone," said Jean-Luc. He looked as disheveled as Consuelo. His scalp hadn't been shaved in a while, and his short thick hair stood in a fluffy black skullcap, just beginning to curl. "We're only taking Spam. Maybe some soup. The passengers, they don't eat that shit, *non?*"

"The passengers are going to have to eat that shit," said Mick. "Starting tonight. Besides, there's an airdrop coming."

"Yeah right," said Consuelo. "I don't trust those *pendejos.*"

The two rogue chefs faced him wordlessly, their hands hanging at their sides with incipient threat, their faces hard. Mick looked back at them, ready to take them on if he had to, but far from sure that he could. They inched closer to him, crowding him, forcing him back into the storage room. Jean-Luc picked up a case of Spam. Consuelo took one of soup and hefted it as if she were planning to throw it at him.

"I don't want to fight you two for some stupid Spam," said Mick, talking fast, holding his ground. "But you can't steal from me. You should have asked me for it. Are we enemies? Why? I did nothing to you. The passengers, they did nothing to you. We're all stuck here together. Why are you making this a war? Put those down. I mean it."

Jean-Luc hefted his heavy box. "We are taking these and leaving those for you."

Consuelo hesitated. Mick saw something in her face. Maybe she was remembering how he'd stuck up for her, treated her fairly. He decided to assume he had an opening and press it hard. He looked at her, ignoring Jean-Luc's mouth-breathing hotheadedness, and said, "We're all stuck out here in the middle of the ocean, and we're running out of food. Can we pool our resources instead of fighting over them? Let's work together, this is stupid."

Consuelo said nothing. She turned and walked out with her box of cream of celery soup. Jean-Luc followed behind her with his box of Spam, and Mick was alone again. He turned off his flashlight and stood in the dark. He wasn't even mad. He felt nothing, in fact. All those years, every day, he had hurled himself into the kitchen at dawn, gone sleepless on the night crew, worked long extra hours without overtime pay, just for the private, dumb satisfaction of flaying himself on the wheel of the mill. He'd seen it as a badge of honor, an accomplishment of will and dedication. He'd believed, stupidly, that he'd be rewarded for it. He'd assumed that there was a point to it, that it would lead somewhere better. Now the whole idea seemed like the punch line to an unfunny cosmic joke on Mick.

The *Isabella* moaned, deep in her belly, somewhere just below his feet: an eerie, prolonged, echoing underwater squeal. It sounded to him like friction and torque between her ribs and her keel, straining at her bolts in different directions, as she rocked gently in the shallow swells. He could feel rumblings along with the noises, the tremors of her discomfort, as if she were waking up from a long deep sleep to discover she was in pain.

chapter twenty

As the high noon sun slanted into the early afternoon, Christine found herself perched on a plush armchair in a big suite on the bridge deck, drinking warm vodka and cranberry juice from a plastic cup and looking up at a framed photo of an astonishingly young-looking Richard Nixon. He had stayed in the suite during a Mediterranean cruise back in the 1970s—before anyone in the room was born, Christine realized—and it had subsequently been decorated in his honor and nicknamed, somewhat ironically she thought, the Nixon Suite. The photograph of Nixon felt like a sly wink. His vilified face looked weary and harmless and almost avuncular now.

Currently occupied by Cynthia Perez, the Mouseketeer turned movie star, it had become the daily hangout spot for the younger passengers. The large living room felt crowded with soft, bright, sweaty faces. A pile of people had deposited themselves on the two enormous beds among many upholstered green-and-gold tasseled pillows, several more were curled into the white space-age chairs and the harvest-gold armchairs and love seats, and the rest of them sprawled on the beige and brown geometric-patterned rugs. They looked charmingly out of place to Christine amid the shabbily futuristic decor. The built-ins were scuffed teak, Danish modern. The kitchenette could have been a set in a 1970s sci-fi movie.

"Why can't we scientifically quantify the soul?" Tye, the Yale historian, was saying, apropos of a hypothetical discussion about death that had been going on to Christine's right. "If we can get to the level of quantum mechanics, if we can identify a quark, why can't we figure out what the hell those twenty-one grams *are?*"

"They're energy," said Tameesha, the singer. "The soul is energy. It goes straight back into the universe when we die."

"But what kind of energy?"

"I read a thing on *Huff Po,*" said Allison, the young piano prodigy. "It said the soul is like our software."

"I read a thing about how we're all just living in a computer simulation," said Matt, the dreadlocked, pudgy trombonist for the Kool-Tones. His skin was thick with sweat. He held a ukulele against his large stomach. "It's a supercool idea. I kind of buy it. A British philosopher came up with it. He says there's a fifty percent chance it's true."

"Right," said Allison. She looked excited. "I saw that too. The designers of the simulation are supposed to be, like, thirteen-year-olds in a basement playing a random virtual reality game after school in the future."

"And if your character gets boring," said Theodore, the married journalist Christine had danced with on her first night of the cruise, "they kill you off."

"I refuse to be killed off," said Valerie with vehemence, turning to Theodore. She'd been talking to the two Russian bartenders who were part of the walkout crew, Christine's old friend Alexei and the bitchy, haughty Natalya, who had evidently been folded into this group.

"Maybe that's what's going on now," said Theodore. "The game-designer kids have shoved us onto an old boat stranded in the middle of the ocean, and they're going to forget about us and leave us here."

"Then we should do something interesting to remind them," said Allison.

"Like a revolution," said Natalya with a languid half-smile. "Teenagers love violence. We could kill the captain. Hijack the ship."

Everyone stared at her blankly, without a spark of interest: violence was not in anyone else's blood, apparently, to Christine's relief.

Natalya looked around at them, disappointed. "You're all little pussies," she added darkly.

Several people laughed. Matt and another Kool-Tone stared intently at each other and played what sounded like part of a song, Matt on his ukulele, the other Kool-Tone on a pair of small drums he held between his knees. Christine felt like the oldest person in the room, a Gen-X outsider in the midst of a tribal gathering of millennials. She could feel how, collectively, they were trying to construct and maintain an abstract wall of words to hold at bay the pressure of their fears about what might happen next. But the conversation did nothing for her own fears except intensify them. She had been trying not to think about Ed and the farm and her life back in Maine, and she had managed this over the past few days by slapping sandwiches together, making lists of stores, chopping limp vegetables. Now, with nothing to occupy her mind or her hands, she felt like a hostage to her own jittery nerves, sitting here among these kids, day drinking, talking aimlessly about nothing. She was in the grip of a visceral memory of planting seedlings in the dirt, the weak spring sun breaking through clouds, the green of the woods a blur beyond the field, the smell of air blowing over the lake, that mineral freshness underlain with the spicy funk of wet, wintered-over, rotting leaves. She yearned for the sensation of digging her hands into cool, rich dirt, even for the clouds of black flies and the stiff ache she got in her lower back from squatting all day.

Christine looked at Valerie, who was taking occasional pictures on her iPhone—she had brought along an extra battery, she explained when someone looked wistfully at it. The other passengers had all turned their mobile phones off right after the engine room fire to conserve power in case they magically came into range of Wi-Fi.

Valerie prowled around the room, looking parched and whip-focused in a black T-shirt dress and flip-flops. Christine couldn't remember the last time she'd seen her friend eat anything, maybe a sandwich two days before. And meanwhile she had been drinking steadily, straight vodka, and had hardly slept since the night the power had gone out, when she'd stayed in bed for twelve hours straight. She said with manic urgency, "After this cruise is done, do you know what they're going to do with this ship? They're going to tow it to Bangladesh to be taken apart on the beach for scraps. And the men who take her apart, the Bangladeshis, they'll breathe the asbestos, the toxic chemicals. Ship breaking is incredibly dangerous work. They pay those men nothing, and a lot of them get hurt and die. That's where this ship is going next."

"Everything is about making money for them," said Tye. "They don't care if people live or die. I heard that too, about Bangladesh."

"I should go there," said Valerie. "Talk to those workers."

"I keep wondering," said Tye, addressing the two Russians. "If there hadn't been a fire and the power hadn't gone out, what would have happened after you all walked out?"

"We would have made Cabaret bargain with us," said Alexei. "They have to please the customers, and to do that, they need us working. We would have made Larry Weiss give us our jobs back with better terms."

"Now, of course, we are fucked," said Natalya. "We had been planning a big thing, a manifesto, we were going to try to get media attention, to make them look bad. But now, *pffft.*" She batted languidly at the air with one hand. "We might as well have just kept working."

"Right. But what else were you supposed to do?" asked Tye. His upper lip was shiny, and his brow was wrinkled with the effort to convey his sympathy for their cause. "I mean, how are you supposed to change anything?"

"History is on your side," said Valerie, snapping Alexei's picture. "And so am I, with all this documentation. It's so frustrating that I can't get this out in real time, show the world what's going on right now."

"We'll be rescued soon, we'll be back on land," said Theodore. He was puffing on a metallic blue tube that spewed peach-flavored vapor. "It's just a matter of days."

"It's weird though, am I right?" said Tameesha. "No signal. You can get a signal even up in space. Like, aren't there any satellites over us?"

"Not in the middle of the ocean, apparently," said Christine.

"This cruise was supposed to give everyone a break from being online," said Tye. "No Internet, no cell phones, a return to the pre-device era. It seemed like a cool idea, before we got stuck out here."

There was a brief silence in the room. It seemed to Christine as if everyone was taking a moment to collectively, silently acknowledge their fear without naming it directly.

"This is totally. Effed. Up," said the drummer finally, punctuating his words with finger-taps on the skins. "Where the hell are we, even?"

"Maybe we drifted into the Great Garbage Patch," said Christine. Everyone looked blank. "It's a massive gyre of trash, something like twice the size of Texas now and growing."

"Oh right," said Allison. "I saw a thing about that. Didn't some Dutch kid figure out how to clean it up?"

"Not yet," said Christine.

"Does anyone else feel weird staring at the ocean all the time?" asked Cynthia.

"It's true, it's like infinite flatness," said Matt.

"Can it make you insane?"

"I read about that in, like, *Salon,* I think. About what happens to the brain when you stare at the ocean. It's called Blue Mind. It's a peaceful state where you slip into a kind of trance."

"Blue Mind sounds like a drug," said Cynthia.

"It's evolutionary," said James. "We came out of the water and we're made of it, and we need it to sustain life. Looking at the ocean makes us calm, like a baby looking at its mother."

"I don't feel calm," said Beatriz. She had been quietly, moodily squinting out the window at the ocean while everyone else chattered around her.

Christine kept her eyes on Beatriz as the voices swirled around the room, gentle, indistinguishable.

"They should study the brain when it's staring at the ocean on a stranded cruise ship for days."

"The water is connected to our emotions. We're not separate from it. It's like there's an invisible umbilical cord connecting us to it."

"In astrology, water signs are considered the most emotional and intuitive."

"I'm a water sign."

"Which one?"

"Cancer."

"Astrology isn't a real thing. There's no scientific basis for it."

"That's your truth. It's an ancient science."

"Word."

Christine missed the galley, missed working. She missed Mick. The vodka was giving her a headache. She was sweating into the upholstery, and she could smell the funk of her own body.

"Hey, I have an idea," Theodore said. "Anybody want to go for a swim?"

Christine stared at him with sharp, grateful relief. "Where?"

"We can't use the pool," said Allison.

Theodore stood up, all purpose now. "I'm not talking about the pool. I'm talking about the ocean! We can jump off the loading bay, the one they use for water sports and excursions and stuff. All the ships have them, they're right at water level."

"Oh my God," said Valerie. "That would be so fucking amazing. I'm so hot. It's like I'm baking internally."

"Isn't it dangerous?" said Cynthia.

"No," said Theodore. "There's no wind and no waves, and we can swim, the ship can only float, so we're faster. Come on, everybody. Get your suits on. Let's go down."

Beatriz finally looked up, something awakening in her eyes. "That is a fantastic idea," she said.

"Drinks for the road?" said Valerie, waving the vodka bottle.

"Maybe not," said Christine as she took it out of her hand. Valerie made a face but didn't argue.

*

Mick lugged three industrial-sized cans of kidney beans out of
the storeroom, opened them, and dumped them one by one into
big metal mixing bowls with all their liquid. He took two latex
gloves from the open box on the counter, snapping them onto his
already hot hands, and dipped his gloved fingers in, tasting one of
the canned beans. He was hungry. He ate another one. They tasted
savory, salty, not bad at all straight out of the can. He caught himself planning the night's menu—a vinaigrette with mustard, some
dried basil and tarragon, a hit of cumin and another of smoked
paprika, sugar, some chopped Spam—as if it mattered to anyone
anymore what he served.

What he needed was a cigarette. He peeled off his gloves and,
leaving the beans to stew in their own juices on the counter, went
out through the swinging doors to the restaurant. He headed for
a table near the empty bandstand, an elevated half-moon with a
canvas skirt, empty mic stands, and sat with his back to the wall,
fishing his cigarette pack and lighter out of the breast pocket of his
chef's jacket. He was whipping through his last few packs, smoking
eight or ten a day. Fuck it. They helped. What else was there to do
in this sunstruck, watery purgatory but smoke? Besides, it wasn't
as if there was some heaven waiting for him when he got back to
land. It was over with Suzanne. There was nothing for him in Budapest either. His father was an asshole. Chef Viktor had died two
years before. His school friends had all married, had kids, settled
down. Everything Mick had in the world was right here on this
ship: his hands, his knowledge, his skills, his experience, and his
dreams of doing something great someday. That was the sum total
of Miklos Szabo, age thirty-four: highly specialized knowledge,
vague and half-baked plans gone awry, and a knot of unarticulated,
frustrated, powerful yearning. For what, though? He had never been
able to act on any of it. His instincts for order and loyalty, caution and sensibility, always trumped his desires and ambitions. He
wished he had known this when he was younger. He should have

accepted his small fate instead of trying to be something better, bigger, more interesting. The Eszterházy, taking over for Chef Viktor, that was the life he had been slated for, suited for, the one that would have made him happiest. He'd overreached. And as always when he overreached, the gods, or whatever they were, had slapped him down. He never learned.

He took a long drag and held the smoke in his lungs for a moment before exhaling into the twilit gloom.

He'd really thought, he'd believed for years, that he'd end up somewhere cool like Amsterdam working under a famous chef like Laurens, that eventually he'd have a restaurant of his own, become a famous chef, himself. Meanwhile, Viktor had retired and sold the Eszterházy to EuroCuisine, a big European tourist chain. They had offered Mick a job, staying on, running the place, but he'd turned it down, even though Viktor had begged him to take it. Mick had probably broken Viktor's heart in at least some small way by leaving, but he'd had to get out, he was on to bigger things. Or so he'd thought.

He had never regretted leaving before now. He'd been too busy sailing around the world, working under celebrity chefs like Laurens, wooing his glamorous intellectual French girlfriend, sleeping in cramped bunk cabins with strangers for roommates, changing ships, changing crewmates, changing bosses, changing oceans, a revolving door of loneliness.

The cigarette smoke left a bitter taste on the back of his tongue. It was useless. He was here, nothing to be done about it.

He was swamped by a powerful yearning to be back there, in the Eszterházy, under the arched beamed ceilings with the wood-burning oven and open-flame grills sizzling with dripping meat fat. He could have saved money, got a business loan and help from investors, bought the Eszterházy for himself. It would have been his inheritance and his home and his future. He could have visited Viktor every Sunday afternoon for coffee, brought him pastries and stories from the restaurant and asked his advice and kept him involved in the place he'd built. He could have married a Hungarian girl, brought his children to work with him. He pictured himself up to his elbows right now in cabbage and dumplings, covered in paprika dust, yelling at his staff in Hungarian, making *mangalitsa,* that special breed of Hungarian pig, a little hairy thing that was totally fucking delicious, cooked in a traditional dish called Gypsy Pork, grilled meat and vegetables on a skewer, like a gypsy might make over a campfire by a caravan.

What a stupid fucking idiot he was. A cold wave of regret hit him broadside and almost knocked him out of his chair. He had nothing to lose anymore. Nowhere to go. He could leave Cabaret, walk off this ship when they got to land, start over. Maybe he would stay in the United States. Maybe get a job in a place in Los Angeles. Or maybe he'd head up to the Oregon coast and live near the beach and cook in a seaside tourist place, read books, take hikes, have his own apartment, find a girlfriend. Maybe he'd go back to Hungary and try to get the Eszterházy back. Whatever he did, it would be something he chose, something better than this. He was not going to fuck this up. He was going to change.

"Smoking alone in the dark," came a deep voice. "How cinematic."

Mick turned to see Sidney the maître d', as tall and correct as ever, moving slowly through the restaurant, straightening the already aligned silverware on tables, adjusting tablecloths a fraction of an inch, lifting glasses to mock-inspect them. He wended his way to Mick's table, picked up the pack of cigarettes, raised an eyebrow as if to ask permission, and shook one out without waiting for it. Mick slid the lighter across the table to him.

"I'll tell you what isn't very cinematic." Sidney sat down, lighting up, his pale blue eyes rimmed with thick white lashes. "Waiting for bloody tugboats to tow us to land. If only we were well and truly lost. No one coming, we're doomed, but we manage to survive by eating the dead while we drift all the way to Hawaii, Japan even." He paused. "Or if the crew had murdered half of us in cold blood and was holding the rest hostage. I'd watch that movie, wouldn't you?"

Mick laughed, out of surprise as much as anything else.

"Look at this," said Sidney. He jangled a set of keys between his thumb and forefinger. "The keys to the kingdom." He rested his cigarette in the glass ashtray and went behind the bar. Mick heard him opening the top-shelf liquor cabinet, and a moment later he reappeared with a bottle and two glasses and sat down again, pouring shots for them both. Mick saw the label: a single-malt Scotch that was more than ten years older than he was. They raised their glasses to each other.

"*Iechyd da,*" said Sidney, in Welsh, presumably.

"*Egészségére,*" Mick replied. It felt good to speak Hungarian. They clinked glasses and drank. Mick rolled the whiskey around his tongue.

"How is your crew?" Sidney asked. "How many do you have left?"

"Five or six, but they've gone off somewhere. I also have a few passengers helping out. Well, lately just one. There's not much to do."

"Yes. I've noticed her." Sidney held his cigarette away from his face, pinched in a leisurely way between thumb and forefinger as he watched the burning end.

Mick nodded. "Christine. She's okay." He took out another cigarette and lit it. He felt his head fogging up, his eyelids heavy with sleepiness, the whiskey, the unexpected intimacy with this intimidating person.

"You're shagging her, right?" Sidney said.

Mick looked at Sidney, surprised. "She's married."

"Don't tell me you've never shagged a passenger before."

Mick looked at Sidney with equal disbelief. Fraternization, especially sexual affairs, between crew and passengers was strictly forbidden. Only the captain and officers got away with it on a regular basis.

"Have *you*?" Mick asked, trying not to sound as shocked as he felt.

Sidney burst out laughing at this question, whose answer was evidently so obvious he couldn't be bothered to answer it, which made Mick laugh too.

"Did you know," Mick said, "that every Cabaret crewmember I've ever met is terrified of you?"

"Well, clearly not enough of them, or the fuckers wouldn't have walked out on me." Sidney took a nip of whiskey and sucked it through his teeth with a grimace of pleasure. "Though I guess it was coming eventually, the way they're treated, poor bastards."

Mick shrugged. "It's the system. We all live with it. Didn't you start out at the bottom and work your way up?"

"In a way," said Sidney. "I was a merchant marine, before I retired to the soft life of cruise ships. I worked for Caledonian MacBrayne, the Scottish ferry company. A rough life in hard boats on cold and stormy seas. I worked winters as a hotel waiter. This is my retirement plan, a cushy job on cushy ships. Well, I've always hoped to die on a ship. It's the only way to go."

"I hope it's not this one," said Mick.

"Cheers to that," said Sidney, filling their glasses again and downing his. He put his elbows on the table as if he were hunkering down in a dark little pub. "Actually, she's a grand old beauty, the *Queen Isabella*. Reminds me of—" He paused, cocked an ear. "Hear that?"

Mick listened for a moment, heard nothing. "What am I supposed to be hearing?"

"A plane," said Sidney. "It's the airdrop."

chapter twenty-one

Down in their cabin, Christine put on her green bikini and waited by the open balcony door in the hot breeze, staring at the ocean longingly, while Valerie changed out of her black bikini into a black one-piece and stood looking at herself from various angles in the mirror, changed back into the bikini again, put on lipstick, wiped it off, draped herself in a gauzy sundress, and reapplied her lipstick.

They climbed down into the ship's belly. As they went along the "B" deck corridor, Christine saw a light ahead and heard voices, muted, almost drowned out by a series of groans and clanks that seemed to come from the ship's frame. The door to the engine room was propped open. Amid the blackened rows of steel pipes and tubing descending, ringed by catwalks and threaded with steel staircases, Christine saw several men huddled on a platform. They were wearing headlamps and holding tools, conferring in low voices near a wall panel of gauges and dials, the glass smeared black with char.

"Hello," Valerie called down into the depths.

"Hello," came a few voices. "Who's there?"

"Passengers," said Valerie.

Christine squinted in the glare of their headlamps. The man nearest her was old, tall, stooped over in a crouch, holding a wrench. She recognized Sasha, Miriam's friend from the talent show. "Are you fixing the engines?" she asked.

"We're banging our heads against the pipes," came a voice from somewhere below.

"It keeps us busy," said Sasha. "If we could just get the desalinator to run. We're waiting for some parts to arrive."

"Well, good luck," said Christine.

As she followed Valerie along the corridor, the smell of old smoke began to dissipate. A stream of fresh air poured toward them. Christine saw daylight ahead, and soon they emerged into a long, narrow room lined with shelves and cabinets and lockers. At the far end, double doors were propped open, leading to stairs down to a small platform extending from the ship's hull, hovering just above the surface of the ocean.

A small crowd of people were already there, looking down with excitement at the calm, still, light-dappled water. The air was soft with spray and haze.

"Look at this," said Theodore to Christine. He gestured outward. "It's our new swimming pool, the biggest in the world!"

He wore old-fashioned olive-green swim trunks that came almost down to his knees. His bare chest was hairy. So he was older than she'd thought, maybe even her own age. Many of the younger men had waxed, hairless chests and wore tight-fitting trunks, neon and bright. The women all wore stylish and no doubt expensive bikinis. Their bodies were soft and unmarked and well nourished, somehow unformed, even the ones obviously honed in the gym, without a shred of wildness or aggression. If they had been stranded in the woods with a signal instead of in the remote ocean, Christine thought, they would have gotten out their iPhones and searched for YouTube tutorials on how to start a fire, how to build shelter, which plants were safe to eat, how to catch a fish. And they would have survived just fine, no doubt.

"I've never swum in the middle of the ocean before," said someone nearby, sounding nervous.

"Me neither. This is cool."

Theodore was the first to jump in. He cannonballed, went under, and emerged with a roar, his fist raised in triumph. "It's great!" he yelled at the people still standing on the dock.

Others gamely jumped in with shrieks and splashes.

"Oh Jesus," said Valerie. "I'm dizzy just thinking about it."

"Don't think," said Christine. "Once we're in, we'll be fine." She held her breath and jumped. Underwater, with her eyes shut, she experienced a brief moment of horrified panic, thinking about how deep the water was below her, stretching miles down into the darkness. Then her head bobbed up and she took a breath, looked around at the sparkling surface of the rocking, gentle bath. She began to move her limbs with pleasure through the salty sunlit water, cool enough to tingle on her skin.

There was a splash beside her, and Valerie was in too, her hair streaming with seawater, her eyes soft without her glasses.

Christine frog-kicked around in a leisurely breaststroke. In the hazy brightness and hot light she saw bobbing human heads, and above, more people on the ship, crowding the upper decks, looking down at the swimmers. She passed a floating plastic bottle, probably thrown overboard from the *Isabella.* Then another. She thought of the invisible cloud of trillions of disintegrated plastic micro-bits interspersed throughout the water, inseparable from it, part of it, like smog infiltrating air. She had seen so many online news stories, TV shows, documentaries that cataloged and exposed humanity's unstoppable destruction of the oceans with images of vast gyres of trash, miles-long oil slicks, bleached and dying coral reefs, seabird stomachs full of deadly plastic, whales and dolphins entangled in fishing nets, algae blooms. She had absorbed all this information with a sense of helpless, grief-sickened rage. It reminded her of reading horror novels as a teenager, unable to look away, sucked in, a stifled scream in the pit of her stomach, eyes shocked wide.

"Hey, Val," she said.

"Hey, Chris," said Valerie, scissoring her legs and making snow angels with her arms, her hair spreading around her head. "I kind of wish I'd brought my shampoo down. My scalp is so itchy."

"Why did you pick this cruise?"

"What do you mean?"

"Why didn't you take a cruise on a new megaship instead? With Wi-Fi?"

Valerie did a couple of slow underwater horizontal jumping jacks while she thought about this. She looked like a giant pale, smooth starfish. "I thought it would be good for me to give up the Internet for a while. I was so wrong."

"Wrong about giving up Internet, or picking this cruise?"

"Well, this cruise was obviously a colossally bad choice. To put it mildly. But what I really learned is that life without the Internet is not very interesting. I just feel like I'm missing out, I'm not in touch, I'm off in some slow lane. What's wrong with being online all the time? It's not like anything is happening anywhere else. Take this cruise. String quartets. Old people. Stuffy food. The library is full of old books no one reads anymore."

Christine laughed. "Philistine."

"I am not," said Valerie, but she laughed too. "The ocean feels smaller than it used to. Everything feels smaller. Doesn't it? Or is it just me?"

"It's just you," said Christine.

They were silent awhile, suspended there together while tiny waves lapped at their skin. Christine looked up at the *Isabella,* feeling like an explorer or an astronaut who'd left the mother ship, ventured away for the first time, and was looking back at it from the void of space. Seen from here, the ship looked small and alone, the only shelter and protection for these hundreds of souls who clung to her creaky old frame. But she also looked reassuring, human-scaled in all that depthless blue, elegant and starkly white in the sunlight, all her curves and stacked terraced decks soaring above the sea surface.

She was aware all of a sudden of music coming from an upper deck of the ship. Two stringed instruments, it sounded like, playing a fugue-like duet that burst on the still, hot air in gusts of notes, liquid and rippling, orderly, resonant, civilized. Under the music, she heard another sound. The engine of a plane, far off. She heard yells behind her and turned to look at the platform. Several uniformed crewmembers were inflating a yellow life raft. As the engine noise grew, drowning out the music, she watched, treading water, as a big cargo plane approached and banked, circling the ship. Then a square door in its rear opened and a large red crate attached to two parachutes came floating down, landing with a splash a few hundred feet away.

As a second crate fell down she heard cheers, whistles, whoops, and yells all around her, as if they were all refugees in a camp or victims of a natural disaster, watching FEMA or NATO trucks arrive with water and bags of rice. As the crew launched the raft and began to row out to the bobbing crates, Christine could feel, vicariously, how exhilarating it must be for them to be headed somewhere, in charge of their own small craft, with a tangible reward awaiting them, not so far away. The plane flew off, its sounds fading to a faint drone, then a buzz, then an echoing memory of an engine. She thought of Mick in the galley, his joy and relief at getting all this food.

*

A chain of workers took boxes out of the two crates on their floating pallets and passed them one by one from the loading bay up to the main galley. Mick stood by the main galley pass, inspecting each box as it arrived. He thought of his predawn food inspection, before the cruise had begun, on the docks of Long Beach so long ago, the oysters and broccoli, steaks and pineapple. This time it was whole wheat sandwich bread, peanut butter, power bars, packages of dried fruit and nuts, baby carrots nestled together like squat orange fingers. Crewmembers came in waves, with box after box, walkouts working together with Mick's team as if they had been one crew all along. Mick heard snatches of singing, laughter, shouted banter in English, Spanish, a couple of other languages he didn't recognize. Consuelo and Jean-Luc joined the chain, humping boxes up the stairwell, conducting periodic quality-control checks to make sure no one filched anything. It all felt surreal, after Mick's morning of near-solitary stasis in the galley, as if he were standing in the midst of a whirlwind ballet of coordinated and kinetic goodwill, as if the plane had miraculously caused everyone to forget his or her own personal grievances and share eagerly in the communal good fortune of them all.

"Heavy one," said Camille as she maneuvered backward through the doors. She dumped her box on the floor and went out again as Mick sliced it open and found it packed with cans of milk.

"This one goes in the breakfast stash," he told a walkout named Kalyani, who had just hustled up behind him. He knew her from the prep station, back in the old days. "With the cereal boxes."

"Milk," said Kalyani with mock-scorn. "Who drinks *milk?*" She gave him a brief frank grin, which seemed to acknowledge that the walkouts had given up, come back to the fold. About time, thought Mick.

"Babies," said another walkout named Chita, breezing in with a fresh box and dropping it with a dramatic sigh as if it weighed a hundred pounds.

As Mick stood up, bracing himself for the next box, he felt a hand on his shoulder. "Do you need any help?"

He turned to see who it was and almost gasped aloud. Christine wore a sea-green bathing suit. Her hair streamed over her shoulders. She was so close, he could smell saltwater, feel the waves of coolness coming off her. A long piece of hair had stuck to her neck like a tendril. She was gorgeous, muscular and fit from physical labor, a real woman with breasts, hips he wanted to rest his hands on, strong shoulders and thighs. He had to blink a few times.

"There's nothing to cook," he managed to say. He could still feel the cool weight of her hand on his shoulder though she'd taken it off. "It's all ready-to-eat stuff."

"We went swimming," she said. "It was amazing. You should go."

"I can't swim." He had never admitted that to anyone before. And certainly not to a woman he was attracted to.

"Oh, come on," she said warmly. "Why not?"

"I never learned. No one taught me. I know, it's stupid."

She didn't hesitate. "I'll teach you."

"I'm a bad student."

She laughed, eyes sparkling. "You're sure you don't need help down here?"

He wanted to kiss her. "No," he replied. "I'm okay, you can take the rest of the day off, too." Why had he said that, when he meant and wanted exactly the opposite? "But maybe I'll see you later, upstairs," he added.

"Okay," she said, already on her way out, over her shoulder. "See you later."

He watched her go, the smooth bare skin of her strong back above her lovely round American ass, cupped by her bikini bottoms. He'd been so oblivious before now. And she'd been wearing baggy shorts and T-shirts.

"Hey, *cabrón.*" Consuelo snapped her fingers in front of his face. "Quit drooling and check this out."

He realized his mouth was hanging open a little. As the woman of his dreams vanished through the swinging doors, he looked down at a box Consuelo was pointing at, packed with cans of crabmeat.

"Who's your girlfriend, Chef?" She grinned at him.

"None of your business," he said, but he grinned back at her.

The next two boxes held dozens and dozens of croissants. Mick chuckled and shook his head. Seriously? Fucking pastry? His earlier solitary depression had lifted, and he now felt all his senses and forces gathering behind one clear and definite thought: I want Christine. No more regrets about the life he could have had or fear of the gods punishing him for overreaching. There was no going back. And there were no gods. Fuck it, he thought. I don't care if she's married. I want her. I want to have what I want, for once in my life.

*

Miriam stood in line near the pool with her paper plate and fork. When it was her turn, the beautiful Indian girl behind the table gave her a scoop of bean salad, which had chunks of some kind of pink meat in it, sweaty-looking, lurid. Miriam waved away the sandwich, a croissant with a white paste. She hated fish salad, unlike every single other Jew she'd ever met. If she had to eat fish, she wanted a filet.

"Can I please have just a plain croissant?" she asked the very tan Australian boy who was handing them out. Her voice sounded creaky, plaintive to her own ears. "Maybe two?"

She took her food over to the old breakfast nook. It was a mess. Most of the deck chairs there had been converted to beds, heaped with sheets and pillows. But there was Christine, sitting sideways on the only uncluttered chair with a plate perched on her knees. Miriam didn't feel much like company right then, but it was too late to pretend she hadn't seen her.

"Hello, Christine," she said. "Can I sit with you?"

"Miriam, hello!" Christine moved over and Miriam sat next to her with her own plate balanced on her knees, and looked dubiously at those glistening chunks of meat.

"How is it?" Miriam asked.

"Not bad, if you like beans," said Christine. She wore a sundress and sandals and looked fresh and clean and absurdly healthy, her hair windblown and sun-bleached. "And croissants with crabmeat." She took a bite, chewed. "Actually, this may be the best sandwich I've ever had in my whole life."

Miriam plunged her plastic fork into the bean salad but couldn't bring herself to eat it. The people around her seemed happy with their food, as if they were homesick kids at summer camp opening care packages full of treats from their mothers. Even Christine seemed thrilled. Miriam felt like a curmudgeon, ungrateful and depressed.

"I saw you all, swimming in the ocean," she said, trying to be cheerful through the sour lump in her throat. "That must have felt so nice and cool."

"It was a little scary at first, then absolutely great," said Christine. "Was that you playing music?"

Miriam nodded.

"It was beautiful," said Christine. She looked closely at Miriam. "Are you okay?"

"Oh, I don't know what's wrong with me," said Miriam. "I don't like crab, maybe that's it."

"You look sad."

"I am sad," said Miriam. It felt good just to say it.

"I'm sorry," said Christine. "For being so cheery. How annoying."

On a burst of affection, Miriam reached out and grazed the girl's cheek with her knuckles, a caress, and gazed into her pragmatic blue eyes. "I'm not annoyed at you, sweetheart. I'm sad at this predicament we find ourselves in. I guess it just dawned on me how really and truly stuck we are out here if they have to send a plane to bring us food. It will be days before we get back to land."

"I know," said Christine, suddenly sober, understanding. "It's serious. I was thinking about that earlier." She yawned hugely. "I'm sorry, I'm so tired, I can't stay awake."

"Of course not. After all that swimming and excitement," said Miriam. "It's cooling off, can you feel it?"

"Yes," said Christine, nodding as she looked around. She stood up slowly, balancing herself on the back of the deck chair. "See you later."

"Sweet dreams," said Miriam.

After Christine had gone, Miriam sat alone with her mound of bean-and-Spam salad. Tonight was Shabbos. The sun was going down. Back in her real life, in Israel, she might have been going out to dinner with her friend Etta, or visiting her son, Avner, and his family in Jerusalem for the weekend, or sitting upstairs on Isaac's terrace with him, drinking a glass of wine while he drank seltzer.

But she didn't really miss the past. In fact, she yearned for the future, for whatever time she and Sasha had together. What would they do together on Shabbos, in Jaffa, that most beautiful, peaceful town? They might walk by the sea at sunset, cook together, invite friends over for dinner . . . It would be heaven on earth.

"Miriam," came his voice from nearby, as if she had drawn him to her just by thinking about him, or conjured him out of thin air. "Miriam."

Sasha made his painstaking way through the crowded slum of

deck chairs and sheet tents toward her. He looked thin and pale and greasy.

"I was just missing you," she said, squinting up at him.

"Here I am." He slid onto the deck chair, behind her. His arms went around her and her head found his chest, the hollow of his neck. He smelled of old sweat and machine oil, both funky and metallic. She nestled against him and inhaled again and again with her nose against his skin.

"Did you fix the engine?"

"No," he said. "They sent parts to replace the burned-out rings and wires and so forth, but the wrong connecting rod for the crankcase. Can you believe it? What a bunch of nudniks. It took us almost three hours to realize, trying to make it work."

"No!" said Miriam, although she had no real idea what he was talking about.

"Yes!" he said. He lowered his voice, but it vibrated with outrage. "So stupid, such a waste."

"Here," she said, handing him her plate. "Share my dinner, you have to eat."

Around them, the air dimmed and cooled. Leaning against Sasha while he ate, she tried and failed not to think about what Flaminia had told her about the patients who'd already died in the infirmary, their bodies secretly taken away, and the ones who would die tonight. And she tried not to think about Larry's helicopter escape three days before, the useless engine parts, the stalled tugboats. She distracted herself from all of it with a favorite memory of her long-dead mother playing Chopin. She had played rarely, only when something inside her seemed to demand it. She'd been a formidably proper woman, but when she sat on the piano bench, she revealed another side of herself: a passionate girl, a sexual, romantic being. Her whole body would sway, her face transported, eyes half closed. She had always poured her entire self into her piano; even when she was rusty, the music was beautiful. Miriam had never loved her mother more or felt closer to her than in those moments.

"We should play something," she said, looking up at Sasha.

He gave a start. "The quartet? Right now?"

"Right now. We should play Rivka's *Six-Day War* Quartet. It's time. If Jakov is able. He's getting worse, I think."

Sasha nodded. "All right."

They found Jakov sitting on his daybed in the living room, drinking from a bottle of water. Miriam handed him the second croissant she'd cadged.

"Thank you," he said with languid melancholy. "This, I can eat."

"That, you shouldn't eat, because it's bad for your heart," said Miriam, "but I am not your mother, and you deserve a treat."

Jakov tore into the buttery pastry with a wolfish, beatific smile.

"So, Jakov," said Miriam when he'd devoured the whole thing, "do you feel well enough to play some music?"

He looked dubious but game. "What should we play?"

"We were thinking," said Sasha with a note of apology, "the Weiss quartet."

Jakov made a peevish face, which luckily Rivka didn't see from her seat on the long white couch next to Isaac. She was surrounded by cushions, facing the balcony doors with her legs tucked underneath her, wearing white silk pajamas and a matching white turban, and she turned to Sasha with her hand fluttering at her breastbone, "Oh, Sasha. That would be marvelous! I had given up hope of ever hearing it played."

"It was my idea," muttered Miriam.

"Everyone," said Sasha. "Get your instruments out. We're going to play Rivka's *Six-Day War* Quartet that she wrote for us, in our honor."

They set up chairs, unfolded music stands, found the sheet music.

Unsnapping her case, taking out her violin, holding it again, Miriam felt as she always did when she was about to play with the Sabra: happy, tense, grounded. Her violin smelled like sweet old wood and rich, oily rosin dust. She tightened her bow, plucked her strings, nestled her instrument between her chin and her shoulder, and held her bow lightly between her thumb and index fingertip as she tuned to Sasha's A.

She looked around at the three others: Sasha, fierce and intent; Isaac, with his serious expression that was always half funny to her, glasses on the end of his nose; and Jakov, golden tufts of hair matted, his face distended with illness, his cello leaning against his shoulder like a small, long-necked, curvy woman, his arms and legs feebly embracing her.

They all looked over at Sasha, bows poised, waiting for his violin scroll's slight lift and dip, which he executed now with a little quirk of his mouth as if to say, *Once more into the breach, comrades.*

chapter twenty-two

It wasn't the best meal in the world, but when it was over, Mick felt an unexpected sense of satisfaction. The food had disappeared as fast as the service team could dish it out. Everyone had eaten well, and they had all eaten together—walkout crew, remaining crew, bridge crew, and passengers—from the same bowls and trays of food. And he'd been told that the walkouts had helped his crew collect the paper plates and napkins and stuff them into trash bags to throw down onto the loading bay. He tried to avoid reading too much into this; their newfound willingness to cooperate might be temporary for all he knew. But he felt encouraged by it, all the same.

When the kitchen was clean and the remaining supplies from the airdrop properly stored, Mick stripped off his chef whites in the locker room. He washed and soaped himself as best he could with a two-liter bottle of water—face, armpits, groin—and wandered up in search of Christine.

It was just after sunset. A crowd had gathered in the glimmering dusk on the solarium deck at the very top of the ship. He saw people lying on deck chairs, riding the stationary bicycles, huddled on the floor, talking in small groups in low voices, cigarette ends and vaping pipes glowing. Mick spotted members of the crew among the passengers, and some of the walkouts too, including Consuelo, who sat next to Natalya over in a corner, talking to several of the younger passengers. He looked around for Christine, feeling like a stranger and an outsider.

"Hey," came a female voice from somewhere around his knees. "Got a cigarette?"

He looked down. Valerie sat alone on the teak decking, leaning against the outer wall of the glass solarium, drinking from a wine bottle.

"Have you seen Christine?" Reluctantly, he handed her a cigarette. It was his last pack.

"No," said Valerie. "But she's supposed to meet me up here. Want a drink?"

He sat down next to her and took a swig while she lit her cigarette.

"So Mick," she said, exhaling smoke. "I think we got off on the wrong foot back there. Remember when I barged into your kitchen trying to interview you?"

"I remember."

"Seems like months ago, right? Anyway, it's okay because I ended up talking to Consuelo, who was super nice and generous with her time, unlike someone else." She gave him a playful nudge.

"I was working," he said.

"So was I," she said.

He gave her a sidelong look.

She grinned at him and cheekily plucked the wine bottle from his hand and tipped some into her mouth. "What are you going to do next? Where do you go after we get off this thing?"

Mick eased back and settled his hipbones on the deck flooring. "I'm not sure," he said. "I'm leaving this job, that's all I know."

"They're letting you go too?"

"No. Not me."

"But you're leaving anyway?"

"Yes," said Mick.

"How come you don't join the other walkouts?"

"Someone has to cook for the passengers."

"Why not let us cook for ourselves? I'm kidding. I'm just trying to understand it from your perspective. Do you think what Cabaret is doing is wrong?"

"Of course I do," said Mick, surprised at the strength of feeling in his own voice. "These are good workers, they've done a good job. They don't deserve to be let go like this. Do you know what they sent in the airdrop today? The supplies they sent us?"

"Yeah. We were joking about that earlier. 'Let them eat croissants.' "

Mick snorted. "Peanut butter, baby carrots, power bars, little boxes of apple juice, like we're a fucking kindergarten at snack time."

Valerie laughed. "Not to defend them," she said, "but they were probably just trying to give us whatever was easiest to pack, the most nutritious, whatever won't go bad right away."

Mick shook his head. "I was hoping at least for real food, some charcoal to cook it with."

"Aren't you glad not to have to cook?" She passed him the bottle.

He drank, wiped his mouth on the back of his hand. "It's much worse if I can't work."

"I hear you, man. Some of us need our work just to get through the day."

"Your friend Christine's like that too," he said, almost as an afterthought.

"She is. I sort of expected when she moved up to the country to live on a farm, she'd relax with the work ethic, but she just channeled it into something else."

"She's a hard worker," he said, feeling for some reason as if he had to defend Christine against her friend, even though Valerie hadn't said anything overtly critical.

They were silent for a while, passing the wine back and forth, listening to the conversations around them. At some point, Mick noticed Valerie's shoulder leaning against his. He shifted away from her to light a cigarette.

"What's that weird music?" she said.

Mick listened. A slight breeze blew the sound to them from somewhere nearby, a spiky, atonal piece for strings, dissonant, shivery-beautiful, squawkingly ugly, terrible and gorgeous in turn.

"I don't know," he said.

It sounded as if the musicians were making it up on the spot. It gave Mick a complicated feeling he couldn't name, the swirling coalescence of everything he'd been thinking about all day, as if they were playing the sound track to the inside of his head.

*

Miriam found she knew the piece almost by heart. They had rehearsed it only twice since they'd set sail, and not for days, but she must have internalized it while she wasn't thinking about it, because her left fingers somehow suddenly knew on their own where to go on the fingerboard, her right hand knew the bowings, the rhythms and dynamics. This had always been the greatest pleasure of her life, losing herself in a piece of music she knew well enough to play without thinking. Now that she didn't have to agonize over the score, Miriam could hear this piece for the first time as it unfolded. Now that she wasn't counting beats and resenting the composer for her diabolical double-stops and pretentious percussive passages, she understood the way in which Rivka had written the narrative of the Six-Day War from start to finish. The first movement described the gathering threat from all sides pressing in on Israel, still vulnerable, the Jews still ragged from the Holocaust, trying to establish their young state. Jakov's cello sent a hostile undercurrent of tremolo from Egypt as Isaac's viola sounded Syria's harsh war cries and Sasha's violins squealed a warning from Jordan, the Arab countries mustering their might to vanquish and exterminate the Jews once and for all. Miriam's second-violin part, she realized, was filled with the quiet determination of a people who had been tested to their limits and tested again, and who had survived, and would survive again. She played her part with a visceral steadiness, holding firm to her odd rhythms, her dissonant intervals a shaky inchoate tremolo growing in force, loudening, resolving into ringing double-stops.

And then came the second movement, Israel streaming into Egypt by air and land. A long silence, suspended, all instruments quiet, and then the violent surprise: first air strikes, then machine-gun fire across the desert. Miriam played, caught up in the drama, remembering the conquering of the Sinai. She'd met Isaac during that quick battle. She glanced at him, sitting just to her left, while they reenacted the skirmish with their instruments. He shot a look back at her, and she knew they were both remembering. Ah, the Jews. A tough, smart little army made up of people like them, classical musicians, scholars, scientists, farmers. And they had won!

Then came the third movement, the second wave of Jewish might and cleverness: this was Sasha's movement, and Jakov's, the air strikes against Syria, the triumph over Jordan, after the Arab world had been told that Egypt had vanquished Israel. Nasser had lied to them, tricking them into attacking a winning army. Miriam felt the power in the ending of this movement, the strong and certain knowledge that Israel would survive.

And then came the last movement, so soon already. Miriam had never realized how lovely it was: the short, sweet, and yet sorrowful sense of vindication, with its theme of "Yerushalayim Shel Zahav," the song written by Naomi Shemer, they'd all sung it after the war: *Jerusalem of gold, and of bronze, and of light, behold, I am a violin for all your songs.* After six days of fighting, one thousand Jews were dead, and many thousand Arabs had been killed. The Jews had taken beautiful Jerusalem from the Jordanians, claimed it as their birthright. Israel was secure. But there was always such a cost. It had been a short but terrifying war, with so much death. Always so much death, with war, whether you won or lost, it was terrible.

When they'd finished, Miriam tucked her violin under her arm. There, they'd played this damn thing for the last time. Rivka, their audience of one, gazed at them all in the light of the candles that stuttered in the breeze.

"Yes," Rivka said. "Oh yes—" She cleared her throat, pressed her knuckles to her eyes. "That was perfect," she said. "You played it as I wrote it. No composer can hope for more."

It was true. They had played it perfectly, and the piece had come to life. Miriam had executed her second-violin part with her jaw clenched on the chin rest, her bow chopping glints of electricity off the strings in the long staccato runs, her fingertips striking the fingerboard with precise deadly blows. She had played her part so well, she surprised herself. A combination of anxiety and fear was a great focuser for the brain and fingers, and for the people in its sphere as well, it seemed. Her virtuosity had forced the other three to meet her there on the plane of pure excellence. Even Jakov, sick as he was. It had always been this way: if one of the quartet played brilliantly, usually Sasha, the other three were spurred to match it. And this time, the brilliant one had been Miriam.

Jakov leaned back in his chair with an expression of stolid exhaustion, his cello lolling between his knees, his hands lax on his thighs with the bow dangling from loose fingers. He had rallied enough to play this difficult, demanding piece. He'd done it for them all.

Isaac put his viola into its open case and went over to sit on the couch with Rivka. Miriam sensed, once more, the two of them enfolded in something private. She had a feeling that something was going on between them, she wasn't sure what. Maybe now that Larry was gone, they were finding each other, finally, just as Miriam and Sasha had. Miriam supposed she was happy for them, but she felt other things about it too.

"Those were such different times," said Sasha. "We were so young, our country was young. We were right, and many of us believed that God was on our side."

"I never believed in God," said Miriam. "But yes, I believed in our right to win that war."

Jakov coughed wetly. "You don't anymore?"

"Of course I do," said Miriam. "But it's all so much more complicated now, isn't it? All tangled up in violence for its own sake, not enough will from the leadership on both sides to resolve their differences and coexist. It's all bullying and lies."

"It was simple back then," said Sasha. He cocked his head at Miriam. "Wasn't it? Even killing, dropping bombs, I didn't question it. We were defending our right to exist. They wanted to exterminate us, but we were strong and smart and we fought for our right to live in our own country."

"Survival," said Jakov. "That was it. That's what we were fighting for."

"The will to survive is eternally strong," said Miriam. "But it's how you do it that matters. And I'm not thinking only of Israel. Yes, you stay alive, but at what cost? What have we become, in Israel?"

"We've done things we should never have done," said Jakov. "Nothing makes that right."

They fell into a tense silence, thinking their separate thoughts. Sasha lifted his violin to his chin and plucked his strings, fiddled with a tuning peg, plucked again. As he played the opening bars of "Papirosen," Jakov lifted his bow and joined in with a rhythmic bass line and sang in his rich, clotted voice that always reminded Miriam of a mournful, passionate walrus: *"A kalte nacht, a nebldike finster umetum, shteyt a yingele fartoiert, un kukt zikh arum."*

Miriam joined in with her clear soprano, two octaves higher, a little wobbly now, *"Fun regn shteyt im nor a vant, a koshiki trogt e rim hant . . ."*

It was an old wartime song about an orphaned boy standing on a corner in the ghetto selling cigarettes in the cold rain, trying not to starve and die like his sister, who had been his only hope and companion in the world. Miriam's voice was that of the ghostly sister, chiming in with the boy's plaint from beyond death, to bolster him. *"Zol der toyt shoyn zumen oykh tzu mir"*: Let death come already for me, too.

Isaac roused himself and picked up his viola while Miriam lifted her violin to her chin again, and they all stopped talking and gave themselves over to their history, their shared knowledge, a musical conversation in four parts they'd held for so many years together. They played "Ale Brider," not a classical piece they'd performed together but a folk song, the music of their parents and grandparents, the music from the shtetls and ghettoes.

During "Flatbush Waltz," Kimmi entered the room with her

accordion and joined in. Then two musicians from the jazz band, the clarinet and trombone players, arrived in time to play "A Yiddishe Mama" and "Raisins and Almonds." Miriam was impressed that these *goyishe* kids were familiar with these old klezmer songs, or maybe they were picking them up by ear. They played with such openness and verve, all of them.

More people arrived, doors and windows were opened, furniture moved to the corners of the room, and people danced. Old people in pajamas chimed in on the songs while younger people watched, listened, clapped and cheered. Allison, the virtuoso teenager, came in and played a Joplin rag on the upright piano by the balcony doors. Miriam's heart beat fast with joy, watching her play, and with such chutzpah!

As the music spooled out into the night, people came from all over the ship, thronged the living room, spilled out onto the balconies, looked in the open windows and doors from the catwalk. There were crew and passengers, young and old, all colors and races, dirty, drunk, sweaty, smiling, draped against railings, raucously singing on the balconies, passing bottles around while the members of this impromptu band shouted out songs and keys, launched into them as if they'd all rehearsed together for years, flying into solos, segueing from klezmer to old jazz standards, the whole room alight with candles.

Cigarette smoke curled, made a haze. Miriam caught a glimpse of Rivka on the couch by an open window with her feet tucked under her like a girl. Here they all were in the owner's suite, Miriam mused, the owner himself gone, and the whole ship joined in music.

Kimmi struck a chord on the accordion. Her singing voice was trained and commanding: *"Sing to the Lord, for he is highly exalted. Both horse and driver he has hurled into the sea."*

"It's Miriam's Song," said Miriam in Sasha's ear. She remembered the quartet's first rehearsal in the chapel, when Kimmi had come rushing in looking for a Bible. Back then, Sasha had been a grieving old man, and Miriam had been Isaac's roommate.

"The Song of the Sea," said Sasha, his eyes gleaming at her, remembering too.

*

Christine resurfaced in her bed in the cabin after being submerged for hours in a profound, dream-filled sleep. She wasn't even sure where she was at first. Lying there, returning to herself, she felt the deep silence around her as a pressure in her head.

"Valerie," she said into the darkness. Her mouth was dry. Her voice sounded like a weak little chirp.

She reached over for her flashlight and splashed the small cabin with cold light, dim now, because her battery was dying. Valerie's bed was empty. The air coming through the open balcony doors was humid and warm and thick as someone's breath. Faint music wafted from somewhere high above.

She threw her blankets off and sat up. Finding that she was still dressed, she got out of bed, slipped on her sandals, and went out into the hallway, spooked by its emptiness, sickened by the stench of raw sewage. Her flashlight lit a murky path to the stairwell, and up several flights. When she emerged onto the aft outside deck, into fresh air and moonlight, she turned it off and saw a warm light coming from one of the high suites above her. She heard people singing, laughter, a violin playing high, fast notes, horns joining in.

She made her way slowly up to the bridge deck and along the catwalk, running her hand along the railing. Candlelight poured from the windows and doorway of the owner's suite; a crowd thronged the living room, spilling out onto the catwalk. She heard laughter and cheers and looked in as Sidney, the maître d', launched into what sounded like an old sea shanty in a loud, rough, but surprisingly tuneful voice, *"Where it's wave over wave, sea over bow, I'm as happy a man as the sea will allow, there's no other life for a sailor like me, than to sail the salt sea, boys, sail the sea . . ."*

Standing at the edge of the crowd, Christine felt invisible, or as if she'd emerged from a coma into a surreal circus, or as if she were still asleep and dreaming. Everyone around her was caught up in the music, drunk and laughing and jubilant.

Theodore appeared next to her on the catwalk, nudged her. "What's up, farm girl?"

"Hey," said Christine. "Have you seen Valerie?"

"Hours ago. Up on the solarium deck hanging out with that crowd."

He handed her a bottle of something. She took a swig and handed it back, feeling whiskey warm her gullet.

*

"Stay here," Valerie said. Feeling antsy, but not wanting to be rude, Mick did as he was told while she went down the short staircase to the bar to get another bottle of wine. The almost-full moon hung low in the sky, splashing the surface of the sea with cold brilliance, turning it into a shimmering, shifting rug. The music coming from one of the suites below shifted to a slow jazz song with a simple but tricky melody. A woman's smoky, rich voice, a cascade of trombone notes, a strong satiny ribbon of violin, twined together and clustered in his solar plexus, forming a knot of feeling that all at once melted into longing. *"Since you went away, the days seem long, and soon I'll hear old winter's song . . ."*

Valerie reappeared, handing him a fresh bottle of wine. She sat down next to him and slipped a cigarette from his pack, handed him another, lit them both. He was well on his way to being truly drunk, and it felt good. Every time he thought about getting up and going down to the party to look for Christine, Valerie seemed to read his mind, and pull him back toward her with the tug of expert redirection. She made him tell her about what had happened between Consuelo and Laurens. Then he found himself talking about his foiled desire to go and work for Laurens in his new restaurant, his failed romance with Suzanne, and his past in Budapest, the Eszterházy, his sister. While he talked, Valerie kept maneuvering her body to keep contact with his, applying pressure with her hand on his thigh, making sure to brush his shoulder with her cheek, taking slow drags of her cigarette so he'd notice her mouth, imagine it elsewhere. He knew this dance. He'd done it before. It always ended exactly where the woman wanted it to end. He didn't know how to bring about any other scenario. Rejecting women who wanted him, walking away from their need, wasn't something he was good at. He wasn't sure he wanted to, anyway. And he knew that Valerie could read this. She had done this dance as many times as he had, she was an expert at spinning the web, and he was caught in it now. The music went on, shifted, got louder and more raucous, then quieter, then the quartet played alone, a moody, sweetly melodic piece Mick didn't recognize because he knew fuck-all about music really, but it was beautiful.

Well into the early hours of morning, as they drank the third bottle of wine, or maybe it was the fourth, they stopped talking. Their shoulders were pressed together. They'd let their knees fall inward so they were touching, too. He felt as if their two bodies had formed a self-contained little cave where they'd taken shelter together for the night, and their conversation had been a stream of words and breath, keeping them warm. He was aware that they were alone now. Christine had never come. The other stargazers, vaping and drinking and laughing on the deck with them, had all left, gone down to bed, or to join the party down below. Mick imagined Christine was down at the party too. He wanted to go and find her. He felt very drunk. On a surge of determination, he pulled himself to his feet, resting his hand against the wall of the solarium, and staggered a little over to the railing.

Valerie got up too, stayed with him.

"Wait," she said. "Can we just take a minute? I feel kind of dizzy."

She leaned into him, looking out with him at the pinkening predawn sky. She slumped, her head lolling on his shoulder. She started to tip over. His arms went around her to keep her from falling down. She exhaled hard, as if with relief, and pivoted to face him, sliding her arms around his neck. The muscles of their thighs pressed against each other. Her body felt insubstantial, droopy, so that he had to hold her up. Her expression was flickering, turned inward. In a flash of intense longing, he thought of Christine, her steadiness and strength, the light in her eyes when she'd promised to teach him to swim. But Valerie was the kind of woman he had always known he deserved, dark and chaotic and bitter. Her mouth tasted like peaty smoke and warm metal. He gave himself over to her with the nihilistic half-sober awareness that the gods were smacking him down yet again.

"Okay," she said with drunken fervor. "We really need to fuck right now."

She put her hand on his crotch and rubbed it slowly, felt his cock harden, slid her hand down his waistband. He was filled with lustful dread, mindless, animal. In a fluid practiced series of motions, she turned toward the railing and lifted her dress and reached behind her and undid his pants and moved her underwear to the side and slid his cock inside her. She let out a low, guttural shriek, not entirely of pleasure, moved her hips backward to enfold his cock as he thrust into her. His mind shut down, floated off like a balloon while he thrust at her and she groaned and mewled and arched her back like a cat.

"Don't come in me," she gasped, finally.

"Okay," he said into her ear, holding her hips still, pulling out of her. He didn't even care if he came, it didn't matter. As he did up his pants, she whisked her skirt down and ran her fingers through her hair. They looked blankly at each other. Valerie's face looked frozen and tired. Mick turned away and oh God, there was Christine, lit by a glimmer of dawn light.

chapter twenty-three

As Christine emerged from the stairwell, she saw Valerie first and then Mick, standing together against the railing by the solarium. Right away she knew they'd been fucking. She felt her stomach clench.

"There you are," she said to Valerie as Mick pushed by her into the stairwell, avoiding her eyes. "I was looking for you downstairs."

"I was up here all night," said Valerie, talking fast, slurring her words a little. "I thought you were going to come join me. Then Mick showed up. We talked. We drank a gallon of wine. I smoked all his cigarettes." She paused and took a breath. Her face looked wayward, challenging. "And then we totally fucked."

"I figured," said Christine. She felt a sting of betrayal but immediately quelled it. What right did she have to feel betrayed?

"Yeah," said Valerie. "It just kind of happened."

Valerie staggered over to one of the stationary bicycles on the deck in front of the solarium. Christine followed her and sat on the other one. She began to pedal hard, leaning forward on the handlebars, as if she could drive the boat with her own nervous energy. She wasn't sure yet how she felt about Valerie and Mick, but her body was tense, and her heart was pounding, so she knew she was upset even though she had no right to be.

"What's going on with you?" Valerie's voice had an edge. She was sitting very still, turned toward Christine. "Why do I feel like I stole him from you or something?"

Christine stopped pedaling and forced herself to calm down.

She took a deep breath. "Of course you didn't steal him, Val. He's not mine to steal. Nothing is going on."

"It wasn't personal, you know. He was there. We're both single."

"I know."

"It's not fair of you to be mad."

"I'm not mad," said Christine. She knew she was lying. "Don't make this into a fight. It's not a fight."

"Mick was looking for *you*," said Valerie. She watched Christine's face closely for her reaction. "And he found me instead. But he kept looking for you, waiting for you, all night."

"Stop," said Christine. She was agitated, on the verge of tears. "Why are you telling me this?"

"It's the truth. Does it upset you?" Valerie looked curious now, detached, as if the journalist in her had taken over at the whiff of a good story. "Are you in love with him?"

"Maybe," said Christine without thinking. She was shocked to hear herself say it. She added in a rush before she could retract or suppress it, "I might be. I probably am."

"Then go and tell him!" said Valerie. "That was just a stupid drunken hookup, it didn't mean anything. He wanted *you*."

"It doesn't matter, he's not the point," said Christine. She paused as it hit her, the answer. "I can't go back to Ed. I can't give him kids. I can't be a farm wife for the rest of my life. I can't do it."

"Oh my God," said Valerie. "Are you serious?"

Christine looked back at her, feeling calm and at peace. "I'm serious."

"But your life is so perfect."

"You can have it," said Christine. She felt so relieved, so light and buoyant, she was almost laughing. "I'll make you a deal. You go live with Ed on the farm, and I'll run off with Mick, okay?"

"Um. Have you met me? I would make the worst farm wife ever."

They both laughed. A wind had picked up and was blowing off the sea, bringing clouds with it. The light from the rising sun was slowly being blotted out by the thickening vapor on the horizon. The air was cool.

"Are you really serious about not going back?" Valerie said at last.

"Yes," said Christine. "I think I am."

She got off her bike and wandered over to the end of the deck. Far down below, in the heaving, foamy water, she saw two tires near a clot of sun-bleached plastic caught in tangled buoys, as though it were some kind of new life form. The water was darkening, concentrating into a denser, colder mass. Waves ran in powerful ripples like muscles under skin while a weird greasy sunlight, diffused and refracted through clouds, slid along the ocean's surface. Out of nowhere, Christine thought of Ariel's song from *The Tempest,* which she had loved once, back when she was young and read books and lived in a world of words. *"Full fathom five, thy father lies,"* it started, and then, *"these are pearls that were his eyes,"* and something about a sea change. She'd forgotten the rest. *"Sea change,"* she thought. That was what this gathering cloud mass on the horizon was, the quickening of the waves, and then she remembered the line that went *"something rich and strange."*

When she turned to look back at the bikes, Valerie was gone.

*

When the party was over and the suite had emptied and people went off to sleep or to look for food, Miriam left Jakov dozing on his daybed, and crept with Sasha into the bedroom and closed the door. For an hour or so, she lay with her eyes closed, naked in bed next to him, too revved up to sleep, her head filled with music, her left fingertips buzzing, her right arm aching a little, phrases of Bach mixing with the staccato of the Weiss and the melodies of the old jazz standards, the lilt of klezmer and folk songs, her inner ear still buzzing with the sound of the clarinet. The windows were open and a cool breeze rushed over her skin. She could hear the sounds of the sea far below, heaving, lapping at the ship, and Jakov, out in the living room, making gasping noises as he snored. He had kept the party going all night long, calling out songs whenever there was a lull, playing with such brio, such gusto, that Miriam had almost forgotten he was ill.

She opened her eyes to find Sasha looking back at her.

"So nice," she said. "It's cooler. Feel the air, it's cooling off. The ocean is waking up."

He reached over and cupped her face with his hand and kissed her. "I was just dreaming about you," he said. He kissed her again. "I dreamed you were living in my house in Jaffa."

They lay silent for a while with the chilly air blowing harder through the balcony door, the rushing, sucking sounds of the ocean. Then Miriam climbed on top of Sasha, stretched herself onto the whole length of him, stomach to stomach, nose to nose. He ran his hands along her naked back and lifted her hips in his hands. They both gasped aloud as he entered her, grinning at each other, holding perfectly still at first, and then gradually moving together. When they were breathless and sweating, she laid her head on his chest and settled her legs to nest in his.

"I loved my dream, Miriam. I wish for that more than anything."

She lifted herself up and looked down at him and studied every wrinkle, every fissure in his face, and her chest ballooned, her head felt light. "I could die right now. Now I've had this, I can go."

"Don't go," said Sasha, smiling at her.

"It's an amazing feeling, to me. I've never had it before."

"Yes you have. It's like klezmer, like Schubert. There's no word for it. There ought to be. Happy melancholy. In German, I'm sure there is a word but I refuse to learn it."

"I would learn it," said Miriam. "Just to say it now."

After Sasha fell asleep, she got up and dressed and went down to the breakfast buffet room to try to find something for Jakov, though she knew he wouldn't eat. She was worried about him. They should never have let him stay up all night. But he had looked so happy. Nobody could tell him to stop.

Coming toward her along the dim hallway was Christine's friend, Valerie. The girl was drunk and lurching, one hand flat against the wall as she propelled herself along. She held something aloft.

"Hello!" said Miriam loudly, as if the girl were deaf instead of merely drunk. "Do you need help?"

Valerie leaned against the wall, her eyes skewed behind her glasses. Her short curly hair sprang away from her head in tendrils. "We've got power bars for breakfast," she said, enunciating carefully, showing Miriam the bar she held, a small dark loaf that looked as if it were made entirely of chemicals. "Courtesy of Cabaret Cruises." She took a bite and chewed with absorbed inward ferocity. "So kind of them."

Miriam took her by the elbow. "Are you okay, sweetheart? Maybe you should get some sleep."

"I am far, far beyond sleep," said Valerie. "I think I'll go back upstairs to think about life." She looked directly at Miriam. "A warning about the breakfast room: it's a shit show. The boomers are in crisis."

She stumbled off. Miriam could already hear voices at the end of the hall. When she reached the open door to the breakfast room, she saw a blurred mass of people all talking at once. They seemed to be directing their comments at Kimmi, who stood alone, cornered, backed up against the empty coffee bar, massaging the air with her palms, apologetically.

"Calm down," she said. "Everybody, please."

A man yelled into her face, "Where are the goddamned tugboats?"

"Why aren't they here yet?" came a voice from the back.

Looking into the crowd, Miriam caught a blurred impression of a helmet-haired woman's toothy grimace, a balding man's wide-eyed indignation, a shocked-looking pink-sunburned man in swimming trunks and polo shirt, a plump woman with a smudge on her cheek and a shock of white hair. She recognized some of them from the party. They'd been singing, laughing, just a few short hours before. Now, in the cold cloudy light of morning, with the wind rising and the temperature falling, everything had changed. The panic that had been dormant, clamped down by the heat, had awakened. Their voices sounded querulous, unhinged.

"When are we getting out of here?"

"It feels like there's a storm coming."

Miriam went over to stand next to Kimmi, hoping that two small women would be more effective than one. To her surprise, it worked. They quieted down right away. "This is an unbelievably bad situation," said Kimmi, her voice clear, sincere, sympathetic. "I know, and you're all being accommodating and patient. But we need to stay organized. We need to keep working together. If a storm comes, there are things we'll all have to do to stay safe."

The crowd had calmed down enough to listen while Kimmi spoke, but now Miriam felt another jolt of panic whip through the room.

"We could be in danger!"

"This whole ship stinks, it's disgusting!"

"We're living like animals!"

"I'm sorry," said Kimmi into the eruption. "I'm so sorry."

"When are they coming?" came a shout from the back of the room. "Why are they taking so long?"

Everyone waited for the answer.

Miriam could feel Kimmi fill her lungs with air, stand up as straight as she could. "Last I heard from the bridge crew, the tugs will be here tomorrow morning. That's all I know. I'm sorry."

Miriam saw fear and disappointment flicker through the crowd. No one had anything to say suddenly; the mood had focused into a compressed paralysis. In the absence of any further answers or reassurances, no one seemed to know what to do or where to go. They were caught in an inward-swirling spiral.

A short man off to the side said, "Is the storm going to be bad?"

"Probably not," said Kimmi. "I hope not."

Another shock wave crossed the room. A woman burst into hard sobs.

Kimmi put an arm around her. "We are all in this together," she said. "You're not alone."

"We're going to capsize! We're all going to die!"

It was starting again, the panic, the shouting. Kimmi stood still for a moment, her mouth open. Miriam could feel Kimmi's internal resolve give way as she turned and walked out of the room, her head down, her face blazing white. Miriam followed her out the door, along the hallway. Outside, on the deck, the breeze blew, almost chilly. From low on the horizon, gold bars of sunlight streamed through dark gray clouds to form swirling vortexes of bruised and gilded air. People had begun moving their bedding and belongings back inside, untying sheets, dragging mattresses, pillows under their arms.

Kimmi took a shuddering breath. "We can't keep track of everyone," she muttered as she walked, as if to herself. "The whole crew is trying. Some people have died of the norovirus and their bodies are down on the loading dock. There's a rumor that someone fell overboard and drowned last night, but no one really knows, it's just a rumor. What if it's true? What do we do? We can't get a new head count, everyone is going all over the ship all the time."

They headed up to the catwalk. Miriam noticed again the hollow sounds that the metal stairs made underfoot, the handrail corroded in spots, rusted dark red where the blue-white paint had chipped off, now beading with water in the rising wind. At the door to the bridge, Miriam paused and looked inside at the several uniformed bridge crewmembers standing watch, staring through the windows. But Kimmi continued on along the catwalk without a word to them.

She stopped at a door at the very end, opened it, and turned to look Miriam in the eye. "I've been living in here," she said as if she were confessing a guilty secret. "In the captain's suite. While the captain has been sick in the infirmary."

Miriam followed Kimmi into the spacious, airy suite. The rooms were decorated in navy blue and off-white, striped wallpaper with oil seascapes framed in gilt, sleek furniture, a panoramic curved window spattered with blowing droplets. It gave a full view of the darkening clouds and the ocean below, foam and spray blown off the heaving waves.

Kimmi pointed to the bedroom. "I have been sleeping in that

king-size bed, all alone, while my crew slept down on the main deck with everyone else. I'm ashamed of myself."

"Well, I don't care," said Miriam. "As for me, I've been living in the owner's suite. And I did nothing. You took charge, it's exhausting."

"It's my job," said Kimmi, sitting on the bed. "I started working for Cabaret right after college. I studied music and theater, since I was like *two* I was always going to be a musical actress. Then I saw a Cabaret Cruise listing for an entertainment and cruise director, and I thought, hey, that sounds fun, traveling the world, making people happy. Didn't exactly work out that way. Eight years ago and I'll be thirty in September and what do I have to show for it? My whole adult life."

"You're so young," said Miriam. "Still a kid."

There was a shout outside the door. Kimmi got up and opened it. One of the young watchmen was rushing by. He stopped and pointed downward. "A ship! There's a ship!"

*

Mick stood down on the little excursion dock in the windblown, drifting mist and spray. They had opened it yesterday to swim, and in everyone's excitement after the airdrop, nobody had thought to close it. A shaft of ocher sunlight pierced the thickening clouds high above and shot down to illuminate the charcoal density all around him, as if he were at the bottom of a coal mine.

He had come down here with the sort of half-idea of throwing himself into the churning ocean. There were worse ways to die. Drowning was supposed to be pretty pleasant, he'd heard. Once you gave yourself over to it.

He pictured his body drifting down through the black depths to the ocean floor. It was so typical; of course he had ended up with the best friend instead of the girl he was in love with. He was always selling himself short, shooting himself in the foot. Just like with

Laurens, with the Eszterházy. He wasn't capable of taking action beyond the bounds of his place in the world. Instead he was stuck watching, standing by, while other people took what they wanted, as if his own life, his own future, didn't matter. And it didn't. Not anymore, anyway.

He shivered. It was getting cold. The waves had picked up and were splashing over the side of the dock, spray hitting his face. He'd eaten so little last night, drunk so much wine. His lungs felt burned. The back of his throat ached.

As he stared into the water, he saw a shadow moving across the dark bars of stormy sunlight. Looking up, he almost fell off the platform. It was a boat, but Mick was sure at first that he was hallucinating. It was a catamaran, with a sleek white spaceship-like cabin sitting between its two hulls. A massive, rigid sail lined with solar panels stuck straight up from its middle like a fin. More solar panels were mounted on the roof of the cabin, as well as two small windmills. Even more surreally, four blond, tanned children stared at him over the side. They were waving at him. Smiling. Holding iPhones, taking pictures.

chapter twenty-four

The *Solar Wind* slid over to the *Queen Isabella* without a sound. No noisy engine, no sails or ropes flapping in the breeze. It was no wonder Mick hadn't known it was there until it was right on top of him. A man waved at him from the cockpit on deck. He was as blond and tan as the children.

"We've been hearing about you guys for days," the man said, shouting over the wind. "I can't believe you're still stuck out here!"

A woman's head, blond also, appeared. "I can't believe we found you!" she said. "Hi! Do you speak English?"

Mick stepped back and clutched the doorway. "Where are you from?" He half expected them to say "outer space."

"Palo Alto," the man called back. "Here, catch!" The man maneuvered closer to the platform, and the tallest of the blond kids threw Mick a line. Mick caught it and tied the end of it to a cleat at the back of the platform, looping it around three times and under itself and tightening the end, hoping it would hold. The man handed the steering over to a teenage boy Mick assumed was another son and went over to join his wife and the other kids at the railing.

"I'm Skip Henderson," he called. His longish hair blew off his high bony forehead. "This is my wife, Phoebe, and our kids. We're on our way to Hawaii."

"Mick Szabo," Mick yelled back. He felt lightheaded, crazed, as if his eyes were bulging out of his head. "I am the chef."

"Beautiful ship!" Skip was looking up at the side of the *Isabella,* leaning back and craning his neck. He seemed very excited to be here. "Is everyone okay on board?"

"We're okay, yes," called Mick. "A lot of people are sick."

"I heard you had a fire," Phoebe said, keyed up, her voice high on the wind. "It's all over the news. I can't believe we found you."

"What a piece of luck, right?" Skip shouted. "We saw some flickering lights last night, and heard music. We thought we were going crazy. But when it got light, there you were."

"Dad," a boy yelled, "can we take the dinghy over?"

"No, stay there, Connor, we gotta book in like three minutes."

Mick heard pounding footsteps behind him. "Hello!" came Kimmi's high, clear voice. "Ahoy!"

Two young men in uniform tumbled through the long, narrow gear room behind her and jumped onto the small landing dock. They had obviously flung themselves down the stairs and were breathing hard.

"I'm Kimmi," she yelled. "And these are the bridge officers, Ivan and Eduardo. The captain and some of the other officers are sick with norovirus."

Mick looked at the three of them on the little dock, seeing them through Skip and Phoebe Henderson's eyes, knowing he looked exactly as filthy, sweaty, and unhinged as they did. It was as if these people had emerged out of civilization, out of real life, a proper well-fed normal family on a clean, modern boat, to find a band of stranded savages, gone mad on their creaky old desert island.

"So listen," Skip was saying. "We're going to have to get out of here pretty quickly. There's a nasty storm on the way, and we have to stay ahead of it."

"A storm," Ivan said. "Is it going to hit us?"

"Yeah. You're going to get blown around some. Do you have any navigational capabilities?"

"No," said Ivan. "No power at all."

"I was just telling Mick here, you've been on the news. Phoebe just put a photo up on Twitter. It's all over the Internet already."

"People are retweeting it like crazy," said Phoebe, looking at her smartphone.

A big swell moved under them, and then another. A wave broke against the low dock, splashing everyone on it.

"This is a total trip," said Skip. "I cannot believe we ran into you. You're on the edge of the void. There's no one out here."

"Except you," said Mick.

"By sheer luck. We were headed for Hawaii but we decided to take a detour because we wanted our kids to see the reality firsthand. We just sailed through hundreds of miles of trash. It's outrageous. Just north of here. Otherwise we wouldn't have run into you."

"You're headed to Hawaii?" Ivan asked.

"Yeah," said Skip. "I wish we could give you a tow. Or take you all aboard."

Mick glanced over at Eduardo, Kimmi, and Ivan. They were all staring at the Hendersons with identical rapt, yearning expressions, hungry to keep them and their boat there, not let them go on their safe and merry way with their radio and food and Internet and children and clean clothes.

*

Christine stood at the portside railing, surrounded by people. The wind blew hard into everyone's faces and whipped them with globules of cold spray as they all looked down at the *Solar Wind* below, the top of its magnificent solar sail reaching almost to their feet.

With warmth, even tenderness, Christine watched Mick among the people below on the excursion dock. His untucked shirttails blew around his torso. She studied his dark, unhappy face as the officers and Kimmi talked to the people on the catamaran.

"What are they saying?" said someone near Christine.

"Look at those kids," said someone else.

"How did they find us?"

"Who are they?"

"They have Wi-Fi," a woman said in a low voice just to Christine's right. She was looking at her iPhone. "Look, I've got a signal."

A flurry swept along the deck as other people appeared nearby, turning on their cell phones for the first time since the power outage, stabbing and mashing at them as fast as they could. Others held them to their bewildered faces as if they expected the boat to be equipped with its very own cell tower as well as a Wi-Fi antenna.

Christine thought briefly about e-mailing Ed, but her mind went blank trying to imagine what she'd say to him. She felt a hand slide onto her arm. Without turning to look, she put her hand on Valerie's and pulled her in close.

"Did you bring your phone up here?" Christine asked. "Everyone's e-mailing. Except me."

Valerie leaned into her. "Who would I write to? You're already here."

Christine silently accepted this as a sort of apology, whether or not it was intended as such, even though Valerie didn't really owe her one.

"Okay, except my editor," Valerie was saying, typing quickly with both thumbs. "She won't believe what's going on, it's such a good story." She stopped typing and stared at her screen for a moment. "Good, it sent. And I can't *even* with all these three hundred other messages, I'm just going to let them wait."

Valerie turned off her phone and put it back into the pocket of her hoodie. Down below, an officer tossed a rope to the man on the *Solar Wind* and it drifted away, bucking and pitching slightly on the waves. The kids on board waved. Everyone waved back at them. The people around Christine seemed to deflate as the Internet connection vanished. But they all stayed crowded together by the railing, watching the boat disappear, first into the fog and spray, where they could still catch occasional glimpses of the tall fin of a solar sail, flashes of white bobbing off in the distance, and then over the horizon, where the sky was lighter, where the storm hadn't reached yet.

*

After Kimmi went down to greet the catamaran, Miriam went back to the owner's suite to check on her friends. Jakov was still asleep, and Isaac's bed was empty. Both bedroom doors were closed. The instrument cases were cluttered in a corner of the room, the *Six-Day War* sheet music still on the music stands.

On her way out to the balcony, she paused to look at Jakov. He lay on his back, his face in profile pale in the stormy daylight, but he was sleeping peacefully for the first time in days. Maybe playing music all night, laughing, singing, had helped after all. His eyes were still, no fluttering. His big stomach hardly moved with his breaths.

She realized that he was dead.

"Jakov," she said, hoping she was wrong, not daring to touch him. "Jakov, wake up."

He didn't move.

"Jakov!" She said sharply, loudly this time. "Time to wake up!"

His arms lay very still along his sides.

Miriam was breathing fast, gasping now. She went into her and Sasha's room. "Jakov is dead," she said wildly. "I can't find Isaac."

"He's in with Rivka," mumbled Sasha, half asleep still.

"In with who?"

"Oh my God," said Sasha, waking up. He jumped out of bed and put on a robe and went into the living room. Kneeling by the daybed, he laid his open palm on Jakov's forehead, his neck, his wrist. He slapped Jakov's cheeks gently, lifted an eyelid and peered at his glassy, unseeing eye. Miriam felt like a coward for not touching him herself, like a terrible friend.

"Jakov," said Sasha tenderly, drawing out the name. "He went in his sleep, without pain. He went in peace."

Sasha started to cry, making small grunting sounds deep in his throat. He put his arms around Jakov and lifted him to hug his shoulders. Miriam stood stone-faced, staring at Rivka's door, willing Isaac to come out. She didn't want to knock, didn't want to know what he was doing in there, what they were doing.

"Isaac," she called finally in a loud, sharp voice. "Isaac! Come out, Jakov is dead."

The door opened, and Isaac and Rivka came into the living room in their pajamas.

"*Achi!*" Isaac shouted. He went over to stand with his hand on Sasha's shoulder, leaning on him for support, offering comfort at the same time.

Rivka went to Miriam and, without saying a word to her, put a hesitant, tentative hand on her back. Miriam felt herself stiffen and start to pull away, shocked, despite herself, that Rivka had spent the night with Isaac.

Oh, what did it matter? Jakov was dead.

She put her arm around Rivka's shoulders and pulled her into the circle, and for a long time, the four of them stood in silence around their friend. Then Rivka broke away, went into her room and got dressed, and went down to the infirmary to tell them.

"Our dear Jakov is dead," said Miriam when she'd gone. "After everything else. After all this."

"It is more than my heart can bear," Isaac said. "Truly, it's too much." He clutched his heart and looked at Miriam. "I feel it breaking. My brother is dead."

"He was my brother too," said Sasha. "And Miriam's. He was family to us all. I never thought he'd be the one to go first."

"Who then?" said Isaac suspiciously. "Me?"

Miriam looked tenderly at the two men she loved most, assessing their health, their spirits, as she had done for so many decades, out of habit, without premeditation or consciousness of doing so. Isaac looked flushed, his hair in more disarray than usual.

"Isaac, were you schtupping Rivka all these years? How could you not tell me? Please don't waffle, just get to the point."

"Nothing happened between us until now," said Isaac. "She was married to our boss. And I had to protect the Sabra. That was all. That was my first and only thought. But Miriam, you always mattered the most to me. So me and Rivka, so what? You and I are each other's family."

Miriam was shocked to find a little tear coming into her eye. "Oh Isaac," she said. She felt so close to him in that moment.

He patted her shoulder and stroked her wet cheek. "But you and Sasha! I never saw that coming, I was shocked, I really was. I was caught off guard. I'm still a little unnerved. I feel a hole in my heart about it."

Sasha was gazing at Jakov. "It's over now," he said with deep sadness. "The quartet. Our brother is dead. It's come to an end."

chapter twenty-five

The rain started in the middle of the afternoon. The sea surface churned with crisscrossing waves of a lucid, eerie green, whitecaps blowing off in foamy chunks. By evening, it was hard to tell the sea from the sky. It was all water and motion and wind, the waves coming from all directions, colliding.

It took well into the night for the storm to reach its full intensity. At least Christine hoped this was its full intensity. She and Valerie were sitting on Valerie's bed, in their cabin, huddled together, staring at each other through the darkness, fully dressed and wearing life jackets.

The ocean moved itself around them, the ship's long body climbing nose first up a mounting wave, then a moment of suspension when it hung on the peak, cresting, and then a lurching drop and a sideways slam against the pavement of the wave's trough.

"Holy shit," said Valerie. "What was that?"

A gust of wind and spray rattled the balcony door. Then came a vertiginous slow spin as the ship swung around and was hit broadside and tipped, heeling starboard, then just as slowly righted herself, then tipped to port. Christine felt her whole body clench in the slow climb up another wave, the brief suspension at the quivering crest, the fall onto the hard sea surface. Then came another roll into the trough and the slow, steady, determined bounce of the old ship, righting herself again, letting out cries deep in her frame that sounded like the full expression of her anger at having to take any more battering shocks to her old system.

Valerie crawled into the little bathroom to dry-heave over and over into the shower while Christine braced herself in bed with her feet against the outer wall, staring through darkness at the black sliding door, her eyes straining, imagining she saw seaweed, flecks, small iridescent fish, bits of driftwood blown against the glass. A few times, she fell into an exhausted stupor that started to turn into sleep, but then another wave came, and she jolted awake again and remembered where she was and what was happening. Any one of the oncoming waves might be powerful and steep enough to swamp the *Isabella,* plow her under with water, keep piling it on, weigh her down until she couldn't come back up, bury her and send her spiraling slowly down to the bottom of the ocean. And after every wave came another wave. The *Isabella* staggered, recovered her balance, suffered another insulting sideways blow, pitched to starboard until it felt as if she'd never make it upright again.

But she always did, rudderless and powerless though she was. She seemed to have an internal sense of equilibrium. Whoever had designed her had known what he was doing, Christine thought. She had been refurbished twice, but the shape of her bones and lines had never changed. Her original designer's expertise was saving all their lives.

As if to prove her wrong, the ship jolted and pitched. Christine and Valerie crashed into each other and the wall. The room tilted. They landed on the floor, rolled, and lay there, trembling, too shocked to say anything for a moment.

"We're going to die," said Valerie. "This is it."

"No," said Christine. "We're going to be fine."

They heard two loud, high blasts, short and long, that signaled an emergency, and then a voice came sharp and commanding over the PA system: *"May I have your attention please. Everyone, go immediately to your muster stations. I repeat, go to your muster stations. Please don't panic, this is a precaution only, we are not in immediate danger, I repeat, this is a precaution only."*

"Oh my God," said Valerie.

"Time to go," said Christine. "Pack your things. Now, Val."

She had already sealed her own phone and wallet and plane ticket home in a plastic bag, zipped into the inner pocket of her jacket. She watched Valerie stuff things into a shoulder bag, her iPhone, notebooks, laptop, jewelry, a cashmere sweater, her expensive Williamsburg designer dress. Christine thought of the green ball gown she'd worn to the captain's table dinner, the gloves and shoes and jewelry, how much they'd cost, Ed's future consternation when he got the statement and saw the amount there among the charges for propane, fuel, and groceries. She saw the ball gown drifting down to the bottom of the Pacific Ocean.

"Should I bring my shoes?" said Valerie. "Shampoo?"

"No!" said Christine. "Let's go."

They went out into the hallway and joined the mass of terrified people making their slow way to the stairs. Christine could hear Valerie's rasping breath behind her as they plunged through the crowd, and then she lost her and couldn't find her again. Emerging from the stairs onto the lifeboat deck, standing in the press of people at Muster Station Two, Christine caught a contagion of hysteria. Her vision zoomed in again and again through a black, cone-shaped tunnel. She felt a hard pressure on her chest, seeing strangers' faces in the blowing rain, hearing a hard wash of waves and the banging and creaking of the crew, their frenzied shouts as they prepared to load the boats and winch them down. Dizzy, short of breath, she lurched against the railing and caught herself. The lifeboats looked like death traps, far too small for the hordes of people being herded into them, strung by cables, hanging high above the churning, dangerous sea surface, flimsy and precarious.

Christine knew all at once beyond a doubt that when her turn came, she would not be able to get into one of those jam-packed capsules. The image of the octopus trapped in its little tank kept flashing in her brain. She looked around for Valerie, but she didn't see her anywhere. The crowd was too closely packed behind her to go back, so Christine fought her way along the deck toward the nearest staircase leading up, where the tide of humans streaming down wasn't as thick, and pushed her way upward. "Excuse me," she said, "sorry," and she threaded through faceless bodies, heard heavy breathing, low moans, keening, the sounds all animals made when they were afraid and in distress.

As she ascended, she began to breathe freely again with relief. Her vision cleared. Bursting onto the catwalk that led to the bridge, she felt triumphant, as if she had escaped to freedom.

*

Miriam, Isaac, and Rivka left the suite together to climb down to the lifeboats, but Miriam was quickly separated from the other two on the thronged staircase. Sasha hadn't come back from down below. He'd gone down at some point during the storm to monitor the engine room's fire-damaged hull, fearing a leak. She could only hope that he'd heard the PA announcement, the clear directions to head for the muster stations. And she hoped even more that he would have the sense to obey it. She made her way through deckwide pandemonium, windblown shouting and chaos, people vivid in the bilious dawn light in their neon orange life vests. In the high winds, the lifeboats shuddered and swayed in their berths against the hull of the ship. Crewmembers had begun to untie ropes and instruct people to embark. It was clear from their gestures and shouted directions to one another that, in the absence of power, they were preparing to lower the lifeboats manually, once they were filled with people, winching them by hand the whole distance of several decks down to the turbulent surface. They looked so frag-ile, precarious, these lifeboats, creaking and swaying as they hung there. And everyone was going to have to get into these things and ride them down to the ocean, trusting in the ability of the exhausted and clearly panicked crew. How the crew planned to get themselves down, Miriam had no idea.

Where was Sasha? She looked around for him and saw only a sea of strangers' faces. She was not getting into one of those things without him, she was not leaving him behind on this ship. They had to go together. Determined to find him, she began fighting her way back to the staircase, beating against the flow of people surging onto the deck.

She hesitated, imagining herself searching for him in the dark labyrinth below. She would never find him. But she could have the bridge crew page him on the PA and tell him to go to his muster station.

Instead of going down, she went up.

*

At some point after daybreak, Mick realized that the storm wasn't going to last forever. And then, just as he was thinking about where to go, the biggest wave of all knocked the ship sideways, kept coming, rolling and tipping the ship until she lay flat on her side. He rolled against the inner wall of the restaurant bar as the side of the ship rose and hung there, suspended. Then she fell back, slowly righting herself as she slid down the other side of another immense, invisible wave. Bottles of booze clinked and rattled overhead. A martini strainer landed on his shoulder. On the other side of the bar, he could hear the tables and chairs shifting, sliding, toppling, plates crashing onto the floor, the wall panels chafing against one another, flexing.

He left the wrecked, tumbled restaurant and made his lurching way through the hallway and up the grand staircase, then along the promenade and up the inner staircase to the bridge. The ship was a mess. It smelled of booze from broken bottles, and shit and urine and vomit. Everything that wasn't bolted down had slid and bounced during the night. Although the ocean was still turbulent, the ship was rolling less dramatically now, so it was possible to walk without falling against the walls. All the sick people had been moved down to their cabins for safety during the storm, but many others were up and about already, restless, panicky. Everyone wore a neon-orange life jacket. Some people stared out the windows at the still-violent sea in the uneasy morning light, huddled together; others crouched in corners, clung to columns, to one another. Some of them had cuts on their foreheads, abrasions on their arms. Locks of white and silver-gray and dyed blond and jet-black hair fluttered and waved and pasted themselves to brows. Voices were quavering, hoarse, shocked.

He made his way, squeezing through the throngs of people, until he reached the staircase leading up to the bridge, then climbed upward as fast as he could go. When he came in, he was surprised to find the captain in uniform, sitting almost doubled-over in one of the bridge command chairs. He looked severely pale and sickly. A handful of other bridge officers were there too, wearing life vests over their uniforms. One of them stood by the PA system. Several others clustered around the doorway. Mick saw Kimmi, clinging to the console under the windows, looking out.

"Go down to the lifeboats," she shouted when she saw Mick. Her cheek was gashed and bleeding. She looked pocket-size, ancient. Her life vest was huge on her. Her twiglike arms stuck out of the armholes. "He's making the announcement right now."

"Why aren't you down there?" he asked her, lurching across the room to stand next to her.

"I'm going soon. The crew is too. Everyone needs to get to their muster stations. There's a U.S. Navy ship coming to pick us all up, just three hours away."

"Why aren't you down there?" Mick repeated.

"Go and get into a boat," said Kimmi.

He turned and staggered toward the door as an old, white-haired man entered, out of breath, soaking wet, his clothes and head smeared with something tarry and black. "I just came from the engine room," he shouted to the crewmembers. "There's a crack in the hull, it's coming in from everywhere, there are crewmembers still down there."

An enormous wave hit the ship. They all went stumbling and hurtling across the bridge. Mick hit the control panel so hard he chipped a tooth. He went temporarily deaf. His arm went numb.

He looked at the others. They looked as dazed as he felt, checking themselves for damage to their bodies and faces. A crewmember helped the captain off the floor, back into his chair. Outside, it was impossible to tell what was happening. Sea and sky had merged, and there was no up or down. Mick's shoulder throbbed. Maybe he'd torn something in there. He stuck his tongue against his chipped front tooth and ran it over the new sharp edge.

"Time to go down," Kimmi shouted.

Another person had come in, an older woman. When she saw the white-haired man, she gave a cry and rushed to him and flung her arms around him. "There you are, oh, Sasha! Thank God I found you. I looked by the lifeboats and you weren't there."

"I was in the engine room," the man said. "We're leaking, I have to go back down."

"No. You come with me," she said fiercely. "We're going to the lifeboats."

"Where are Isaac and Rivka?"

"Down at the muster station. I came to find you. I won't leave without you."

Mick was making another attempt to stagger toward the door when Christine burst in on a fresh wet gust of wind. "Good morning!" she shouted.

He couldn't believe his eyes.

"Hello!" he shouted with half-hysterical, giddy abandon. "Beautiful day, isn't it?"

Christine laughed, beaming at him with a jaunty hilarity that was completely at odds with their predicament. Mick felt a rush of love for her so intense he thought his heart might explode. Swimming through the pitching air, he threw his arms around her. She hugged him back hard. They stood for a moment, swaying with the force of their contact. Her body felt strong and warm. He never wanted to let her go.

"When we get off this ship," said Mick into her hair.

She pulled back to look into his face as the ship bucked again. "Yes," she said clearly. Holding on to each other, arms tightly around each other's waists, they each shot out a hand to steady themselves on the console panel, tumbling into the elderly couple.

"Miriam!" cried Christine. "Sasha!"

"It's you!" said Miriam. "Go downstairs!"

The wind died abruptly. The rain all but stopped. The ship went quiet. It was just the pitching waves, the roar of the surf, far below. The air in the room was charged with negative ions, dim and cool and humid.

Kimmi came to stand at the console with Mick and Christine, Sasha and Miriam, the five of them shoulder to shoulder, looking out through the salt-crusted windows at the wild foam and water, expectantly, as if they were all waiting for something.

"They made us read a horrible thing in Bible school when I was a kid," said Kimmi, out of nowhere. Her face glowed in the stormy light. "Revelation 8:8: 'And the second angel poured out his vial on the sea; and it became as the blood of a dead man: and every living soul died in the sea.'"

"That's terrible," said Christine.

"I know," said Kimmi. "What the heck kind of story is that to tell small children?"

"The Song of Miriam is better," said Miriam. "That's a song of redemption and hope. I loved the way you sang it."

The *Isabella* moaned and gave a little heave to port, rocked by a monster swell.

"Listen to her," said Kimmi. Her teeth were chattering, not from cold, Miriam thought, but from a strange excitement. Miriam felt it too. "All night, I kept telling her, 'You can do it, Izzy, just hold it together, come on!'"

While Kimmi talked, the ship was hit by another wave, smaller than the last one, but still powerful enough to make the ship lurch. Mick tightened his grip on the hand railing below the console. He felt something wrench and twinge in his right shoulder. He held on so tightly his knuckles cracked as the ship slowly, shudderingly righted herself again and everything quieted.

"No way," said Kimmi. "Over there. Look!"

They all looked in the direction she was pointing. Far away, a streaming bolt of sunlight lit up a patch of stormy ocean, the rain and spray creating a dazzling column of air, shimmering almost gold.

"It looks like the ladder to heaven," said Christine.

They all laughed, no one knowing quite why, apart from the fact that it felt good to laugh.

"We can't climb it," said Sasha.

"But what a beautiful sight," said Miriam.

Just as quickly as it had appeared, the faraway shaft of sunlight was swallowed again by the clouds. But somehow the air on the bridge seemed brighter. It was so quiet, they could hear the ocean running against the hull far below. The *Isabella* listed, just a little, but they all felt it.

"Are you guys ready to go downstairs?" said Kimmi. "We should go."

"What is that?" said Christine. She was staring straight ahead at a wide, dense, blue-black mountain of a wave veined with white coming toward them. It grew as it came and filled the windows until it blotted out the storm. The *Isabella* tilted upward, rising easily into the air as if a hand had reached down and lifted her from the sea.

"Here we go," said Mick.

He held his breath and felt a swooping in his stomach as the ship climbed the marbled face of the wave, up and up. The *Isabella* seemed to balance on the crest, trembling and weightless. The windy green-and-white foam disappeared and the whole world went gray and silent.

Mick looked at Christine in the sudden hush. Her mouth was open, her face astonished and full of anticipation. He wished he could stay up here with her forever, and never come down.

ABOUT THE AUTHOR

Kate Christensen is the author of six previous novels, most recently *The Astral,* and the memoirs *Blue Plate Special* and *How to Cook a Moose. The Great Man* won the 2008 PEN/Faulkner Award for Fiction. She has written reviews and essays for numerous publications, including *The New York Times, Vogue, Elle, The Wall Street Journal,* and *Food and Wine.* She lives with her husband in Portland, Maine.